Praise for *Is Just a Movie* by Earl Lovelace

"*Is Just a Movie* confirms Lovelace as a master storyteller of the West Indies." —Ian Thomson, *The Financial Times*

"Funny, moving, endlessly inventive." —*The Times of London*

"Lovelace's fiction is deeply embedded in Trinidadian society and is written from the perspective of one whose ties to his homeland have never been broken. In his new novel, he turns his attention to the remote fictional village of Cascadu and the lives of ordinary individuals whose relationship to politics, their peers, and their own weaknesses provide fascinating material. . . . Lovelace is bursting with things to say about this complex, heterogeneous society in the late twentieth century. This he does with a flair that at its best reaches a soaring rhapsody. The scabs of racial tension are cautiously peeled back and we witness the community's loves, aspirations, and machinations; their little victories and defeats, their best selves and worst selves. And when things become too difficult, there is always the spirit of Carnival that presides over their lives: recuperative, cathartic, communal, celebratory."
—Bernadine Evaristo, *The Guardian*

"Vivid prose that seems to stroll effortlessly across the page. Lovelace's writing is meticulously crafted but it retains its casual elegance." —*The Times Literary Supplement*

"Earl Lovelace's genius is revealed in his capacity to consistently write characters of complex sophistication that remain fully believable as products of their landscape and time even as the author conjures up riveting and often unusual circumstances in their lives. Lovelace's characters are compelling because of the care and profound empathy with which he explores their thinking and their feelings. Lovelace understands Trinidad and its people, its music, its history, and its psyche in ways that have made him one of the most important writers to have emerged from the Caribbean in the last seventy years. *Is Just a Movie* manages to combine all the elements of the best calypso—a postmodernist sense of the world, an earthbound wit, a capacity for complex tragedy, and a haunting humanity. Lovelace makes you want to be Trinidadian."
—Kwame Dawes

"The publication of a new novel by Earl Lovelace is an event to celebrate. This satire, while biting, is tempered with a pathos and humor which direct us to the fundamer
to recognize in all of Lovelace's writin
—Lawrence Scott, author, *N*

"More than any other writer, the prose of Earl Lovelace is 'Trini to the bone.' And like the famed Cascadu river fish after which the village in *Is Just a Movie* is named, once its sweet flesh is tasted, the reader is destined to return to its shores."
—Robert Antoni, author, *Divina Trace* and *Carnival*

"Earl Lovelace is arguably the Caribbean's greatest living novelist. In *Is Just a Movie*, he writes at the top of his considerable literary powers, picturing the Caribbean's poor and powerless defending their ever-embattled humanity with resourcefulness and tenacity."
—Randall Robinson, author, *Makeda*

"Music, broken hearts, revolution and scandal sway through the novel, which, like all of Lovelace's books, is forged in the dizzying heat of Carnival and the hotbed of post-independence politics."
—*Metro* (London)

Winner of the Grand Prize for Caribbean Literature from the Regional Council of Guadeloupe

Praise for Earl Lovelace's earlier novels

"*The Dragon Can't Dance* is a landmark, not in the West Indian but in the contemporary novel. . . . Nowhere have I seen more of the realities of a whole country disciplined into one imaginative whole." —C. L. R. James, author, *The Black Jacobins*

"Generous, torrential prose that seems to hold every complexity— of history, of ethnicity, of reason and magic alike—within its rushing energy." —*New York Times Book Review*

"*Salt* is a book of great beauty and force which is going to take its place as one of the classics of twentieth-century world literature."
—Judges of the 1997 Commonwealth Writers' Prize

"Lovelace expresses powerful and often subtle ideas with memorable directness." —*Chicago Tribune*

"A defining and luminously sensitive portrait of postcolonial island life. . . . A poignant, beautifully crafted tale." —*Kirkus*

"[Lovelace is the] consummate Caribbean man-of-letters."
—*Publishers Weekly*

"Distinguished Trinidadian novelist Lovelace writes fiction as syncopated, sinuous, and irresistible as the calypso music that punctuates the lives of his poor but proud characters. . . . Lovelace peers beneath the rigid structure of island society into the desiring hearts of men and women struggling for recognition, respect, and love. . . . As Lovelace masterfully choreographs the dance of each of his finely drawn characters, he reveals the conundrums not only of Caribbean life but of the human condition itself."
—*Booklist*

"*The Dragon Can't Dance* is a wonderful work filled with depth, insight, and truth. While the story is grounded in the milieu of Trinidad, its message is universal and timeless." —*Multicultural Review*

"Superb lyrical writing and a moving sense of history being enacted in the lives of individuals." —*Mail on Sunday*

"A deeply affecting and satisfying novel distinguished by intense lyrical writing." —*The Observer*

"Carnival leaps out of these pages with deafening steel bands, pageantry and dance." —*The Daily Telegraph*

"Lovelace writes with a singularly truculent acuteness, both in narrative and in the dialogue which captures West Indian speech rhythms so convincingly. . . . The Schoolmaster is quite unlike anything a British author could produce, being its own enviable thing, absolutely." —Robert Nye, *The Guardian*

"Earl Lovelace's writing has a picturesque yet dark energy, with a carnival snaking through the novel like a dangerous spine."
—*The Guardian*

"Earl Lovelace writes like a man who has just discovered language and is amazed. Each word is a revelation." —*The Times*

"A novelist of intelligence and sensibility." —*Sunday Times*

Is Just a Movie

EARL LOVELACE

Haymarket Books
Chicago, Illinois

This edition published in 2012 by
Haymarket Books
PO Box 180165
Chicago, IL 60626
773-583-7884
info@haymarketbooks.org
www.haymarketbooks.org

Distributed to the trade in the United States
by Consortium Book Sales and Distribution, www.cbsd.com.

ISBN: 978-1-60846-175-2

Published with the generous support of Lannan Foundation
and the Wallace Global Fund.

Cover image by Jed Nichols.

Printed in the United States.

Library of Congress Cataloging-in-Publication data is available.

2 4 6 8 10 9 7 5 3 1

In memory of Errol Jones

For Funso Aiyejina
And for Tiy, Maya, Lulu, Che, and Walt—and all those
who have waited long enough for this book to finish

ONE

I, Kangkala

My name is Kangkala, maker of confusion, recorder of gossip, destroyer of reputations, revealer of secrets. In the same skin, I am villain and hero, victim and victor.

I am a true-true kaisonian.

I reduce the powerful by ridicule. I show them their absurdities by parody. I make their meanings meaningless and give meaning to meaning. I dance bongo on top the graves of the mighty. I am the Dame Lorraine presenting in caricature the grotesque of the wicked, the deformity of the stupid, the obzocky of gluttony. I show the oppressors themselves misshapen: gros toto, gros titi, gros bondage. Yes, I portray the big-stones man: a bag of boulders bulging from my pants, I am the big-foot, sore-foot man, the big-bottom, big-breasted, big-belly woman. I am the dispenser of afflictions.

But I was born again by a slip of the tongue when one night in the kaiso tent, as I am preparing to sing my song, for the benefit of foreigners in the audience, the Master of Ceremonies introducing me, proceeded to make his announcement with an American twang. He said, "Ladies and gentlemen, this is the song, and this is your singer, King Kala."

So, suddenly, in the interstice, or shall I say the *interspluce* of this mispronunciation of Kangkala brought on by this Trinidadian fella wanting to sound American, calling Kang King, I was reborn to a new vision. It was in the middle of the time of the uprising we called Black Power. I

5

don't remember exactly what song I was going to sing, which big shot I was going to lash, whose business I was going to expose; but, that night, inspired by the MC's error of my name, a grander role fell to me. The mockery was over, the double entendre at an end. I take off my jacket and roll up my sleeves. I would become the recorder of the people's story, singer of their praises, restorer of their faith, keeper of their vexation, embalmer of their rage. I became the poet of the revolution.

Then the state of emergency was declared. The heroes made their triumphant surrender. Then they disappeared. Some skipped over to religion, some ran back to their trade union, some fly back to Africa, some sailed into electoral politics, one take up a piece of chalk and with the walkway his blackboard began to lecture in the university of Woodford Square. But the stage was no longer our own. The show was over. I tried to sing them into presentness, to invoke them with song:

Oh, Mastifay, Mastifay, meet me by the Quay d'Osay
Cutouter, Cutouter, meet me by Green Corner

But everything was against me. I was singing, but nothing came of my songs. Then that too ended, not a sound came from my voice, not a new note spun from my head.

I looked around to see those who had dreamed with me steaming into safe harbors. They rebuilt the pyramids, they reconstructed Hanuman, they parted the ocean and stuffed the Middle Passage back into oblivion. All that time my aunt Magenta is wrestling with the angel, saying with a fierce loyalty and hope that I could not fathom, "I will not let you go until you bless me." The angel continued to struggle. I didn't know what to do. I thought it was I alone who was left believing – in believing. I was beginning to panic. I didn't know where I was going. I begin to look around for a harbor. And then I witnessed the exquisite choreography of Sonnyboy's dying.

Starring Sonnyboy

When Sonnyboy Apparicio hear the government had declared a state of emergency and was arresting leaders of the Black Power demonstrations that our most illustrious historian had christened the February Revolution, his first instinct was to run. He exchanged his dashiki for a long-sleeved white shirt, patted down his halo of hair to fit under a bebop cap, left Rouff Street where he stayed by his brother Alvin when he was in Port of Spain and dodged his way to the village sleeping on top Hololo mountain to hide out by Daniel, an Indian pardner, where he felt sure the police wouldn't look for him, there to wait for word of the resistance that the Black Power leader warned would follow, *as faithfully as night follows day, if the government take God out their thoughts and try to stop the onward march of Blackpeople.*

Throughout that day Sonnyboy listened to the radio give details of leaders captured, of leaders surrendered, of leaders on the run, and he spent a sleepless night on the canvas cot in Daniel's front room, agonizing over the likelihood that the Black Power rebellion, after months of roaring, was whimpering to its end. But when next morning he see in the newspapers the compelling poetry of his leaders' surrender, their clenched fists in the air, their bodies bristling with the authority of their outrage, the very policemen that had arrested them gazing at them with awe, it became clear to Sonnyboy that the *Brothers*, as he now called these men, had not crumbled, but, like the Flounce dancers in the Guyana masquerade, had leapt

9

from their humbling to a more invincible height. Wanting to take his place beside them, Sonnyboy take off his bebop cap, pushed it into his pocket, teased out his hair to the previous halo of its fullness, said goodbye to his pardner on Hololo and rushed back to Rouff Street to wait there for the police to come to arrest him. But, at Rouff Street, the fellars usually congregated on the corner had melted and the few gathered there were not all that familiar with him. Not wanting to be arrested on a street where people didn't know him, Sonnyboy take a taxi to the town of Cascadu, where he had lived in the house of his grandmother since he was fourteen, where he was sure he would find a multitude appreciative of an event as important as his arrest. In Cascadu, people who saw him out in public were alarmed at what they thought to be his foolhardiness, and his good friend Gilda grabbed him by the collar with an excess of force he expected to be excused because of his good intentions:

"You crazy or what? The police looking for Black Power people, why the arse you not in hiding?"

Sonnyboy portrayed himself as smiling and saying to Gilda and the people with him: "Don't worry. They could kill me, but they can't kill the revolution," words of courage that so moved Gilda and the people with him that, at the risk of themselves being arrested for what was now unlawful assembly, since the state of emergency was in effect, they shepherded him into his grandmother's yard and crowded around him with a sense of awed and prideful jubilation to wait for the police to come to arrest him.

His grandmother, whose pride in him had ballooned almost to bursting over the months of his involvement with Black Power, thrilled that he was going to be arrested for championing a cause more noble than the personal misdeeds that usually landed him in trouble, cooked for him a pot of rice and pigeon peas with ochro and saltfish, enough to offer the crowd that had gathered in her yard to witness the occasion of Sonnyboy's arrest, to eat.

No police came that day, or the next, and the cheerful faces of Sonnyboy's waiting supporters began to droop. They began to speculate that the authorities doing the arresting had him lower on the list for martyrdom than he had led them to believe he merited. They began to drop words for him:

"Like they forget you, boy?"

"How come you ain't get hold yet?"

Faced by the prospect of being marooned in the freedom of oblivion, Sonnyboy decide to take matters into his own hands. On a brilliant Sunday afternoon when most of the villagers were heading to the parched savannah to see the cricket match between Cascadu and Dades Trace, and others were on their way to the blue sunshine of the beach, he laced up his boots, put on his black headband, his red dashiki, his green dark shades, and, with the halo of his hair like an open umbrella over his face, set out for the police station, behind him his grandmother, his good friend Gilda, another pardner Dog and in the back of them a group that was making the journey to see him brought low.

"I hear all-you looking for me," he said to the single policeman on duty.

And to avoid the indignity of being asked who me was (since, at his words, Constable Stephen Aguillera, the policeman on duty had raised his eyebrows in puzzlement) he added his name: Sonnyboy Apparicio. Without a word, the policeman opened the huge station diary in front of him and began turning its pages. Sonnyboy held his breath. And he only exhaled when Constable Aguillera raised his eyes to his.

Five years earlier, hearing the news that Ramona Fortune, the girl he loved, would be leaving for England on the day immediately after Carnival Tuesday, Constable Aguillera, himself a youth just two years on the police force, had left the Matura Police Station unattended, released the single prisoner whom he had made promise that he would return by the midnight ending of the festivities, and had gone to look for *Bucco Reef*, the McWilliams Carnival band in which he was told Ramona would be playing. He spent half the day searching for the band and, when he found it, trying, without luck, to get past the guard of relatives and friends surrounding her. When he returned to Matura just after midnight, with a heart dripping with grief, it was to find the station blazing in light, and waiting for him the corporal in charge of Matura Police Station, the sergeant and inspector up from Sangre Grande, and the prisoner he had released, back in his cell, on a new charge of wounding.

Pleading guilty to Dereliction of Duty, Constable Aguillera at first accepted the penance of his exile to Cascadu as punishment that was deserved and had worked hard to make up for that single blunder by efforts to present himself as a conscientious officer. His boots, belt and buttons were always shining, his stance erect, his voice firm, his notebook in order, the language of the charges for misdemeanors clear; and in less than two years he had Cascadu straight, his presence enough to bring calm to the

12

bedlam of Main Street on a busy payday Friday, a flash of his eyes sufficient to direct men to give over money due the mothers of their children who had come to the rum shop to intercept them before the rum shop or gambling club take it from them, and a voice with the quality of force and sternness to order the most enthusiastic troublemaker to go to the police station charge-room and sit there and wait while he made up his mind what charge to place him on.

But when Constable Aguillera observed that his good works had gone unrewarded, and officers his junior with nothing approaching his record of arrests were promoted ahead of him, a certain resentment began to eat at him. For two years and a half he went on a spree, drinking rum, gambling and enjoying the favors of women who, drawn to the neatness of his uniform, the uprightness of his stance and his overall power and good looks, were falling all over the place for him. At one time he found himself friending with a woman in nearly every village of his district and had two of them at the same time big-belly for him. He mended his ways somewhat when six months after the two babies were born, the mother of one brought the baby to the police station, put him in his hands and walked away. He gave the baby to his mother to mind, cut down on his drinking and made an effort to keep his head straight when he see a nice woman passing. However, the unfairness of the administration still rankled and he continued to refuse to arrest anyone. Fellars used obscene language within earshot of him. Taxi drivers double-parked, and numerous skirmishes took place within clear sight of him. On Main Street, two badjohns, Big Head and Marvel, had a fistfight that started in front the gambling club and ended up in front the rum shop where he was drinking, bottle and stone pelting, people dodging, the whole street in disorder for an hour and fifteen minutes. Constable Aguillera maintained his resolve not to make an arrest until justice was meted out to him.

So, on that Sunday, when he looked up from the station diary, it was with a sense of personal relief that Sonnyboy's name was not in the book. But, hearing the disappointed grumble of Sonnyboy's supporters, and the hum of jubilation from those behind them, he advised that if Sonnyboy wanted to be sure of his status, he should go to the savannah, where he would find the corporal in charge of the police station looking at the cricket match; or he could sit down and wait, on the chance that the inspector who was handling the Black Power business might drop in and clarify whether or not he was to be arrested. "*Or, you could go home.*"

Sonnyboy recalled smiling. Even the police were doing their best not to see him. He decided to wait.

I would meet him sitting on the bench in the charge-room when I was brought in with two revolutionary brethren, Ibo and Marvin, who, bad luck for us, were apprehended in a roadblock on the Toco Road as we were making our way to the hills of the remote village of Kumaca. As soon as I sit down, Sonnyboy strike up a conversation with me, affecting a familiarity that we really didn't have, and he continued talking to me for the half-hour it took for the three army officers to come to fetch Ibo, Marvin and me to detention on Nelson Island. As they signaled for me and my two brethren to get up and follow them, Sonnyboy, still talking to me, got to his feet as if he was one of our party and calmly strode out with us to the waiting army jeep.

As we were about to enter the jeep, the newspaper photographers who had been waiting outside the police station to catch a glimpse of the Black Power detainees, as we were called, aimed their cameras at us. I was tired with worry. I turned away, to give the impression of nonchalance but really because I didn't want my photograph appearing in the newspaper with me, a revolutionary, looking so harassed.

But Sonnyboy, not quite smiling, brought himself erect, lifted his right hand, fist clenched, above his head, and with a sense of honor, and a deserved delight, shouted, "Power to the People!" in a salute so rousing that I thrust my own right hand, fist folded, in the air and shouted: "Power!" When I looked, I saw that my comrades had done the same.

I didn't know Sonnyboy all that well. I knew him as a badjohn, a man who had his problems with the law. I had seen him at one or two of the Black Power rallies in Port of Spain and, meeting him there in the police station, I assumed he was one of us, one of the detainees. But later, when I heard his story, I was glad that my presence there that day had enabled him to save face before his grandmother and his brethren and allow him, for the first time, to enter into the custody of the police not as a common criminal but as the freedom fighter he knew himself to be.

Poet of the Revolution

When I am released from detention, Port of Spain is a
changed place. The People's Parliament where in the
time of Black Power we had assembled before we set out
on our daily marches is back to being just Woodford
Square. The day I went there, the roar and babble of
brethren at the gate, passing out pamphlets for rallies, is
replaced by neatly dressed women and men silently
holding up copies of the religious magazine *Awake*. At the
side of the fountain, where the Grecian nymph is turning
a dirty green under the unsteady drip of water, the leader
of a band of Shouters, barefooted, in a yellow robe and
red head tie, is delivering a sermon to a single diligent
listener, a vagrant whose torso, arms and legs are wrapped
in cellophane, bulking him up to look like an astronaut
without a helmet. On the railing near to the urinals, a
gray-haired man, his hair plastered down on his skull and
his beard neatly trimmed, is arguing for the divinity of
Marcus Garvey and the immortality of Haile Selassie. I
look in the listening crowd for regulars from '70, men who
had talked revolution, who had raised their fists and
shouted *Power*. One is selling snow-cone, another one have
in his hands a book of lottery tickets for sale, and one is
sitting on a bench by himself alone, curled up and quailed
like callaloo bush in the hot sun, the heave and bounce
gone out of his step, the light in his eyes dimmed, about
him the exhausted look of a routed combatant glad to
embrace the chastening rebuke of his defeat. None of

16

them seem to recognize me and I choose not to trouble them. I their poet and prophet was now a stranger.

For Carnival that same year, in the Victory Calypso Tent where I had spent the last five years as the lead calypso singer, the crowd no longer want to hear my songs. They sit quiet enough while I am singing, and continue their forbidding silence when I am done, and it is only out of his sense of gratitude that Jazzy, the manager of the tent, is keeping me on the program, since, thank God, he ain't forget that in the two years leading up to '70, I was the big name pulling in the crowd. But even Jazzy's loyalty was wearing thin.

This night he called me into the little booth he called his office and he say to me, "King ..." That is how he call me: King. That is how he call those of us who win the Calypso crown already.

He say, "King, how you feeling?" in this tuneless falsetto that put me on my guard right away.

"How I feeling? Since when you is a doctor, Jazzy? Tell me, Jazzy, how you expect me to be feeling? No encores, no appreciation. Most times I feel like I singing to myself."

"King, don't think I don't appreciate the songs you singing." His words slow, heavy, like they weighing down his head, have him looking not at me but down at his hands, the fingers of one pulling carefully at the others, like a pay-master singling out and counting hundred-dollar bills.

"Jazzy, why you don't stop beating around the bush and tell me what you have to tell me?"

And now he drop the bomb: "King, we going to have to put you on the bench."

"You taking me off the program, Jazzy?"

"Because, King, the revolution, the rebellion, it finish, it done. And, those songs you singing, the people ..." pausing for the eternity of two-three seconds, his eyes flashing, his voice going up with the scratch of a new harsh rhythm (and I could hear him forcing back the distaste, the disappointment). "The people, the people," straining to restrain himself lest his blood pressure boil over. "The people?" In his voice a chuckle, a sneer, steering him away from the chasm of his disappointment. "The people paying their money, they have the say. You have to give them the songs they say they want. That is democracy. Left to me ..."

"Left to you? Jazzy, *it is* you it's left to. And look where you put me – in the calypsonian's cemetery."

"Cemetery, King?" with a sense of hurt that make me lighten up.

"OK, purgatory."

Jazzy smiling his contemplative Jazzy-smile at the clever-ness and accuracy of my retort, "You good, you good ... Left to me ..." spreading open his two hands, palms upward to demonstrate his good faith, his voice soft like a baby's, so, if you don't know the hardhearted fucker you dealing with, you'd think he going to cry.

"Left to me, I'll keep you singing until these people come to their senses and start applauding you. But they say they want calypsos to make them dance. They leaving here and going to the other tent. You see our tent last night and tonight, how it empty? We have good calypso, but the people say they want to dance. You have any song for them to dance to?"

"Jazzy, Jazzy, Jazzy. I tell you this already. Let me tell you it again. I am a poet. A poet, you hear? And the reason

18

I sing calypso is because poetry don't have no real following here in this island. Lots of calypsonians recite their calypso, I sing my poems."

"Poet?"

He look up at me as if what I say sweeten him and he start to smile – not yet to laugh. "Poet and Prophet, eh," rubbing with an open hand one side of his face, the better, I suppose, to contemplate the idea: Poet and Prophet.

"Poet," he say again, opening his two empty hands in what I suppose he expected me to interpret as his pantomime of regret at not having the fictitious money that he acting as if I asking him for. "Don't vex with me, King. We have to wait on the people."

"Jazzy, how long I singing in this calypso tent?"

"King, if is reproach you come to reproach me, now is not the time. I trying my best. For the tent. For everybody."

"No, Jazzy. Tell me how long I singing here."

"How you could ask me how long? Is right here in the Victory Tent that your career begin. Nine-ten years ago, without a calypso name. Is I who give you the name Kangkala. Come in here a slim little fella with your cap turned backwards and your head tie-up like a Baptist, singing something about the Blackman cry. And though it was no big song, you had a voice, you could carry a tune. And after that you sing something about racial unity, dress up like a Indian bridegroom, a *doolaha* with a little Indian dancer dress up like the *doolahin*. And then with Black Power, you start to sing about the injustices to Blackpeople, Black is beautiful and that big one about South Africa. People full up the tent to hear you."

"And you know why, Jazzy? I show people who they really is. I show them that they bigger and more grand,

19

that they have more heart and guts and stones than what people give them credit for. I show them what nobody else show them."

"King, I didn't call you here for a lecture."

"No, you call me here to tell me you taking me off the stage."

"We have to survive, King. The tent have to survive. Calypso have to survive. People don't want those Black Power songs again. People want a break from this seriousness, King. I running a calypso tent. I can't tell the people what songs to like."

So now I am a reserve calypsonian at the Victory Calypso Tent. No room for me on the singing team.

I have a couple new songs I working on. But for some reason they not coming out right, and in any event I not getting the chance to sing them. Eventually, one night I get called up to sing; Jazzy conscience pricking him. He call me up. And I sing one of the new ones which I entitled "Nobody Will Tell You Who You Are':

Because they want to own you, they want to control you
No matter what you show
you will be the last one to know that you are a star.

And I could hear the crowd. Like the truth of my words embarrass them, they just waiting for me to finish the song for me to disappear. I make it to the end and out of respect for me, the band start up, playing the refrain of my song, and in the audience the scattering of people who remember me when I was king – like they sorry for me – start up clapping in a rhythm that leave me unsure whether or not they want to call me back for an encore. And the hypocrite MC, his voice dripping with this false magnanimity, like he is a captain in the Salvation Army giving out charity, call out my name, "King Kala!" And all is left for the people to do is to speed up the tempo of their clapping to demonstrate their wish to have me back on stage to sing another verse and, as it were, take a bow, since they know this is what calypsonians sing for, to satisfy the patrons, to make them want to hear our song again. I stand up on the edge of the stage ready to go back on, waiting on the people.

The people? The people just remain silent, the drops of applause tailing off one by one, like rain in the hot sun. So, if I didn't know it before, the message reach me loud and clear: *King Kala, you have to get out of here. Get out.*

That night after I come off the stage, I lean-up by the bar, sipping a beer and watching the people in their chairs, trying very hard to be amused, and the entertainers on the stage singing song after song attempting to amuse them. I feel a presence at my side; when I look round, is Jazzy standing next to me. He have a Malta in his hand. He doesn't drink hard liquor – his pressure. I don't even want to look at him, I so vex.

"The people not conscious like you, King," he say in his soft, pleading baby voice so I can't tell for sure whether is sympathize he sympathizing with me or is fuck he fucking me up.

He speak again, talking to himself more than to me, "The music change."

"Yes, Jazzy," I tell him. "The music change. The music change."

I had to get out of there. Jazzy was right. Black Power was done; the shouting of *power* hadn't brought the old house down. The raggedy voice of the people was indeed the voice of God. The revolution was over. The world some of us had set out to change in order to claim our place in it was pretty much the same. For just a moment, we in Black Power had parted the silence that curtained the biggest issues in this land – the dignity of Blackpeople, opportunity, equality, what was to be done, how to go on.

"It coulda been worse, King," Jazzy say, like he read my mind. "Nobody is in prison. The fellars that they lock up, they now free ... I think in all is only one fella get killed, and the only tragedy it have is the few crazy fellars out there parading as guerrillas on the hills. The army and police closing in on them."

"Tell me something I don't know, Jazzy. My cousin is one of them."

I wasn't really listening. I needed a rest. It was getting harder to sing. Even I didn't like how I was sounding. I had to stop punishing myself. Yes. I had to get out.

Is Just a Movie

Right after Carnival, a fella from America come down here to Trinidad, say he making movies in the island. Big announcement. Big write-up. Front page. He building up the movie industry. Big talk. Local talent wedded to foreign technology, the set of shit you hear already. But with the help of the government and the business community, the movie gets under way.

They have auditions. I set out to go. As a well-known composer and singer of calypso, a real calypsonian, not just a fella who sing other people songs, I don't expect a problem. I will show them. Forget calypso. I will be a movie star.

So I go down at The Carib where they picking people for the parts. Stanley, Errol, Claude, Wilbert, Ralph, fellars who act with the Theatre Workshop, all of them there. Fellars from Strolling Players, Best Village people: the Talent. The fella from America, he have his people, *foreign industry*, that he bring with him. They give all of us a little test, the audition. To recite from a literary work. Ralph do something from *Hamlet*, the big speech, "To be or not to be." Errol do something from Derek Walcott's *Dream on Monkey Mountain*. The Great Makak speech:

> *Sirs, I am sixty years old,*
> *I have live all my life.*
> *Like a wild beast in hiding.*

And I do for them a piece of my Midnight Robber speech:

23

My name is Kangkala,
maker of confusion, recorder of gossip,
destroyer of reputations, revealer of secrets.
In the same skin, I am villain and hero, victim and victor,
I reduce the powerful by ridicule.
I show them their absurdities by parody.
I make their meanings meaningless and give meaning to
    meaning.
I am the Dame Lorraine presenting in caricature the grotesque of
    the wicked, the deformity of the stupid, the obzocky of
    gluttony.
I show the oppressors themselves misshapen, gros toto, gros titi,
    gros bondage.
Yes, I portray the big-stones man: a bag of boulders bulging from
    my pants,
I am the big-foot, sore-foot man, the big-bottom, big-breasted
    woman.
I am the dispenser of afflictions.
I dance Bongo on top the graves of the mighty.
    Yes, Kangkala is my name.
    But I was born again by a slip of the tongue
    when one night in the calypso tent, as I am preparing to sing
        my song,
the Master of Ceremonies introducing me decided to make his
    announcement with an American twang.
He said, "Ladies and gentlemen, this is the song and this is your
    singer, King Kala."
So, suddenly so, in the interstice, or, shall I say, the interspluce of
    this mispronunciation of Kangkala brought on by this
    Trinidadian fella wanting to sound American,
calling Kang, king,
I was reborn to a new vision.

I had to find new histories to write, ignored heroes to celebrate.
I began afresh to sing.
I became the poet of the revolution.

"Marvelous," the director say. "You fellars have talent."
Talent, yes! So they pick me. So I have this role.

The role they give me, the same one they give the locals, is a role to die. Local talent. Our role is to die. The rest of the people, they bring from America. They is the stars, the ones that have lines to speak, lives to live, in the movie of course.

Though, to read what the newspapers have to say you would swear I had top billing: LOCAL CALYPSONIAN FEATURED IN FOREIGN MOVIE. Yes. And now when I walking the road people looking at me, *The Feature, The Featured*, pointing me out to their friends. Woman who never talk to me waving at me, going out their way to come and ask me for my autograph: nice woman. Local movie star. Me.

So, I get this job to die. Is a kind of jungle picture, with a river in it and a trail and a rope bridge and a love story and natives with headdresses of colored feathers, their splendid bodies bare except for grass skirts, carrying bwana packs over the mountains. And they have donkeys. I mean, we have donkeys. Some of us tote the loads on we head. Around us is the enemy, another warring tribe. In the bushes. Crawling on their bellies. Shooting with expert marksmanship. They just shoot you and you supposed to fall. These shooters ain't missing at all: the script.

When you're a little boy and you playing stick-'em-up, the shooter does miss a few times at least before he connects. It is part of the convention of the game: the shooter shoots; you fall or dodge the bullets and make

25

your escape. And since it is not real, since it is make-believe, it is left to you to confirm his marksmanship by agreeing to be wounded or shot dead. There is a certain give-and-take, reasonableness, like in a fiction, rooted in the idea that life gives everybody a chance, that leaves everybody satisfied, whether you are the one shot or the one doing the shooting. The shooter must miss a few times, since it is quite fatal when he connects. But here, in this movie, the fellars who shooting, they not missing at all. The only people who they missing is the fellars from the States: the stars.

"Their lives are charmed," Errol says smiling, talking about the stars. "Their lives are charmed."

Errol is an actor who looked on at the rebellion of '70 and kept his distance. He feels deeply. So much of life pains him and delights him. He is alarmed, astonished, outraged and for him that is enough; I mean, he doesn't feel the need to go beyond feeling to action. His job is to feel, to bear witness with his heart. He emerges less a moral superior than a barometer of emotion. Now he had taken grief to a new height. His words sound like poetry. His laughter is deepest pain: Their lives are charmed.

I going over this ravine on a rope bridge. *Blam! Blam! Blam!* Shots all around. Fellars falling, except fellars from the States. All around me fellars falling, left and right. *Blap! Blap! Blap!* Like flies. Like how you see natives fall in a Tarzan picture. As the people shoot, they falling. They falling. They dropping dead just so. Then I get shot.

Even in a movie, I don't want to die on a rope bridge with bwana pack on my back. But this is the script. They shoot you, you have to die. That is what they paying me to do. To die.

I get shot. I hold my shoulder, wounded, and I scramble across the bridge and Blam! They shoot again and I start to fall. I have to fall. But something holding me back. My conscience, my pride. Something is not right. And I look across at Stanley and Errol and them for a cue, how to die, since they are experienced actors, real actors. But Stanley and Errol, all of them, all these fellars, good men, good actors, they just falling down and dying just so. And I in confusion looking at them fall, thinking how could an actor, a man like Errol, fall so? "But wait!" I say when it hit me what was happening. "Wait! Wait! Wait! Wait! What is this?" And for a moment, I am torn. I don't want to upstage Errol and Stanley and them. But same time there is a voice in my mind shouting, *No. No. No. No, I ain't falling so.* I can't follow them. I ain't dying so, No, man. Um-um. No.

Even when I was a kid playing stick-'em-up and I get shot, I composed my dying like a poem. There was poetry in my dying. When I get shot and I start to die, I hear the theme music of the movie, I turn to the bite of the bullets, my knees buckle, my hands reach out and I hold on for the last, a little piece of the world – the sky, the air, my eyes open and I fill them with the wonder of trees, singing birds in the verandas of their branches, the roar of women in the marketplace, the noise of children at the playground, people quarreling, lovers undressing each other, I move into a dance, feeling the blood of life leaving my head, I breathe in, the fragrance of ripe guavas turning to the smell of crushed corraili leaves, hearing the last drumroll, cymbals crashing, seeing the lights growing dim, waves beating onto the shore, fish leaping silver. That was when I was a little boy playing. Dying was a performance. I was at the center of my own dying.

Now, here was I, a grown man, in a real movie and I was dying like ah arse, like a fool. And I actually see myself beginning to fall, following the lead of fellows who I respected. I see myself falling when, out of the corner of my eye, I glimpse this man, one of the fellars, one of our fellars get shot. And this man flings up his arms as if he is lifted by the shot. And he holds them spread out there above his head like a stickfighter whose charge is arrested by his parrying of a blow and he sways, stretching them away from his body like he crucifying a cross or like is Carnival day and he playing a big mas, a big hooray of a Wild-Indian – The Rise of Montezuma or something – with a tepee for a headpiece, the tassels on the sleeves of his jacket hanging down like a curtain of fern, his cape spread out behind him, the music blaring *dar-da dar-dar: dar-dar, dar-dar*, and he in front the audience in the savannah and he straining to hold the headpiece, to hold it steady to prevent it from toppling. And he remained balanced there for an eternity, then he sink down slow to his knees, his hands on his heart, the blood leaking out his chest, his eyes gazing at the ground with that look that those paintings show Columbus and Cortez and those conquistadors have in their eyes when they about to kiss the ground of the land that they just discover and conquer and claim in the name of Isabella the Queen of Spain. But this fella's eyes is not an ocean of arrogance; they don't have in them the greed, or bombast; in them is the piety, the awe, the pity, as if just as he was discovering the land, discovering life, he had to leave it. I applauded him. There was the death I would have died.

The man dying so magnificently, the author of that extravagant and magnificent dying, was Sonnyboy. Inspired,

28

I fling out my arms too in the beautiful movements of the dance of my childhood and begin the exquisite choreography of my dying.

"Cut!" the director says. Cut it. Because the director don't like how we dying at all. He doesn't like it. And even the fellars there, the same fellars, my countrymen, who go through a boyhood like my own, and who should know, who must know the conventions of the shooting game, the same very fellars looking at me and Sonnyboy, as if we commit some kinda crime. The quality of our dying is an embarrassment to them. We dying too slow. We wasting too much of the Whitepeople time.

"Too extravagant," Errol says. "Too colorful!"

"Rookie," Claude says.

As if they have some superior notion of how a man who is shot is supposed to die, all of them start to laugh that *heh heh heh* laugh by which the less courageous of us were subdued.

"What you expect from a calypsonian?"

I spoke to them. I said, "Gentlemen, I want you to know that this is the last moment of my life. This is the last moment. This is not my dying. This is my last living moment."

But no. The director don't want it so.

"No?"

"Sir," I ask him. "Sir? You think it is fair to ask somebody to die just so, to fall and crumble just so without leaving at his dying some memorable gesture? You think it right in a situation where all that you have been given to do, where the total span and compass of the work you are employed to perform is to die, to do it, to die so ... so unremarkably?"

But he swing his head and toss his mane. Budget.

29

Shooting schedule. Time constraints. He believes that that kind of dying, that expression of meaning belongs to the stars. He has stars to do that, he tell me.

"But," I pointed out to him, "I do not see the stars getting killed." Something that we in this part of the world have been familiar with over a lifetime of watching movies: Star-boys don't die. They are the ones that endure. And even at the end if one dies; if perchance, according to my friend Bispat, quoting what he remembered of his Shakespeare, if perchance one should be killed, you know him, he doesn't need his death, you have seen him live his life. I am the one dying. I need my death to live.

"And, sir," I said.

"Call me Max," he says.

"Call him Max," the Trinidadian natives echo, jubilant as if they just get a holiday.

"Max," I said, the word like a weight on my tongue, "Max, I feel misled. Here I am a native, robbed of my life and now of my dying. Remember," I continued, "that after this death I have no further part in the picture ... unless you need me to die again. I know is your picture. I know I am not the star-boy. But, even so, you can't rob me of that ... of that ..."

"Honor?" Errol challenged, his voice gurgling with sarcasm, his cheeks bunching, his teeth showing.

"Not honor. *Right*. No matter what your plot, we are human who would each like to leave our individual mark, our human signature, on our efforts and it is as human we must die."

"Hear! Hear!" cried Wilbert and Claude in unison. "Hear, hear!"

"You talking, boy!"

Yes, I was talking now, I was speaking. In full flight, I had a voice now, I was on the floor:

"And if it is your pleasure, if, according to your script, according to your script-writer, if is your pleasure that I must get shot ... if I get shoot ... if you shoot me, indiscriminately and casually, letting me die so obscurely that people watching this picture can't even see me in the background in the bush toting the loads for your expedition on my head ... if you say I must die, at least allow me the space to die how I want to die."

But he wouldn't budge. And the Trinidadian fellars, my countrymen, not giving me no support.

I tried to talk to them, "Listen, fellars," I say, "Stanley, Errol, Claude, Ralph, Davindra, Errol, is like you don't know who you are? You are among the best actors in the world. You have, at least, earned your dying. Don't let this joker treat us so."

"It is just a movie," Errol say. And as if to point us away from the pathos, the pain in the statement, he say it again, this time with half a laugh to give us the direction we should take: "*It is just a movie.*" And you had to listen past the chuckle in his laughter to the subtle agony bubbling in his voice, the sadness, the grief, the truth, the tears of a capped-down rage: "*Is just a movie.*"

"Let us get together," I plead, "and live the last moment of this life with some dignity. He can't fire everybody."

"It is just a movie," they answer in chorus, something between the corrective sternness of a parent and the mindless recitation of children on a school stage.

"Max is the director. He is the boss," they chorus.

"Max is the boss," Errol says with that double and triple meaning.

31

"And you?" I ask. "Who are you?"

"We?"

"I?"

"Me?" *And I could hear the metallic ring of the me, like a note struck on a steelpan*: Mee-ee?

"I just putting in a day work."

"I can't sing calypso, like you."

"And I certainly not a badjohn. Like your revolutionary pardner Sonnyboy."

Now they were ridiculing me. "Heh heh heh," they laughed.

"Worry with Sonnyboy," they said snidely. "Sonnyboy just doing this for kicks."

"For the excitement."

"For sport."

"Sonnyboy just showing off."

"You getting pay to die how the director say to die."

Now they were vexed with me. And more vigilant about the man's business than their own.

"Just dead and get on with it before you muddy the water for everybody else."

"If you want to die in style, make your own picture."

"Yes. Star in it. You and your pardner Sonnyboy."

"Heh heh heh," Errol say again and the others laugh: "Heh heh heh."

"Yes. Is just a movie. You don't need to make style."

"Style? Style? Style? You want to deny me style? Errol, I am dying and you want to deny me style?"

"What he so serious about?" they ask.

"What else do I have but style?"

"Yes, what you so serious about?"

"No, no, no, fellars, what else but style?" I found myself

32

screaming. Then I caught myself. Yes, what was I so serious about? What the hell! I mean, I didn't want to appear to be superior to them, to embarrass them. They were my pardners. I wanted to be one of them, one with the crowd. And for a moment, I try. I seek refuge in laughter, in the joke that would absolve me of any deeper responsibility and give me the support of their company.

"What they paying you to do?" they ask.

"They paying me to die," I said loudly, my whole head on fire, the crowd spurring me on: "I will die how he say to die. Yes," I say aloud. "It ... it ... it ... It is ... it is ... It is just ... It is just ... It is just ... It is just ..."

"Yee-es!" they encourage, relieved that I had fallen in line.

"Yes," they cry. "Yes. It is just a movie."

"It is just ... it is just a movie." And I join them in the laughter, "Heh heh heh!"

But I still uneasy.

Then in the next scene, we had to die again. In the bush this time, obscured by plants and vines, part of the foliage. I am just a blur in the background. Just ahead of me is Sonnyboy. And the shooter, a native from another tribe, release bullets to his heart, to his head, the shots so intense that he start jumping and dancing and walking in that electric break-dance spasm like you see those fellars perform in gangster movies when shots slam into their body, and the inevitable death is delayed by this frenetic dance in salute of life. And in the middle of his ballet, the director calls:

"Hey, you. Cut! Cut! That is not what we want."

Sonnyboy does not move. He stand up there, his body coiled in an inexpressible anger and outrage and surprise

33

and grief. I thought he was going to speak. Sonnyboy is calm. He lifts both hands, palm open. Like in surrender.

The cameraman stop filming. They turn off the lights.

The men look at each other.

And right there Sonnyboy take off the feathered headpiece of the costume, unhook the rings from his nose. From his waist, he unbelts the band of the grass skirt they had given him to wear and he drops them with his spear – his spear – right there. And for a moment he stand-up there in his shorts, slightly comic, looking bemused, as if he had surprised himself, and now didn't know what other move to make. It was as if the spontaneity of his action had faced him with the self hidden in himself. It was a self that he was thrilled with and alarmed by, and almost in a daze, as if he now had no choice but to be the fella he had unclothed, he made one step, then another, and with that fella's legs, he walked away.

I could see the others, the crowd of them, their grass skirts below their bellies, gathered together like the members of a choir of penguins in a helpless flutter of alarm. Sensing what might have been his bewilderment, they gather the courage to laugh at Sonnyboy, at the fool he had made of himself: "Heh heh heh!" Until I begin to take off my headpiece too and my nose rings and my amulets and my leggings and my grass skirt. We stand facing each other, me and they, as in a pantomime in which they are portraying the righteous members of a tribal council and I am the dissident member they are ordering into exile. In a pantomime, I would leave the stage for this number and would return for the next one. But I am not going to return. This is not a pantomime. I am not playing. As I walk off, I could hear them serious, then outraged, as if I had assaulted them, the laughter dying in their throats. I hear Errol's voice, frustrated, angry, insistently pleading what he believes to be a truth I had not grasped:

"It is just a movie, King! It is just a movie!" screaming the words at me, tears in his voice. "King, it is just a movie." As if he is pleading for his life.

I felt quite sad. I didn't say anything. I hated to leave Errol like that; but I had to. Because I had my point too. How to say it: *Yes. Yes, because if ... if indeed it was just a movie, did he, did they not consider that I was ... we were just actor?* But I didn't say anything. I didn't look back.

I was outside the building when I heard my name called. When I look around, it was Sonnyboy. He was leaving as well.

"King!"

"Listen, pardner," I tell him. "You don't have to leave your job because of me. You're working. I don't want you to jeopardize your employment just for me."

He didn't respond immediately. He just looked at me with what I suppose was patience. I had totally misread the man. "Sorry! Sorry!" I said. "Sorry," I said again.

"Yes," he said, talking to himself. "You hardly know me."

Rouff Street

Before he came to stay by his grandmother in Cascadu, Sonnyboy lived with his mother at Rouff Street in Port of Spain, up the hill, behind the bridge, between the sounds of the goatskin drums from the Shango Yard by Ma Trotman, the shouts and pleas breathed from Mother Olga's Shouters church, the staccato of cussing, the grumble of anger, and the screams of grief that would lodge in his brain and give him his ear for rhythm, so that later, when he started to beat iron in the steelband, what he produced was not the insistent percussive sound to keep the band on the beat, but the discordant chiming clanging clataclanging that opened up the belly of the music to make woman start to wine, young fellars square off to fight and big men put their two hands on their head and weep.

Childhood polio had made one of his legs shorter than the other, and had given him a slight hop-and-drop walk that was in tune with the music in his belly; and he balanced himself with the awkward elegance of a king sailor on the unsteady deck of the world, out of time with its rhythm, wondering, as he walked through Rouff Street, what disaster had brought him to this place where his ears always ringing, his head always hot, his mind thinking to get a penknife to cut, a stone to pelt, a bottle to break, trying to understand how he was to be Christian and human in this mess.

At Escallier RC, where he went to elementary school, his surliness brought him to the attention of the headmaster

Mr. Mitchell, who called his mother in to complain about his inattention, the hostility inside him that set him fighting, that make him one afternoon take up the school bell while classes going on and start to ring it, *balang! balang!* like he summoning a set of dangerous and rebellious spirits. After Mr. Mitchell call her in for the third time, she put Sonnyboy to sit down and explained to him what Mr. Mitchell in his way had tried to tell him but didn't have the language to get across:

"They put you here in this boiling heat to live, not because this is some wonderful cleansing fire out of which they expect you to emerge productive and restrained. They put you here to kill you. For you to dead. To give you so much pressure that you will turn their brutality against your own brother so that their prophecies would be fulfilled. And the reason why you must listen to what Mr. Mitchell tell you is not because your obedience will bring down blessings from The Most High, either in this life or in the one to come. And not because the mighty will unleash their harshest punishment on you if you break their commandments. They doing that already, and you have done them no wrong. The reason you must stay Christian and human in this place is because, for all the sermons they fling in your direction and the tears they shed in your name, they so expect you to fail, they have a cell and a number waiting for you in the prison and a place to bury you when you dead. Yes, they counting on you to turn up in their jail and on their gallows. Your mission, if you decide to take it, is to disappoint them. Let them claim their victory somewhere else. Leave them with their money and their baubles and their Babel. Leave them with what they have. Don't give them the pleasure of seeing you inhabit their prison or their hospital or their grave. Do not let them see you vagrant in the road begging them for the crumbs of their pennies. Stay up, so you could watch the surprise in their eyes when they see you still here, when they see they ain't kill you, when they see that you not dead. Let them marvel, 'I wonder how this one escape?' The world is a more than beautiful place. It doesn't belong to them more than it belongs to you. Yes, to you. Wickedness can flourish, it cannot reign. Things can change. And if all you have to fight with is yourself, don't do their work for them. Stay strong. Don't drag down yourself with foolishness."

She put her arms around Sonnyboy and hugged him to her bosom and he put his arms around her neck and he stay there, hearing her heart beat, feeling her body heave, tasting the tears dripping down from her eyes onto his face before she break away, blinking and laughing: "Go and eat your food. Hold up your head. Look at me. Look!"

Sonnyboy had looked at her live these lessons, herself scrubbing and washing and wrestling the two rooms they lived in into a home, with red lavender in buckets of water, with gully root and sweet broom and blue soap, the four corners of the house smoked with incense, the floors brightened with linoleum, the windows with curtains, the furniture with varnish and the walls with paint, the troughs of earth in the little space in front the house planted with aloes and ginger lilies and wonder of the world, with marigold and zinnias and croton and Jacob's coat, the plants at her front door flowering with a joy as fertile as the faith she expressed in her singing and her contagious laughter: the scandal of her jokes doubling over the women fetching water or washing or bathing at the single standpipe on the street, lifting them in these magical moments above the mud and the rubbish gathered in the drains, to a height from which to look squarely at the world that looked down on them, the women holding their bellies with two hands to keep from bursting with the sweetness of the pain of the dotishness that flowed from human beings, all of them joined now to a sense of community. Among them the wonderful simplicity of human exchange, plants for their front gardens, remedies for illnesses, consolation for the mother of the girl who get catch with a belly, compassion for the mother of the boy gone off to jail, the exchange and generosity: a dress, a pair of shoes, exchanged, one keeping the children for her neighbor so she could go and release the pressure, dancing to the music of Fitz Vaughn or Sel Duncan; his mother waiting her turn, returning fortified from the standpipe by which she had to bathe, with a bucket of water, her petticoat dripping, the form of her body outlined underneath it, without apology to anyone except perhaps Sonnyboy's father, the man she had enlisted to help her save herself and him. From her own strength, doing her all to prevent the place from weighing him down, seeing that his shirt was ironed without a crease, that his food was secure, protected from flies underneath the wire netting of the safe, giving him the last of the cocoa or coffee and she and the children drinking teas from shrubs in the yard, vervine, carpenter grass, and Sonnyboy's favorite, fever grass, consoling him when the fella he was working with as a mattress maker and upholsterer of chairs wouldn't pay him the money he work for, agreeing with him that "Lance, man, you not cut out for this shit. You have too much talent. You too good-looking to take this set of pressure. And, boy, you have a good voice, you could sing."

She watched other women watching him when they went to a dance, her mother babysitting the children. He and she in the same color and styled shirt and pants, dancing, her two hands round his neck and the comfort of her bosom against his chest. She watched him move among people with his movie-star smile and relaxed stance, confirming her thinking that no, this cell and prison of Rouff Street is no place for you, expecting him to take off and go away and get out of this place and praying for him to stay, no family to help them, the four brothers of his, each with his own battle to fight, the one older than him who fancied himself a singer, setting out every morning, decked in his white ruffle-fronted shirt with the puff sleeves red, his guitar round his neck, to the Botanic Gardens or the Lady Young Lookout to find tourists to sing them verses of popular calypso or made-up ones of his own on the beauty of the tourist woman, the cleverness of her husband, the loveliness of the island. After they give him some change, going back in time to clip tickets for the 12:30 show at the Pyramid cinema where he held down a job as a checker; another brother, George, the saga-boy, dapper, pants seam cutting, shirt collar upturned, gold chain on his neck, gold teeth in his mouth, every time you see him is with a new woman holding on to him as if she fraid he will fly away if she let go; Calvin, the sportsman, good at cricket and football, going every day to the savannah to play one of the games, sometimes with a bat in his hands, always his wrists bandaged, a knee band or ankle band on, walking with a limp to draw attention to his dedication to sports as well as to his heroic survival; Bruce who coulda been a heavyweight boxer find himself in prison for beating, one by one, seven fellars who sampat him after a dance; and Lance, he, Lance, the one with such good looks and talent and all the promise, stay anchored here making mattresses and upholstering chairs, not, as she thought at first, because of her and the children. Because of a steelpan.

Pan

Lance have this pan, a carbide pan, big enough to sound, big enough so it could play two notes, then three, Borborpee dorp! Boborpee dorp!

Every Monday and Tuesday midday he would go to the empty train carriage at the railway station to jam with the fellars from the abattoir, each man beating out the rhythm on his own pan or calling out the ringing rejoicing spirit from his own piece of iron.

One day Lance forget his pan in the train carriage. When he get it back two days later he discovered from its face and sound that someone had beaten it out of shape and out of tune so that it didn't give him the usual sound when he struck it. He was ready to kill. Thank God Lance didn't find the man who commit this brutality on his pan.

"Thank you, Jesus!"

She had watched Lance come home with this bruised and wounded pan and begin to pound it to get it back into shape so he could get the lost notes of the rhythm. After days of hearing him pounding and pounding, she tell him, "What you doing? You not going to get it to sound the same way again, you know."

"I know."

"You know? So what you doing then?"

And is then, before he could answer, it hit her: somewhere in pounding to find the lost note, Lance had begun to hear a note that as yet hadn't made a sound. And what he was doing now was trying to get not the note he had lost but the note behind that note, a note unsounded and sacred and surprising and potential – to get that note to sound.

Now Lance in a trance. Lance is a sculptor of iron. Lance coming home early from work to work on the pan. Afraid it would burst from his pounding, Lance build a fire and he heat the pan and when the metal hot and soft he push out the note, not the note yet, a little bump on the face of the pan, making the bump bigger little by little by little and then another bump, each bump a note, a sound, she and Sonnyboy watching the whole operation, Lance hammering again, pounding and pushing out the metal, shaping the notes to fit on the face of this pan, tightening the space or widening it, flattening it or deepening it to get the note to correspond to the sound in his head, in his heart, in his belly, in his stones, Lance envisioning a whole new world of sound, taking the music of the drum to another pitch, another plane, Lance going over the whole process again and again to get this new and audacious music out of his drum. And all this time, her mother and those neighbors, who know the trouble she seeing, looking from Lance and his patient tenderness with the pan to her to see what she doing with this man, and she could hear them thinking, *if he had with you the patience he have with that pan, if he had with his children, with work the patience he have with that pan* . . . She tried her best to be supportive. She wanted to assist. But, they were right. She couldn't help but observe his patient tenderness with the pan, and she find the same words leaving her head and finding her voice: "If you had with me the patience you have with that pan . . . If you had with work, with your children, the resolve you have with that pan . . . If you had . . . if you . . . if you . . . if if if . . . if . . ." And although in her belly she could feel the value of what

Lance was doing, in her mind she wanted from him an explanation to help her mother and the world understand what a woman like she was doing with that man; but, Lance didn't have the words to answer, and instead of sitting down feeling guilty and small, or struggling to find the words to console her, anytime she start up, started to talk, he would get up and leave and go to the empty lot across the road and sit down on the boulder underneath the mango tree where a growing congregation of idlers were cheering him on as he journeyed into the heart of the pan. When she look at him, the man she see in front her was not the man she know. That Lance was gone, this man was spirit, Ogun.

But the world don't stop demanding money for things. The children have to eat. They have to get uniform and shoes to go to school, she tell him, not just to reproach him about his neglect of her and the children, more to get him to appreciate the role she was playing to free him from the death and defeat of this place; not, as she said with the undertones of jubilation and triumph and frustration at being put into this situation, not to do all this for you to spend your time reshaping a steelpan, but to be a man to make a dent in the iron of this beast of a world. She wanted him to say something, to make clear his position. But he wasn't hearing. He couldn't hear. One day when he was with his congregation in the yard across the road, she take Sonnyboy and his brother Alvin with her and go by her mother further up the hill in Zigili Trace to stay, making, after she cool down a little, the occasional visit back to him with a bowl of pigeon peas and rice or dumplings and saltfish, offerings of her goodwill and also to see if it had left him, this pan jumbie, this spirit that had claimed him;

and when she discovered that it had not, she pick up the rest of her clothes and go back up by her mother, this time to remain. And it would be there eventually he would come to see her, at first with a promise to change, but, later – as someone surrendered to a more urgent calling than seeing after the welfare of she and his children – to bring little gifts for the children, a toy on a birthday, two-three copybooks at the opening of the school term. Once he brought them each a pair of gym boots into which he had placed a dollar bill, the magnificence of this gift lighting up Sonnyboy's face and bringing tears to her eyes, because she was glad to see Lance trying, for by then he had made himself not the principal individual responsible for the well-being of his children, but one of many contributors to their welfare. Sonnyboy watched as the hill wrapped itself around his father, feeling at first resentful of the community for taking his father away from him. But, later, as he realized that in giving himself to the community, his father had given the community to him, Sonnyboy began to feel a sense of belonging. He began to hold himself a little more upright, to set down his feet with more careful steps that carried up his shoulders and crafted his limp into the delicate rocking, crawling dance of the king sailor navigating the perilous tightrope of the hill, his mother knowing the trouble such a dance attracted, watching, proud and frightened, speaking to him with a calming gentleness, asking "How school going? How your shoes fitting?" Her gentleness deepening, as she felt the weight of her children's upbringing falling more and more on her single shoulders, taking him up the hill to the Shango yard by Mother Olga where she begged Shango and Obatala to intercede for him, and the better to cover all options, she

45

tied her head and mounted the hill with him to the Shouters church for Mother Olga and Mr. Trim to put their hands on his head and pray for him. But things didn't change. At home she began to hum the hymns of resolve to keep off despair, as a declaration that for all her burdens she had not surrendered:

Jesus on the main line, tell him what you want, tell him what you want right now.

But even that would not sustain her, and she had her eyes open now out of necessity for another man, not as pretty. Fellars start to come around, and she find herself accepting favors from a fella she would have rejected a few years earlier as too tame, too surrendered, but was glad he was a little more stable, less inclined to roam, would care for her, didn't have no steeldrum beating in his belly, wasn't carrying no lost note in his stones, accepting this change as part of the life she was born into, having discovered some time ago that it was useless to complain, not only about him, the man, Sonnyboy's father, but about anything around her, the roads, the houses, the area, the schools, the violence, the hard times, each article of frustration linked to the chain of strangulation that was this hill. Everything was on her shoulders, and when things didn't work out with the fella, she sang to Jesus, wishing for the miracle of winning a lottery, for her aunt in the States to send for her. In a rush of optimism, counting the money she would make working over there in the States, dreaming with the children the things she would buy for them, the butter to put on their bread, the leather shoes, the shirts, the pants. And all this time making miracle after miracle to create the magic of a meal from the scraps she could

46

afford in the market, until one day after the market, she put down her basket, she sit down on her front steps and when she go to get up she feel the whole town pressing down on her. Yes, it was too much and she came to the realization that really, yes, she really was not able. This thing that she find herself having to face was bigger, more monumental and rooted than she had imagined. It was not just a challenge, not just a test of endurance and strength that could be overcome by work alone, or by faith or by fortitude. This place? This place was something that was set up and maintained by the great spite and wickedness and – let me give her a word – cynicism of a pitiless Power. It was not something she could change by herself alone. This was a place she had to leave. Sonnyboy noticed her change of rhythm.

He recognized that she had replaced the cheer with which she lifted up herself and the neighborhood with a new triumphant resolve to escape this place, to leave it and go.

Every other day she was at the Post Office sending a letter to her aunt in the States or inquiring about one she was expecting as she sang:

Jesus on the main line tell him what you want,
tell him what you want,

with a kind of upbeat defiant joy in order to coax good fortune into her life, making dance steps while she washed the clothes or cooked so as not to be forsaken by joy, while three streets away his father pounded and tuned the instrument they called the pan, working for the day when the new notes would fly out from the nest of metal, slip off the face of the bowl of steel and rise into flames of sound, the first steelpan notes in creation. Sonnyboy listening for the sound too, for the note, beginning to rush home from school to go to the yard in Zigili Trace, to be there when at last his father would play the notes that he had carved on the face of the steelpan and music would fly out and angels would rejoice and his father would come home, bringing food for the table and a ham for Christmas and his mother wouldn't have to leave and go away to America.

Mammie

And then, that evening, Sonnyboy going home from school, walking up the hill that branched into Rouff Street when he hear his name called. When he look around, it was his mother, behind him, returning home, hurrying up the hill to catch up to him. She had left that morning to go to Maraval to check out the possibility of a work with a woman who wanted a housekeeper to live in. She had gone, expecting to convince the woman who wanted the housekeeper that she could do the job without living in, since she had children of her own to mind. She had walked to go and walked to come back the four-five miles since she didn't even have money for car fare (buses did not run there). The woman was sympathetic, but she really had to have someone to live in. However she had a friend, she said, higher up the Maraval road, who wanted somebody. The woman give his mother the address. It wasn't very far, she tell her. If she catch a taxi at the corner, she will get there in five minutes.

Taxi?

"Yes," his mother tell her. "Thanks. Thank you."

But she didn't have money for taxi, so she had to walk back home and it was there she was heading when she see Sonnyboy. She would go and see about the work next day by taxi, but, the *taxi fare?* The only person she could think of getting it from was his father. So, she had steered Sonnyboy in the direction of Rouff Street.

"All I want from your father is taxi fare to Maraval.

Nothing else," speaking out loud as if she wanted to make it clear to herself as well as to him that she wasn't doing this to try to get back with him. "And if he don't have, for him to go and get it borrow from his brother or one of his friends."

When they reached Rouff Street, Sonnyboy see in the yard his father, sitting on a big stone underneath the mango tree and around him the congregation from the neighborhood, all of them hushed and waiting.

He watched his father take up the pan and set it on one knee and with a stick in his hand begin beating the pan, coaxing out the notes,

pam pam pam paddam pam
Pam pam pam pam

that when he hear them is the melody of the hymn that for years had been sounding in the ears of the hill from the church of Mother Olga and Mr. Trim:

I am a warrior out in the fields,
and I can sing. And I can shout ...

And everybody waiting for the absent sounds to enter the world, to enter life. And his father, hitting each note to establish its presence searching for the sequence of notes that would produce the melody of the song.

And I can
And I can
And I can tell
And I can tell it tell it tell it,
And I can tell it
and I can tell and I can
I can I can I can,

the sounds called forth from their slumber, sparkling, clear-eyed into the world:

And I can tell it
And I can can can tell it
And I can tell it
And I can tell it all
About ...

And everybody waiting for those notes, like a family waiting for a relative they had never seen but would recognize when she came:

And I can tell it all about
that Jesus died for me
When I get over yonder
In the happy paradise,
When I get over yonder in the fields.

And Sonnyboy hear the notes flying out like flocks of birds from the nest of the pan, like a sprinkling of shillings thrown in the air, like a choir of infants reciting a prayer. He hear them again, like a rush of butterflies in a swarming dance, angular and precise like sharpened steel knives, soft like rain falling on a galvanized roof, like dragonflies dipping their tails into the water of a pond, the first steelpan notes in creation. And his mother grip his hand and stand up there, looking on as if this man, his father, was a stranger she was seeing for the first time and he knew, Sonnyboy knew, without a word from her that she wasn't going to ask his father for the taxi fare to Maraval. After he play that tune, people lift him up off the stone into the air and when they set him down, they put the pan in his hands. And like the congregation was waiting for this occasion, fellars pick up their own drums, some of them bring out pieces of iron, some dustbin covers and anything that could sound, could ring, and they went out on the street and down the hill, everybody following, Sonnyboy and his mother standing there on the same spot; until, with the crowd gone, she hold him round his shoulders and he put a hand round her waist and the two of them set out to walk back home to Zigili Trace, the two of them so wrapped up in each other that they didn't see Miss Catherine at her window looking down at them in the quiet street, until Miss Catherine called out to his mother, to them, with the gentleness of a blessing, *Lystra and her big son*, the words remaining long seconds in the air, Sonnyboy hearing them too, huge and gentle, fulling up his head, his heart, his belly: *Lystra and her big son.* And his mother answering, yes, in that moment hugging him with all her fear and fragility and her wanting and her love, "Yes, me and my big son."

And they didn't good reach home when they hear down the hill the police siren wail and the sound of scuffling and the metallic clang of pans hitting the ground and after a while screams and grunts and the animal panting of men running, and, coming up the hill, a relay of voices shouting the story in the one word: "Police!"

A little later Sonnyboy's father came to the house to ask his mother if they were all right. He was barebacked. His head was bandaged with the jersey he had been wearing. He was smiling as he tell them how he get away from the police by pushing the pan under a house and crawling in beside it. He was lucky. Sonnyboy felt his head grow big and his eyes begin to burn. He was waiting to hear the rest of the story. But that was it.

52

The day of creation was the day of humiliation. His father was angry, but nobody was outraged. Nobody. Sonnyboy felt his heart drop into his belly. And that was when the words that would pass his lips many times in his lifetime entered his heart, unfurled like a banner, "I not fucking taking that." Next day he carried them with him as he walked to school with the awkward elegance of a king sailor dancing on a stage by himself alone. Later that day as he discussed with Blackboy, Redman and Ancil and George the events of the night before, he said the words that in repeating he was claiming, "I not fucking taking that," only to be overheard by the headmaster Mr. Mitchell, who called him up to be punished. Asked to stretch out his hand to receive six lashes from the strap, Sonnyboy put his hands behind his back, shook his head and made his announcement to the astonished schoolmaster that was his declaration to the world, "I not taking fucking that," and he walked out of the school never to return.

Two weeks later his mother get the letter that she had been waiting on from her aunt from the States. On a Saturday afternoon she take him and Alvin and walk with them up past the savannah by the Botanic Gardens and the zoo. She buy each of them a snowball and sit down between them, on a bench and read for them the letter that she had just received from her aunt in the States. Her aunt was sending for her. She had to go. She would leave Alvin with her mother and send Sonnyboy to stay with his grandmother in Cascadu.

Remember the Singing
Rooplal and the Cascadu Years

In Cascadu, Sonnyboy would get a work first on the
Carabon cocoa estate, where he would do some cutlassing
and weeding, addressing his tasks with a sullen labored
care, slower than nearly every other worker, but twice as
neat, the grass he cut piled in different-sized artistically
shaped heaps, the hedges trimmed neat, the tools washed
clean after use, his mouth pushed out, his face severe, his
manner abrupt, as if he needed a mask of grumpiness to
compensate for the extraordinary diligence of his work.
He would carry his slow spiteful thoroughness to the
variety of odd jobs that fell to him thereafter, as a yard boy
at Choy's grocery, as a helper at Tarzan's tire shop, as a
laborer at the building sites, where he mixed cement and
sand under the impatient supervision of his uncle
McBurnie who found his thoroughness commendable Yes,
but, Jesus, man, at the rate you working you will put me
out of business. Sonnyboy happy to leave that job for one
in the sawmill where he could take whole day to clean the
machinery, tidy up around the building and bag sawdust
for sale. Later as he grew in strength and years he would
take his ceremonial thoroughness to the grappling of logs,
and canting them, mora, crappo and tapana, onto the
platform to be cut into boards or scantlings, as dictated by
the owner. On a Saturday afternoon he would head for the
river that flowed through a lullaby of bamboos, where
with the same labored care he would wash the sawdust

out his hair, excavate the sawdust out the cup of his ears and from underneath his fingernails, and fresh and clean set out for the Junction with the tiptoeing walk of a king sailor, muscles rippling, his chest outlined in the new jersey he had bought from what remained after he give his grandmother money from his pay, arriving at the corner to stand and watch cars pass and to smoke a cigarette and drink a beer with Gilda and Terry and Dog, and if he still had money left, cross the road and join the fellars gambling under the Health Office building. And when – not *if* – he lost, return to the consolation of the Junction to listen to Dog talk about the exploits of badjohns from the city, Gilda tell again the story of *To Hell and Back* and *Shane*, Gilda demonstrating the action and whistling the soundtrack to *Shane*, becoming Audie Murphy crawling on his belly through a hail of bullets, or Jack Palance, with the smooth stutter of a footballer taking a penalty kick, getting off his horse in *Shane*. He would draw closer to the circle of fellars listening to hear Terry, with subdued laughter, his hand over his mouth at the choicest parts, tell of his adventures with the women he had encountered in the hot dimly lit gateways of the city, detailing the time he and Ralphie meet this woman in a gateway and after haggling with her over the price of her company, following her on tiptoe up some rotting stairs into a dingy room on George Street where, with a lighted cigarette burning in her mouth, she lifted her dress and perched herself open-legged on a stool, blowing out smoke leisurely from the cigarette between her lips while Ralphie did his furious business between her thighs. When it was Terry's turn and she saw the equipment he was toting, her eyes opened wide and her voice rose in rebuke, "Where you going with that?" And, in a sterner voice, "You not putting *that* here, you know," closing her legs, getting off the stool, fixing her dress, *I better get out of here,* clattering down the steps, grumbling with an intimidating fierceness about their inconsiderateness, their money tucked away in her brassiere.

With nothing sensational to contribute to the evening's entertainment – he did not have the gift of retelling movies, and the intimate experience he had with women was almost nil and so not something he wanted to reveal – Sonnyboy found himself telling of the first time his father went on the road with the steelpan he had tuned and was attacked by the police, of his own astonishment and outrage as he watched the people unable or unwilling or afraid to retaliate, establishing that episode as the basis of his own resolve, *I not fucking taking that,* a declaration that even the fellars recognized as his way of sharpening his determination to stand against humiliation from any agency, be it individual or the state. They didn't burst out laughing like at Terry's salacious tales or feel the need to draw imaginary guns from their hips as at the adventures of *Shane.* They listened somewhat uneasily, sensing that Sonnyboy was waiting for the occasion to prove how ready he was to confront the world and they took note to make sure not to be the ones to give him the provocation they believed he was seeking.

And he went on growing into his manness, nurturing his resentment at the world, waiting for it to provoke him, ironing and seaming his trousers and stepping out with what would become his trademark neatness, his long sleeves folded at the cuffs, his handkerchief flapping over his back pocket, his hair in a muff, a little face-powder to take the shine off his forehead, making his way to the fêtes in the RC school, daring the girls to refuse to dance with him, waiting for a fella to oppose him and so provide the confrontation he was inviting. But he was lucky, and the only trouble he get in was a few skirmishes with fellars over gambling and a few over girls at a dance, nothing major, until the stupidest thing get him the trouble his grandmother tell him he was all the time looking for.

One night he and some fellars see this drunk Indian man by the shop, one of them search his pocket and they shared the few dollars found on him. Robbery with violence was the charge. His grandmother couldn't save him. That was the first time he went to jail, to the prison for youths where he would learn to box, would discover his aptitude for drums and his ability to wring a thrilling delighting power from his favorite percussive instrument, the iron. When he got out two years later, he had this nervousness about him as if he was spoiling for a fight, with a kind of aggressive listening and an ear tuned to pick up any slight, and it would be that keenness of hearing that would get him in the next set of trouble. Some obscenity about his mother. In this one, Marvel had a bottle and he had a knife. Marvel get cut. When he come out of jail, he had added a greater deliberation to his movements and stillness to his stance. He became a fella who although he did not appear to be looking, took note of everything around him. Later, this alertness would grow to become the foundation of a new sense of ease that helped him to control his aggression and banished his nervousness when he began to speak. For this development he had to thank Victor Rooplal, a dougla fella, who the first day he appeared in Cascadu, approached the Junction with a sense of ease, his two empty hands swinging, the pale flabby muscles of his arms displayed in a sleeveless merino, with a tailor's measuring tape hanging around his neck, and beside him, but not looking at him or speaking, as if they were having a disagreement that they had not resolved, a good-looking, brown-skinned woman, *a Spanish*, with long black hair, Marissa, a thin noisy battleax of a woman, who could have been at least ten years older than him, carrying in one hand a paper bag with what the town of Cascadu would discover later contained the few clothes she had hurriedly grabbed when she made up her mind to run away with him before the man she was living with came home from work and in the other hand a cage with a young parrot that Rooplal had won some days before in a dice game from a woodsman in Navet, Sonnyboy and the fellars looking out from under the Health Office building where they were playing the gambling game *wappie*, uncertain of any connection between him and the woman until she stopped, reached into her bosom, took some money out of her brassiere and give it to him without a word and continued walking toward the gas station where it was discovered later a relative lived, while Rooplal crossed the road to the Health Office building, in his hand five single-dollar bills smoothed out and packed together to make them look like a million, fellars seeing him coming, thinking he's easy pickings made a place for him. He find a place to sit down and begin to call his bets with the careless confidence of a man who know what he doing, and by the time the sun went down that evening he had everybody money in his pocket. Next weekend he would do it again, win-out everybody, leaving fellars to wonder if he was all that lucky or if he had a system of marking cards that nobody could detect. So that after that Saturday the only ones to bet against him were strangers and thirsty, impatient young fellars like Sonnyboy, who initially refused to be intimidated by his apparent skills, but who would in time discover that betting against him was throwing away money.

Rooplal settled down in Cascadu in a little house not far from the RC school, making a living gambling and ministering to distressed women needing help in matters of love, the steady stream of them going to him for bush baths and love potions, women talking of him in whispers, his notoriety spreading among them as an obeah-man, a seducer, whose magical charms none of their gender could resist, and the young fellars of the town holding him up as their authority on women, politics, gambling and race.

Rooplal was of mixed blood, African and Indian, this happy convenience making him welcome in each camp, entitling him to shower abuse on members of either group with a coarseness they tolerated from no one else, no side able to accuse him of prejudice since he shared his heritage with both; in his case, the two bloods canceling out each other, as equally potent warring and destructive poisons whose only virtue was to produce an offspring that was acceptable to both and that could be claimed by neither. Under his influence, Sonnyboy told the story again of the incident with his father, but where in earlier recounting he shared the blame between the people and the police, under Rooplal's prompting, he now put the responsibility almost solely on the people. Rooplal, it turned out, was also a tailor of some reputation, but had to leave his sewing machine behind because of the circumstances in which he ran away from Navet. By judicious management of his funds, Marissa saw that he paid down on a new sewing machine and did her best to encourage him to give up obeah and gambling.

He worked at tailoring for a little while, but he couldn't sit still for long in what was his tailor shop while card was playing out in the town, and eventually he spent most of his time gambling and the rest of it dodging men who came looking for him to get the clothes they had paid him to sew. Marissa, who had to bear the brunt of their anger because she was the one they met when they went to his home, now began to appear at the gambling place to call him, with some sternness, to come and complete the work he had accepted down-payment on. She was also not happy with his relationships with the women. She herself had gone to him for help to get her husband to pay her more attention and had ended up leaving the man and running away with him. The less Rooplal listened to her, the more she nagged. She began to reprimand him in public and to do everything in her power to shame him into becoming the man she wanted him to be. They were well matched in the department of stubbornness, he with the ability to ignore her and she with the tremendous power to nag again. She would leave him eventually after years of pulling and tugging, the final straw discovering he and a woman, both of them naked, in a secluded area on the bank of the river, in what he insisted was part of a ritual of healing. That night during an argument with him she burnt herself attempting to lift a pot of boiling water off the fire to pour on him. After that, he became very uneasy in her presence, and their relation went further downhill. One day after another quarrel, while he was under the Health Office gambling, she gathered up her belongings and put them in a paper bag to publicly display how little she had profited from being with him, next, she poured kerosene over all the clothes he had in the house, piled them in the middle of a room and left a lighted candle in the midst of the pile so that by the time it burnt itself out and caught the clothes on fire she would be far away. In a rush of spite she opened the cage and let out the parrot that Rooplal had come to treasure since he had fed it hot peppers to make its tongue flexible and had taught it to use obscene language, but the bird flew around the house for a while and then returned and stood on top the cage. In the end she put it back into the cage and took it with her to the taxi-stand where she stood waiting for a taxi and relating to anyone willing to hear all the intimate business that went on between Rooplal and her, while the parrot who answered to the name Cocotte went on cursing in its cracked voice the private parts of everybody's mother, until a policeman came. He couldn't do nothing because the woman was not cursing and there was no law under which he could arrest a parrot. And she went on telling to the crowd that had gathered the terms of endearment Rooplal had used to woo her, the darlings, the sugarplum, the ointments with which he would anoint his body, the places on her own that he would kiss, what he would do with his tongue, where on the bed he would place her, her helplessness in the situation because of the powers to charm that he possessed. She was still carrying on when her taxi came. She had just put one foot in the taxi when the onlookers were attracted to the appearance of a stream of white smoke in the air, somewhere in the vicinity of the RC school. Thinking that it might be a fire, people moved toward it to be sure of what was going on. Marissa coolly

61

completed her entry into the vehicle, the driver moving off slowly, to give occupants of the car the opportunity to see if it was indeed a fire and Marissa the occasion to wave cheekily at what was now becoming a blaze, then, speeding away in the direction of Cunaripo.

After Marissa left, many of the women of Cascadu saw Rooplal as a man to avoid and forbade their female relatives to look him in the eye. For protection against the force of his magical charms, they bathed in water perfumed with sweet broom and red lavender and doused themselves in prevention powders they got from another more reliable obeah-man, kept their heads straight so as not to meet his eyes and fingered their rosaries when they saw him passing. But to another set of women, Marissa's revelations had added to Rooplal's mystery and appeal and his home-lessness now offered an occasion for their solicitude. After she left, there was a steady stream of women of all levels of maturity who came by with rosaries or ohrinis or religious tracts, about them the soft grace of angels of mercy, shyly asking directions to where he might be found. Many of them offered him temporary accommodation, others offered him food, and some brought clothes. He accepted the full package of accommodation, food and clothes from Miss Zeena, a widow, a soft-spoken big-eye Christian woman with long hair and a body not so much weighed down as propelled by the sincere and muscular roll of a formidable bottom. After six days in which no one in the town saw him, he moved out of her place and settled into a two-roomed house behind the gas station.

With Marissa no longer there to harass him, and without the sewing machine to distract him, Rooplal gave up tailoring, but exposed the town to his other skills. He spoke on the political platform of any candidate who came to Cascadu and who would pay him. He made or pretended to make counterfeit money, and endeavored to find every means of making money without the inconvenience of orthodox labor. He linked up with Alligator Teeth, a loudmouthed big-eyed fella, a mouther whose claim to notoriety was his fearsome-looking teeth, loud voice and his boast that he was not too squeamish to scratch out the eyes or bite off the parts of any man who was so foolish as to get into a fight with him. With him, Rooplal roamed the countryside presenting himself as a maker of counterfeit money and trying to sell people the idea that there was treasure buried in their yards. In support of his claim, Rooplal produced two gold coins, which he said had come from a certain piece of land nearby, from treasure buried in the seventeenth century by Blackbeard the pirate. For a small fee, he was prepared to unearth the treasure. Some people chased him out of their yards, but there were the few who believed they were getting a bargain and paid him to dig, which he did, until they turned their back and he and Alligator Teeth disappeared with whatever money they had been given.

By the time Sonnyboy fell in with them, they had pretty much given up those moneymaking schemes and were focused on the more legitimate activities of gambling. Rooplal's disregard of the consequences of his actions on himself or on others was what principally fascinated Sonnyboy, and as he listened to Rooplal's stories of his escapades, the cards he marked, the women he fooled, the people he fleeced, Sonnyboy glimpsed in that approach to life something liberating, and Rooplal, sensing a willing apprentice to his methods, drew Sonnyboy to him.

Soon Sonnyboy became one of the party, going with them to whatever festivity was taking place in the town and its surroundings: to wakes, with two decks of marked cards and two packs of candles to provide light, at village fairs and sports meetings and harvests, with a folding table on which to play Over Under and Lucky Seven, or the Three Card game, with he, Sonnyboy or Alligator Teeth taking the role of the lucky punter, the decoy, pretending to be the one who could spot the Queen. They took their crooked games also to the various venues for horseracing, the savannah in Port of Spain, Santa Rosa in Arima, Skinner Park in the south of the island and at the open-air venues for Kiddies' Carnival. They went to Tobago only once and were chased away from setting up a game of their own by the Tobago hustlers and they ended up bathing in the sea and eating crab and dumplings from vendors on the beach at Store Bay. And so he had gone on, guided by the philosophy of how to get his own way and what it is he had to do to end up with a dollar in his pocket.

For Carnival, Rooplal and Alligator Teeth continued their hustle in more artistic vein, taking the role of Midnight Robbers, Rooplal adopting the persona of "The Mighty Cangancero" and Alligator Teeth that of "Ottie the Terrible." They left Cascadu and headed for Port of Spain, stopping at towns along the way, engaging each other in mock confrontation, drawing audiences at every street corner and coming away with purses full of money.

Hear Rooplal, The Mighty Cangancero:

Away from the dark lagoon of gloom came I the Mighty
    Cangancero, the most notorious criminal grand master.
With my every step, I cause the earth to tremble, my smile brings
    rain.

64

*My laughter causes the heavens to rumble, trees to fall, rivers to
overflow, animals to stampede and human beings to look for
shelter.*
*I am known in Mars, Jupiter, Saturn and the planet they call
Uranus,*
*I am the intergalactic bandit whose face is on the Most Wanted
list of bank robbers, kidnappers, plunderers, assassins and
bounty hunters.*
I traffic in precious metals, rubies, diamonds and pearls.
*For I am the most notorious criminal that was placed upon the
face of the universe. Everywhere I go the police and secret
services of the planets are on the lookout for me.*
I am Public Enemy numbers one two and three.
So bow, Mook-man, and deliver your treasures unto me.

And Alligator Teeth, Ottie the Terrible:

*Are you not afraid to walk this long lonely road, where I this
bloodthirsty terminator performs his daring crimes. For I live
today when men who seek to destroy me are all dead. I can bite off
a portion of the moon and shorten a season. A breath from my
nostrils can melt the north pole, inspire raging torrents, overturn
continents and cause islands to disappear. A wave of my hand can
stop rain, and cause, in what was once luxurious green, the panic
of deserts to appear. Women moan and children groan when
meeting me, this criminal master, so for your own good, I ask you
to seek my sympathy and bow, Mook-man, and deliver your
treasures unto me.*

Sonnyboy did not go with them. He headed directly to
Port of Spain to link up with his brother Alvin and other
relatives who from whichever part of the island they lived
would find their way into Tokyo steelband, all of them, the
whole Apparicio clan, the older ones holding aloft bits of

65

shrubbery, the younger ones waving handkerchiefs, the streets of the city their own for this one time of the year, so they have no fear of nothing, nobody could touch them in this band, people had to clear the road for them; Sonnyboy himself lined up with the rhythm section, the assembly of hard-muscled men, there to keep up the tempo and maintain the rhythm, as the guardians and force of the band, armed with an instrument that had the heft of a weapon they could employ if the need arose to fight. But fighting was out now; their mission was to give life to music, to make the rhythm sing, to draw people into the Festival of Spirit, into the Orisha of dance, into the defiant consolation of song, so they could know that poverty was not strong enough to overwhelm them, nothing could subdue the freshness of their enduring, nothing overwhelm the monument of their spirit, or overturn the cathedral of their dreams; Uncle George, the smooth one, the saga-boy, older now, with what remained of his hair still black, still slicked back, still neat, with two gaudily dressed and made-up women holding on to him, but not with the desperation of those of an earlier time, more as if supporting him; Sonnyboy's uncle Egbert, the one who tried to be a calypsonian, his shirt open showing his chest, portraying a wounded soldier, dressed in an army jacket, his head bandaged, embodying the response to the unutterable poignancy of the occasion by drinking to excess and wanting to fight, less to inflict hurt, it turned out, than to engage another human being, to let out this thing he couldn't express, this love that he was trying to find a way to give, in the end quieting down like a child, collapsing with that rubbery yielding, embracing the very ones a moment before he wanted to fight. Sonnyboy watching the pantomime of grief and nostalgia as Egbert staggered along, his arms thrown over the shoulders of the two men carrying him, not knowing what to do with himself, wanting to challenge the world, to fight with it, wanting it to know that he hurt, that something was missing. Sonnyboy held the tears inside himself, cradling the iron and looking across at another uncle, beating iron beside him, Bruce, a big strong man who Sonnyboy see one time bathing at the standpipe, having soaped his skin, lift a tub of water and pour it over his body to rinse off, Bruce now with the iron up under his chin like is a violin he playing, except that instead of sawing across the instrument, beating down on it, his arms curled and glistening, his shirt front wet with sweat, the music in his head, in his ears, in his belly, in his stones, and Bruce looking across at him too, striking the iron with a fresh resolve to challenge and encourage a new intensity from him to match and counterpoint his beating, Sonnyboy calling upon his muscles for the effort, feeling them respond, the iron ringing afresh, *clatack, clatack, clatacanging* with a new triumphant benediction. And behind them, in the band, people flowing with their soothing rousing dance, every triumph and disappointment and pain understood, a fella with the mincing, zany elegance of the king sailor, moon-walking across the street, the sweet obscenity punctuating the sober poetry of his uncle Egbert's challenge to the world: "Beat that! Beat that!" opening his arms and pointing to the pans, to the music, to the dancing: "Beat that!" *Beat that!* Wanting an enemy to fight, finding a brother to embrace. Because this morning he could fly. No army could defeat him, no force could keep him down: *Beat that!* And his friends would

67

come and hold him and embrace him and understand his tears and rage and pride: *Beat that!* And, bearing him up, they would flow forward, linked together with arms on shoulders and hands around waists, and he, Sonnyboy, beating the iron, *clakatang clakatang,* still beating when somebody put the mouth of a bottle of rum to his lips and he throw back his head and drink two-three gulps, still keeping up the rhythm for the band, and next to him his uncle Bruce, with the iron up under his chin, *balang balang balang balang bang,* everything else forgotten. And that would be Carnival for Sonnyboy.

And he would go back to Cascadu refreshed, renewed, to the sawmill and to the outings with Rooplal and Alligator Teeth, the dance of his king sailor walk giving him a certain unbalance that brought mystery and authority to his bearing, so that Rooplal, ever on the lookout for new moneymaking schemes, seeing him walking said, "Wait. I have the exact job for you. We could start a church. We could make bags of money with you as a pastor."

"And you collecting the tithes?" he said, turning it into a joke. But it was true. Rooplal was his friend, but Rooplal had not seen him either. Fearful that if he was not careful he would fade into the nothingness of the town, roused from slumber by his one day of Carnival, Sonnyboy grew quiet. He began to cultivate a way of speaking that muffled his words so you not sure exactly of what he saying. He developed a gruffness of manner as the best face with which to face this world, his arms folded across his chest like a genie, his voice clear and decisive when he had to speak, in his eyes a look of inquiry, to keep people on edge, deliberately stepping into their space to unsettle them, to have them shifting and uncomfortable. There were young

68

fellars who were ready to fight him just for that challenge, but his own readiness to oblige them gave them pause. Fellars had to take their time with him. Conscious of his power, he stepped off even slower now, his elbows turned outward away from his body, one foot rising and falling in sync with the other in the rolling motion as if he was pedaling a bicycle, so that even his grandmother find that for a big man he was walking too pretty. And he only begin to think of his future when, participating in one of Rooplal's audacious schemes that had to do with counterfeiting money, he found himself with Rooplal and Teeth in a room of a house somewhere in the countryside, in the middle of nowhere, while Khalid, the man who had brought them there, lay sleeping. Earlier that evening Sonnyboy had watched him sharpen his cutlass, then release his five pit bulls to patrol his yard. He had then invited them to dine with his family of a wife and five daughters. It was a delicious dinner of curry duck and steamed breadfruit. Khalid had paid Rooplal to produce 1,000 dollars of counterfeit money. Rooplal take the man money and had not delivered. He had danced the man until the man catch up with him. Now he had to produce the money by morning. There was no way that could be done since the whole thing was a con job gone bad. At the dinner Rooplal reminding him again that while he was overwhelmed by his courtesy he did not believe it was really necessary for them to remain. Khalid had in his possession the device to produce the money. All he would have to do would be to open it after the 12 hours. Yes, the man tell Rooplal. But I don't want to make no mistake. I would rather you remain. And he showed them to the room in which they were to sleep. As soon they enter the room the man give them to sleep in, Teeth start to tremble and then he came up with the idea that they should join hands and pray.

Sonnyboy had actually begun to pray when Rooplal let go of his hand, put a finger over his lips and stepped lightly out the room. He was following the trail of the aroma of desire left by one of the daughters who as they were having dinner had made the fatal error of looking into his eyes and had fallen under his magical spell. He found her in her room quite awake, fully dressed and with a suitcase packed, waiting to be rescued from the boredom of her village and taken to the places of excitement she had seen in his eyes. She was prepared to lead him past the dogs on condition he take her with him. He agreed, and while the rest of the house was asleep, she led Rooplal and his party out of the yard, into the road and to freedom. Rooplal tried to explain to her that life with him would most likely be hard and that he couldn't immediately provide anything comparable to what she was leaving. She didn't want to hear anything. She put one arm around his neck and clung to him. She would go wherever he was going. As soon as they walked out of the yard, Alligator Teeth started to run. Sonnyboy followed him. At some distance from Khalid's house they stopped until Rooplal came with the girl clinging to him and joined them and they set out walking in the direction of Cascadu, until a truck taking produce to the Port of Spain market stopped for them. Rooplal, the girl and Teeth proceeded to ride the truck all the way to Port of Spain, but Sonnyboy got off at Cascadu. He had decided to leave the association with Rooplal and Teeth for good. It was only after the truck had gone that he pushed his hand in his pocket and realized that Rooplal had not given him his portion of the money. Next day, knowing that Khalid and his men would be looking for him, he headed for Port of Spain to cool out by his brother at Rouff Street.

A few weeks later he would hear that Teeth playing badjohn at an excursion in Mayaro had his left hand chopped off just below the elbow by a young fella from Tunupuna whose name he didn't know was Blade. Rooplal, he would hear, had migrated with the girl to Canada. Sonnyboy would begin a new life as well.

In Port of Spain, Sonnyboy met Big Ancil, who was originally from Cascadu but now was a supervisor on a project in Port of Spain. From Big Ancil he got a job as a laborer on the project and he went about his work with few words and his trademark diligence. Struck by his strict mumbling tone and his diligent, if sullen, performance as a worker, Ancil had made him a foreman. He had managed the men under his control with a stern and intimidatory appearance and a minimum of words, spoken in the same mumbling indecipherable language, a display that so impressed Big Ancil (who was also a moneylender) that he employed him to extract money owed him from delinquent debtors. Later, delighted by his success in this very important matter, Big Ancil, who at that time was supporting the National Party, engaged him to provide protection for their supporters at their meetings in opposition territory. There he ran in once more to Big Head and Marvel, who were doing the same protective work for the Democratic Party. They had allowed their diligence to get out of hand and at their meetings actually began to jostle people who too vocally opposed the party they supported. Sonnyboy was clear. He didn't want any war with them. "Live and let live," he tell

71

them. "All of us getting a bread from the politics. We not here to kill nobody." And he exacted a truce from them.

One day Sonnyboy was riding in the car with Big Ancil when Big Ancil, who was announcing the details of a political meeting, seized by a fit of coughing, handed the microphone to him. After the shock of discovering how odd his voice sounded, Sonnyboy went on, with the approval and encouragement of Big Ancil, announcing for the rest of the evening. After that, whenever Big Ancil was tired he handed the microphone to him. At first Sonnyboy gave the information of the meeting, the time, the speakers, the venue; but, bored with repeating the same things again and again, he began to talk about things that interested him, about labor, about workers doing a fair day's work for a fair day's pay, about the pressure placed on people who he called the underdog in society, about how it was only one set of people the police arrested. He spoke about the difficulties his mother had to mind him and his brother and of her having to go away to get a better life. He told again of what happened with his father the day he put the notes on the steelpan and how Blackpeople didn't raise a hand in his protection. All that, Big Ancil came on to say, was what the National Party was going to change. The reason they were voting was to get that better life here. So between he and Big Ancil there developed a dialogue in which Sonnyboy outlined the problems and Big Ancil came on to say what the National Party was going to do about them. Big Ancil was finding driving the van too exhausting and he encouraged Sonnyboy to get his driving permit so he could take over the driving. It was while on his way to have his birth certificate reissued to him at the Red House that Sonnyboy, walking through Woodford Square, came upon the arguments and discussions on religion and politics and race relations that men were having in little groups all over the Square.

With the experience of speaking on the microphone announcing meetings behind him, and with the freedom to speak with authority that he had developed in his association with Rooplal over the years, Sonnyboy entered the discussions confidently. He discovered that there were people saying the same thing he had been saying for years: *I not fucking taking that.* And he marveled that they didn't have to tiptoe around the issues. They spoke out bold: I not accepting the world as you have laid it out. These fellars had better words and more history, but the sentiment was the same.

And he told again the story of his father and the inaction of the people and set off a big argument in the Square about whether Blackpeople were to be blamed for their own bad situation. There were those who agreed with him, but others were astonished at his ignorance of a history that had also made Blackpeople their own worst enemy. Blackpeople needed to see the world through eyes of their own.

After that day, Sonnyboy returned to the conversations in the Square, and over the months he began to see the world through eyes of his own and to join in the idea that they had to take power to take back themselves from that terrible history. He was there to see the numbers grow at the meetings and the Black Power movement begin. Sonnyboy joined the Black Power marches to Woodbrook, St. James, Diego Martin, there in the Carnival of claiming. Space and self and voice, history beginning to belong to him. Sonnyboy felt himself coming alive, felt that his arms were now more his own, that there were things to be done. He explained to Big Ancil that he had to say goodbye to the announcing, he had to move on. And since in his own mind he was a soldier, he began thinking of the struggle as something that would pit muscle against muscle. He convinced the Black Power people of his ability as a fighter. They appointed him bodyguard of one of the leaders. They equipped him with a pair of binoculars for him to bring faraway objects near, and he walked around with his king sailor walk, his arms folded across his chest, and a face more serious than anybody's own, one of the most conspicuous fellars there. But, he didn't care; he was part of an invincible army, part of the making of a new history. He watched the police vans trailing behind them as they marched to San Juan, Maraval, Cascadu, Couva. He watched the soldiers nodding their heads at the thunder of the speeches. And he with his arms folded, or with the binoculars glued to his eyes as he searched the crowd, for what, he wasn't clear. And, how quickly things turn around.

Nelson Island

Before his detention on Nelson Island, Sonnyboy had been to prison – not for thiefing, not for chopping up people in a dispute over ownership of land, or taking part in some big racket, defrauding the treasury; he went to jail for fighting, for defending himself against the disrespect and terror of a world that was ready to starve and stifle the underdog. Yes, he went to jail for fighting – on the streets, in the gambling club where he bust Marvel head with a bottle and, yes, a couple fellars feel the taste of his razor. But, there in political detention, as he listened to the Black Power leaders exchange stories of themselves and present insights from Frantz Fanon, Malcolm X, Stokely Carmichael and Walter Rodney of the violence rooted in the colonial situation, he realized that his *I not fucking taking that* was no different to fellars shouting for Black Power. He began to see that his lived rebellion had given him a place not at all inferior to that we had claimed for ourselves. He saw himself as a revolutionary like the rest of us. But even there, not many of us shared his view of himself. I myself didn't really take him on until the day he said something that made me look at him again.

He was sitting just above the beach, looking down at the sea. We had been talking about the steelband movement, about the difference between rebellion and revolution. He said, "You know this is the first *real* jail I make. This detention here as a political prisoner is the first time they put me in prison for doing *something*. The other times was stupidness. Fighting Marvel, cutting a man. Stupidness."

I took note of it, but didn't say anything. However, I noted that he had taken the opportunity to present himself as someone on our level. We were the revolutionaries and although we were willing to grant him a role in the revolution, his being a badjohn did not quite qualify him as a revolutionary.

When the period of incarceration came to an end, we said our goodbyes. Fellars were going back to their various jobs, some as teachers, some as civil servants, some to the university. Sonnyboy felt a sense of adventure, not as if he had come to an end, as if he was now beginning. In his last week of detention, he had received a letter from his mother. It had made him feel a softness to family and he spent that week thinking of all of them, his mother, his brother and his father.

He decided to stop first at the home of his father, who had moved out of Rouff Street. Sonnyboy found him in a new housing settlement that had already begun to grow old. It was as if the architects had decided to reproduce Rouff Street, the same narrow streets, the same tiny rooms, little concrete boxes steaming in the day and damp at night, no playground for the children, no allocation of space for business, no new vista from their surroundings, here their humbling renewed.

When his father opened the door and see Sonnyboy standing in front of him, he didn't immediately invite him in. Finally when he did, he greeted him with what Sonnyboy believed must have been a prepared speech:

"I allow you to come through my front door because you are my son, but I want you to know that this hooligan business of burning and looting, of mashing up a place where the people is trying to build, is something I can't uphold. I hope you will get a job now and settle down. This badjohn business not going to pay."

Sonnyboy felt ambushed. He felt as he had done at times when he had stood before a magistrate who was convinced of his guilt even before he heard a word of evidence. He searched his mind for something to say. He pushed his hand in his pocket. His fingers touched the letter he had there. It was one he had received from his mother a week before the end of his detention.

"Ma write a letter."

And he said the same thing again in different words: "I hear from Ma."

And when his father didn't say anything he said it again: "Ma write."

His father still did not speak. Later, as if he believed he had made his own point with enough clarity and could now condescend to speak on other matters, his father said, "You hear from your mother, you say. How she?"

"She say she want to come for Carnival or Christmas."

"Is how many years now she saying that?"

"She say if not Christmas, this Carnival for sure."

"Lystra always saying that."

As if those words, his own words, had the effect of softening him at a time when he didn't want to be softened, when he didn't want to yield, he looked at Sonnyboy, with what Sonnyboy thought was disappointment, as at a project pretty much lost, as someone who had taken a course that he was helpless to redirect, that regrettably he had to hold himself against; so when with no less sternness he said to Sonnyboy, "You want a beer?" it was not an offering of peace and conciliation; it was a gesture to fill, until Sonnyboy left, the space that had arisen between them.

Sonnyboy accepted the beer as a gesture acknowledging the calm they had reached with each other and went to the doorway and drank it, commenting, because he needed something to say, on how well his father had kept the plants in the trough of earth in front the house.

"But they need some water," he said.

"Yes, I have a little fella does come by and water them but I ain't see him for days."

He stood before his father, wanting to hug him, afraid to even offer him his hand to shake. And wanting to do something, to give him something as a mark of some kind of connecting. He felt in his pockets. All he had was the letter from his mother. He took it out and handed it to his father:

"Here is the letter from Ma."

"But it is addressed to you."

"Yes. But you keep it. She ask about you."

He made his way down the narrow street to the main road where he got a taxi, a little sad over his father, but consoling himself that he was on his way to Cascadu and a new life. In Cascadu he went into the gambling club with the intention of making peace with Big Head and Marvel, his opponents of long standing. But that didn't work out either.

A Sad Reception

I was in Cascadu already when Sonnyboy returned, about him a watchful quiet as if he wasn't quite sure how people would receive him, his hair tall, his long sleeves folded at the wrist, more restrained than of old and in a way more at ease, hailing out to everyone with the accommodating pleasantness of a man who expects to be honored, greeting people in the exuberant falsetto of the new salutation that he had picked up from brethren in the Black Power movement, "Power to you, Brother. Peace, Sister," carrying a breezy confidence wherever I see him, at a football match, at the draughts games in front Cushe Barbershop, in the rum shop with his old friends Gilda and Dog, quick to put his hand in his pocket and sponsor a flask of the white rum that fellars were drinking, waiting for the acknowledgment to come, that he was one of our heroes, showing a new allegiance to Cascadu as if to make sure that his presence registered; so that for Carnival, although he went to the city to beat iron in Tokyo steelband and join his brother Alvin and the rest of the Apparicio clan, on Carnival Tuesday he was back in Cascadu with us for the stickfighting and the parade of the two-three bands that made up our carnival, and for the first time beating iron in the Cascadu steelband. Still, Sonnyboy find the open arms he expected closed to him, most of the people he meet drawing away from him in search of a new distance from which to engage him, as if he had become a man who suddenly win big money in a lottery or a hero who managed some great achievement that put him on a plane different from the one ordinary people on. Others, seeing him, looked up from playing cards or drinking or whatever they doing, trying their best to give the impression that nothing remarkable had taken place around him, and he begin to wonder if he had returned to the right town.

"Don't worry, man," I tell him. "People don't have anything against you. Is just that you land up here in a confusing time. Everybody have to work things out for himself. Because you change doesn't mean that people change."

When I passed in front his grandmother's house where he lived, I see him clearing the adjacent plot of land, to do some planting.

"Food," he said. "Cassava and corn and pigeon peas and sorrel."

When next I see Sonnyboy, he is driving a van owned by Gilbert Perry, a well-known supporter of the National Party, distributing various food supplies to shops around the countryside, talking still in the falsetto of a man who been away. He would still be driving the van when the canvassing started for the general elections. This time, the van had a loudspeaker attached to it and Sonnyboy was giving out pamphlets and announcing the meetings for Crispus Perry, the National Party candidate. I was surprised.

When I first saw him driving the van, I took it as just a job he was doing. I had assumed that his involvement with Black Power had created some distance between him and the National Party. He didn't give me any explanation for what I saw as a new development in his political affiliation and I didn't ask for any. I wasn't thrilled about it. I had my own feelings about the politics. However, I didn't have a job to give him. I tried to see his new activity not as his surrender, but as contributing to his efforts to get people of the town to see the man he really was. I looked on. I went to a couple of the meetings he had advertised. It would be at one of these meetings that he would start the fire that would spread and burn down almost the entire commercial sector of the town.

At that meeting, the speakers introducing the Prime Minister had such a long list of his titles to enumerate, so many of his enemies to identify, such a wash of his great achievements to praise, that by the time it was the PM's turn to speak, the two gasoline lamps illuminating the platform began to sputter, the signal that they would soon go out. Not a soul there had gasoline to fill back up the lamps and the single gas station in the town had closed in the time the earlier speakers were speaking.

"Candles," suggested Crispus Perry, the candidate for our district, then a slim, cheerful, fresh-faced business graduate who the PM had selected from the university to demonstrate that young people were about more than fruitless rebellion.

"Candles?" Aunt Magenta and Mr. Oswin Tannis had together made the same exclamation. And Mr. Tannis, a retired sanitary inspector and a veteran party supporter who had been responsible for bringing in two busloads of supporters from Laventille and San Juan to bolster the crowd in attendance, still smarting from being rejected by the PM as the candidate for the constituency in favor of young Perry, just sucked his teeth in disdain and turned away, leaving Aunt Magenta to explain to Crispus Perry that the sight of lighted candles at an election meeting would give it the look of a wake, symbolism the Opposition would be only too happy to seize upon and make merry with.

It was then that Sonnyboy stepped in with the suggestion that as an alternative they use the flambeau, a simple device consisting of kerosene in a rum bottle, with a strip of cloth inserted to serve as the wick. This, he reminded them, would produce a light that would not only shine more fiercely than the candles but would give that more militant an ambience to the meeting, since, on the authority of the eminent anthropologist Dr. JD Elder, the flambeau was the light used by Africans released from enslavement to celebrate, symbolize and commemorate Emancipation. With their agreement secure, Sonnyboy, with his demonic efficiency, flung himself into action right away. He went next door and knocked on the side window of the shop, which was legally closed at that hour, and without much trouble persuaded Lutchman to open up and sell him a gallon of kerosene, the accommodating Lutchman – "Anything for you, boss" – going out of his way to give him a number of rum bottles into which to pour the kerosene.

And is only after Lutchman close back the window, smiling with his splendid teeth to himself, no doubt, with what must have been the mischievous satisfaction that his help had not fully aided them (*Let them take that if they want to believe that because I is Indian I against them, let them take that*), that Sonnyboy made the unsettling discovery that he had kerosene and the bottles, but no cloth for the wicks.

The PM had been waiting to speak. With the formidable

contempt for inefficiency, and the monumental appetite for spite that had made him the most exemplary political leader in the Caribbean, feared by cabinet ministers and worshiped by the rank and file, the PM had noted, with an impatience bordering on vexation, the last brilliant gleam of the gas lamps flaring to their death. Without surrendering his irritation, he shifted in midstride so to speak, the way a great batsman adjusts to the demands of the moment, he put the notes to his speech in the bulging pocket of his black jacket, stood up, cleared his throat and to the consternation of party organizers, though not to people who knew the kind of bad mind he had, was about to deliver his address in the darkness when, with the gesture of sacrifice that was to surprise everybody, Sonnyboy, who had done so much work already, ripped one pocket off his shirt, rolled the fabric lengthways, inserted it into one of the rum bottles filled with kerosene, set it alight, and stood with self-satisfied repose looking at the rest of the men to follow his example and tear off their shirt pockets for use as wicks. The young candidate, Crispus Perry, was wearing a necktie and blazer that had him sweating, and offered up the handkerchief he had been using to pat his brow; the two older men, Thom and Tannis, with no such expendable item to hand, hesitated at the thought of ruining their good shirts and looked resentfully at Sonnyboy for putting them in the awkward position of having to choose between loyalty to the party and the well-being of their clothing; however, they began to empty their shirt pockets, albeit slowly. But Sonnyboy, anxious to emphasize the urgency of the need, snatched at the other pocket of his shirt, with such determination that he ripped the shirt itself, only to discover a split second later that his calamitous action had been in vain and that had he waited for just a moment longer he would have been rescued by the resolute action of my aunt Magenta.

Music and Magenta

My aunt Magenta wanted three things from life. She wanted a son to see about her in her old age, a daughter to go out into the world and do the things that for one reason or other she didn't have the chance to do, and a man, good enough and strong, whose face she would be glad to see when she get up in the morning. It had fellars who buzzed around from the time she was nineteen, good, able-bodied working man who didn't have gold teeth in their mouth. It had fellars with jacket-and-tie ambition, and one who was a singer, not of calypso, of sentimental songs. They were OK fellows, but they didn't move her.

The man who moved her was a charmer, a fella who had this rascal power from the start, a quality barely camouflaged by his police uniform, his eyes a little brighter, his voice a little smoother, his gaze a little more unsettling, setting off the alarm in her belly and a flash of roasting heat up her neck, causing her to bite her lip and breathe in deeply to prevent herself exploding. People warn her about him. Everyone know he was a womanizer and a heartbreaker, but Miss Know-It-All see only the set of his broad shoulders, the high cheekbones, the smile, the long legs, the smooth steps of a foxtrot dancer, all flowing together to give him the name they called him, Music. She thought it was love. She believed that she alone by herself could be the world to him in the way he was her world. For this miscalculation, from Mr. Music, she had a son. She was twenty-two. He stick around long enough to see if he could give her the daughter; but by that time she was a little wiser, and she watched him drift away with the smooth deceptive motionlessness of a sailing ship leaving harbor, looking like it not moving at all, and when you look again it gone, leaving her with a tied-up story that she didn't even try to decipher – scholarship, study, a friend in England, immigration. She was a nurse already and she had to get married or resign. That was the rule. And she wasn't vexed with Music, and she wasn't sorry for herself.

She turned to Jesus and to her church, hard work and dreams elevating her from Sister to Mother. The only man to interest her was a man she had to stand up on tiptoe to see if she could see. But she hear him in the meeting at the Junction, talking with the rough smoothness of a badjohn, of the changes he would bring to the islands. And just so, she fall in love with this man she didn't even see, who people say was an obeah-man, Shango-man, Shouter Baptist leader and Oxford University doctor all rolled in one. So now she had in her life Jesus, and this brilliant man, who had come to make a better place not only for her but for the whole island.

But things didn't change, at least not quick enough for some people. Opportunity still had to do with the color of your skin, with a history that try its best to make you shame for the brutality somebody else inflict on you. You was in a place that didn't reward you for your labor, that give you the worst of everything and expect miracles from you. And while it had a few people who make the miracles, it was too much to ask of everybody. And she was there to sing with people and to console and to cheer.

In all her struggles, she had her child behind her until he reach the age to be on his own. The boy was Franklyn, and when she look at him she see the same smooth dancing movements of his father, except that where the father's smoothness was in sweet talk and scampishness, the boy smoothness come out in the texture of his skin and the poetry of his batting.

Franklyn could bat.

Franklyn Batting

In Cascadu, when Franklyn went in to bat, around the ground the talking would stop, people would look for a good place to sit, and from the savannah the word would go out, little fellars taking off running in different directions to make the announcement, "Franklyn batting! Franklyn batting!"

Through the whole village it would go, *Franklyn batting*, and before she go out her door, Miss Dolly would pull out the firewood from the fireside and add some water to the pot she cooking so it would bubble slow while the wood glowed to ashes, Rabbit and Jerry would get up off the bench in front the rum shop, people buying in the grocery would hurry up with their message and even down Eight-mile it would reach, Kenny slowing down his taxi to shout out as he passing to the people bathing by the spring, "Hey, all-you, Franklyn batting! You hear what I saying: Franklyn. Franklyn batting. *Franklyn batting*," and would drive maybe another five minutes, making the announce-ment, before he turn around and pick up those who ready and carry them back up to the cricket ground. Old cricketers like Housen and Montiqueu and Hercules would leave from in front Cyril house where they stand up talking and Bank and Pico and Copper and George, from different starting points, not even knowing exactly where they going, seeing people moving, would feel the tug of a grand event and begin to follow and only after they on their way they would ask, "Where we going?" and the answer would come, "Franklyn batting. Franklyn, yes, batting."

In the club, fellars playing knock rummy would take up their money and pack up the cards and head for the savannah and even Melda, clerking in Mendoza shop, would ask Ross to hold on for her with the selling so she could go and see Franklyn bat. Just for one over. Just one, holding up her finger, "One, Ross. One." And Ross would hold up his finger too and his eyes would open and his moustaches would tremble, "OK. One, you hear. One."

And in the gallery of the house behind the savannah, Manick father, off today from driving the steamroller, sitting down in his hammock, would make sure he have a big cup of water and peanuts in a bowl beside him on the floor so he wouldn't have to move while Franklyn batting. In the savannah, people there already on the mound of the hill that was the pavilion would dress-round to make room for old man Castillo and his two pardners and feel the pathos as these men contemplate then laboriously engage the herculean task of sitting down, their bones creaking as they hold out their hands, feeling for the ground and with a sigh in salute to the pain in their knees, in their bones, would ease themselves down, *Ahhh!* on the grass. The girls who had been modeling their lithe limbs and their Sunday fashion would settle down in front the community center near where my aunt Magenta was selling coconut drops and soursop icecream and nobody would say nothing, just watch Franklyn with the bat in his hands walk out to the ground with his slouching walk, bending and unbending his shoulders like the two ends of an accordion, lifting his knees high, one first then the other like the limbering-up exercise of a high-jumper. Then he hold himself down and walk off again, nonchalant, this time, like a prince who never see a day of trouble, his head in the air like he walking on a rope stretched across the sky, so confident his balance that he not even looking down to see where he putting his foot. After he mark with chalk the spot on the matting where he would take his stand, Franklyn would settle over his bat, casting to one side, with a shrug, the cape invoked on his shoulders and look now at the bowler run up to release the ball.

People look at cricket for the runs, but with Franklyn it was the runs, yes, it was runs, but his batting wasn't only runs, it was the spring in his step, it was the dance of his body, the confident readiness of muscles to move forward or sideways or back: to tiptoe or pivot or kneel or duck; and then the ball would come and he would leave it alone, just that, watch the ball and withhold his bat from it. And although it didn't show in the score book, that was a stroke, that was a statement, that was an acknowledgment of the bowler and an announcement to the world that we here. We have eyes. *We ready*, just to hint to them that they can't play the arse, that they have to put it on a length, we not going powerful-stupid chasing after wide balls. *Put it on the stumps. Put it on the stumps. Until I ready for you.*

Franklyn had three leave-alones. He would leave alone in acknowledgment of a good ball, not even having to shake his head, not even doing nothing like that, just a ordinary leave-alone, and he would leave alone as a warning to say don't put it there again. Sometimes with a smile, to mask his perplexity and to acknowledge that the pitch of the ball or its flight or its pace deceive him a little, a wee bit, he would leave alone, measuring the distance from the ball so as to know exactly what to do when the bowler put the next ball in the same spot. He had a lot of no's, that is, when he actually play the ball for no runs,

"Noo!" He had a lot of no's. As if he knows that it have time in the world. And all that is batting and he ain't even start to score yet. I not even talking yet about Franklyn going down on one knee and sweeping to square leg or climbing back on his back foot and slapping it back past the bowler, not a man move.

I ain't talking yet of Franklyn up on tiptoes, his eyes fixed big on the ball he been watching its whole journey from the bowler's hand, and even after it pass his waist and look like it about to go past his wicket, he had already pivoted like he doing a bullfight dance and just when the keeper feel he have the ball in his fists, his bat come down sweet and long, long and sweet, slap, between the keeper and slips, *How you going to stop we? How you go keep we down?* And all round the wicket, each in its own time, each off the chosen and appropriate ball would be the music of bat on ball, punctuated by the chorus of our applause; though, it wasn't Franklyn alone we were applauding. When Franklyn batting we were the ones batting, and in the mirror that he had become we would see ourselves in contest with the world. He was holding the bat but the strokes was our strokes and the bowler was England or Australia or Pakistan: the world. Yes, the world. It was ourselves we were applauding. And when he finish batting, when he get out, a curtain of silence would fall like when the evening sun that you know going to rise tomorrow goes down.

Nobody would move yet, we would wait and watch him come back under the mango tree like a dancer who just finish dance a set and is walking the girl who partnered him back to her seat, and put down his bat and sit down and take off his pads and then you would hear the voice of

91

a mother – Miss Ruby – calling her boy-child Glen to come now and do what she tell him to do so long before but which he must do now. And if you look across at the gallery of Manick house you would see the father putting on his slippers and taking up his cutlass with a sense of urgency, as if Franklyn's batting had imposed on him and his family and indeed the whole community the need *to do* something, to exert on the world an equivalent force and style. On the mound, with the same herculean straining, the old men would push themselves up with their hands to their feet, making sure of their balance on the slippery deck of age. People would start talking again and Pico would reassemble the Four for the knock rummy and Melda would run past everybody, her slippers flapping, screaming, "Ross going to kill me," but in her heart knowing that Ross will understand how she lose track of time, and a girl and a boy would walk slow close-close together and shy, their swinging hands touching, holding just briefly and letting go so as not to make a spectacle of their feelings.

Rain could fall now. And gradually argument would start up again in the rum shop, the Four would reassemble in the club, music in the snackette next door would begin to play and the old men, walking slow, would lift up their hands in a hello, walking a little straighter today, and that night men and women would make love as if they have the world of time, paying attention to details, to the no's and the yeses as of a Franklyn's innings, and others, in company, over a nip in the snackette or with their elbows on the wappie table in the gambling club would take their time with one another, *Nooo!* And people would restore in themselves the patience, the un-hurry, to let a slight pass, to leave a bad situation alone, to not be inveigled by shit, to resist having to agree to stupidness, to say no, thank you. No, and lift a glass to their lips and down a drink in salute of each other, with the same smooth un-hurry of Franklyn dispatching a ball to the boundary.

To my aunt Magenta and, indeed, to all of us in Cascadu, it was just a matter of time before they would call up Franklyn for a trial match to represent the country in cricket. We were waiting, all of us.

Black Power Comes to Cascadu

Then that Saturday afternoon. It must have been March month. Cricket in the savannah. The day bright, hot, sweating. Aunt Magenta is cooking, and she hearing from the cricket ground behind her house the noise of silence and intermittent applause from what she supposed was the supporters who had come with the visiting team, the noise too soft for it to be Cascadu team batting. Then she hear this other sound, of drumming coming toward her, like the wind groaning, the noise growing louder and nearer, until is like the drumming happening inside her house, inside her head, and when she look outside it was to see Blackpeople with flags and banners, marching in the street. And right away, Aunt Magenta remember the dream she had dreamed three nights straight: the flags and the people and she naked from her waist up, covering her breasts with her two hands, and a beautiful black girl with long hair and a long dress and beads round her neck walking with Franklyn. Still struggling to remember the details of the dream, she went outside to see, yes, the Black Power demonstration that had come to Cascadu. In one panoramic sweep of her eyes, she see Miss Janice in her yard standing up with her mouth open, holding the dress she was going to hang on her clothes line, Manick father out on his gallery with a cutlass in his hand, Miss Ruth who had some rice paddy drying on some bags in front her yard, rushing out to pick up the bags, terror in her eyes, one of the Black Power fellars saying to her, "No,

94

Mother, we haven't come to harm you, but to liberate you." Cricketers and spectators were pouring out from the cricket ground to see this congregation of Blackpeople lifting their folded fists in the air and shouting "Power!" She watched the march go past and she go back inside the kitchen to finish grating the coconut to put in the pigeon peas she was cooking. And while she there in the kitchen, through the window she see Franklyn and Evrol (who had come out with the cricketers and spectators to watch the procession) coming back from the road, with them is a girl, beautiful, a stranger to her, with hair loosened and a long dress. When she look again, it was to see Franklyn outside by the barrel in which she collected rainwater dipping out water with a calabash. With him is the same girl drinking water, and Franklyn looking at her with a look she had seen before in the eyes of his father when she Magenta was the girl and he Franklyn was his father, Music. While she there watching, Franklyn looked up and see her and he call out, "Ma, this is Marcia. Marcia, this is my mother," and the girl waved at her and she waved back at them and when she look again, she see him and the girl walking toward the road, slow and distant like is a dream.

She never see the girl again. And the next time she see Franklyn was when the police bring him down on a stretcher, dead, with a cloth band around his head and his mouth still open. He was in the bush, they said, in the hills. A revolutionary in the hills. And five bullets in his body.

And thank God for Clephus.

One day before that Easter, she in her yard, near the front steps, throwing corn to see if she could get the chickens to come close so she could catch one, see this man, whose name she don't yet know is Clephus Winchester, going by with his springy tiptoeing walk, his shoulders spread out around him, his pants stick up in his crotch, its seat tight across his bottom, as if he in the grip of the arresting hand of the police, saying good evening in his slow Tobago drawl and when he nearly finish pass in front her, he stop and look at her, his face stretched in his broad Castara Bay smile, his teeth, white like the surf, suddenly filling up his whole mouth, and his eyes on me, not as if he was looking at a Mother in the Church, but like he measuring me to see how much cloth it will take to make a dress to fit my body, and look at me again in a kind of worshipful confusion and I fighting to keep my face serious, like how a Mother in the church supposed to keep her face, asking in what I hoped was my stern Mother Magenta voice, "Mister Gentleman, is me you watching?"

And she watched the most delighted smile bathe his face as he nodded, "Yes, Miss Lady, is you I watching," his eyes open looking on her with such adventure and boldness, causing me to step out my prison:

"Well, don't stand up there watching, help me catch this chicken."

And from that beginning, through the terrible sorrow with Franklyn, with the police and the wake and the burial, he would be the man to stand beside her with the armor of his shoulders, the peace of his countenance and his shy Castara Bay smile, his pants stick up in his crotch and his two left feet spread out to balance him.

She waited, after Franklyn's death, for somebody from the government to come and tell her something. She went to party group meetings and she give her support. She went to rallies. And she waited. Aunt Magenta get thin.

She put back on some size. She dry up again. She start talking to herself. Sometimes I would find her in the kitchen, talking to the absent Franklyn, asking him how he could do this thing, how he could run away from his future, how he could leave her in such pain and the cricket field without his light, or asking the Prime Minister to explain the reason for the killing of her son *who was a good boy, who was only standing up for the same freedoms that you preaching.*

"How you expect him to be less than the man you paint in your speeches? What you expect when he hear you talking about what it is to be free? And how, if Franklyn didn't bow down to anybody in cricket, who you expect him to bow down to in life?"

She blame the crazy police, the trigger-happy one they call Kojak, with the bald head and the gold chain and the dark shades and his shirt collar turned up like a badjohn. She quarrel with Franklyn for allowing "the stupid company to inveigle you to go to the hills, Evrol and the girl with the long dress and the long hair that she see in her dream. Yes, Evrol, your pardner. Who the government take and make a senator."

Every time she speak, another name was added to the list of the guilty. The only innocent as far as I could see was the PM. What was she waiting on him for?

To answer my query, she went to her Bible and when she open it, her left hand fall on Genesis, chapter 32, and her right hand settle on verse 24:

And Jacob was left alone; and there wrestled a man with him until the breaking of the day. And when he saw that he prevailed not against him, he touched the hollow of his thigh; and the hollow of Jacob's thigh was out of joint, as he wrestled with him.

And he said, Let me go, for the day breaketh. And he said, I will not let thee go, except thou bless me.

The words that would guide her. She had to hold on to him until he give her the blessing.

So when she hear people saying how he was acting like a badjohn, she tell them, "Yes, he's a badjohn for the big shot and them, not for me and you." And she point them to the Bible and she preach it as a sermon to let them know that Jacob didn't get his blessing because he was a good man, it was because of his struggle. Whole night he had to fight with the very Angel that would bless him.

Now, the PM was in Cascadu. She wanted to see his face when he say what he had to say about the killing of Franklyn. And how would she see his face, if there was no light.

Confident that her age, size and status placed her beyond the necessity for modesty *and in any event we is all big people here*, she lifted her dress and tore off a huge strip of her cotton petticoat, which she then tore into smaller strips to function as wicks. These she gave them to stuff into the bottles with kerosene to be set alight. And there was light. The lighted flambeaux were handed out to the party faithful and they took up positions around the stage in such a fashion that the light would be cast upon the speakers on the rostrum.

Except for the stream of smoke they gave off, the flambeaux gave good light; and the only manipulation needed to keep them from going out was that the bottles had to be tilted every now and then to keep the wicks moistened and the flame alive.

The Fire

Sonnyboy Apparicio was at one end of the stage, holding up one of these lighted bottles and fighting to keep his two eyes open. For the last twenty-one days, he had been campaigning with the National Party through the surrounding villages, supporting the candidacy of young Perry, the nephew of the owner of the van he was driving, announcing the meetings on the loudspeaker and giving out pamphlets with details of the place and time of the meetings. In addition, he had that very morning helped to build the stage, decorate it with dried coconut leaves, stems of green bamboo and giant heliconias and to erect the banner welcoming the PM and speakers to Cascadu, all of it done with the taste and thoroughness that in all his changes had not left him.

He had also spent the last seventeen nights not in love-making as that sensational scandal sheet, *The Cannon*, later reported as it sought to pin the blame for the fire on him (NATIONAL PARTY ROMEO SETS MEETING ABLAZE), but walking back and forth and back again a total of eight miles each night between his grandmother's house where he was staying and the home of the woman he was tracking, four miles to go, four to walk back; so by the time the meeting got under way that evening he was so fatigued that all he wanted to do was go to sleep. However, he continued to hold up the light, not only out of duty but because Aunt Magenta had confided to him that his name was going to be called publicly and the work he was doing on behalf of the party acknowledged by one of the speakers. He had remained attentive to the speeches so as not to miss his name, nervous like if they were going to call him to make a big speech or something, lifting the flambeau higher so that, without anyone noticing, he could check how under his armpit was smelling, wondering if when he get to the podium he should wave with a flap of his hand, open-palmed, as he had seen the PM do, or hold up his two hands like a hero, like a victorious weightlifter at the Olympics, or lift just his right hand with two fingers spread out in the V for Victory sign, like the leader of the Opposition did.

Up to the time the PM got to the podium, none of the speakers had mentioned Sonnyboy's name; and the only person left with the option of paying tribute to his worthiness was the PM himself. However, as the PM spoke in the wobbly blaze of nearly a dozen flambeaux, of the monumental deeds to be undertaken by his government: the International Monetary Fund to appease, the National Debt to service, the civil service to downsize, the disease of rampant individualism left over from colonialism to eradicate, the African, Indian, Chinese, European, Lebanese and God knows what other peoples to weld into one nation, the commanding heights of the economy to wrest from the clutches of foreign interests, the restless Black youth seeking deliverance in mischief and slogans to be guided back to the path of responsible citizenship, Sonnyboy, listening to the volleys of applause that punctuated the PM's speech, felt himself so reduced in significance and his claims for acknowledgment so minuscule, that he prayed there would be no mention of the little work he had done. And he stood at his post, heroically, tilting the bottle and righting it as the flame burned, no longer listening for his name, but breathing in and out deeply to dispel exhaustion, relax himself and shore up his energy for another night of adventure with the woman who of all the people he had met in Cascadu was the only one who, despite the misgivings of her mother, had seen him as the man he wanted to be and had encouraged in him the delightful idea that she could be his girl.

Sonnyboy Apparicio did not know when he dozed off with the lighted bottle tilted in his hand. The meeting observed that the backdrop of dried coconut branches and bamboo leaves behind the speaker was ablaze. Yet, not even those with him on the platform made a move, because they believed that the fire was a demonstration of the magical powers that for twenty-five years the people of the country were led to believe the PM possessed. He was credited with having the ability to change his shape to any animal of his choosing, a pig, a donkey, a ground dove, to disappear from one place and turn up at another at times nobody expected. And while there were the skeptics who believed that, even with his brilliance as an academic, he was still too young to have acquired the powers of a shapeshifter, a *lagahoo*, a number of people pointed to his close friendship with Mr. Buckett, the healer of Matura, and Papa Neeza, the most powerful obeah-man in the country, and the fact that he had never lost an election, as evidence of his special powers. As a result, people who were in any way opposed to him took precautions to ensure that he didn't know their secret thoughts. Certain members of his own political party, who at that time were sitting around in their living rooms making remarks critical of him, seeing a strange dog appear in the yard, began to speak in whispers, members of the chambers of commerce seeing a black and white cat enter the room began to laugh loudly to obscure what they were saying, the Save Tobago Society and members of the Oilfields Workers Trade Union, the Sugar Unions and certain members of the civil service, so as not to be caught off guard by any of his unannounced visits, had adopted the stratagem of designating at their meetings one of their number as a watchman, arming him with a big stick and giving him the responsibility to alert them in the event that any strange person or unfamiliar animal appeared, the stick to be used to chase the creature away, not to hit it, at least not too severe a blow, since they had put too great a value on the Prime Minister to have him suffer injury. So they watched the fire blaze and continued to listen to the PM and to applaud even more vigorously, their applause drowning out the crackling noise of the fire. The PM unloosened his tie and continued speaking until, feeling himself broiling in the sweat of his black jacket, he looked around to try to identify the source of the heat and saw that the actual structure of the stage was ablaze. The PM let out an oath, turned and ran. It was then that the mesmerized onlookers felt power return to their limbs. Some followed the PM's example and tried to get away from the stage, but others, believing that his attempt to escape the fire was simply part of a larger performance, stood their ground, applauding in anticipation of the spectacle they expected to follow, and they continued to applaud until my aunt Magenta pointed to Sonnyboy Apparicio at the far corner of the stage, leaned up against a post, sleeping, the flambeau that must have lighted a path away from him smoking on the ground beside him. People wanted to wake him, but others were holding them back from interfering, sure that he was part of the performance still to be completed, and it was only when Aunt Magenta, screaming at the top of her voice, with Clephus at her side elbowed her way to Sonnyboy, roused him from sleep and dragged him away from the fire that people turned grumblingly and reluctantly to see if they could put out the blaze. No one was able to call the fire brigade in the town fifteen miles away, since the only working telephone in the town was consumed in Lutchman's blazing shop and the other one, the one in the police station, had been dead for months. It had no water in the taps. The night was dark. And by the time we were able to organize a bucket brigade to get through the track to the river the fire had spread. Wee Lee Laundry, Dulcie Roti Shop and the wooden float and accra stand where Eileen sold peppered pomme citre and fried fish and bake, were all ablaze, bottles of rum were exploding from Lutchman's burning Rum Shop and Grocery, things were fizzing and bubbling and bursting in colors of red and yellow and green from the drugstore, and flames were roaring and leaping high from what a few moments earlier was Toro Tire Repair Shop.

But, strangely, as he watched the town ablaze, what he found himself thinking was that he couldn't continue to walk those distances to see the woman he wanted to think of as his girl.

Sweetie-Mary
Don't Make Me Stop Loving

A few months after Sonnyboy began driving the van, he had come upon her sitting dreamily behind the counter of the little shop run by her mother, a quiet place, one of a handful of houses scattered along the stretch of road leading to Cascadu, the shop itself an extension of what was their house, the little place stocked with fruit from the lime, orange, chenette and mango trees in her yard, the rest careful purchases, bread, cakes, sweets, sweet drinks, drinking chocolate, coffee, tins of sardines, nothing bought that would not sell, each lonely item of commerce laid out with space around it on the shelves like prizes at a village fair, the mother, meditative almost, her head tied with the cloth of her Shouter Baptist faith, her face serene, on it a kind of battler's acknowledging smile, respectful of her marvelous opponent, a world that had wrestled her down and was watching her strain to rise again; her whole history there in her face, her good looks, the admiration from men, the parties, the good times, the first man, the first child, then the second, and now the chain of four remaining children, three daughters and a son, her beauty passed on to their faces now, the flare of nostrils, the full lips, the nearly sleepy eyes, her consolation and pride that this was her own place, something less to develop than to guard, her few pennies lifted and weighed with a scrupulous accounting, the dribble of customers petted, fussed over and fed arresting bits of village gossip to keep them returning, and all the while, her eyes open, sizing up the men who passed through to discover which among them she would find acceptable for her daughters, and who the good-for-nothings that had only trouble to offer, interrogating them if they so much as glanced at one of the girls, "Who is your family? What job you doing and for how long?" Questions she should have asked their fathers, her judgement immediate, so that some men passing through, truck drivers transporting gravel to Cunaripo, drivers of vans laden with plantains and sweet potatoes and dasheen, going to the Port of Spain market, found her hostility unaccounted for and others, in a hurry to get on with their journey, found themselves delayed by her offer of a drink to quench their thirst or her plea to sample the cake one daughter made or taste the crab and callaloo cooked by another, she herself doing all of this with a delicious charm that revealed more and more of herself until first one, then another, of the men began to eye her as a prospect for romance, a regard that when she realized it brought first a smile then made her look at herself again, the idea of her desirability tempting her, and eventually taking root in her mind, so that she took to wearing dresses that revealed the heft of her bosom and outlined the thrust of her bottom until the men went beyond admiring to putting question to her that she pretended not to understand. For months she was the star of the show and was on the verge of surrendering to Alphonse, who every day dropped in to see her and who she had begun to believe she could share a life with, when, pressed to declare his intentions, in a fit of honesty, he confessed that he was already living with a woman. This brought her back to her senses and although she tried to smile it off, her spirit was damaged and she looked at every man that came in with suspicion. That was the state she was in when Sonnyboy Apparicio came driving the same van, which would later be used in the service of the National Party. He was distributing chocolate bars, black pepper, seasonings, red mango, and paradise plums. He had stopped the van and got out to sell to the woman homemade chocolate bars and black pepper and paradise plums; and, still facing the van, had called to her in his important salesman's voice to find out what else she wanted and to reel off for her the other items he had for sale. He had turned toward the shop, the goods she ordered in hand, and with one foot flat and the other on tiptoe was about to step toward her. And there, in the shop, leaning over the counter, her hand under her chin, was this girl, woman, her eldest daughter, he would learn afterward, one he had not seen before, looking at him, seeing, he thought, when he replayed that moment later, everything his pose of importance was trying to conceal, that his right foot was shorter than his left, that his effort to sound clever was to let people see the man he was, that he was lonely and dying for someone to love.

And don't you know, said her smile, *that I am here waiting? Don't you know?* But he couldn't be sure, as he called her mother to come for the things she had requested, whether her smile was part of the general disposition with which she faced the world or a greeting composed just for him.

He stand up outside the van not daring to move because he didn't want the girl to see that one of his legs was shorter than the other and that he limped like Legba. And before he had time to argue himself out of his deception, he drew himself into a military straightness, made the few steps forward, careful not to reveal his impediment, and after the transaction, the selling, stiff as a toy soldier, made the same effort to get the few paces back to the van and go on his way.

As Sonnyboy tell me, he dreamed of her.

"I dream of her," he tell me, amazed that something like that could happen to him.

"You dream of her?"

"I dream of her," a wistful astonished delight at his own surprise that she could so get under his skin to his feelings: "I dream of her," surprise turning to the confirmation of the possession of capacity that had not shown itself before … "I dream of her."

For weeks, he stopped at the shop without a word spoken by either of them. Just her eyes seeing inside him. He listened to what her mother called her, so he learned her name was Sweetie-Mary. He put together bits of conversation he heard and deduced that she had lived away from home for a number of years and had come back here at her mother house after her failure to make a life of her own; though, from looking at the set of her body, at the dreams that would cross her face, it was clear to him that she had come for shelter, not in surrender. She did not speak, yet he felt her watching him, not knowing whether she knew of his limp and was secretly laughing at his efforts to hide it. He would know better if he heard her speak. He wanted to hear her speak.

"Talk to her," I tell him.

"In front of her mother? The mother don't trust me. I am not you, you know. I don't have a set of woman running me down."

"Write her, then."

"Write? I will talk."

Away from the shop, in the van on the road, Sonnyboy practiced what he would say to her to show himself serious. He would tell her that she made him feel he was real, that the salesman's voice of importance with which he had armed himself was not his true voice, that he was searching for his real voice. He had disguised his limp because he was afraid she wanted a perfect man and he wasn't the perfect man.

"This love business is hell," he said.

But he couldn't shake her from his mind. In another mood, as he drove the van through the shady roads past the cocoa estates and the immortelle trees of the countryside he practiced jokes he would make with her, to calm her. Silly nonsense, things like *Habla español? Bien. Gracias, claro!*

He had to laugh at himself. Still, when they were alone, he continued to present the salesman self, the bluff, the loud, the confident self, feeling himself sinking deeper into a pit of deception, while his real self remained hidden away like his limp without the confidence to be revealed.

Every time he returned to the shop, Sonnyboy Apparicio felt transparent and under suspicion, and from how they watched him, he suspected that between the mother and the girl he had become a subject of conversation. Then he noticed that whenever he arrived the mother managed to find some reason to absent herself and he would be left alone with the daughter. He wondered if that change was something that she had argued for, or if it was a test set by her mother.

In the beginning, when he found himself alone with her, the very thought that he was being given an opportunity that he was expected to seize, that he wanted to seize, made him cautious, self-conscious, and he did what business was to be done not so much with indifference as with circumspection, watching as she cleaned the counter and rearranged the shelves and swept the shop, and wiped out the icebox and attended to customers, in her eyes an amused superiority at the blindness of people who did not see the wonderful world of her dreams.

"And are you one of the blind?" asked her eyes.

He felt transported in her presence to another place, another world where he dangled in space, uplifted by the light that flooded the shop at her smile that stretched her lips, tentative at first, like a careful bird poking its head into the open. He studied her, what she was wearing, the polish on her nails, the curve of her breasts, the music of her movements, the teeth in her smile, her butterfly eyelids. He inhaled her scent, watched her hand giving change to a customer, her fingers closing around a reel of thread; he watched everything, and he stepped out of the shop, resolutely trying to hold himself straight.

On one of the days that he found her alone, although neither of them said a word, he felt, as he steadied himself and walked toward her, that she was seeing right through him and he went into the shop, exaggerating his limp, and when he saw her looking, he reached for one of the jokes he had developed to ease his embarrassment.

"I was in the war," he said, with half a laugh, bending and touching the calf of one leg. "Lucky they only blow off a piece of this leg, but my other legs are good."

"Legs?" she laughed. A little too loudly, he thought, with a sliced sweetness that displayed the space between her upper front teeth, dissolving his fears, giving him the opening he had been seeking, making him want to keep her interested. And he began to talk, in the falsetto of importance of his salesman's voice, about his leg, of his schooldays, the nicknames they give him, Pretty-foot, Hop-and-Drop, and of his mastery of repartee in order to counter the jokes made at his expense. This very exercise had sharpened him, had given him the mental quickness to extemporize as a calypsonian. As demonstration, he made joke after joke just for the delight of watching her suppress her smile.

"I bet you don't know this one," he said. She raised her eyebrows.

"Why is a post not like a sleeping man?" Of course, she didn't know because it was something he had made up. With a show of knowledge he told her, "It is standing up, *comprendo? Habla Espanola?*"

She shook her head.

"Just say something and I have an answer," he prodded. "Just say anything."

And she did smile.

Now he said, "There are two things I want. One is to claim my life ..."

"And what is the other thing?"

"To meet a nice woman like you." And he could see behind her half-smile the wondering if he was a man she could take a chance on.

"But I hardly know anything about you."

"Well, let me tell you."

Sonnyboy told her the story of his life. He talked about the insult and blindness of not been arrested on his own merit, of the sadness over the business with his father.

"Don't make them make you stop loving," Sweetie-Mary said, her voice thin and trembly and as if she was saying these words not so much to him as to herself, their

110

eyes linking. She surprised him. She really was listening. That was when he knew it. Yes, this was the woman.

Yes. With renewed pleasure.

"And you?" he asked. "You went away and come back. What about you?"

"Me?"

Sweetie-Mary Tells Her Story

After she leave Cunaripo Secondary School, with a pass in Religious Knowledge and Cookery, Sweetie-Mary look around Cascadu to see what she could find to do. The only employment was in the government works project, keeping the roads clean and the hedges trimmed. Agriculture was dead, and in any event that was not a sector her education had prepared her for. She wasn't qualified to be a teacher. She wasn't qualified to be a nurse. She feel she was too good to be working in a store, if she could get even that, and she know that if she was to make something of her life she would have to leave Cascadu.

So, she headed out one Monday morning in her best dress, something off-the-shoulder, with two straps to keep it up and a little blouse over it, with her red high-heeled shoes and her handbag with her birth certificate and her General Certificate of Education with her two passes, Cookery and Religious Knowledge, to Port of Spain where she get a job to sell beauty products that had her going from door to door trying to sell people the idea that it is nice to look nice and smell sweet, advising them which shade from among a range of lipsticks suited their complexion, she herself smelling of the perfume she was selling, her face smoothed over with the makeup creams, her hair falling around her face like a model in a fashion magazine, sweating (though she can't allow herself to sweat) in the hot sun in the outfit she was required to wear, balancing in high heels to represent glamour, her own language reformed, refined, the clothes she wearing costing more than a month's pay, the more time she spend doing this job the more into debt she falling. People find she looking nice and staying slim, not knowing that it is because she hardly eating. Sometimes she dress up like Christmas and she don't even have money to take a taxi home, and she didn't have to have a pass in mathematics to understand that she was not working for money but working to be working, to keep up the appearance of doing something. There she was, a woman alone, far from the strictness of her home. No religion to save her, no protection of family to shelter her, free, alone, every temptation she have to deal with by herself alone, every move a fella make to interpret for myself, nobody to decipher anything for her, a whole world to face in freedom without support or cover. And she have no money. She owe the company for the dresses she wearing, for the shoes, for the hairdo, for the brooch. The only thing free is the perfume and the cream she was selling. To have any money she have to take advances on her salary; and because she don't have money anyone that offer her something, she looking at them with suspicion. She start to be afraid of men who look at her too hard, to swell up her face at fellars who wanted to talk to her. She start to close up, to get dry. She dream that she was pregnant. She dream she was falling. She look around her, nobody to give her rescue and she realize that she was alone and that the world didn't care. It didn't care. People smiled or cried, the world didn't care.

With the little pittance that they give her, she keep up the pretense that this was a great city and a great world and she made her appearance in Cascadu in the high-heel shoes and the pretty dresses that she didn't tell them that

113

she did not own, with presents for her mother and her little sisters, not big things, little things, a ballpoint pen, a nail file, ribbon for the hair of the one still in school, candy, to make them think things was all right with her, all of them waiting for Saturday afternoons for her to come out the taxi, everybody shouting *Mary Mary Mary*, all of them standing around waiting for her to open her purse and take out the little nothings, all of them believing that she was more than OK, that she was good. Many times when things get hard, she thought of going back home to Cascadu, but when she think of the sight of her sisters' faces as she dip into her bag those Saturdays and bring out the little square chocolate in the pretty gold paper or the little rubber doll or the bodice, she couldn't do it. She think of it, but she couldn't do it and she bear what she had to bear alone. She blamed herself for not learning in school. She blame herself for not signing up to be a security guard like her cousin Janice who at least had a uniform and a baton. She blamed herself for not being brave enough to open her mouth and let the people employing her know the pressure she was under. And men, she stayed far from men, because it was one thing to get pregnant in Cascadu but even worse to get pregnant in Port of Spain. She looked around at the girls cheerfully selling in stores, girls prettier than her serving in snackettes, at people passing chatting with each other in the streets – where did they get their smile? How did they keep the rhythm of their body? What it is give them their pep, their bravery? And what to do? She changed her hairstyles but that didn't change her. She begin to feel odd, like the only person in a Carnival band without a costume. Where was she living? First in the hostel for women and then in a little place up

Belmont Valley Road that she could barely afford, where it had no lights, the water was at a standpipe in the yard, the only furniture a bed and a table that she used to iron on. And who to talk to? Her neighbors in the apartment next to her room, Miss Elaine and the man she living with, a seaman, Jose, a smiling Spanish fellow who was always home, waiting for a boat, from the moment he get up from sleep, smoking cigarette after cigarette and every day discussing a different part of a woman's anatomy to the mechanical amusement of his pet parrot that he had trained to laugh at his jokes, *Ha ha ha,* and to say the only other words in his vocabulary, *Excuse me! Excuse me! Ha ha ha excuse me.* In the upstairs apartment was a newlywed couple whose names nobody knew because they called each other by one name: Darling. I'm going out, Darling. Bye, Darling, Hello, Darling. To save money, which she didn't have, she started to carry a sandwich to work; and to kill two birds with one stone she started to go to the Roman Catholic cathedral around lunchtime to eat her sandwich and to pray. One midday as she come out the church, she meet Miss Waldron, a woman who worked same place as she, stylish, well put away, everything in place. She too was leaving the church where she had gone to pray. They start to talk.

"No, girl," Miss Waldron tell her, after she tell Miss Waldron how her life was going. "Nothing ain't wrong with you. You just young. You just totally new and free and modern. You is the first free woman in the world, no man, no family, no religion, everything to fight for, everything to replace or reject. Everything to build. You is new. You can't want to give up even before you begin. And looking for a man wouldn't help you. You approaching it wrong.

You frightening life. You making life nervous around you. You not giving it a chance to help you. If we have a responsibility to this place, to this business, then it have to have some obligation to us. If we put our labor here, it is here we have to look for our future. Where the cow tie is there it have to graze."

It was after she talk to Miss Waldron that she raised with her supervisor the question of the money being deducted from her pay for the clothes they give her to wear. She talked to them. They danced her for two months.

"We striking," Miss Waldron tell her.

"Two of us?"

"You want me to do it alone?"

The next thing Sweetie-Mary know, is she and Miss Waldron on the pavement in front of the business place, she that first day in her nice dress and high-heel shoes like she going to a soirée, and Miss Waldron as usual well put away. At the end of that day her feet killing her, she sweating, she tired, she thirsty. With that experience she and Miss Waldron learn that you can't go on strike looking like you just step out the pages of a magazine. Next day they gone back in more comfortable clothes. They stay in front that place on the pavement for three weeks. They had started off, she and Miss Waldron, in their feeble, uncertain voices whispering the words that people on picket lines used:

Don't buy, Pass by.
Don't buy, mamaguy.

And singing even more feebly the hymn sung by trade unionists, "Hold the fort for I am coming," timid, like she doing some kinda wrong. Then it hit her, *Girl, what you*

frighten for? You ain't thief nothing. If you open your mouth and talk,
the police can't hold you. So what you handcuffing your mind for?
And what you have to lose?

And it hit her that all she have is her love.

"And each other," Miss Waldron tell her.

Next day, she upped the volume of her singing and she
get into the rhythm of the song, *Hold the fort for I am com-ing*,
like she is a roadside Shouter Baptist, until people start to
look at them, some to smile and some even to join them in
the chant:

Don't buy. Pass by.
Don't buy. Mamaguy.

And is so her employers hear them. So when they call in
she and Miss Waldron with the offer to give them a few
dollars more and to deduct only half the cost of their
clothing from their pay, she decided that she wouldn't take
it. She would leave the job. She wanted to do something
for herself. She could cook. She was young enough, she
could start again.

Sonnyboy was hearing what she was saying, but, even
more, he was listening to the spirit in her, feeling from her
the humor, the joy, the faith, the life.

The Love Song of Sonnyboy

Sonnyboy couldn't help a smile broadening his face.

"So what you grinning at?" she asked him.

"We should be together," he said, and when she said nothing: "You is just the woman for me. Can I come for you and take you for a drive sometime? I sure you never see all the places around here. The beach, the waterfall."

She looked at his leg.

"My foot," he said in explanation. "It got short." He pronounced it *shot*. "I was going through the Nariva swamp trying to save one of my buddies when the enemy tossed a hand grenade. I'm lucky to be alive today."

"You was in a war? In Trinidad?"

"In a battle. You never hear of it, the Battle of Nariva?"

She looked at him suspiciously, "No. I never."

"It's a joke," he said. "That is what I tell people when they ask me about my leg."

"Fool," she said. "Whose van it is you driving?" asked as if the question was not her own; and he notched it as an inquiry inspired by either her past or by her mother.

"You want to go for a drive?"

"Drive? I in enough trouble already. If I leave here for any drive, my mother ... I don't want her to be talking, telling me anything."

"So how I will see you, then? The cinema? You go to the cinema? If you want, I could ask your mother if you can go for a drive with me. You want me to ask your mother?"

118

"No. She wouldn't want me to go with a break-foot man."

But you're a big woman, he thought to say. Instead, he said, "In the war I got the medal of honor for bravery," still trying for a joke. "You sure I shouldn't ask your mother?"

"She wouldn't understand. Is better not to tell her anything. She would love to be able to say that I run away with you. She will feel better. It will make people feel sorry for her, for her troubles, her children.

"It will be a Godsend to her, her daughter running off with a short-foot man, a break-foot man, and a badjohn to boot."

"Badjohn? That is how you see me? A badjohn?"

"So, you not a badjohn?"

"What you think?"

"I don't know."

He swallowed his disappointment and tried again. He said, "So how will I see you?"

She didn't say anything.

Then she turned to face him, to study him, and suddenly he saw in her eyes the mischief and daring, as if a fresh thought had just jumped wild into her head: "Though if you come in the night when my mother sleeping ..."

He turned back to her. "When can I come?"

"Any night," she sang.

"Good," he said, too quickly, not wanting to ask for details lest she discover a difficulty and withdraw her invitation.

And is only afterward that Sonnyboy discovered that he didn't know when to go. Any night was so imprecise. What hour? When did the mother go to sleep? And Sweetie? How would she know when and where he would be waiting? He didn't want to wait for another two weeks when he had legitimate reason to visit the shop.

119

That night Sonnyboy put on a black beret, a black sweater and black pants so as to blend in with the darkness and set out on foot to Sweetie-Mary's house. He had no idea of how he would see her or what he would do. But as he walked, all the music he had known flooded his brain, his being and he started to whistle. He wanted to whistle love songs that would expose his feelings, but the tunes he found himself whistling were tunes played by the steelbands on Carnival Monday when the city was a stage and symphony, thick with music, overflowing with love. And that night, on the four-mile stretch of road leading from his grandmother's to Mary's mother place, Sonnyboy whistled song after song after song from those mornings. He whistled "In a Monastery Garden." He whistled "Lebensraum." He whistled "Back Bay Shuffle" and Puerto Rican mambo. He whistled "Eine Kleine Nachtmusik," "Minuet in G," "The Flight of the Bumble Bee," "Roses from the South," "Skokian," "The Bells of St Mary's," and when he got to Sweetie's he whistled "With a Song in My Heart," the tune that Ebonites mash up town with, when he, Sonnyboy, was a barebacked fella in the steelband, beating the iron, tasting the music, sweat flowing down his face, feeling the heat and the strain of his arms and the sweetness of belonging, and by his side big hard men who have no fear for nobody, who ain't 'fraid nobody in the world, who will pelt bottle and stab and cut and butt and cuff, these big men marching down the road to their own rhythm, their feet dragging in that sweet hallelujah nonchalant rhythm, as if they own the world and the road ain't big enough to hold them, so they walk, not side by side, but singly, one behind the other, with space around each, as if they were each costumed in a big mas, a King of the Bands costume that would require the whole road for them to display their power and beauty. All the dancing in their heart, in their pores, in the grains of hair on their head, in the stirring in their stones, and all they could do to express it was this chip chip chip, chipping down the road, part of this multitude, with their arms spread open like in a crucifixion, as if to say *all this is we, all this is fucking we, all this, listen to it, listen to your heart and your stones.* And in front the band, dancing the love is a woman with the flag, she jersey tie-up halfway up her belly, below she breasts, her bottom out-jutting, her foot planted so she could get a grip on the ground and bring forward the power and space to wave the flag and display all the fecundity and love in her dancing; and behind her the crowd, the band, just flowing, just chipping, everyone swept along by all the love a moment could hold. All that love. Lord! And that was the nature of Sonnyboy's whistling, all that was his love song.

Every night the whistling would pierce the darkness, come out from the trees along the road and Sweetie-Mary would hear it, along with her mother and her brother and her three sisters. She couldn't move because the whole household was awake, listening. When he went to deliver goods, her mother was present and he didn't get to talk to her to firm up an arrangement as to when he would see her, so he continued his whistling. After three weeks, Sonnyboy was on the verge of giving up expecting Sweetie-Mary to come out and meet him because even he was aware that everyone was hearing him; but he kept on whistling "With a Song in My Heart," whistling all the parts of the Ebonites Jouvay morning arrangement whenever he got in the vicinity of the house, because at least he knew she would be hearing. And then one night in the middle of his whistling, she appeared smelling of the cleanness of honey and the sap of trees, and so as to not alert the neighborhood that anything different was happening he went on whistling and walking away from the house, she walking with him, because by then her household had grown accustomed to hearing the whistler and the mother no longer alert at the whistler's presence had gone to sleep. And that was the pattern of their meeting. Still, every time he thought to touch her, she countered by a change in her posture and another story about her life, of the fellow she thought loved her, of the mistakes she made, of the wait she had decided she must wait, of the care she had to take of the difference between love and love, Sonnyboy all this time trying to calm her until his eyes began to close on him, forced open only because he knew he had to walk her home and then walk back by himself and get a little sleep and go and drive the van. But Sonnyboy had already had his answer from her. He was happy to be with her and really pleased that he could just enjoy her presence, his heart and head so full that sometimes he didn't have anything to say there was so much, so that sometimes he just nodded and said *yes* aloud, as if, yes, this was right, this surrender.

"What you want with me?"

"I tell you already," he said.

"Tell me again," she said.

He looked for words: "I like you," he said, knowing that those did not convey the weight of his feelings.

"Like?" she asked.

"Yes, I like you."

"You like me? Man," she said. "You have to love me. And show it to me every day." And as if not to discourage him, but wanting to alert him to her ambition, she said, "I have my plans. To open a little business. I can cook."

Sonnyboy didn't say anything. He had wanted with her words to hold her, to draw her to him and to embrace her, but he resisted the temptation, careful to not make a wrong move because she might still be thinking of him as a badjohn. So, waiting for her guidance, they walked on in silence. Sonnyboy felt himself in an unfamiliar world and that he was being led by this woman. He was not unhappy to follow. He was thinking how to make her see him, wondering what to do. He wanted to be himself. But what was himself?

When he was going back home alone, he began to feel that his caution was not enough. Just to follow where she led was not enough. He had to find a way for himself, to expose to her what he had in him and what she meant to him, how to let her see the space in his stomach, the melting in his heart, how to let her know that he knew and liked her smell and the curve and color of her lips, her eyes and her smile and the feel of her soul. And that was how he started to listen and to melt, and to think and watch her lips and teeth and smile, to see, to see and feel it, whatever it was he didn't quite know yet, but he was beginning to feel it coming inside him, not even patience, not only respect, something that later he would understand as cherish, slow and clear, a light coming inside him how to cherish and love. And just like that he held her hand and she folded her fingers about his own and he begin to discover what fingers is and hands and arms were. He touch her face and he begin to learn what face was, what flesh was and what hair was, all that he learned, marveling with each discovery, oh lord, and he didn't say a word those times. And next day the world opened up for him, the colors of flowers, the shape of leaves, birds whistling their own tune, dancing their own dance, and insects, so intricate the patterns on their body, fragile like lace, exquisite like gems. He watched the way branches bent, and lonely bare trees standing alone. And he knew now what a flower was and what was a leaf. These things, it had taken him all his life to know. He began to feel himself coming alive in a new way, to a new world.

"Lover boy," fellars teased. "Lover boy."

Lover boy?

But he didn't let their mamaguy bother him and he didn't tell them of the sweet hard delight he was experiencing. Over these nights now and again she would let him hold her in his arms and for a moment she would sink against his chest and he would feel the heft of her body, or sometimes she would just accidentally stumble against him and he would feel the firmness of her hips and the world wobble and melt and the weight of a wonderful tormenting urgency in the pit of his stomach that made him feel as if he had no time left to live, and only her embrace would save him. Now even as he dealt with the weight of his urgency he found that in his arms she too was trembling and gasping for breath. As if she too was growing weaker, she would push him away less and less firmly until she was more in his arms against his chest, her breasts, her breath, the scent on her skin. These moments were happening more and more often. And they began to walk now further and further away from her house as if they had to keep in motion to escape drowning in the pool of urgency, walking one night in one direction and another night in the opposite one. One night they walked and walked until he found himself in front of the house in which he lived. He pointed out the house. That is where I live. Not daring to suggest that they go in, not wanting to make any move that would make her think of him as crude or uncouth, wondering how to be other than himself. He didn't know how long he could keep this up. Another night they pass it again. It started to rain lightly. Neither of them wanted to acknowledge it.

Finally he asked, "You want to go inside?"

"No. I want to stay in the rain and catch pneumonia."

They went inside. She sat on the bed. He changed his shirt that had been soaked by the rain. He offered her a T-shirt of his own. She shook her head no. She watched him, his muscles. He didn't touch her. He kept his distance. With his shirt changed, he sat on the other side of the bed, away from her. They said nothing. And just when he felt that the urgency in his belly would overpower him, he said, "Let's go."

He really didn't know how long he could keep up this.

The PM's Promise

This was never going to happen again, the PM said, at his next meeting, as he stood on the platform constructed on the site of the disastrous fire, shouting to be heard above the steaming hum of nine gasoline lamps.

"Because as wonderfully as these gaslights shine, if we are to enter the modern epoch as a contending force that the world shall respect, if not honor, we shall have to equip our communities with more reliable light. So tonight I make this solemn pledge to you, the first thing I am going to do in my next term as your Prime Minister is to ensure that every rural community be given electricity, a fire brigade be set up in every town with hydrants and standpipes and a twenty-four-hour water service. The colonial order developed the cities and left the countryside to languish in backwardness, leaving you only the monuments of their dominion, their churches and their police stations, the busts of their heroes. So this is where the concentration of our energies shall be. What they left untouched we will develop, what they scorned we will exalt, what they sullied we will wash clean. Here in these villages we will pitch camp and all the angels of hell shall not prevail against us. Come hell or high water, we are not going to leave you without water nor in the dark again. Not in Egypt village, not in Guayaguayare, not in Blanchisseuse, not in Matelot and, God willing, ladies and gentlemen, certainly not here in Cascadu."

The PM had said nothing about Franklyn's death.

126

By the time the applause to the PM speech died down, the site of the fire had been cleared of rubble, surveyors and architects and builders had appeared with hard hats and tall boots to construct a complex that would house a new grocery store, drug store, hardware and department store. A week later Mervyn Aladdin, a fire officer from San Fernando, appeared in uniform to interview young men of Cascadu who would form the volunteer fire brigade that the PM had mandated.

We watched from the roadside as he put them through their paces on a Friday evening, climbing and descending a ladder and then go marching through the town. I never see them touch a hose and they had no fire hydrant to open. They had no building of their own and no equipment except for a ladder, which they borrowed from the Department of Works. They got no pay but were promised a fireman's uniform at the end of their training and the opportunity of graduating to the ranks of the professional firemen when the Fire Station was opened in Cascadu.

Since the fire, Aunt Magenta had thought of acknowledging, if not rewarding, Sonnyboy for the good work he had done for the party during its victorious election campaign and (she didn't put it quite in this way) for his role in starting the fire that had shown itself to be so beneficial to the development of Cascadu. She took her concern to the party group, and after agonizing over what reward to offer Sonnyboy, Mr. Tannis came up with the idea that Sonnyboy should be invited to train as a fireman, after which he would be employed permanently as an officer in the fire brigade that the PM had said would be built in every town.

At forty-two, Sonnyboy Apparicio was just over the age and one inch under the acceptable height required to join the Fire Service, and with the impediment of his foot, slight as he made it out to be, he did not qualify. More importantly, he did not have any desire to join the Fire Service; so when Mr. Tannis made him the offer, Sonnyboy looked at him in astonishment.

"Fireman? Me? A fireman?"

"What he wants to be, Chairman of the County Council? He lucky he not charged for arson," Mr. Tannis complained to my aunt Magenta.

Sonnyboy came to me.

"King, give me your opinion. You could see me as a fireman, eh? Tell me! You could see me climbing down a ladder from a burning building with a man on my shoulder?"

His new beginning had fallen through and he would have to look for a new job too, because Tannis's uncle, who owned the van he was driving, had decided to get out of the transportation business and had no further use for his services.

Sonnyboy spoke to Sweetie. She knew about the fire.

"A fireman?" Sonnyboy mused.

Sweetie-Mary heard the pain in his voice.

"Don't make them make you stop loving," she said.

"This is a sign," he told Sweetie, "for me to begin my life by myself, independent of anybody."

She took his hands in hers. She stroked his fingers. "You know," she said, almost gaily, "if you want you could run away with me."

He looked at her again: "You serious?"

"Try me."

And that was how a few nights later he came on her street, driving a car and pulled up and parked it nearby, with the engine running, not only to signal his presence but because he was not sure that if he turned off the ignition it would start again, hoping she would hear him whistling "With a Song in My Heart" above the sound of the beating engine.

It was an old car that had passed through many hands, that had spent just over a year in the yard of the mechanic Freddie with a FOR SALE sign on it. Freddie had allowed him to drive it, *so you could see how good it working.* Since Sonnyboy stopped driving the van, he had been thinking of driving taxi for a living and had been looking for a car he could afford. This car was a bargain, and what made it so good a bargain was that "you have your mechanic right here," Freddie tell him. "Whatever little repairs, I right here to fix them," Freddie said.

The car, also, of course, was a demonstration of Sonnyboy's ambition.

So when Sweetie-Mary came out, he showed her the car.

"It is an investment," he said. "I could run it as a taxi and if anything wrong I have my mechanic Freddie to fix it. I bring it to show you and also just in case."

"Just in case what?"

"Just in case you ready to run away with me."

"You asking me to?"

"You ready to run away with me?" he asked

"When?"

"Right away."

"Wait here," she said and she walked away from him back to the house.

"I couldn't believe it," he tell me. "I couldn't believe it. The woman go inside with the same heartbreaking walk

129

that I could make out even in the dark. Next thing I see is the lamp go on and I there in the bush, keeping out of sight, thinking is some big secret thing me and the girl was doing. Then a little while after, this time surrounded by her family, all of them there in the front room, she, the mother, the sisters, all together, holding on to one another, like they saying goodbye. Then Sweetie come through the front door walking bold-bold with her suitcase in hand, all of them still around her, as if they were seeing her off.

"And I there in the darkness hiding. I feel stupid. I feel like a arse."

But he didn't say anything, even when she get into the car. And she, sensing something wrong, had the bravery to ask me what happen. "What it is happen? Tell me, Sonnyboy, what happen?"

Until finally he had to answer: "I thought you was running away with me."

"And I am," she said.

"And your mother? You tell your mother? You tell her?"

"Yes, I tell her."

"So, so they know everything?" Sonnyboy felt even more of a fool.

Then is when she tell him that running away was not even her own idea, but her mother's. For years she had made it clear to her girl-children that as long as they lived in her house, if any one of them was to become intimate with a man, "Is either he marry you or run away with you."

All the way to his house Sonnyboy again wondered whether he had made the right decision or if he had allowed himself to be entrapped by Sweetie and her mother. He did not say a word.

"You vexed with me?" she asked. "You want to take me back home? I put you through a lot of trouble?"

He still didn't speak. He didn't touch her either. For three days.

And his uneasiness didn't leave him until the night he awoke to find her sleeping in total abandoned and contented slumber, her head on his shoulder and her legs sprawled all over his body. He removed his arm from under her head and he fixed her head on the pillow and held her loosely, wanting to draw closer but not wanting to surrender his vexation until he better understood the situation that had caused it. She threw an arm around his neck and drew him closer and held his head to her bosom, and bit by bit, without a word spoken, they negotiated a settlement that left them in the arms of each other, climbing into an imminent tomorrow and swimming together to a shore that was on a far horizon and an arm's length away, going together into a forever place whose name was on the tip of his tongue but that his brain would not allow him to say. And Sonnyboy did not know that the sounds of their celebration had reached the world until next morning when he encountered his neighbors, he find each of them looking at him with a knowing grin. He continued to smile back at them in perplexity until one of them couldn't keep it any longer: "Last night," he said, "we nearly call the police."

Sonnyboy's embarrassment turned to alarm at the thought that his grandmother had heard them. And he was thinking to avoid her, but Sweetie-Mary, feeling it would be better to apologize, went to her.

"Sorry for the noise last night."

"What noise? Around here, with dogs and birds and

traffic, to get my sleep, every night I plug my ears with cotton wool."

Mary's mouth dropped open and the smile of joy coursed upward from her belly and without thinking or anything she reached out and hugged Sonnyboy's grandmother; she felt the muscles on the face against hers. The grandmother was smiling. That was the beginning of their friendship that was to delight Sonnyboy and give him a focus that he had never had before. Sweetie-Mary had brought him something. He wasn't sure exactly what to call it. He called it luck. Mary had brought him luck. Now he would show Cascadu the man he really was.

One day he came home to find Sweetie-Mary and his grandmother clearing out the front gallery. They intended to make it a vegetable shop and much more. Together the three of them agreed on a plan. Sweetie-Mary and his grandmother would manage the vegetable store and he would pay down on the car and run it as a taxi.

Of course they had other plans for the car. On weekends they would be able to go to the beach. For Carnival they could go to a fête, to calypso without having to worry how they were going to get back. They could go to see cricket in the Oval. With the money he brought in they would renovate the place, stock the store, extend the gallery, put a couple chairs and tables and set up an eating place where Sweetie-Mary who was a good cook would prepare food for sale. Bit by bit they would pave the yard and extend the eating section, so by the time the electricity promised by the PM came to Cascadu, they would be ready to open a first-class eating place.

TWO

The Man He Wanted Them to See

In the three years it take for electricity to come to
Cascadu, Sonnyboy, his grandmother and Sweetie-Mary
transformed the gallery in the front their house from
what was a stall with its few bananas and tomatoes into a
vegetable shop that also sold homemade fruit juices,
cakes, fried fish and bake, and whatever dish Sweetie-
Mary was cooking on that day: fish-broth, oildown,
saltfish and provision, pelau. During the week sales were
slow, but on weekends, when people stopped on the way
back from the beach, the three of them were busy, and
the business would have been profitable, except that it
also had to pay for repairs to the car that Sonnyboy
bought to run as a taxi.

The car was running good. Sonnyboy drive it to Mayaro
to the beach for them to dig for chip-chip. He went
Rampanalgas with Sweetie-Mary for the Fishermen fête.
He drive it to Port of Spain market to buy fresh vegetables
for the shop. He drive it by Sweetie-Mary sister in Diego
Martin. All that time, he owing Freddie for it. The minute
he pay off Freddie for the car, it start. Bushings for the
starter want changing, gear box want overhauling, the
accelerator cable break, points, coil. The battery need
recharging. I don't think it ever again make a complete
trip to any destination without breaking down, and the
people of Cascadu get accustomed to seeing it on the side
of the road with its hood open and Sonnyboy stand up
beside it, waiting for some good Samaritan to give him a

push or for his mechanic Freddie to arrive with his bluster and bag of tools to get it to run again.

And is now Freddie tell him: "The car is a old car. What you expect? We have to fix it."

"You get trapped already," Sweetie-Mary tell him. "Is better you just sell it."

"Sell it," his grandmother agreed. And even though nobody asked his opinion, his friend Gilda looked at the car and said what he had said the first time he saw it, "Old car is trouble."

Sonnyboy held on to the car.

"People laughing at you," Sweetie-Mary tell him.

"Let them laugh," he said. "They just jealous."

Sonnyboy kept the car. Through his mechanic Freddie he found secondhand parts for its repair, Sonnyboy upholstered it and painted it over in a brilliant yellow that hid the scars of the numerous welding jobs done on it, and applied his famed neatness to its upkeep. It looked good, cared for; apart from guzzling gas and drinking oil, the only problem was it took time to start on mornings. In the night he parked it at the top of the incline on the street where he lived so that he could kick-start it by rolling down the hill. Even that operation did not always work and many times the car would tumble, start briefly, flutter for a few moments then cut off as it rumbled downhill. On the flat, it needed a push to start it. After a while he enlisted Sweetie-Mary and his grandmother to help him. It was an adventure that his grandmother relished. She didn't know how to drive and had never sat in front a steering wheel before, but because she didn't have as much strength to push as the others, she got the delightful task to steer while they pushed and when Sonnyboy shouted "Hit it," to come off the clutch, put her foot down gently on the brakes and if it didn't quite start, to come off the brakes, give it gas and go back to the brakes again. "Clutch, brakes, gas," she recited. It became part of the ritual of starting the car on a morning. But despite his grandmother's exhilaration on those mornings, she saw that the expenses for the car was bleeding their takings and she had to agree that he should get rid of it. Sonnyboy argued to keep it. Yes, it was an old car. But, what it needed was care, a good overhaul, a tune-up and it would be ready to rumble. And there would be little trouble because – and this was his ace – he had a good mechanic. Neither Sweetie-Mary nor his grandmother said anything. True to his word, Sonnyboy dropped by his mechanic Freddie almost daily to have him repair whatever problem had developed, replacing broken parts with those he (Freddie) managed to get from derelict vehicles parked in his yard. When Freddie did not have the parts, Sonnyboy himself searched for them by tracking down vehicles from which he could find the various screws and bolts that were missing from his, and soon he knew the location of every Avenger in nearly the whole East of the island. This experience of scouring the region to find car parts brought him into contact with fellow sufferers like himself who held on to nearly useless machines as symbols of their place in the world. Sonnyboy felt admitted into their society, so to them at least because of his suffering he was seen less as a badjohn and more as one of them. He came to feel himself so much part of that brotherhood that even if he was traveling in a taxi, at the sight of a car shut down, he would persuade the driver to stop and he alone or both of them would go over to render if not assistance, consolation.

One day with all three of them in it, the car shut down

in the middle of Cascadu. Sonnyboy and Sweetie-Mary got out, and with his grandmother steering, they pushed it into the garage by Freddie where he left it for repair.

Sonnyboy turned his attention to the vegetable shop, where his help was needed. He did the running around during the day, worked at nights while Sweetie-Mary and his grandmother did what else had to be done. Without the daily problems with the car and with the additional time he put into it, the business began to prosper, Sweetie-Mary to cook more often, and the ideal of having a restaurant in Cascadu took shape. Customers who had left because they didn't have this and that in stock, seeing the flutter of life in the place, started to return. In addition, the brotherhood of used car owners who saw him as one of them began to patronize him.

One afternoon his two good friends Gilda and Dog appeared carrying two small benches, a draughts board and a flask of white rum. Following them was a small group of men. They had come to set up in front of his place of business and to engage their passion of playing draughts and drinking white rum which they chased with plain water. Pretty soon draughts and the discussion of the game dominated activity at the shop. From the very first day she saw them, Sonnyboy's grandmother warned him that having draughts-playing at his business place would bring bad luck.

Sonnyboy saw it as an attraction, as an indication of people accepting him. Bringing people to the shop could only help him.

"Help to sink you," his grandmother said. "What they buying? You don't sell rum and the water that they use to chase the white rum you give them free. What is your profit?"

"I don't want my friends to think I behaving like a big shot," he said.

"You have to stop them," his grandmother said.

But Sonnyboy didn't have the heart to do so.

It didn't take a month for the first signs of the blight that his grandmother prophesied to appear. At first it didn't seem a big thing. A few houses down the street, Rosie Ramroop put up a roti stall selling fruit juices and doubles and barra. Two weeks later, the van that brought his stock of goods was sold to new owners and they refused to allow him the kind of credit facilities of its previous owner. In the week following, Sweetie-Mary's nephew Patrick pushed a marble into one of his ears and had to be taken to the hospital in Port of Spain to have it removed. Two weeks later, Rosie Ramroop, who made and sold roti and potato pies, brought a fridge run by kerosene and started selling trays of ice, and even Sonnyboy's grandmother who liked a cool drink began to patronize her. Sonnyboy's customers began to drift off to Rosie Ramroop's place. Sonnyboy finally began to believe. He approached Gilda and Dog in a roundabout way, pointing out to them that his customers were drifting away. They had noticed it too, they told him. But they did not even think that it had anything to do with them, and they continued to turn up every day for their game. Sonnyboy didn't want to resort to violence. He didn't want to get ignorant as everyone expected him to. He decided to wait. His grandmother wasn't waiting. She tried her best to make them as uncomfortable as she could. She wrapped her head in a blue head tie and burnt incense in a homemade censer and trailed the smoke around them, all the while reciting the Magnificat. She placed cloves of garlic and the cut halves of yellow limes where she knew they would be sitting. She scrubbed the floor with gully root and water reeking of red lavender and asafoetida, but succeeded only in chasing away customers. Gilda and Dog kept on coming. A huge Coca-Cola sign with the single word ROSIE's, that could be seen from a distance, appeared in front Rosie Ramroop's place identifying her shop as a bona fide business place. Customer after customer made the journey to Rosie's.

One day, when it had one sweetbread left in the glass case and the last potato pie had stiffened like a piece of board and the bhajee was dry in the bin and the few ochroes had grown black and soft with fungus, and the only thing they had for sale was the three slices of fried fish in the glass case and the roasted bakes that Sweetie-Mary made, Dog, about to complete a series of moves that would wipe out Gilda, raised his head from the draughts game for the admiration of the spectators and saw that, apart from Sonnyboy, the two of them were alone. "Wait," he said. "Where is everybody?"

Sonnyboy didn't have the heart to answer him. But his face must have revealed his pain.

"Like things going bad, boy?" Dog said. "Pressure?"

Sonnyboy nodded and with his last ounce of patience he smiled. "Yes," he said. "Pressure!"

Gilda, contemplating the draughts board, realized that he had lost the game. He stretched and yawned. "I hungry," he said. "I wonder what Rosie have over there to eat?"

Sonnyboy did not speak.

"Well," Dog said, "let's go and see."

And it was so that Gilda and Dog gathered up the knobs, took up their benches, their draughts board and made their way over to Rosie Ramroop's establishment where they set down their benches, placed the draughts board on their knees and organized the pieces for their game. Sonnyboy made the sign of the cross.

Believing this was a sign that his bad luck had ended, Sonnyboy decided that he would celebrate by taking his family to the beach that weekend. Every week for months every time he saw Freddie, he would be told to expect the car that weekend. There was some one part that he needed to get to finish the job. He knew where to locate it, but, *the time, boy. The time.* He set out to see Freddie to hurry him up so he would get the car for the weekend. And so that she would share in the good news he expected, he got Sweetie-Mary to go along with him.

He found his vehicle hoisted on bricks and blocks, stripped of wheels and rims. When he turned the ignition to start it, he heard no sound. He lifted the hood. The horn, the carburetor, the coil, the battery, the accelerator cable, the fan belt, the generator, and he didn't know what other parts – all had disappeared. Freddie, it turned out, had been plundering his car to service other needy vehicles.

"Freddie?" Sonnyboy pleaded. "Freddie."

Thank God Sweetie-Mary was there. She hugged Sonnyboy and half-carrying him, she dragged him away until they were a safe enough distance from Freddie, then she put one hand round his neck and the other around his waist and took him home.

The Hard Wuck Party

Sonnyboy had barely finished thanking Sweetie-Mary for saving him from getting himself in trouble when there appeared at his business place John de John, the novelist from Matura, with him Didicus West of the Hard Wuck Party and a band of his followers, each of them in green T-shirts and short khaki pants. They were on a recruitment drive throughout the island and had been directed to Sonnyboy as a businessman who had the social conscience, the fighting spirit and might want to throw in his lot with them, not just for the upcoming County Council elections but for *the long haul.*

The Hard Wuck Party, Didicus West explained, had fought the last two elections without any of its candidates winning a seat and only the leader receiving the five percent vote entitling him to get back his deposit. That did not worry them. Because what it showed *was either the people didn't hear us, or how far in advance of the country we of the Hard Wuck Party are.* They were not perturbed either to be described as a group of intellectuals who spoke a language people could not understand. "Since when do we have to apologize for intelligence, for intellect, for insight, eh, comrade?"

And they were continuing with electoral politics not only to see how many seats they would win (to be frank, they didn't expect many) but to discover how far the people themselves had advanced in consciousness since their last trip to the polls. So the real politics could begin.

"We have spoken and written about the solutions to the nation's problems. The only reason we can ascribe for the people's response is that they do not understand that they possess the solutions in their hands. The politics can only make sense if the people accept themselves. That, Brother, is our message. Believe in ourselves. That is the message. And that, Brother, is where you come in. We need people who people understand. Who can translate ideas to the masses. That is why we need you."

This show of confidence in him, absurd as it was, cheered Sonnyboy. He felt himself in good company. The people of Cascadu had not understood him either. As he said to the leader of the Hard Wuck Party:

"It is like me. I have been trying to show them me. They don't understand me either. And I not using any fancy language."

"Yes," said the leader. "We need to look around us with our own eyes, to take our own inventory of the place, of what is available to us, what use we can make of things, how we can use things different to the way they have been used before. Knowledge and imagination. We need to know the names of the birds that fly around us, the plants, the weeds, what are they saying to us as well as what they can do for us. Did you know, comrade, that there are in this country 93 species of mammals, 93 species of reptiles, 432 species of birds, 37 species of amphibians, as well as 644 species of butterflies and 2,555 species of plants. And we are still counting. We have been looking outward at the other, not inward at the self. We have no sense of the sacred, no sacred space, no sacred icons."

"And how do we change it?"

143

"We. I'm glad you said *we*. Comrade, the new politics is to help us break the old molds and set ourselves free to create in Independence. We have to cease to play the same roles we were brought here to perform. And that is why, Brother, we want you to throw in your lot with us. We believe in the hard work, not the shortcuts."

By the end of the session, each one of the members was introduced to Sonnyboy and Sweetie-Mary. They wanted Sonnyboy to represent them in Cascadu, to sell the party's newspaper and attend their meetings in Arouca.

Sonnyboy was taken entirely off guard. Here, totally unexpected, was the opportunity he had been waiting for, to show the man he is. Now they would see him for what he was: a revolutionary, not a badjohn. But as he shook hands all around, he caught a glimpse of Sweetie-Mary's patient consoling eyes looking at him and in one little part of his mind, a little voice squeaked, *Sonnyboy, they trap you again*. He pushed it aside.

"How many newspapers you taking, in a town this size?" Didicus West asked. "Twenty?"

"You have so many?"

"Ah-ha. You good," the leader said, admiring his quickness. "Ten? Fifteen?"

"Yes."

"Yes, what?"

"Ten."

When the Hard Wuck people left, Sonnyboy found himself still ruminating on his own witticism – *You have so many?* And what caused him to lean toward the Hard Wuck Party was the quick-wittedness of its leader: *Ah-ha. You good.* But then he came back to earth to figure how, in the community where no one read, he

144

would get rid of ten newspapers. He should have decided on five.

In the months to come, Sonnyboy sold three newspapers, one to Mr. Tannis, one to Manick and one to me. The others he kept on display, spread out on a string in the vegetable store, eventually to be given away to customers who needed wallpaper. Sonnyboy attended the regular meetings of the Hard Wuck Party in Port of Spain and Arouca, and brought back the hard work message to Cascadu, telling people who came to the shop about the need to educate themselves, *to accept yourself just as you are,* telling them to discover the names of birds, to identify your sacred spaces, to move from being just workers in the place to becoming guardians of the space. In these causes, the intellectuals of the Hard Wuck Party were turning things over and helping people to see the world anew. Revolution, they said, was the turning over of things. And even before it happened, they had to see it. Teaching steelband playing in the schools should be seen as the steelband yards becoming schools, taking calypso to church meant that the calypso tents must be places of worship. With this orientation, ideas that had been easily accepted before were scrutinized and turned over. They renamed the seasons to fall in line with common usage. Instead of wet season and dry season, we were now given mango season and kite season. They used as well the language of sports and childhood games like pitching marbles to describe the attitudes to everyday life and political gambits. They took the vocabulary and symbolism which our education had ignored and gave it a new importance. *Chinksing, buttards, fein, zantay,* all found their way into the language of politics. Following their lead,

Sonnyboy utilized the stickfight dances and movements as the basis for physical exercise. Twice a week he assembled his grandmother and other party group members in the yard of his place of business to sing stickfight songs and to strike stickfight poses and go through the movements of the stickfight dance until they were sweating. Cascadu was on its way to becoming the intellectual and spiritual center of the island.

In the years I had known Sonnyboy, this was the first time I see him so enthused, so confident that he had a part in the building of something that would take him, take us, to at least a more interesting place. He was like a big Boy Scout, overflowing with belief. And it was the force of his enthusiastic belief that made him the rallying point of the Hard Wuck Party in Cascadu. In the beginning some people laughed at his passion and winked at each other as he spoke, but he did not see or acknowledge their cynicism. He set up a party group in Cascadu with himself as chairman, and as secretary/treasurer Brinsley Brown – a small pig farmer, a former supporter of the Butler Party, one of the unfortunate car owners waiting on Freddie to repair his vehicle; as committee members, he roped in Gilda and Dog, who while supportive of him had remained playing draughts in front Rosie Ramroop's business place without afflicting her with any discernible sign of blight.

About him and indeed about them all was a sense of performance that attracted people. The Hard Wuck Party was fun. In the party newspapers there was a column on medicinal plants, one on native birds, another on sacred spaces. With his new concern for the environment, Sonnyboy joined a group of hikers. Some Sundays he would take Sweetie-Mary, his grandmother and the children and go to the forest, to waterfalls, to beaches. He returned from these adventures with plants, with feathers, with shells, with stones. He began writing little epigrams that he plastered over his shop. His delightful madness drew visitors on the way to the beach and made his shop the place for the people of Cascadu to congregate on a Saturday afternoon or a Sunday morning. People came to the shop just to read what, inspired by the intellectuals of the Hard Wuck Party, he had written.

He gained an even wider audience for his work when *The Cannon* featured him in a story with a picture of him in stickfight pose taking his supporters through their paces and a list of the thoughts credited to him, entitled SONNYBOY SPEAKS.

The voice of the people is the voice of God.
Righteousness shall prevail.
We shall overcome.
Who don't want to hear will feel.
I will not let you go until you bless me.
People do to you what they already do to others or to themselves.
You are not the enemy.
Accepting yourself is accepting God.
Denying yourself is denying God.
Monkey does always climb the right tree.

These were not ideas he had copied, but positions he had arrived at on his own. And it was with that sense of self-discovery that Sonnyboy and his few party members, without feeling intimidated by the greater intelligence of party intellectuals who were expected to have all the answers, began to ask questions of themselves aloud for the first time.

What is Life?
What is the Good Life?
What is Community?
Why Democracy?
Who is a Representative?
What is a Citizen?
How Do We Learn Our History?
The Basis of Land Distribution?
Should Everyone Have a Home?
What Is Development?

These provided the subjects for discussion. Soon the party's name was on the lips of everyone in Cascadu, first as a kind of joke, but then because it suggested delightful serious fun. They gave parties, not grand affairs but nice. They invited me to sing old-time calypsos and had people singing along. They had cookouts and family sports day with greasy pole and running races. More and more people appeared wearing with pride the short khaki pants and green T-shirt, with its arresting slogan: *Power to the Hard Wuck*. And although my aunt Magenta had no intention of abandoning the National Party, she asked me to get her a pair of khaki short pants and one of the green Hard Wuck T-shirts. Because of the activities organized by Sonnyboy and his group, Cascadu, a town unknown to the Hard Wuck Party in fifteen of its sixteen years of existence, came to be mentioned by the Hard Wuckers as one of their strongholds, one of the few constituencies where their candidate had a chance if not of winning a seat in the general elections, certainly landing one in the County Council elections.

When the question of a candidate to stand for County Council elections first came up, Sonnyboy's was the only

148

name offered by the Cascadu party group. The fact that he had been to prison did not seem to bother them. Sonnyboy, the secretary of the Hard Wuck Party group, Brinsley Brown argued, was a freedom fighter like Butler, like Mandela and other leaders who were imprisoned for resisting a system that was working to subdue them.

But this characterization did not find favor with Mr. Tannis. Perennially overlooked by the National Party for every position he offered himself for, he was outraged that Sonnyboy was being compared to Mandela or Butler. "Sonnyboy had a prison record. The man is a badjohn," he said to my aunt Magenta. "Maybe I should have trained myself for politics by cuffing-down people, eh? Maybe instead of going to school and getting an education I should have learned to use a razor."

As an organizer, Sonnyboy had exceeded by far the expectations of the Hard Wuck Party. In addition to organizing Cascadu, he had shown he could hold his own in an argument with any representative of the other parties. But, the Hard Wuck Party supporters were concerned that they would lose votes if they put up Sonnyboy. Indeed, they were concerned whether, as someone who had been to prison for criminal offenses, he could be allowed to stand for elections at all.

In the meeting that followed these revelations, the leader of the Hard Wuck Party, Didicus West, pointed out that what they had before them was a situation in which a resistance fighter was being seen as a delinquent. That was the absurdity of the present politics, he said. It was clearly a battle that he and the Hard Wuck Party must promise to fight – after the elections. Meanwhile, in the interest of time and resources and for the good of the party, he saw no other course than to ask Sonnyboy to withdraw from contention and give his support to a candidate other than himself.

Claude Cruickshank was the one screening committee member that disagreed. As far as he was concerned, the question of Sonnyboy's eligibility to stand for election was one that needed to be answered immediately. If the Hard Wuck Party wanted to bring attention to the situation, and strike a blow for the real politics, there before them was a golden opportunity to make the eligibility of Sonnyboy the central theme of their election campaign or be accused of the absurdity of excluding the revolutionary from the revolution.

"Comrade," Didicus West said to him at that meeting, "I am afraid that we shall have to live with the absurdity until we get into power."

"Look at that, eh," Sonnyboy said to me when I went to see him. "The revolutionary is banned from the revolution. I not surprised. Why should I be surprised?"

I could feel his pain.

And Sweetie-Mary, feeling for him, had responded with her mantra, "Don't let them make you stop loving."

"Why should I be surprised? You know what hurt me?" he began.

"You know what hurt him?" Sweetie-Mary said.

"Nobody tell them, 'You can't treat Sonnyboy so. After all he do.' Nobody say, 'You can't do Sonnyboy that.'"

They were looking at me.

"You can't do Sonnyboy that," his grandmother said.

"But I am bigger than that," Sonnyboy said.

"Don't let them make you stop loving," said Sweetie-Mary. "Let us show them. Let us work to elect whoever they choose."

"Yes," his grandmother said. "Show them the man you is."

The committee hadn't yet chosen his replacement. There were two candidates. One was Carlos Nan King, a geologist and a part-time resident, whose relatives owned a fifty-five-acre farm on the outskirts of Cascadu. He was an avid Carnival player and a sportsman who had represented T and T in rifle shooting and had self-published a book of poems entitled *Chin*. Few people of Cascadu knew him. The other, the one who was well known to Cascadu and who they would eventually choose, was Manick.

Manick

For all the boys who lived in the Settlement, the savannah was a place to play. For Manick, it was a place to graze the cow. He would walk the cow along the edge of the savannah in the part near the forest where the ground was swampy and the grass tall and let it graze, happy to field a ball when it was hit his way, running it down and heaving it from there on the boundary sometimes into the hands of the wicketkeeper. If his father wasn't home he would take a chance to take his turn at bat. In that situation, not looking at the ball closely, lashing out at it and getting out quickly so he could hurry back to the cow on the edge of the savannah, accepting I suppose that he was not free to bat like Franklyn and Berris and Evrol and the rest of us who lived, like him, surrounding the savannah, and who were free to play uninterrupted on weekday evenings and, if a match wasn't playing, nearly whole day Saturday, going on until awakened from the trance of our play by the voices of mothers or grandmothers bawling: *Evrol! Beresford! Regis!* And then you'll hear one of the boys scream and the others take off running, because Miss Ruby or Miss Ruth had arrived with a switch or a belt. Miss Pearlie didn't shout, she just appeared with whatever instrument of terror she had to hand, a broomstick, a scrubbing brush, a pot spoon, a side of slippers, a wet shirt from her washing, the only warning of her presence the gasp of anticipation when she was near enough to Evrol to deliver the blow, and all you'd hear is *whoosh*, as Evrol disappear. Sometimes, to play a joke on Evrol, one of the boys would steal up behind him and make the heaving breathing-out sound of his mother and Evrol would bolt. Aunt Magenta hardly ever called Franklyn and me to come home, and the two of us would stay in the savannah till it was too dark to make out the ball. Ramesh and Soogrim didn't have a cow to graze, but they didn't let dark catch them in the savannah. If you wanted to see Soogrim run all you had to do was say, "Soogrim, look, your father!"

Manick father was not so strict.

He had arrived at the Settlement a few years earlier, sitting on the high seat of a steamroller, steering its massive wheels back and forth over gravel and asphalt and stone, and had cleared the plot of land in the bush behind the savannah, and then we see him and maybe two other men passing along the track at the side of our house, and next thing we see is a building, a wooden house with three rooms and a gallery, with a hammock and a bench the only pieces of furniture we could see from the road. From that location, he would edge himself into the consciousness of the Settlement, not so much as our neighbor, as a man living in our neighborhood, doing nothing to change his status of stranger beyond his mumbled good evening to my aunt Magenta as he went through the track that passed at the side of our house, stamping his presence on Aunt Magenta as ... a lonely man whose heart and homeland was somewhere else, showing no interest in nothing Cascadu had to offer and offering nothing himself, displaying no symbol or evidence of belonging to anything we could recognize; in his yard no cluster of jhandi waving in the breeze. From his house no sound of prayers, or of Indian music, no offer of parsad at Eid, no deyas for Divali, no a beer staining his clothes for Pagwah and no preparation for Christmas or Easter or costume for Carnival either, not showing any interest in the old churches or the new, neither Catholic nor Anglican nor the Adventist nor the Pentecostal that had begun to sweep up all the souls in the Settlement except my aunt Magenta and her flock who was Shouter Baptist, his only interest the cricket matches played on the savannah, and even those from the distance of his own house, so that I often heard Aunt Magenta wondering as she looked out in puzzlement from her kitchen at his lonely house whether he might not be a fugitive from justice, a fella who chop up his wife and run away with another woman or commit some other heinous criminal act like burning down somebody house and coming to hide out here behind the savannah, *You think I making joke?* To her, this idea not so far-fetched, since there was nobody in Cascadu who knew him or knew anyone to whom he was related or where he come from, all she (and I suppose the rest of Settlement) could see was that he had a woman that hardly ever leave the house and a girl-child that nobody ever see on the road, the two females going out not even to the shop, the only one to provide a sign that it had people living there, this boy, Manick, seen toting water or grazing the cow, going to the shop, going to school, the only one of the family whose name was known to Settlement, so that we referred to his father as Manick father and his mother as Manick mother and his sister as Manick sister, all of them, except, in time, the sickly mother (who one Saturday in the middle of a cricket match appeared astraddle Manick father back, the father staggering under her weight as he toted her along the track by the side of the recreation ground to Ram taxi waiting on the road to take her to the hospital) visible only on weekends when Settlement Cricket Club was playing at home, and you see them in the gallery of their house, the father lying in his hammock from where he could see the game, on the floor beside him his newspapers and his slippers so he could read or get up and go and do whatever work he had to do whenever he wanted to do it, and Manick and his sister sitting on the bench, all of them, we would learn from Manick later, waiting for Franklyn to go out to bat and when he did, when Franklyn start to bat, the father not moving, saying nothing while the crowd roared in acclamation at the genius strokes Franklyn made, clearing his throat uneasily, the words that he seemed to want to say filling up his mouth, choking him, so when he did speak it would be in a hoarse voice, asking Manick or his sister to bring a cup of water for him please; and he would drink the water as if to wash down the words that had stuck in his throat, without shifting his eyes from Franklyn out there in the middle.

When Franklyn get out after batting, Manick father would look around as if for something he had misplaced, heave himself out the hammock and with a new force and drive, slip his feet into his slippers and hurry outside to tend the tomatoes or the baigan in the backyard, or trim the fence or cut grass for the cow, all of it done with a sense of urgency as if he, his family, the community too and the whole district, if not the world, needed to immediately exert some equivalent force and style to match Franklyn's batting; so that Manick and his sister felt compelled to find something useful to do, so that at the fall of Franklyn's wicket, Manick would rush to get a book to read or a bucket to go for water or a knife to go and cut grass for the cow, his father still mumbling with an acknowledgment magnified by what Manick at first thought was either envy or regret: *That boy could bat.* The little bitch could bat, a verdict that he must have contemplated and thought on and weighed from watching Franklyn match after match and from looking after each game to find out if that judgement still held good. *He could bat,* saying it to himself more than to any in his house, each time with more admiration and regret and certainty, so that it appeared to be a conclusion that he would have preferred not to have to come to, his regret at Franklyn's ability suggesting to Manick that he (his father) had set himself the task of finding a deficiency in Franklyn's batting, and finding none had to look again to see if he could discover the flaw that he wanted to be there but that was not there, at least, not yet, not even to his own eyes, his assessment of Franklyn's batting having more weight because it was arrived at not with any cheer or from any generosity, but was forced out of him only because he could find no evidence to the contrary. And it must have been this – what by then had to be incontrovertible evidence of Franklyn's superior ability – that must have caused him as time went on to be a little more civil especially to Aunt Magenta who he must have found out was Franklyn's mother, looking at her, when he passed in the track at the side of our house, to see if he could spy out what she might have contributed to the genius of the boy or to discover in her the flaw not immediately evident in Franklyn's play, this look, looking, making my aunt Magenta a bit uncomfortable, causing her to remark, "I wonder what this Indian man looking at me like that for?" Alarmed that it could be intimacy he was seeking ("I wonder what kind of woman he take me for?"), not knowing then that intimacy was the last thing on Manick father mind, coming only later to appreciate the explanation put forth by Clephus, that for him (Manick father) Franklyn's batting represented the people of the Settlement, not only talent but application, discipline, and to accept Franklyn was to remove any impediment to accepting the community that Franklyn represented and from which he (Manick father) had held himself aloof. And it was in order to justify to himself his keeping his distance from them that he continued to carry on his weekly examination of Franklyn's batting with the objective of finding grounds to reject them or (and this he said with a certain caution, thinking it was better to err in the direction of Manick father's rejection than to assume he wanted to be one of us) that he was sitting there using Franklyn's batting as the measure by which he would measure the people of Settlement not because he wanted to reject them, but because he wanted to join them (he too had heard unflattering stories about them), and Manick must have been in the same quandary because he had looked on in bewilderment, not sure how he should relate to us, uncertain that he had his father's permission to enter our world, feeling himself in a limbo place with no guidance how to move.

When Manick was thirteen his mother died and two years later his sister get married. For her wedding, his father sell the cow. His sister moved out, and for a while he and his father watched the cricket together, the father in the hammock and he on the bench, until one Sunday close to two years later, his father returned from a river cook in Salibia with a band of people that included Elsie, a young woman smelling of rosemary and perfume, with two big deep pools for eyes and a face on the verge of mischievous laughter, her hair not oiled like his mother's used to be but open and fluffy, her lips red, her stare bold, her voice thinner, higher, like the whine of a mosquito, but sweet, like she was a singer. A month later, Elsie moved in and his father changed from the man who busied himself working most of the time Manick knew him to a fella who on an evening bathe and put on a short pants and a sleeveless merino and stretch out in the hammock with Elsie sitting beside him in the same hammock, cracking the shells of peanuts she had parched and feeding the nuts to him, or when balata was in season opening the ripe fruit and slipping the berries one by one into his mouth, the operation broken off now and again with he tickling her and she catching fits of laughter. On a weekend her family would come to visit and Manick father would send for his single village friend, Mr. Alan, a Black man, who himself was a loner, having nothing much to do with the village either or with Carnival or the church, his garden his religion, to partner him in a game of All Fours against whoever Elsie family bring, the talk about food and cooking and cricket, all of them dismissive of the politics, the whole world out of order for them, his father especially with a sense of superiority, making a joke of everything, talking as if to convince himself that nothing here was worthwhile, nothing worth the effort, sweetened by his belief that it had a pack of arses running the country, ruling the population of jackasses, this opinion presented so insistently that none of his mates (if you could even call them that) dared to disagree with him and he would carry on with his commentary while the others grinned and looked for ways to accommodate his opinions without the offense of disagreement while out of concern for his blood pressure (for he managed his emotions poorly, and his laughter often turned to rage) Elsie would leave her cooking to sap his forehead with Limacol or massage his neck and shoulders with coconut oil and soft candle.

On the occasion of Hindu feast days, his sister and his brother-in-law Doon would come and bring sawine and sweetmeats for them, but Doon wouldn't stay.

One day, Manick came upon his father and Elsie in the hammock, Elsie feeding him peanuts and he tickling her. Seeing Manick witness to such an intimate exchange, his father said to him, "You not going to go to the savannah and play cricket?" as if it was something he permitted him to do regularly. Taken by surprise, Manick stood open-mouth before his father, struggling to find what to say until his father waved him away. "Go."

So it was that at a time when his boyhood was nearly spent, and with the pent-up enthusiasm of years of being on the edge of the boundary, Manick found himself at liberty to go to the savannah to play cricket with the boys of the Settlement. And whether it was from his years of watching from his gallery or from the closeness of the boundary where the cow grazed the grass while he fielded and heaved back the ball for the players, Manick found that he not only had a good throwing arm but as a cricketer he had talent, he could play. We welcomed him, happy to have an extra man for our games.

And so he went through the initiation of becoming one of the boys, the butt of our jokes, the one to be ordered about, engaging in our quarrels, our many near-fights, our running races, cultivating his cricket until he began to bat, not with the easy disdain of Franklyn but with great care, little chance-taking, protecting his wicket, with a careful flourish all his own until the team became confident that he could anchor an end. Yet there were occasions when something dangerous and daring would come over him, and with a gleeful spite, as though trying to break out of the very mold in which we had set him (and in which he had established himself), he would start to lash ball from off the wicket with a fury that silenced everybody and made us look at him again, and begin to see him (I thought) as one of us and someone quite his own. And when eventually we picked him for the team, it was as much for his patient plodding as for his moments of crazy hitting.

So Manick was one of us, playing cricket and later joining us under the streetlamp where we practiced karate and ballroom dancing, where we sang love songs and old calypsos, and shared with each other our dreams, our world opening up to him, leaving him to feel what he would describe later as a certain indebtedness that he found no way to address until his father get married to Elsie and he invited the boys to the sit-down part of the wedding, the eating part, with buss-up shot roti, baigan, tomato choka, chataigne, curry mango and curry goat. He was always on the look out for another occasion to invite us home by him, but none would come; and we would remain in this one-sided relationship, linked by cricket until Black Power come to Cascadu and meet us on the corner under the streetlamp sifting the matter between reality and dream, every one of us wanting to escape Cascadu, I on my way to Port of Spain to become a calypsonian (I am putting myself there on the street corner with them, but in fact I was away quite often); Romesh, the only one of us who didn't have a lot to say, with his hands

160

in his pocket, twenty years old, getting ready to married. Beresford thinking about going away to Canada, Franklyn just waiting for them to call him to cricket trials to represent Trinidad and Tobago, then the West Indies and tour England and bat at Lord's, the Mecca of cricket; Soogrim, waiting for his then bedridden father to dead, everybody about to go off on his own, and he Manick working as a Public Works checker, keeping a record of materials brought in for bridges and roads, saving up his money to go away to study in England, saying again and again how great it will be to be there in England to see Franklyn when he come to play at Lord's. Franklyn. At Lord's. At the Mecca of cricket.

"To see you there, boy! To see you. *There.*"

By that time I was spending more and more time in Port of Spain, making my way as a calypsonian, where I get involved with Black Power, ending up in the days I was in Cascadu organizing our own demonstration to add to those taking place in all parts of the islands.

The Red Flag

The night before the Black Power demonstration in Cascadu, I had arrived with Ibo and Marvin to talk to fellars of the cricket team gathered under the streetlight at the corner and to give out placards for the march. Right away Romesh remembered he had to run an errand for his father on Saturday morning; Soogrim explained that his mother was distressed about the violence on these marches and was concerned that he would be arrested. Although I explained and they knew that we never supported any burning or looting and that in all the events we had throughout the island is only one bad-lucky fella who get killed, Soogrim did not believe he could convince his mother to allow him to go. It was clear that Romesh also wanted out, so it didn't surprise us when Soogrim and Romesh get up and leave. I didn't look at Manick. But I paused, waiting to see if he too would get up to go. When he didn't, we started to give out the placards. Franklyn selected one marked *Power to the People*, Evrol get one marked *Change is Nothing to Fear*, Beresford had *After Four Hundred Years*, Marvin had one *Nobody Will Tell You Who You Are*, Ibo handed Manick the one marked *Africans and Indians Unite* and Manick take it. But you could see is not what he wanted; he look around with what I thought was a feeling of unease, wondering, I supposed, if he was offered that one because he was the only Indian present, which was true but was not how we would have liked him to see it. I for one didn't see him as the token Indian made

162

to carry the placard on race relations, but still he was an Indian and I could see how Ibo would give it to him. Seeing Manick's hesitation, Ibo tried to cover up what he now must have felt was his error: "You don't like that placard? If you don't want that one, you could get another. Which one you want? You want *Power to the People* or *Change is Nothing to Fear?* You could have any of them. Maybe you want *People of the Caribbean you do not know who you are and Nobody will tell you who you are.* If you want you could exchange with Marvin."

When I look at Manick I see he is not looking at the placards; he is looking at the flags. Ibo see it too. And, right away, I know is trouble.

"It have these three flags," Ibo said. "The red flag is for the blood that has been shed in this struggle and the blood that might still be shed in the struggle; the black flag is for the land, for the place, for the people who we fighting with and for; and the green flag is for the peace that will flow afterward."

Manick is looking at the red flag.

"The red flag is the one for war," Ibo say quickly, cautioning. "The green one is the one for peace."

And, yes, just as I wondering where this talk was heading, I hear Manick saying, "You know what I want. I want to carry the red flag. Give me the red flag."

At first I thought Manick was making joke. But when I look at him I see the man is serious. He wanted to carry the red flag.

"The red flag?" about three-four fellars asked.

"That is what I want to carry."

Then it entered my mind, he is the only Indian here, how could we allow him to carry the red flag, the principal

163

symbol of the Black struggle. And how could he, knowing the situation, *want* to carry the red flag?

But if, and this must have popped into his head same way it popped into mine, if he couldn't carry the red flag, then what was he doing there? What was his purpose?

Because if he was one of the fellars, one of us, if we were in this together, how come he wasn't allowed to carry the red flag? And, if he couldn't carry the flag, what was his position in this demonstration? Why should he be in it at all? Was he there just to support us? Or was he there as a separate revolutionary in his own right? What did he want? What was his position?

I waited for Manick to say something. I kinda hoped he would see the awkwardness of the situation and withdraw his request and leave us to ignore those hard questions. But he said nothing. I didn't speak either.

And after more silence, as if he had come to his own decision, he stood up. I suppose we all thought he was about to leave. Ibo chuckled. And whether it was from a feeling of being offended by Ibo's chuckle, or that in fact he was already on his way out, Manick walked away without a word. I didn't try to stop him.

It would be after he had gone and the rest of the placards given out that I learned Manick had prepared a speech, which he had hoped to deliver on the march. He had learned it by heart and had recited it for Beresford. Something about Africans being emancipated to nothing, and, in a society facing at Emancipation the prospect of change, Indians brought into the plantation country, not to change the society but to keep it from changing. And they were granted the instruments to make them more properly part of the system by having a contract (bad as it was) and being granted land in lieu of passage back to India. Africans were set adrift. There was no burning economic reason to grant them compensation or land. There was no economic reason for their condition to be addressed. The reasons were moral. And the colonizers' moral best had already been done in the name of Emancipation.

Indians, he said, had played their roles well. They worked hard, took over the sugar industry, developed agriculture, and through sacrifice certainly, but also already shaped by a system of labor, they turned to small business, while the system continued. Many of them had become fervent supporters of the system. Since Emancipation had not liberated the society, they now needed to come together with Africans to work for its liberation.

As I say, I didn't hear the speech myself, but it did not surprise me. That was the season of speeches. Everybody was making one. Black Power had placed each of us with enough courage and conviction on a soapbox with a microphone before us and an audience ready to cheer. Young, idealistic, each of us wanted to be part of the roaring, of the awakening that was sweeping the country's youth. What Manick was reported as wanting to say was not entirely new. It was what we in Black Power were saying. The great value of such a speech from him was to put Africans and Indians side by side in the liberation struggle – at least in Cascadu. That was what I, for one, was fighting for.

But I couldn't call him back, because I still wasn't sure that it was appropriate to let him carry the red flag. The fellars were as confused as I. In the end, I left it alone.

165

On the march next day, Manick did not appear at the demonstration. He did not come. I did not see him at any of the other rallies either.

Then it had ended, the state of emergency, the arrests. He was not arrested so he was denied being a hero. Ibo, Marvin, Sonnyboy and me (those of us arrested) had become martyrs after a fashion. Franklyn went up into the hills to his death, Manick did not seek us out. And when I saw him we said little more than hello. I didn't think of it this way at first, but increasingly I wondered whether he really believed we had wronged him. I had many questions: Was there something he believed would have been achieved by his carrying the red flag? Would he have stayed and made the speech if we had let him carry the red flag? It troubled me. I had to consider whether the price he had set for telling what we all knew to be a historical truth was that he be allowed to lead the march.

That incident remained between us. He never volunteered an explanation and I did not seek him out to give one, though the story I heard placed him in the role of victim who along with Romesh and Soogrim had been excluded from the march by those of us who wanted to see it only as an African thing.

His brother-in-law Doon was gleeful at what he chose to interpret as our lack of regard for Manick. "They spit you out like a plum seed," Doon tell him. "That is what you get from *them*."

Doon was a strong supporter of Mr. Bissoon and the Democratic Party. He had erected in his yard a cluster of jhandis. In his mechanic shop, his radio was always on the station playing Indian music, at volume not only to allow

166

him to hear, but for all around to know that he was listening.

What effect Doon's observation had on Manick, I do not know. When I returned to Cascadu after Nelson Island, he had moved from the district.

The Doubles Man

Manick left his job as a checker and for a time more or less managed a hardware store an uncle of his had opened in Curepe. While there, he started a correspondence course in law from Wolsey Hall in the UK. He joined a cricket club in Tunupuna, where hearing the favorable comments on his playing encouraged him to put more effort into his game and he was called up for trials for North Trinidad, though by then his best days had gone, but he wondered what he would have accomplished had he started out in the savannah earlier. What would have happen if his father had let him out earlier and he didn't have the cow to graze? If he was free to play cricket like Franklyn, how would Cascadu have looked at him?

"You woulda been our hero. Like the great spin bowler, Sonny Ramadhin," Doon tell him, in a tone that left him unsure whether Doon was commending him or mamaguying him.

Our hero? That was not the answer Manick was looking for. But he didn't tell Doon nothing.

Manick left the job in Curepe and returned to Cascadu. He bought a secondhand van and went into the business of transporting household items, beds, fridges, and later he bought chairs and tents and tables which he rented out for weddings and parties. The old cricket team had ceased to function and his business begin to claim him and for a time he turned his attention to his nephews, Romesh and Sunil, Doon's two sons. On weekends he went over to the house of his sister and brother-in-law Doon with bat and pads and wickets. And he started.

He showed them how to bat, the various strokes. But he also spoke to his sister about their diet, about their freedom, their self-confidence. Seeing how strict she and Doon were with them, he sought to intervene: "Allow them to break a glass, to walk inside without wiping their foot at the door. Let your children branch out, let them go, don't hold them back, yes, see 'bout the shop, the food, the education, see 'bout the cow," he said, remembering his own childhood, "but set them free." And for a few months he was very attentive to them, buying balls, giving them the benefit of his experience as a cricketer, batting the balls away from them and having them run from one side of the yard to the next, pick up the ball and hurl it back at him, teaching them to watch the ball as it was released from the bowler's arm, requiring them to tell him which way it was spinning, showing them how to move their front foot to get to the pitch of the ball, how to point the elbow, how to grip firmly the left hand.

"You go kill them fellars," Doon said, referring to his sons.

"Nah, man."

"Yes, you go kill them. With all that running."

Now, after some time, whenever he went over to Doon's the boys were not available. They were either inside the house doing home lessons or in the yard helping their father fix a car, since by then Doon, who had learned his trade by being apprenticed to the town's mechanic Freddie, had established a shop in his yard and even on a Sunday the boys would be tinkering with one of the cars left there. Believing that Doon had agreed with his Indian cricketing star project and was happy that his sons were first to benefit from his coaching, Manick complained to him about the unavailability of the boys, only to discover that Doon had other ideas for them.

"Doctor and lawyer," Doon said.

And, as if to justify his decision, he said, "You feel you could just practice and go out there and beat people? You need self-confidence. What we need is an Indian Prime Minister to give Indians the self-confidence to make us feel a part of this nation. Come with us and work for the Democratic Party and elect Mr. Bissoon as Prime Minister."

Manick took his plan to another level. He offered his services to the schools in the area, the Hindu school, the Muslim school, the Presbyterian school. He decided to offer prizes, to give away bats and balls. To honor his generosity, the schools invited him to address the children. He told them about Sonny Ramadhin and Rohan Kanhai, Garfield Sobers, Viv Richards and Alvin Kallicharran and other great batsmen, how widely they were respected, how they belonged to all the people. "You can be that too." He told them about practice, and another idea he had picked up from reading books on coaching: "Visualize," he said to them. "See yourself at Lord's," he said, remembering Franklyn.

He roped in some of the Settlement players as coaches. Whenever there was a Test Match in the Oval, he organized the hiring of a bus to take the boys to the cricket. He carried on with such enthusiasm that he came to be known in all the schools and cricket grounds in the constituency.

"Come out into the open, let loose, compete. We have done well in business, not by just hanging back but by going out and competing, and now we have to compete in other areas. Some of you may not like cricket, but it have other sports." He gave support to sports in general, karate, weightlifting, and boxing. Everything counted. And when a girl at one of the schools asked, "What about us?" he went to the schools, he talked to the teachers. Why were Indian girls not playing netball, volleyball, cricket, athletics? Why were Indian girls not playing? It was as a result of one of his speeches that he was invited to be a judge in the beauty contest to select Miss India Trinidad that would bring to his attention the startling beauty of Petra Ramnarine who was parading as Miss Delhi. As soon as he saw her, he set his mind on making her his wife. He bribed the organizers to let him give a prize and allow him to crown the queen who he was sure would be she and indeed it was. Miss Delhi first beating out Miss Uttar Pradesh and Miss Bombay respectively.

He was so carried away by the opportunity to speak in her presence that he became extravagant and his words ended up in the newspapers under the headline

INDIAN BUSINESSMAN SAYS
WE DON'T WANT NO INDIA IN TRINIDAD

"What we want more than a Miss India in Trinidad is an Indian Miss Trinidad and Tobago, someone to represent the whole nation." And he used the occasion once again to plead with the audience, to "send out your girl-children, let them loose, don't hold them back."

Mr. Bissoon demanded to know what place he had in mind to let them loose into. "The Creole bacchanal? That is where you want them to go?"

Manick compounded matters further in an oblique

171

reply to Mr. Bissoon at a school function at a Hindu school that won at cricket at primary-school level for the first time: "We have to go out into the wider community. We have to go out into the Creole world like our foods, like roti and doubles, foods that had become national dishes. When people eating them, the last thing they think about is that it is an Indian that make them."

It was this speech that was taken up by a media happy to have an Indian openly challenging Mr. Bissoon on racial unity. But even more than that the idea was made the subject of a chutney song on doubles sung by Soogrim nephew Baldeo:

> *Doubles in trouble they don't know my name*
> *Doubles isn't only Indian food again*
> *Creole like hot pepper, anchar the same*
> *Doubles in the nation not Indian food again*
> *I went by my boujee, boy she in pain*
> *I is not a doctor, girl don't complain*
> *Doubles isn't only Indian food again*
> *I want you remember doubles is the nation, not only the name.*

It was a big hit, made bigger still when Baldeo persuaded him to accompany him at the chutney competition, where he was introduced on stage with a bicycle with a large wooden box on the handle, portraying a doubles vendor. It won the competition and catapulted Baldeo into stardom, the tune popular not only with the regular chutney crowd but played in dancehalls all over the land. Manick benefited from the popularity of the song and it was due to all that publicity that the Hard Wuck Party chose him over Nan King to be its candidate for the County Council election. Immediately I thought of the speech he was to have made in 1970. I thought of telling him I was sorry, but he had responsibility too. I was glad he had another opportunity to deliver it. If he delivered the same speech that was reported to me, then I was ready to apologize to him and do what I could to get him elected.

When I did get to hear him at one of the Hard Wuck Party meetings, the speech I heard was different to the 1970 one:

Brothers and Sisters, he began. *We the people of Indian origin were brought here to save the plantation from ruin and we did a great job for the society* ... I listened for the part about changing the society, about joining the resistance and turning it into construction. But he spoke about the need to access the professionalism produced by all in the society and to elect our best representatives in the same way we picked the best cricketers for our cricket team, without reference to their ethnic origin.

I turned away from it, feeling disappointed. I don't know that the people who heard him were all that moved either. I followed him throughout the campaign but he never strayed far from his ambiguous position. It seemed to me that it was not so much what he was saying, it was what he was not saying. So although Sonnyboy donned his green T-shirt with its forceful slogan, *The Power of the Hard Wuck,* and went with Manick through the district from house to house, reminding them of the adventure of self-development, of the need for sacred spaces, and the delight in finding names for native plants and the birds, something was missing. Manick didn't have the fire to inspire them with anything more than his sense of efficiency and, some felt, the idea that he was ready to go beyond the narrow vision expressed by Mr. Bissoon. He didn't have the fire.

The campaign changed from dream to the practical, as if he too was not allowing himself to cut loose. I attended meeting after meeting, waiting to see him cut loose, who I saw was the patient careful batsman who didn't want to get out. I still did not believe he had revealed himself to us. I couldn't help him.

Sonnyboy himself looked spent. It was as if the fun was gone. The game, I thought, was at an end. The Hard Wuck Party had become *hard work*. The adventure, moved by the spirit of Sonnyboy, was over. Manick, however, had made a showing good enough to encourage the optimism of the leader of the Hard Wuck Party.

"Brother," the Hard Wuck leader said to Sonnyboy, "we are getting there. We are overcoming tribalism with ideas, with mission. The country is advancing, eh, comrade?"

When Sonnyboy did not answer immediately, the leader of the Hard Wuck Party prompted, "Eh, comrade?"

"Yes, Chief," Sonnyboy answered. "We advancing. *Slowly.*"

"And that was when I know I was bigger and more real than these highfalutin intellectual people," Sonnyboy told me. For him, the Hard Wuck Party experience had reached its end.

The Coming of Electricity and Clayton Blondell

On his home front, the car Sonnyboy had bought to run as a taxi was a memory, the business was in need of his attention, his grandmother had aged rapidly and began to carry on conversations with her deceased husband, Horace Apparicio, who was a soldier in World War Two, fighting in Egypt. They had been talking of going to Tobago when he returned and having a second honeymoon. They would take the island ferry. She would purchase the tickets and book the hotel, so she wanted Sweetie-Mary to get information on the times the ferry left Port of Spain for Tobago, its cost, and details of the hotel where she and Horace intended to spend their honeymoon.

She had taken to going on long walks by herself and sometimes people had to bring her home since she forgot not only the place where she was going or coming from, but what day or month or year it was. Just before Christmas that year, Sonnyboy returned from the Cunaripo market to find Sweetie-Mary frantic. His grandmother had not returned from one of her walks. After hours of searching the town, they found her sitting in the shade of an umbrella on a bench on the bank overlooking the old railway station. She was there she said to meet her husband, Horace Apparicio, who was returning from the Second World War on the last train. Sonnyboy and Sweetie-Mary suggested to her that it would be more comfortable for her to wait for him at home.

They brought her back home and sat her on the rocking chair on the veranda, where she was to remain waiting for Horace in her best clothes, singing the World War Two calypso composed and sung by Lord Executor:

Run your run, Kaiser Wilhelm, run your run
  Hear what Chamberlain say, Cheer, boy, cheer
With Charity and humanity we go conquer Germany

At times she seemed to catch herself, aware that something had gone wrong in the world, but what, she couldn't for all her trying work out.

Then she stopped singing and sat there half-asleep waiting, sometimes on her face a look of perplexity, for an event her mind had misplaced, now and again getting up and going to look through the window to investigate a sound only she had heard, sometimes calling Sweetie-Mary or Sonnyboy because your eyes are better than mine to tell her exactly what was going on in the world outside, because she couldn't make out everything clearly. One day she thought she heard a noise outside. "Yes, Ma," they said. Yes. But what they heard was not her imagination, it was the long screaming wail of whistles and the abrupt thunder of an invasion, and when they looked through the window, it was to see a convoy of trucks and tractors and cranes, with tanned and muscled men, with power drills to tunnel into the roads and backhoes to scoop earth out the holes in which to set the tall balata poles. The electricity promised by the PM had arrived. Excited by this vision, Sonnyboy hurried to the center of the town, wanting to be there among the people when the trucks and equipment went by. And it was a good thing he did that because he was there to see the caravan toting electricity poles and equipment for the road works, and, following it, merchants, sellers of cloth, pots and pans, electric irons, television sets and stereo systems and behind them the religious people, fastidiously groomed Pentecostal preachers in three-piece suits and silk shirts with a flatbed truck bearing huge tents, Adventists, Hindu pundits, Muslim imams slim in long gowns, Hare Krishna in saffron robes, Shouter Baptist mothers with enormous bottoms and loose dresses, exquisite in red and white, Shango leaders with the slow powerful walk of weightlifters and the shuffle of stickfighters, all the elements that were to take the town into modernity. And when he figured that this new invasion was over, there appeared the big event, the great show, Clayton Blondell, at the head of a group of women and men variously dressed in army jackets, in dashikis, some with caps, others with dreadlocks, others in turbans, Clayton himself bareheaded, shirt collar open, a pendant in the shape of Africa on a chain on his chest, a silver bracelet on his left wrist, the tapestry of healed cuts and bruises that gave his tanned face the toughened look of a street fighter, a gold crown on a front tooth that made his smile sharper, more menacing, with the movements that in another fella might have suggested the exhilaration of dance, in him the loose pugnacity of a swagger, something deliberate and rehearsed, planting his feet down with the authority of a gunfighter who had just tethered his horse, his hands sliding across his hips to touch his thighs as if he wanted to make sure his guns were there in the event that he needed to draw, so that fellars talking about him later said he rode into town. *He rode in*, evoking the horse, the gunman, the woman to be saved, the bad man to fight. But if was fight he wanted, he had come in the wrong time.

The whole town had come out and I was there sitting around a table on the balcony of the recreation club with Sonnyboy, who had left his own place to come out on the main road to see what was happening.

Five, four years ago any one of us would have offered to fight Clayton immediately, just for the swagger of his walk. Then this town belonged to us, or so we thought, and a stranger entering had to know how to walk into it. Now there was nobody to stop anybody.

I saw the genesis of this abandonment of responsibility to the town as connected to our questing for Black Power.

Our novelist John de John wrote in one of his occasional newspaper articles:

In asking for Power we would discover we were indicating that we didn't have any; in articulating our need for power we had emphasized our powerlessness, so when in an earlier time we felt the town was our own, and therefore to be defended by us, now we couldn't defend a place we had come to believe we did not own. We had surrendered what we thought we never had. And yet, who among us would not have in that time cried Black Power!?

So we watched this man come in uninterrupted, with such arrogance that Constable Stephen Aguillera in his white tunic and white helmet, keeping duty at the junction, felt a challenge to his resolve not to arrest anyone and although this man didn't do any act that could be called unlawful, he went over to him to see what misdemeanor he could at least caution him on. He noted the pushcarts, their contents: incense, oils, sandals, belts, sculptures of lions, of Haile Selassie, Marcus Garvey, of Ethiopia; books, *The Philosophy and Opinions of Marcus Garvey*, the sixth and seventh Book of Moses, *The Tibetan Book of the Dead*, *The Destruction of Black Civilization*, *Signs and Symbols of Primitive Man*, books by Ouspenksy and Madame Blavatsky. He picked up book after book.

"You have any banned books here? Any seditious material?" he asked, trying to get him to respond in a hostile way to give him the opening he sought. But the man was careful enough in his answers, and Constable Aguillera walked away without finding any reason to arrest him, leaving him free to walk with his own brand of cockiness onto the veranda of the club where we were drinking and saunter past us with barely a nod, on his way to the bar. So that a little later when Sonnyboy went to the bar, I was not surprised to hear his voice rise in rebuke:

"You walk in here like a hero. Nobody doesn't know you. And you talking louder than everybody else."

The noises grew louder. Fearing that Sonnyboy would lose his cool, I went to the bar to see what was taking place. Sonnyboy was getting ready to confront him. I took my drink and encouraged Sonnyboy to return with me to our seat on the veranda. He was still fuming. A little later, the stranger whose name we did not yet know, on his way out, stopped at our table and introduced himself. His name was Clayton Blondell.

"Brother," he said to Sonnyboy with what I thought was false gentleness, "Brother, I am sorry if I offended you, but there is no cause for you to insult me."

And turning to me he said, "You see what is happening? The brother is reprimanding me and he doesn't know me. He doesn't know anything about me. All I was trying to do was make a little conversation. My brother, we have to be careful with each other. My brother, you see what they

179

have done to us? We have lost respect for one another. And why? We were kings, man."

"Brother?" he said, addressing Sonnyboy. "Brother, can I sit down?" Disarmed, Sonnyboy said nothing and Clayton sat down and began to speak.

To me, it was as if this man had swaggered in directly from the late sixties or early seventies, the declamatory language, the missionary sense of self-righteousness, the sense of injury, the colossal self-confidence deriving from a certainty of being in the right, the very attitude that we had lost, had left behind, this man had retained. The very period of our history that we had let slip by, this man had decided to resurrect. It was as if he had been asleep and had awakened with potency and zeal without realizing what time of the century it was. Later, as he spoke, we learned that he had been in the USA in the late sixties, he had listened to Ron Karenga, Stokely Carmichael, Malcolm X, and he had the books of Marcus Garvey. He was a sculptor and artisan. He had returned to Trinidad just after Black Power and had thrown in his lot with the artists and craftspeople housed in booths along Independence Square by the name The Drag Brothers. He was leader of a commune that had come to establish itself on an old cocoa estate in Cascadu.

It was clear that he had much to say. As he spoke, I heard the tone of impatience, of accusation, the words, images, Pharaoh, Nile, Egypt, Black. Once or twice I tried to interrupt, to ask for clarification, to get him to focus on some particular; but he refused to give way.

"Listen, brother," I said. "I too have a point of view."

He had heard that I was a calypsonian and he had some advice for me. Here we were, he said, a black people forced to rebel against a black government in order for the society to extend dignity and justice to Blackpeople. We have to get out of Babylon, to flee.

"Listen, brother," I said. "It is more complex than that."

"Complex for you, but not complex for any other people. We are the most complex people on the planet."

"Brother, I am just trying to understand you."

"You do not understand?" He turned to the gathering (for by now he had attracted a crowd): "What have I been saying that any of you do not understand? You don't understand? OK, then I will explain. Let me explain." And he was off again: "I am saying," he said without taking breath, "I am saying that you have surrendered to being less than anybody in this land."

I could see I was being maneuvered into the position of opponent for his purposes. He had surmised that I had some weight among the men in that gathering and in besting me in an argument he would establish himself. At first I was annoyed and bemused and tried to fight it, to speak; but then recognizing that I was simply a prop for his performance, I let him speak. And as he spoke, batting aside interruptions, I detected no new message, but if his objective was to become the center of focus, he achieved it.

"And what about you?" I asked, after he had attacked government, the men, the schools, everybody.

"Me? Don't mix me up with you-all. I am African."

Africa. He was an African.

"Brother, we have to reclaim ourselves as African people, lay claim to our ethnic space. Everybody came here as different ethnic groupings and everyone was allowed his religion, his festivals, except the African and this is what we must reclaim."

181

These were words I myself might have used, but hearing them from him, there was a taint of patronage, of being superior to us. I wanted to oppose him. That is what he evoked in me: the desire to oppose him. But there were men who immediately sang his praises and identified with his sentiments and were ready to support his arguments.

Thinking later about what had made him such an arresting figure, I concluded that it was not only because he did not allow anyone else to speak, not certainly because we believed in the simplicity of his accusations, but because we had nothing to say, or, rather, we had been saying nothing. Clayton was filling a space. He had arrived at the moment of our greatest weakness and uncertainty.

I saw that I had to be careful.

In the months to come, Clayton settled into the town, and soon he became a regular at Sonnyboy's and I was forced to defend myself against his wisdom, his certainties, his abuse, his insults, his Africa. On more than one occasion I had to restrain myself from offering to fight him. He attacked my calypsos as too tame, too concerned with having fun. "How can you have fun when there is so much to be done? How can you dance when your people are at the bottom of the ladder and slipping down further every day?" He attacked our involvement in Carnival as a frivolity we could not afford. "Look at your homes, your families, your children's education. Where are we going?"

"Tell me," I asked him in one of our exchanges, "how do you return to being African in this place with so many mixtures?"

"Return? You have never not been African."

"Look, we can't give up the future for a past."

"And you can't have a future without a past."

The idea of needing to come together to build a nation, he laughed at.

"You alone. Look at the others. Here every creed and race see 'bout itself."

Around me people buzzed with agreement and admiration at his wisdom, his courage and forthrightness, for saying things they all thought but he alone was courageous to say. I was trapped. So I watched him grow, his power, his truth, his forthrightness, his honesty, his simplicities, his shifting, his songs about our failure, our shame. I listened to him present his Africa, the sphinx, the pharaohs, the pyramids, the kings and queens of Egypt, its sculptures, its peoples.

And what did I have to show?

The steelband, the Carnival, the calypso that I had been so fond of invoking as symbols of our achievement in this new world began to seem thin, small, light before the monuments of his Africa.

He was commissioned to construct, John de John told me, a representation of the sphinx monument to display in Port of Spain at the Emancipation Day celebrations, to correct the impression that we were a people without history.

"But which people do not have history?" I asked.

"The colonizers did a good job on you," he replied.

In all these exchanges, I felt myself losing ground and the listeners looking at me with new suspicion. How could I question Africa? How could I deny Africa as dream of potency to people who had been robbed of Africa? I shut my mouth. But it was strange that now when at last we had the opportunity to claim Africa we would want to do so at the expense of all we had created here in the Caribbean.

In the arguments I had with Clayton, Sonnyboy was nodding less and less to the points I made and listening with greater interest to what Clayton was presenting. One day when I went to Sonnyboy's place, I found Sweetie-Mary and him dressed in the most splendid and, I imagine, expensive African clothes. And here was the irony: the man who had influenced me to give up my costume of native was now in a costume of his own. There was a new sign on the place:

OUR ITAL SHOP

"Our Ital shop," I said, reading the sign.

"King," Sonnyboy said, sadly, detecting the query in my tone. "It is a pity that a man like you is not one of us."

In the months to come I began to see another Sonnyboy. It was as if he had joined a priestly order. That year he decided against taking part in Carnival. Because the Blackman can't waste money, the Blackman waste too much time already, the Blackman watch other people grow rich. The Blackman had to stop this Carnival mentality. The Blackman had to leave Carnival for those who could afford it and see about his family. All of it said with the passionate righteousness of a convert. I couldn't help feeling that this enthusiastic rejection of all he had been associated with before was not only his way of signaling his elevation to a higher status but his way of punishing the community that had refused to acknowledge him the way he felt it should. He had new friends, strict, zealous converts like himself, who exhibited a new energy for progress. Sonnyboy had joined the existing order. He had fitted in with people who Gilda and Dog couldn't take on and with whom Sweetie-Mary didn't have much in common.

Sonnyboy had been a badjohn, a rebel, a revolutionary, he had appeared as a member of the National Party, he had been the local organizer of the Hard Wuck Party. All in an effort to win acceptance from his community. I felt he was done with trying. He had found a secure place as an African.

We had gone forward to right back where we had begun.

Africa

Sweetie-Mary wasn't happy with all these changes. She had little life beyond working in the shop and minding her children. And although Sonnyboy had taken her only once to the Oval to see Test cricket and two times to a calypso tent, those were great events in her life and had given her a base from which to contribute to discussions on cricket and calypso as an equal. Also, her excursions with Sonnyboy in the steelband on Jouvay morning was still one of the sweetest times she had had with him. But his changes in attitude had left her with a feeling of unease and she showed it. Now and again I would hear Sonnyboy grumbling about *her behavior*: "She start back eating meat ... She want more jewelry ... Buying a set of clothes ..."

I overheard her: "But, Sonnyboy, Africa is not a prison. You can't make Africa a jail."

Sonnyboy sought my opinion: "King, what it is she want? What she want?"

"Man," I tell him. "If I was you I would just go in the Carnival band and beat the iron and let the woman play her mas."

He looked at me as if he wanted to hit me.

"King," he said sternly, "Sweetie-Mary is an African woman."

"If you know who she is, then what you asking me?" I didn't usually talk to him so sharply. But really I wasn't joking.

I had to say goodbye. I felt a certain sympathy for Sonnyboy, and admiration, even. I do not mean to sound superior. However, I expected that Sonnyboy would occupy the exile of his comfortable harbor until he saw something else to move on to.

Aunt Magenta was puzzled at my concern for Sonnyboy. "Donny, Sonnyboy is no revolutionary, he is a badjohn. What you expect from him?"

The heroes we had inherited had it easy. Distance had crowned them with haloes. Sonnyboy was in the here and now. In the brilliance of this light, we could see his every flaw.

I know Sonnyboy was a hustler. He had lived a twisted life, I know, there was nothing pure about him. I knew his story. But he stood for something. And I was beginning to see that however twisted he might be, what he had contributed to us was a No. *I not fucking taking that.* That *no* joined the No's our heroes had said to the colonizing world. His No was directed at his brethren, not only from a point of view of not wanting what was on offer, but in the suggestion that there was something else we had to build. That was his importance to us. And that is why I had to have us see him not in terms of delinquency, but as serious actor and cause.

I didn't know if I was making myself clear. My aunt and Clephus continued to criticize me for holding up Sonnyboy *as some kind of hero.* I know they meant well, but I also knew that they were responding with the prejudices of their education, our education. But I had to go on. However, I didn't quite give him up. I would drop in to see him. We would chat. I would invite him for a drink. This was just a phase he had to go through, I thought. It would soon come to its end.

I was wrong. Clayton's Africa was gaining ground. Everybody was seeking public ethnic recognition. In Cascadu, Carlos Nan King spearheaded a move to have the day the Chinese arrived in Trinidad declared a public holiday to match Indian Arrival Day and Emancipation Day.

Romesh had become one of the school of home-grown Hindu holy men barebacked and wearing dhoti like Mahatma Gandhi and in the absence of the river Ganges cleansing themselves in the Manzanilla sea. A new African society validating and accrediting individuals and institutions had arisen, with Clayton having the prestige of being installed as its first chief. I saw him in his regalia of chieftainship, his chin tilted upward as his subjects made their obeisance to him. Every tub was sitting on its own bottom, everybody was finding his own ethnic harbor and those of us left outside were suddenly nowhere. But Clayton didn't pose just an abstract challenge, he had attracted to his attention Dorlene Cruickshank, the most beautiful woman in Cascadu and the bright spot of my world.

Dorlene

Dorlene that time was employed in the library in Cascadu,
an elegant polite woman, her hair pulled back off her face
with a simplicity that was more challenge than style, since
she felt no need to create any illusion, having already
established in her mind that no stranger would be visiting
the library and there was not a man in Cascadu worthy of
her, an idea planted in her mind at eight or nine soon after
she came home from school one rainy Monday to find the
fence mashed down and a piano settled on the veranda of
her house and her father up from the garden inspecting the
house to see what had been broken, while Mr. Alliman
Brown, the truckdriver, who had been engaged to take the
piano on the truck up the hill, stood in the road, looking
down over the hibiscus hedge that separated them from the
road, at the piano, asking Dorlene's father if anything was
broken and blaming the misfortune on the Englishwoman
Miss Phyllis Dorset, the woman who had paid him to get
the piano to her house up the hill, saying with a performed
outrage, "What the hell she want a piano for? These people
come from England and bring everything with them, why
they don't look for things we make here instead of having
me carry that big-arse piano up that hill to mash up my
frigging engine?"

"Well, thank God nobody ain't get kill. Eh, Mr.
Cruickshank? Eh?" And when her father, the Mister
Cruickshank Alliman Brown was addressing, made no
answer, he continued in the same irreverent fashion:

"From what I could see, this piano reach where it going. It can't move from here," his voice louder now because he wanted to be sure that he would be heard by Phyllis Dorset, who had parked her own car and come fluttering up to join him, "What happen, Mr. Brown?" Alliman Brown not even bothering to explain the obvious, saying, "You lucky you wasn't driving right behind me. The piano break the rope and chain and slide off the truck and slide down the hill and break down the man fence and nearly break down this man house and kill everybody inside. You lucky you wasn't up in my tail."

"You think he will let it stay there for the night?" Phyllis Dorset talking.

"I suppose I could come down and give piano lessons here. If we can't move it and if it is all right with you, Mr. Cruickshank."

"Piano lessons! You want to give piano lessons. You want piano lessons, Mr. Norman?"

And Norman Cruickshank, Dorlene's father, standing and looking around with a sense almost of apology, as if it was his house that had moved out its way to intercept the piano; while Mr. Brown: "You can't see it now, but just touch that piano and it wouldn't surprise me if the whole damn house don't come tumbling down."

"Well, can I just leave the piano here?"

"Well, what you expect him to tell you. Of course, you have to leave it. Norman, you going to have to keep the piano."

So that was how Dorlene's family found themselves in possession of a piano. In order to move it, Norman Cruickshank erected two huge pillars to give additional support to the house, decided to reinforce the house so

190

that it would be able to stand up on its own when the piano was removed. Before he could remove the piano, he received a letter from Phyllis Dorset who frequently went sailing up the islands that she was in St. Vincent and would be staying there for a while longer and could he please keep the piano until she returned. That while longer stretching into years. By this time the father had enclosed the veranda and made it a living room with the piano as the centerpiece, more as a monument to be tended than an instrument to master, and although the owner did not return to claim it, Dorlene's people never quite felt they owned it. The only one of them who would venture to play it was Dorlene herself because she was the youngest and because her father could deny her nothing.

It was the prestige of this possession that her parents would take to heart and set themselves apart from the town and encourage Dorlene to think she was better than other people, an idea further consolidated by her beauty, and advanced even further when she passed with superior marks the examination that would take her to secondary school at St. Joseph's Convent in Port of Spain, my aunt Magenta obtaining the news while she was searching the newspapers for the names of children from Cascadu who had placed in the Common Entrance Examination, a habit she had inherited from her mother who had looked in vain to find Aunt Magenta's name in what was then the College Exhibition Examination.

"Poor thing," my aunt says, looking up from the newspaper, not overly joyful at all, but sad for the girl who had grown up remote from our world. "She will not know the bush teas and the songs and the dances. She will live on the edge of the world that is her world. My Lord, how sad it is that so much will be lost to her, will be lost to us."

So from early I was mindful of Dorlene as someone disadvantaged, someone in need of sympathy. I wanted to embrace Dorlene, to make her aware of the world to help her bear the burden of this being here and not here. I imagine myself her protector. I want to speak to her, but we do not know each other really, except from this distance. I watch her walk past the corner, her white bodice immaculate, each fold of the pleats in her skirt in place, dispensing the charity of her smile, the smile widening as she grew because by now it was clear that she belonged elsewhere.

Yet in my heart is this sympathy for her.

"How terrible it must be for her," Aunt Magenta said. "Her only sin is she just happen to pass an examination that her schooling was preparing her for. And it will take her away and keep on taking her away if she unlucky enough to pass another one, and she will go completely if there is another one after that. That is education for you. Is a lucky thing you ain't have none."

All those growing years I watch her from a distance, *good morning, good evening.* And she makes her way to the cocoon of her world of family, the cousins, the aunts, the weddings, the christenings, the Christmas dinners, where they all get together to eat pancakes, to play Scrabble, to count the deceased, to get news of those who have gone away to England and to be brought up to date on the year's scandals, her mother the resident historian quoting from the stack of newspapers she saves to read up on the murders, the embezzlements, the political scandals that supported her proposition that independence was something *they* not ready for.

When she left school, Dorlene would have loved to get a job in Port of Spain. Instead, the job she got was in the library in Arima seventeen miles away. The librarians there agreed that nice men did not read, and, in order to expose themselves to a wider pool of a suitable set of men, had organized a program to invite poets to read their work in the library, calypsonians to sing, and John de John the novelist from Matura with thirty-five unpublished novels to read from his current novel, which he had been finishing for forever, Dorlene herself appearing on the program playing the piano and beating the tenor pan. I was one of the calypsonians invited. It was a successful project. At the end of the series, one of the librarians was engaged to be married, one of them had moved in with a man, and a man moved in with one. Mabel, a girl who had started same time as Dorlene, was pregnant and Miss Trim, the head librarian, who had been most skeptical of the idea, had found romance. In her youth she was one of the most beautiful women in the island; her problem, she could not find a man worthy of her. Hassled by men who found her so attractive and desirable, she had gone through life trying to hide herself to make herself a little less obviously desirable, but the clothes she chose refused to cooperate and nothing she wore could contain the scandal of her body and the scent of mornings and rivers and swamp lilies that she left in her wake. Not knowing what else to do, she became a born-again Christian and began to wait on the only refuge she could imagine, age. But age came slowly and ripened her into a more formidable beauty, her presence so heating up the church that the pastors stumbled over their sermons and wives were cold to her. She moved from church to church, increasingly uncomfortable, sinking herself into an even more glamorous piety in an effort to diminish her attractiveness and keep herself out the mouths of wives threatened by her presence. Even she found love. She discovered that one of the poets best received was a weightlifter who lived next door to her brother. He was a vegetarian and an avid hiker. By the time the series was over, she had begun to lift weights, to hike and to cut meat from her diet. The man who was interested in Dorlene turned out to be not the calypsonian he had presented himself as being but a fella on his way to becoming a priest. That was when she met me. She returned on weekends to Cascadu, where she attended the Roman Catholic church, distant, remote, pious, chaste. Feeling somewhat disappointed that she had not met the man worthy of her, she teamed up with Cynthia de Leon, a red woman like herself, a singer from Maraval, with her head shaved clean, her shaved eyebrows replaced by a long blue line. She had been one of the discoveries of the literary program and had joined Dorlene to take cheer to the unfortunate and the sick, Cynthia singing and she accompanying her on the guitar. They made a good pair, Cynthia de Leon with her voluptuous body, her extravagant gestures, and Dorlene, sober, laid-back, intense, each one giving balance to the other, each one almost laughing at the other so that on stage they would appear to be enjoying the show at least as much as the audience. Dorlene found herself thinking more and more of her music and the orphans and the sick and of joining the nunnery. The idea of her as a nun flattened her mother, who on the weekends they spent together tortured her with her tears of disappointment and prayers to find a man to bring her grandchildren. Her brother who had come back from studying and was about ready to take up a government posting in the Ministry of Agriculture did his part by setting her up with friends of his. She dressed carefully for these dates, not wanting to look too stuffy, and went to them with an attitude to enjoy them, but they never got past the fact that it was a set-up and she went back to finding her mother dismissing her opinions, because as bright as she was she couldn't get a man. She began to panic. She saw her parents growing old and began feeling as surrendered as Miss Trim might have felt. She listened to her parents laugh and talk as if the world outside was dangerous, some place that could claim them anytime unless they were vigilant. Her mother with the newspapers saved from years before as if she found the past vastly more interesting than the future, her brother, impatient, demanding as if the world had not turned out quite as he had expected it to. And what was her life to be? Dorlene enrolled for music classes at the university on evenings, and during the week traveled down from Arima to St. Augustine.

She was on her way to Rio Claro to perform at a concert when, as she was traveling by taxi along the Cocal road, a coconut fell off one of the trees that lined the road and smashed the windscreen. In the multiplying fractions of the seconds during which the driver struggled to bring the car under control, to avoid hitting a coconut tree and to escape collision with an oncoming truck, Dorlene saw the swirl of sea, the fins and fans of coconut trees, the blue arc of sky, she saw the mangrove on stilts, on grids of roots and the gulls and the gaulins with long feet and with the bags underneath their beaks, heard in her ears such a rush and roaring of life, of stars of eternity stretched out seamless and everlasting and endless and the color of speed and the radiance of sand all in a moment that she prayed to God that if He spared her this time she would spend the rest of it in His service. She didn't say it in her prayer, but she was thinking definitely of the nunnery. When, after an eternity, the car righted itself, inches from the trunk of a coconut tree, she found herself where the impact of swerving and braking had thrown her, in the back seat with three other passengers, in the lap of Pauline Mendoza, a fisherman who was on his way to Manzanilla Police Station to report the sighting of a strange abandoned vessel that had run aground on the reef. She felt his breath, his arms, the grizzled scrape of his beard, the fiber of his muscles. She smelled the beautiful stink of fish and knew that she was alive. She saw the coconuts for the first time, the beach across the road, the weeds growing on sand, she saw the endless awesome infinity of space and time, she saw the gulls and the seaweed floating on the seawater and shells of shellfish, ants balancing on leaves sailing, she saw the mangrove and the small crabs and puddles left after the rain and knew that she was part of this magnificence that she had never before imagined, and she knew then with a beautiful impatient certainty, her blood roaring inside her ears, that this life was something that had been given her to live and she felt that service to God could be undertaken in a variety of occupations and His praises sung best by her living. She had escaped without injury; even her guitar miraculously remained unbroken. She untangled herself from the embrace of the fisherman and beaming the widest and most brilliant of smiles she made the sign of the cross, got out the taxi, and crossed the road to wait for one going in the opposite direction.

196

It was after that event that for the first time I saw her at a dance at the community center. She came over and spoke to me. She remembered me from the program in the library. We danced. We talked. She talked. She told me of her work in the library in Arima. She told me the story of how they got the piano into their house. She told me of her near-death in the car in Cocal. She told me of her love for the piano, for music. She lived here but she didn't know the place, she was ashamed to say.

"If you want a guided tour, I can show it to you."

"You serious?"

"Yes."

I wanted to impress her. I talked of my writings, my singing, the difficulties of being a poet in this place.

"And I thought you were a calypsonian."

"I am a poet. I only sing calypso because poets can't make a living in this island."

We became friends. On weekends when she came up from Arima I would show her Cascadu. I invited her to hear me at the calypso tent. We went together to Siparia fête, Fisherman fête in Toco. She joined the Cascadu steelband, wanting to play pan. At dances well-dressed strangers came over to dance with her. She loved the attention, especially from fellows not from our town. I could see her discovering herself, becoming aware of the power of her charms, the intrigue of her silences, the various effects of the looks in her eyes. One by one, we fell in love with her, but none of it registered on her. We were her chums. None of us was intimate with her and none would be. I watched her fall in love with strangers. Smooth fast-talking fellars, fellars who were nothing – who in any arena of male tussling I would mash up –

would become giants, gods, because of the blessing of her love.

When she fell in love, it was an event. At such times she would become feminine, wear her best dresses, makeup, all the things she did not do ordinarily, and there would emerge this woman, her eyes sparkling, her very skin breathing out her magical femaleness. None of it was for me, for us. I had to listen to her talk about these fellars, blowing them up to a bigness they did not deserve. All the insights she displayed in our discussions on other matters deserted her when she talked of them. And in spite of my misgivings, my own sense of these fellars, their inadequacy, their lies, their bullshit, I was forced to try to see them through her eyes, their style, their fashion, their intelligence, their sexiness.

I watched Dorlene grow slow, silly, dreamy, helpless, as she fell in and out of love, wounded and miserable as she suffered the pangs of heartbreak and disappointment. At these times, she became unreasonable, demanding, childlike, impossible. For days she went about sick, as if about to give up the ghost, her heart bleeding. She wrote poetry, she recited poems, she posted letters. She made entries in her journal. She grieved, she cried, she didn't eat, she stopped talking to friends, became critical of us, she pined, she beat herself and I had to pamper her and coax her back to normalcy. Gradually my role became that of consoler. As demonstration of my goodwill, my caring, I had to listen to the stories of the men, their shortcomings, their intelligence, their selfishness, their arrogance, not allowed to say to her a word critical of them unless prompted by her to do so. Ordinary, stupid fellows taking up my time because they had become gods by virtue of the blessing of her love. Even when she was done with them, they remained in my eyes men marked with a status that outranked mine. I felt myself dwindling. I felt myself disappearing as I nursed her back into the world until, at last, when the love waned, she became human again, she became reflective, began to accuse herself of foolishness and to laugh at herself and to destroy the fantasy that was the love and the myth that was the man. And what about me?

"Look," I said. "I feel uneasy. I feel that I have to protect myself."

She laughed. "Donny, you have so much woman. What you going to do with me?"

And so she put me off. But, "No. No. I mean it. I have to protect my feelings. I feel uneasy, like a fraud. People believe I in something with you. And I am not."

"Why are you getting angry?"

"I am not angry."

"You are not?"

"You making this a joke."

She took my hand, looked into my eyes. "But, Donny, you are my friend."

And so she charmed me. I was her friend. And that is what I would remain through the years. If I sound like a nice forbearing guy, forget it. I was doing this for me. I was sticking around waiting for her to see me, to see that I was more, could be more than a friend.

When Rochard appeared on the scene from England, she introduced me to him.

"Oh, I know you," I said, a bit too quickly.

"You do?"

"Maybe I don't," I said.

"He lives up the hill from us," Dorlene said.

"Near the woman with the piano?"

"Yes," she said. "You remember."

I remembered.

I had seen him driving a truck through the town, stopping it, his brakes squealing, and jumping out importantly like he was going to arrest somebody or out a fire or something.

"You like that fella?"

"What kind of question is that? Of course I like him."

It didn't make sense to me. Other fellars flattered, they lied. They affected a kind of polish: bullshit, but polished. They performed for her. She was a lady to be wooed. Rochard didn't believe in this *lady* shit, he was a Trinidadian, a Trini, he said. The best of human beings in the best place in the world. And he was not to be fooled. Trini women liked their bacchanal. He was short-tempered, as if he was always ready to brawl, to fight. Loud as if his right to be heard was more urgent than anyone else's. And, for peace, I found myself forced into a role of the agreeable. I was the one to keep my voice down, nod my head, let him talk. I shocked myself. I found myself reining myself in, the consciousness of what I was doing getting me angrier and angrier the more I said nothing. To my shame, I talked not in front his face, but behind his back I complained to Dorlene.

And Dorlene acknowledged that he was a nice fella but that was his way. She told me of his support for cricket, his old-mas playing, his impatience with the way we were developing. "You know he has read the entire *Guinness Book of Records*."

"The whole thing?"

"The whole thing."

He knew everything. In his company, you felt you couldn't talk for being so often corrected. Whenever Dorlene tried to talk he interrupted her. He mimicked her if he disagreed and she laughed. She looked at me with complicity as if to say, "You see. *His way*."

But maybe he loved her. He was planning to propose marriage to her, she said. I had the feeling it was the threat he suspected from me that pushed him to propose to Dorlene. But the proposal didn't take place. Three days before the event, with his same Captain Marvel, Superman bullshit, he went hunting in the forest with his some friends of his. He got separated from them. Not able to find him, the pardners made their way out the forest. Five days later, some fellars planting marijuana in North Manzanilla would bring him out to the seaside town, bleeding, bruised and babbling out his head.

That was the end of that. Rochard's family surrounded him and a month later Rochard left for Miami. He never returned. And so began the story that soon everybody in Cascadu would be repeating: Something was not right with Dorlene. She was never going to get married.

"Poor thing," Aunt Magenta said. "Something is not right with her."

Even though Dorlene had disappointed me, I couldn't leave her at that time. Dorlene was hurt. That was when she threw herself into the steelband. And began arranging tunes for them. Music became her life.

On occasions, I went with her to the movies, to a party, but I was more her escort than her lover.

"Donny, you think something wrong with me?"

"Wrong? Nothing ain't wrong with you."

But I could see that the confidence she had begun with was dented. I thought that now with this experience she would favor me, that she would at last see me, appreciate me, to think that maybe I could be the one to comfort her on a more permanent basis. I felt myself edging closer to her. We talked of life; I showed her the calypsos I was working on. But I did not push. I, too, had to get accustomed to the idea of she and me. I had of course become quite uncertain. I didn't want this to fail. And in some way I must have communicated this to her, for she too began to measure how much of herself she would give to me. She began to relax in my arms, dancing, but the relaxedness had brought her close to me and I was gentle with her and she would nestle close to me and I would put my arms around her, and as if alerted to some deep sense of danger, she would pull back to some sense of carefulness, and then she would hold my hand and tell me what a good friend I was. I waited.

Clayton and Dorlene

We were at a fête in the community hall when Dorlene first saw Clayton. He was standing a little to one side of the band, ostensibly listening to the music, bristling with an importance that he must have believed everyone was aware of. She was standing in his line of vision. She expected him at least to smile at her, but he ignored her. And for that insult Dorlene decided that she would pursue him.

"You know him?" she asked me.

"In a way," I said.

"You don't like him." It was a statement more than a question.

"I didn't say that."

"You didn't have to say anything."

She was attracted to him, but, also, I felt there was an arrogance in him she wanted to punish. She wanted him to want her so she could reject him. And that was their beginning. She found her way next to him, they got to talking. After that they saw each other, and soon she became one of the group that gathered around him for the sermons he delivered.

I have tried to think what was the motivation. Passion? Love? Guilt?

At the dances in the school he came and folded his arms and listened to the band play. Dorlene who used to so love to dance stood up at his side talking. I asked her to dance, she looked at him, she looked at me. She hesitated. She moved toward me just as I turned away.

She would be angry with him one day, the next she would be singing his praises. I waited for it to end.

One day she gave me a letter and asked me to give it to him.

"I don't know if I should be doing this," I said.

She could see on my face that I wasn't happy.

"I don't think you understand him, Donny."

She told me how he had come here, his life story, of all the things he had done, the things he wanted to do, the struggle he had to escape the chain of being just another fella to get a job and stay out of trouble, as if staying out of trouble was a vocation. Stay out of trouble? Let trouble stay out of me. Those were his words. He had come from a poor family, ordinary people, no better than anybody. All politics had given them was the right to vote; that was all. You have to understand why he is so angry with the world. The disrespect he had to endure; and even worse, people expecting him to accept it, to accept being second-class. You can't understand what he had to put up with. No, you don't understand. You can't understand.

"I? I cannot understand?"

"Donny, you are a successful calypsonian."

I listened to her talk.

"How could you have asked him to accept being second-class?"

"And wasn't it so for all of us? And we don't demand to be kings."

"And why not? Why shouldn't you? Why shouldn't you demand to be kings? You were kings."

"All that we left behind ... The glories of the Nile, the pharaohs. We represent people stripped of name and rank, people who have no badge that makes them superior to anyone."

"Independence has failed him," she said.

"Failed him? We haven't even begun. Failed him? What you expect? To find a ready-made country. This is something to build."

"But you have accepted it. He has not."

"I hear you."

"That was why he formed the Black Power movement."

"Formed? He formed it? He didn't form the Black Power movement, Dorlene. He wasn't even in it."

"Formed it, joined it. Why are you against him?"

"Did he tell you he formed it?"

"He is fighting for his life. He is fighting to be himself, to restore himself to his fullness."

"He said he formed it?"

"To be a person free to enjoy the best the society has to offer."

"He said he formed it? He told you he formed the Black Power movement?"

"Donny, he made me see myself, how I grew up, where I lived, what we wanted, what we believed, what we were taught."

"What were you taught? What were we all taught? To be better than Blackpeople?"

"To not look back."

"To not look back?"

"He made me see that the more we advance, the further we grow away from Blackpeople. We become lost to Blackpeople. He made me see how lost I am."

"Great." However, I didn't want to go on. I didn't want to appear self-serving or to be bad-mouthing him. I

205

listened to her talk.

"Could you give him this letter for me?"

I take the letter. I hold it in my hand. I tried to control my temper.

"Could you give him this letter for me?"

"So that is what you think of me."

"What are you talking about?"

"So you think I accept this second-class position? Look." And I gave the letter back to her.

"You not taking it to him for me?"

I shook my head.

On her face I could see, as she took the letter from my hand, a new interested look at me, settling on what I thought she thought was my jealousy. But then she grew so quiet, appeared injured, I was almost moved enough to take the letter and be her messenger.

I felt myself a traitor to myself. Next day, I wrote to her:

You have ignored me for strangers, for people you don't even know. You take me for granted because I am here. Did it ever occur to you that I am better than those fellows, that it is I who love you? Have you ever really looked at me, listened to me?

"Donny," she said when she saw me, "Donny, don't be angry with me."

But I was not angry with her, I was angry with me. I had to let her go and I had to hope that maybe if she saw Clayton, rather, if she saw through him, she would see me.

I didn't talk of my feelings to Dorlene. But she knew me and, seeing me in that mood, as if to placate me, she invited me to her home.

"Fine."

On previous occasions when I went to her home, her

mother had received me with suspicion, if not hostility. She would leave me standing in the yard while she got Dorlene; she would never know my name, I had to give her my name again and again. She would sit there while I spoke to her daughter, looking through the old newspapers she had accumulated over the years, cutting in now and then as if I still was not present, to point out some article on murder or robbery or deception that had to do particularly with young men, or suicides, or chopping that had to do with Indians, or some other, commenting favorably only on the industry of the Chinese, addressing me only indirectly to say to Dorlene, "You don't find he resemble the Birchwoods or the Douglases," until later she would come out with: "Well, who is your family, which part you from?" Already as if the very threat of the question was enough to dissuade me from pursuing any relationship with her daughter. And I got the impression that Dorlene herself was waiting to hear what I would say, as if this was an examination that she hoped I would pass.

I had developed an uneasiness with her. I figured that she felt that not only was I taking Dorlene away from her, I was taking her to an inferior place.

But this time she was welcoming. It didn't take me long to work out why. The threat of Dorlene with Clayton Blondell had made her fall back on me. I suppose I was the lesser of the evils. "Come in," she said, and she called out Dorlene. She offered me a drink and she sat down to talk, spoke to me about calypsos and wanted to know if I sung with Lord Kitchener. Here again, I was second best, the less formidable threat. Instead of this pleasing me, it made me realize how weak I must appear to them.

"I want you to sing at the wedding," Dorlene said.

207

"Which wedding?"

Then she told me, "Clayton and I are getting married."

"Going to help him build the Sphinx?"

"I'm not joking."

She took my hands in hers. "Donny, I'm not getting any younger, you know."

"You going to do it?"

She nodded. "I want you to sing at the wedding. It's the least you could do for me."

"Girl, you really know how to punish a man. But I'll think about it. I'll see if the date suits me."

I had a gig in St. Thomas with Lord Superior, the calypsonian. I wasn't sure of the dates. I hoped I would be away. I didn't want to be present when she gave herself to him.

Wedding

On the Monday morning of the week of the announcement that Dorlene Cruickshank would marry Clayton Blondell, the postmistress, Beryl Dove, discovered on the steps of the post office the head of Sonny Lalloo, a greengrocer of San Juan, in a cardboard box marked Pure Soya Bean Oil. On the Tuesday, Flavius BonAventure, a security guard with the Electricity company, climbed up a telephone post and decided he would remain atop it until his wife, Celia, returned to him. Wednesday, Oliver Kanhai was speeding to his eighteenth-birthday party when he ran into an oncoming vehicle in a smash-up in which three people were killed. Thursday, Yvonne Peters, a dancer, was stabbed thirteen times by her common-law husband who drank Gramoxone after he had done the deed, dying while she was in the hospital fighting for life.

So, the Friday announcement of the wedding found priests, pundits and other holy people from the town offering prayers to remove the band of misfortune that had surrounded the community. Women and men who had not gone to church in a long time heeded their call to attend the crusade the Church of the Open Bible was conducting. Everywhere you turned that week, you could hear singing, chanting and praying. Aunt Magenta, a mother in the Shouters church, not to be left out, tied her head, band she belly, take up her bell and other accoutrements of her worship and set out with a small flock of her congregation for the four corners of the town to toss out the evil spirits.

In that week the streets were empty after six, as if we were expecting a storm. Men went directly home from work. Even the young men playing football and cricket in the savannah cleared the railings where they usually sat after play. The town was so depleted that in the rum shop Constable Stephen Aguillera found himself drinking in company with Aaron and Isabella, habitual drunks, the only other citizens not seeking redemption. Contemplating the rash of righteousness that had overrun the town, Aaron offered what Birbalsing the shop owner took to be a most insightful remark (which he would write out in his own hand and put up as a sign in the rum shop):

Without sin, I shall surely die.

Fellars who used to frequent the rum shops shepherded by their women passed in their best clothes with Bibles in hand on their way to the Crusade and their way back to God. From the veranda of his gambling club, Constantine Nieves, biggest gambler in the district, took in the week of prayer with an amused sadness, thinking that this too was life. Although he had announced that in that week drinks would be free from 7 to 8 and the table stakes for poker would be reduced from twenty dollars to ten, coming up the steps to the club was the smallest trickle of men who looked so far gone that they did not think even prayers could help them.

"And you know," he said aloud, "with all the fuss they making, there going to be no wedding."

Japan, the other great gambler in Cascadu, a money-lender, nearby on the big wappie table, playing a game of single-hand rummy with a stranger we knew only as Sailor, was quick to respond: "You betting on it?"

"You damn right, I betting. What odds you giving?"

"Even money," said Constantine.

"With so much people against the wedding?"

"The bride and groom practically in the church already," said Constantine, "I would be a fool to give you odds."

"The man could skip town," said Japan.

"And leave that woman? No."

"Or an accident could happen to him."

"Even money," Constantine said.

When Japan finished the game, he called to Constantine, "How much you putting?"

"On what?"

"That the wedding not going to happen."

"Whatever you have," Constantine said.

And that is how Cascadu came back to its senses.

Once the news went out that the two biggest gamblers in the town were laying bets on whether or not there would be a wedding, first, those keeping vigil under the telephone post where BonAventure was fasting made their way to the gambling club to lay bets, some with Constantine, some with Japan. As others followed, the town began to feel once more in charge of its destiny. All over Cascadu people gathered up money to put with that of Constantine Nieves against the heap that Japan was anxious to lay on the table. Japan who had bet on the couple getting married was no fool, and to ensure that no accident happened to Clayton, he detailed Big John to follow Clayton and Oliver to follow Big John, and asked Sonnyboy to keep an eye on the two of them.

"So where you putting your money?" I asked Aunt Magenta.

"There will be no wedding."

"No wedding?"

"Half the town against it and every day her mother down on her knees in front half a dozen burning candles and a picture of the Virgin Mary, pleading for Dorlene to come to her senses and call off the wedding."

"You don't think is too late for that? I know Dorlene, how she stubborn."

"And I know the mother," my aunt said.

Dorlene's Wedding Day

So I was there to see Dorlene, in a white bridal dress, its train carried by Mercury Allgood and her sisters, then small beribboned children, present herself at the church for the purpose of getting married to Clayton Blondell, a man disliked by more than half the town and hated by Dorlene's mother who, since the announcement of the wedding, each day went laboriously down on her knees before a burning candle and the picture of the Virgin Mary to plead for Dorlene to come to her senses and call off this wedding.

Up to the morning of the wedding day, Dorlene had not relented. The villagers, packed in the churchyard and hanging from the vantage of its walkway's two enormous mango trees, were there to see the guests arrive from their respective worlds: Dorlene's relatives, in private cars, their clothing displaying the self-assuredness of their class, duty-bound to put a brave face on the occasion, as if whatever objection they had to her choice of mate was less to be emphasized than the superiority of class and the solidity of clan; Clayton's family turned out in the shiny extravagance of the poor, their chariots, the grandest taxis money could hire, in wondrous costumes they had gone into years of debt to afford; Aunt Magenta, draped in a buxom splendor of her own that matched theirs, a fan in one gloved hand, the other hand linked to the muscular arm of her escort Clephus Winchester, who was making his first public appearance with her.

Half an hour after Dorlene's appearance at the church,

213

there was no sight of the prospective bridegroom, and Aunt Magenta, who is telling me this part of the story, in the church now, fanning herself with the letter-sized invitation (she had lent her own fan to Clephus) as she stewed in the luxurious vapors steaming from bodies enveloped in finery around her, was beginning to wonder whether the man would turn up at all, or if the candle that Dorlene's mother had burning on his head had had its effect so that even as they waited he was on his way out of Dorlene's life back to the depths of hell where the mother believed he had come from. Just then, Big John and Oliver, stiff-looking, in their formal wear, one in a green suit, the other in a brown one, appeared with Clayton just a step or two ahead of them. We would learn later that at the time when he ought to have headed for the church, he discovered he was nearly an hour too early. Not wanting to appear too anxious, he had asked the taxi to let him off at the gambling club, a place where nobody would look for him since he had never gambled in his life. There he was introduced to the playing of the card game wappie. He took off his jacket, rolled up his sleeves so that the elbows of the shirt would not be soiled rubbing against the card table, and sat at the table. Fellars anxious to benefit from beginner's luck encouraged him to cut the cards; he did, successfully, and went on to make nick after nick. He was still nicking when Big John and Oliver entered the club. They had looked everywhere else. And it was only when Clayton turned and saw them dressed in wedding clothes that he was brought back to the present.

"What time it is?"

"They waiting for you in the church."

"Just let me wash my face."

He stuffed the money in his pockets and went to the washroom in the back where he splashed his face, unrolled his sleeves, buttoned them at the wrist and put on his jacket, and he walked out, leaving the club buzzing over his amazing run of luck.

In the church he went past the whispers of the spectators, up to the altar to meet Miss Dorlene as the steelband began again to play "Here Comes the Bride" for the last time that day and they stood together before the priest, not meeting each other's eyes until the priest asked the question, *If anyone know a reason why this man and woman should not be joined in matrimony speak now or forever hold your peace*, heard the silence settle like a roar in the church. At that point a troupe of women stood and made their way up the aisle, beside them their children ranging in ages from perhaps twelve months to twelve years, each one with Clayton's long head and fierce eyes. The congregation groaned. It was Clayton's children and their mothers.

In the silence, Dorlene's mother made the sign of the cross and her scream rent the air. Dorlene stood in front Clayton. She lifted a hand to strike him. At that moment four pigeons flew into the church. Just for an instant Dorlene began to tremble and then all at once she stood calm. "Sorry," she said, and still holding the bouquet she walked out the church, the three little Allgood sisters, not aware that anything was wrong, hurrying behind her, carrying out their office with the same fluent and rehearsed ceremony, the steelband breaking out into "Claire de Lune" and the mother, her lips smacking nervously, lifting her head to see Dorlene standing before her with an icy calm. "You satisfy now, Mother? You pleased?" And she pushed the bouquet into her mother's hands and left the church, the mother stilling her own trembling lips to say softly words that only those near could hear: "Is not for me you do this, you know. Is not for me, you know."

And then there was confusion with the money that people had bet.

The man holding the bet had been flanked by Mr. Constantine and Japan. On seeing Clayton enter the church, he had given over the bet to Japan and Japan began handing over various sums to those who had bet along with him. Now Mr. Constantine wanted to get the money from Japan. In the episode that followed, Japan, accompanied by Big John and Oliver, went up to Clayton. They wanted to beat him, but Japan who now had to collect the money he had held only briefly, told Clayton, "Maybe is best for you to leave this town." And they should have realized that something was wrong because Clayton just went on smiling and putting forward his arm to shake hands. And it was only afterward that they realized that Clayton wasn't hearing them. He had tripped off into a world all his own.

Even then, we didn't know how deeply wounded he was. We would understand the seriousness of his condition only later, when the next day at the same hour of morning Clayton visited the church in his clothes of a bridegroom that he had not changed, shaking hands all around. For the rest of that weekend and for some days in the new week, Clayton went through that same exercise. By then it was clear, from the scent emanating from him as he extended his hands for the umpteenth time, that he had not taken his clothes off since the day of his aborted wedding.

"That is what you get when you hang your hat where your hand can't reach," Aunt Magenta said.

I was surprised at her lack of sympathy.

Seeing that I wanted to speak, she looked at me sharply. "You have something to say?"

"No, no," I said too quickly. Then, on reflection, "No, it is a terrible thing. Plenty people sorry."

"I sorry too," in her tone more triumph than sorrow.

"I suppose," said Clephus, spitefully, "Sonnyboy will have to finish build the sphinx now."

But I wasn't amused.

Up the Hill

I had seen Dorlene grieve before: anger, vexation, self-pity, her eyes brimming with a soft unutterable hurt, accusing you, making you feel, no matter how innocent you knew yourself to be, that you were a part of the world that had hurt her. But this time she didn't cry, she didn't scream, she didn't curse. In the months after the scandal of the aborted wedding, she endured the presence of Clayton in Cascadu, overhearing him ridiculed, teased, the whisperings when she passed, the *poor thing* mouthed by sorrowful shakes of the head, endured the *how nice you looking* from people glad to see her taken down a peg, not because they bore her any particular ill will, but because this rejoicing at someone else's sorrow kept it away from their own door. Then he left Cascadu, but that didn't end the attention from the town. She tried at first to hurry past the comments, and when she couldn't she decided to be deaf, not hearing, and then to be blind, not seeing, and then she was dumb; so that when I saw her walking in the market, drawn to her full height, her chin tilted upward, her eyes fixed on the horizon, she didn't see me. She didn't look healthy. It was as if she was stuffing herself with the wrong foods. Her face looked swollen. Her hair was straightened, its silky ends, curling comically around her temples, like the relaxed feathers of a dusting broom. She was wearing a tailored suit to camouflage the size she had put on, but it did not hide much. Her neck had grown bigger, her back and shoulders had thickened and the flesh

218

of her arms bulged over her sleeves. "Hello," I said, intending to stand and talk to her. She contrived an off-putting smile and continued on her way briskly, I am sure to avoid having to speak to me, but also in a backhanded way, I thought, to see if I cared enough to pursue her. I didn't know what to say. I felt guilty, helpless and responsible. The disaster of the wedding had saddened me and I saw that she needed someone, she needed me.

It was a week or so later, I went to her home. I had the correct excuse to do so. I had received an invitation from the Culture Ministry of Grenada's Revolutionary Government to visit the island to take part in a grand event involving artists from the Caribbean. I had listened to reports of the revolution from afar, had followed the events, the seizing of the police stations without a shot being fired, the banning of the newspapers, the formation of the militia, the people's revolutionary army, the defiance of the USA. I had gone to hear their leader and prime minister Maurice Bishop speak when he came to Trinidad, and had been impressed by his charisma, hopeful that here at last in the Caribbean was a group of persons prepared to tackle the silence that had continued from emancipation.

When I got to Dorlene's home, she wasn't there. I met her mother sitting on their veranda in her rocking chair staring ahead, the old newspapers that she must have been going through scattered around her feet. Weeds were overgrowing the garden to the side of the path, a cat was asleep on the steps.

Her mother recognized me: "Dorlene is not here," she said.

As I turned to leave, I asked her if she knew where she was.

Then her tears, her grief began to flow: "I don't know. She didn't tell me. She doesn't talk to me. She doesn't tell me anything. She leave me here alone. I am not well. I am a sick woman. Sugar. Pressure. Why she doing this to me? I am not guilty of any wrong. I am not to blame."

"Do you know where she might be?" I asked.

"She left three days ago to go by her brother, I am not sure. She was talking about going to find Clayton. Up in some dangerous place. Exactly where I do not know. Her brother in Woodbrook should know. You know her brother Claude?"

I remembered him as the one member of the Hard Wuck Screening Committee who had spoken in support of Sonnyboy's candidacy. I had the impression that he was no longer an active member of the Hard Wuck Party, but I didn't know for sure. I had lost interest in the organization and it seemed to have abandoned what it called electoral politics.

"Yes, I know Claude."

"You going to look for her." It wasn't a question. And it required no answer. "Tell her for me I sorry, am not a bad woman. The best is all I want for her. That is all. That is my sin: to want the best for my daughter."

"But I don't have the address of her brother," I said.

"It is Woodbrook. Let me give it to you."

She wrote out the address for me. So I was in it now. After I left her, I went to see Sonnyboy to find out if he had an address for Clayton. Sonnyboy didn't have Clayton's address, but he wanted to come along to see how Clayton was doing. That was fine. Early next morning we set out for Port of Spain. We found the Woodbrook address easy enough and we met Claude. Dorlene wasn't there. She had gone to visit Clayton, he told us, but he had the address. Laventille. His first impulse was to give us the address and leave us to find our way, but in the little time we spoke, he changed his mind. I suppose the fact that we were from Cascadu had something to do with it. Now, he wanted to go up the hill. It was something he had always wanted to do and he was glad for the opportunity to see the hill of resistance, the birthplace of pan. He didn't want to drive. We could take a taxi down town, then walk up the hill. Did we mind walking?

It was all right with me and I suspected that although Sonnyboy didn't say anything, he didn't mind either. As far as I knew he had, in the last years, not frequented the place where he was born and spent his early years. I didn't know what to expect or how he would respond.

Going up the hill was going into a world that the rest of the city had left behind. It was an old part of the town, with posters plastered on the walls that hugged the margins of the street, announcing the showing of movies from cinemas no longer in operation, of fêtes featuring music bands no longer in existence, the only current items the smiling faces of the candidates for elections: Vote for Oswald Sanguinette Your National Party Candidate. Vote Machel Des Vignes for Labor Party. Vote for Wilson Toppin. Of the faces of promises, one candidate had an eye gouged out, another had his teeth blacked out, one candidate had been given a beard, another a pair of spectacles. The only pristine face was that of the National Party candidate looking out contentedly, his victory assured.

The place looked aged, bleak, its architecture faithful to the template of poverty, neglect, the new houses painted in the same colors of the old, matching the feel of decay, or garishly highlighting it. The first person we saw was a man alone standing before a half-built house, contemplating the unfinished building, the holes of the windows, the doorless openings, the absent steps, the unpainted pillars, the boxing with the lengths of steel into which the mortar is to be poured, his collapsed shoulders holding up, in faith, the faith. You couldn't call out to such a man to ask him directions. And we walked on up the hill until we got to a corner where another alley disappeared and saw on the other side of the street a young fella with the sharp eyes of a hustler and the air of a fugitive, alert to run, and, I suppose, intuiting that we were not the police, inquired, "You looking for somebody?" in that double-, triple-speak, partly to put us off, partly to intimidate, really to discover who we were.

"Yes. We looking for somebody," Claude answered. "Clayton. Clayton Blondell is who we looking for," speaking with the self-assurance of an experienced adventurer.

"Clayton Blondell? Clayton Blondell?" The young fella sounding the name for it to register.

"Who they looking for?" Another fella, older, a turban on his head, dark shades, a military jacket, had materialized.

"Blondell. Clayton Blondell."

"Blondell, Blondell, Blondell? Oh-ho, Sharkey brother. The mad one. What you want him for?"

"He's a friend."

The man with the turban looked at me again, recognition in his eyes.

"Wait! You is . . . don't tell me – calypsonian? Kangkala?"

"King Kala," I said.

"King Kala, yes."

As if to confirm his discovery, he began singing one of my calypsos:

Nothing is changed
Not the silence not the shame
It can't be humans living up here
Conditions so bad
These people forgotten
In this dream they calling Trinidad ...

"You remember that calypso? Nearly win everything with that one song: Panorama, the Road March. The Monarch competition."

"Yes," I said, flattered, but not wanting to make too much of it.

"And you are?" I asked.

"Jeremiah Jerry, Mayor of this republic here on the hill, Black Power activist in '70, former member of the Regiment. Drummer. Agitator. Painter. Singer. Revolutionist. Artist. Guide to this treasury of our country. Gentlemen," he said, turning to his fellows (for another fellow had materialized from the side street), "we have royalty in the house. A king of calypso." And back to us, "Gentlemen, welcome. You looking for Clayton. I will show you where he living. I going up the road. Come."

He came over and shook hands all around, pausing before Sonnyboy, screwing up his face trying to remember where he knew him from. But Sonnyboy didn't give anything away.

And we set out again, up the hill, past the guardians of the street corner selling ganja, the suspicious eyes wondering what was our business, were we the police, what were we selling. And I am thinking of my guide, who

223

is he? How much will he expect us to pay him? Should we offer him money? Will he be insulted if we did?

And our guide questioning, seeking to locate us more precisely, "So where you know Sharkey brother from?"

And once we tell him Cascadu, he set about telling us about Clayton's family, from his grandfather Matthew who build the first house on the hill . . .

without no tractor or crane, tote up a little track he himself made, the lumber and the galvanize piece by piece and cement and gravel and sand, bucket by bucket and bricks one by one, he alone, the workman and the builder. And after he finish build the house went and take up this strapping, smooth-skinned, black Vincelonian woman, Gracie, whose beauty he spied out first in the bustle of traffickers on the wharves when she get off the schooner with her bags of ground provisions and avocado and ginger and later where he see her selling at the Port of Spain market and bring her with him up the hill where he install her as his queen and who returned the blessing of his adoration by selling in the market and minding the five children she make for him plus another one he already had with another woman, this child who when the other five leave and go away would be the one to take care of both Matthew and Gracie in their old age and build a Shouters church and make three boy-children for a man who was working on the railway, one who would be the captain of the steelband . . . one would be a policeman and the other was Clayton –

"Look," he said, interrupting his history to tell us of the people and the places we were passing.

That is the place there under that mango tree where Spree and some young fellars carve out the first notes on the face of a steelpan

224

... And over there on the other side on Rouff Street another fella Lance was doing the same thing. Shango and Shouters, poets and artists, journalists and mas men. Everything that this country throw up, you could trace it to this place here.

We walked in the bright morning along the winding road, past houses that had grown gray, precarious like spinning tops sleeping at standstill before they fall, up past standpipes without water and roads without asphalt, past people their eyes inquiring, *What you want here?* Our guide answering the unspoken questions: "They looking for Clayton."

"Clayton?"

"Sharkey brother. The mad one. Miss Gracie grandson."

And we continued on, past the street blocks, each one manned by a more serious band of silent watchful men.

I saw scrawled on walls the faded signs of Black Power, the portraits of Malcolm X, Martin Luther King and Makandal Daaga, on a little further to the likeness of His Imperial Highness Haile Selassie emerging out of the head of a lion, the poster of the National Party across which efforts to erase what was written had left a F—. And beyond that, across the road the steelband yard:

... where the players beat out the tunes for Carnival. The whole hill assembled to go down with them to cross the savannah stage so we could show them that we here. Now, look what happening! You could hardly get fellars to play now unless you hand over cash ...

At the corner, I see the single Blackman's shop barricaded with iron mesh. Who was he barricading his business from, I wondered. I watch the grimy apartment building, with barebacked children gambling on the steps,

225

their eyes cold as concrete, their language with the same metallic ring and thrust of iron.

... Now we have to protect ourselves from our own children. Because they have guns, not old guns, new ones in the plastic casing, because what we sell them is not their life, but another life, is not love, is the fight-down and the bling.

It was hot. I wanted a beer. I also wanted to offer our guide a beverage. We went into the shop.

"This is Mr. Mackie, the shopkeeper," our guide said. "Mr. Mackie," he said, calling to a stringy exhausted-looking man, "Mr. Mackie, look who I bring here: King Kala the calypsonian."

"Yes?" said Mr. Mackie, scrutinizing us from behind his wire cage.

Mr. Mackie used to bring out a dragon band. His brother, Tank the stevedore, used to play Robber: "Stop, I say stop, you mocking pretender. Bend your knees and drop your keys and call me the master. Because if I stamp my feet, I would cause disaster...." You remember that speech, Mr. Mackie? Bat, devil, dragon, jab molassie, all used to come from this hill. Today if you see one dragon you see plenty. My uncle Hector was a tailor. He used to play Black Indian. Prince, the joiner, was the leader of the Fancy Indian band. And we were ready, eh, Mr. Mackie? ...

"Years ago," said Mr. Mackie. "Those days, mas was holy, was sacred. You didn't just put on a costume and jump into a band. The costume was only one part. King sailor had to dance the sailor dance. You couldn't just pick out a sergeant costume and wear it, or be a major just because you like it, or because you could afford to pay for

226

it. You had to dance to get your rank. Bat, Dragon, Imp, Jab Molassie. Everything you play, you had to master the movements, the song or the speech. Mas of beauty and purpose. It was serious business."

The streets of the city was our own, eh, Mr. Mackie? George Bailey, McWilliams, Cito Velasquez and his King sailor, Terry Evelyn, Errol Payne, and all the other mas, Dragon, Robber, Bat, Wiley, Jab-jab. We had the steelband moving to perfection. We were ready for Independence, eh, Mr. Mackie?

"All that beauty, all that power, all that imagination, that community, that love," said Mr. Mackie. "What we do with it? What happen to it?"

"What stop it, Mr. Mackie?" Our guide was asking the question in my mind. "Politics stop it?"

"We get trapped, all of us," Mr. Mackie said.

Every year, for years, the big-shot people try to waste us down, "what we doing playing mas when we hungry, when we have no money," as if they were so concerned about our welfare. We didn't take them on. We know that what the mas was doing was fortifying a community, was holding up a people their system had set about to waste down. We know that celebration was not just mindless fun, it was rebellion, it was community, it was creativity. And we keep on, eh, Mr. Mackie? Until, yes, the people we vote for, the politicians come with the same sad song, "we should look to our education, together we aspire together we achieve," and a set of talk without a dream. "Because there is nothing more to rebel against," they tell us. "We independent now. This is the time for construction not rebellion." So, we surrender. We give up rebellion. We give up the mas. Eh, Mr. Mackie? Mr. Mackie is our historian. And we wait for the construction.

And Mr. Mackie: "We didn't give it up. They stifle it."

We had the Bomb Competition pan musicians, showing their genius on an instrument, that could master any music. We had the people pushing pan, celebrating community, inventing. It was something that we had control of. They invite the steelband into the savannah and start the thing that they call Panorama that would take the pan out the street Carnival and put it on a stage, we the supporters following them there, eh, Mr. Mackie? And for a moment we try to carry the streets onto their stage, but that stage was too small for all the people . . .

"It was the pans they wanted on their stage, not the people."

And that is when everything start to mash up: they separate the musicians from the movement, the community gone to one side, the youth off to another, the old stagers gone to the savannah trying to keep faith with their bands, all of us left as spectators.

"I tell them vote for somebody from up here, get somebody from up here who know what people feel, who know what people do, what people go through, who appreciate the value of the things we do."

And we do it, Mr. Mackie. We vote for one that is supposed to be our own. We put up a fella from up here, Mr. Mackie.

"Mr. Gentleman," Mr. Mackie said, looking directly at me, "let me give you this advice: Beware of people who think they know you. We put up a fella from up here. But that is the worst thing we do, because he know us too well. He see what we put up with, so he believe we will settle for a place without lights, without water. He see

228

that we could make the magic of making bricks without straw, we could tote bags of cement and buckets of gravel and sand through a track up the mountain. He see us making miracles and believe we must continue to make miracles.

"Now, look at us. What was performance in Carnival is now the reality of life. The devil is no longer in the make-believe of Carnival, he is right here on our streets. The Midnight Robber is not a character in our fiction, he is in possession of real guns."

The people to represent us must be people who see that the monuments we have created is bigger than the pitch lake and the oilfields and the sugarcane plantations. They must see us.

"The people," said Mr. Mackie. "The people to represent you is you.

"And even you have to know who *you are.*

"The hope?" Mr. Mackie continued, turning to Claude. "*You* asking *me* about the hope?"

I was hearing another verse of my calypso:

Imagine, if you will, the conditions of people on top this hill
People whose offerings make us see
Our common humanity
Give us the pan, give us the mas
We leave them in the labasse to catch their arse

I saw the mountains of filth, the film of heat, the dogs, the youth with their eyes alert watching, with an old caution and defense and calculation, past the signs of The National Party Forever and torn posters with pictures of the leader of the political party, across which someone had painted in the one expletive FUk. And further up, the last stage of despair and affirmation and release, the final statement for everybody to see. On the wall with the leaders and the chiefs and the politicians, somebody had drawn the likeness of a pistol and underneath it had written in an artistic cursive handwriting: *Everybody muddercont.*

I looked at Claude. He had gone quite gray. "What do you call this place?" he asked the guide.

"This is the part we call Congo," Jeremiah Jerry answered. "Up there," he said, pointing at another hill, "is Beverly Hills."

Coming out the trace was a woman stately like an orchid, her shoes held in one hand to save them from the mud. I heard the tinkle of the steelpans, of rain, of drizzle.

We walked past the standpipes without water, the children agile and bony and up to the flags and the hut, our guide waving his hands, calling the name, *Clayton*, sent on again. Through this dark bright place damp, where water had made its own meandering tracts, here and there a child pushing a roller, little boys in a box cart, a yard with a little lawn, a yard with a coconut tree growing. And then the house with the flags of the Shango palais in the yard.

"Over there," said our guide, pointing to the yard with the flags.

"Over where?"

"Over there, the house in the Shango yard."

It was one of the yards with a flower garden, marigold, Jacob's coat, wonder of the world, zinnias. Dogs lay silent, serene almost as if nothing was to be allowed to disturb their leisure. There was a calabash tree and sugarcane plant and soursop, a sense of peace. As I stepped into the yard, the dog didn't bark. A woman came to the door with a sense of inquiry and then as if she knew who we were and was expecting us, she smiled.

"We looking for Clayton," I said.

"I am Clayton's mother."

She came outside to meet us and took us into the building at the side of the house, the palais, with its earthen floor and its benches arranged up against the walls. Dorlene was there, sitting on one of the benches, and she introduced us to the mother. Clayton was inside the main house, resting. She was sorry. He had just taken medicine, which got him groggy and made him sleep. She was sure he would like to see us, after we had come all that distance. She was thinking to wake him.

"Don't wake him," Dorlene tell her. "They could come back."

"You will come back?"

"Yes, we will," Claude answered.

We didn't stay long. Soon we were ready to leave. Dorlene decided to leave with us.

"Take care of her," the mother said.

Dorlene said her goodbyes and we walked out together.

"Take care of her, you hear. Take care," the mother said.

The scent of marigold, the sound of whispers, the light growing dark.

"And I am sorry," Dorlene called to her.

"Don't worry, darling. God is love. He'll be all right. We working on him. He will get better."

A taxi was going downhill with space for one passenger. We put Dorlene in it. We thought of waiting for another taxi, but we didn't want to split the party up, and it was I who now wanted to walk.

We set out downhill. No one said anything, but we were all touched. I could feel Sonnyboy uneasy as if he felt he should make some response to revisiting this place he had in some ways escaped. He didn't say anything. I had many questions for him, but I didn't ask them.

And we walked in a silence that I soon realized was due to the absence of the running commentary by our guide Jeremiah Jerry on the way up the hill. We continued down the hill in silence. I was waiting for Sonnyboy to say something; but, it was Claude who began to speak.

Claude's Belonging

Claude didn't just love those he called *the people*; he wanted to be one of them. "And you would understand my predicament," he said, "if you grow up with a piano in the living room of a house that none of the villagers would be invited to enter and into which none would come, even on Christmas Day when its doors were thrown open and the table laid for them, with ham and ponce crema and sorrel and ginger beer and rum, and you would hear the people festive on the street, cuatro and shack-shack and guitar and parang singing sweetening the air, as they go to every house in the neighborhood except your own, deliberately passing it straight because your father had made himself custodian of a piano that by accident had fallen onto his veranda, making the possession of the piano that he couldn't even play puff him up with such self-importance that he shut himself and his family away from all but the most essential contact with the village." So that Claude had no playmate who was allowed to enter his yard and none he could leave the prison of his yard to go out to.

So, after he put down his book and examined the moss on the trees, after he dig up the earth for worms to inspect and dissect, he would watch birds head for nest and the evening surround the forest and night spread over the land, and hear the breathing of the trees and the hoot of spirits out there in the dark, the douens with their little children bodies, their broad straw hats and backward-turned feet calling, *hoot! hoot!* Hoot, like jumbie birds, as

233

they ran through the forest playing, Claude trembling at the thought of being outside in the dark peopled by spirits at the crossroad, La Diablesse, the lagahoo, soucouyant, and the phantom dragging along a coffin by a chain, all that to be erased by sleep, morning bringing him the world anew, and he would go past the bay leaf tree, through the gate, out into the day, past Pory land and Sylvan garden and Carabon estate, glad for the sun, for the light, for the tadpoles flitting across the shallow pools made by rain in the track marks of tractors, for the bridge and the river below it, flowing clear and glassy, the bands of tireless silver fish bunched together like racing cyclists, the coscorobs, drifting by solemn like monks, a single guabine in the lightly striped suit of a prisoner, its mouth open, like it dreaming, drawing him into its timelessness, until the horn blast of a passing truck remind him that is school he going to and he would set out again, carrying the timelessness with him into the morning sun and the noise of traffic, trucks carrying gravel and sand and lumber, vans transporting bananas and oranges and yams, on his way these formidable women dressed in green, in black, in white, in red, their heads tied with bulky colored kerchiefs, the scented oils on their skin smelling of mystery, of magic, of obeah, saying *Good morning, Miss Gloria; Good morning, Miss Dolly, good morning, good morning*, not only out of politeness but from a respectful fear. These women could put a light on you. You could go blind for looking them bold in the eye. *Good morning, child; good morning, darling. Good morning, Sweets.* And the men on his way, Hailings and Carlton, Ottie and Sylvan, fighters, dancers, pan men, cricketers, all of them with this power of belonging, of ownership, behind them this world of spirit, of mystery

234

that he, Claude, was only able to navigate because of the guidance of Orville, a boy his own age, one of the tribe of Bascombe children, grouped by the town under the single name *Baachac*, a species of destructive brown big-headed ants, the indomitable nest of them living three-four houses down from him. Orville could whistle through his fingers, Orville could make flips without his hands touching the ground, Orville could run faster than anyone else, Orville could play a flute, Orville could drum. It was Orville who cautioned him not to point his finger at a funeral, otherwise the pointing hand would rot, who instructed him that if he went out in the night, when going back home, he should enter his house walking backwards so as to fool the spirit into thinking he was going in the opposite direction. It was Orville who let him in on the rites to avoid a flogging, the words to chant, the number of stones to throw over his shoulders as he approached his home – *by St. Peter, by St. Paul* – the leaves of which plant to pick. So when Claude hear his mother saying, as she watched Orville or one of his tribe go past her fence, "Be glad you not like those people," he knew that she didn't understand. The truth was that he felt that theirs was not a life from which he had been saved, but an adventure of which he had been robbed. Orville had an uncle named Sandy who for Carnival blackened himself with black grease, strapped two horns on his head, reddened his tongue and played jab molassie, Orville blackened too with a tail made of bobbins strung on wire getting to play too, going with him all over town, beating with two sticks the pitch-oil tin in the compelling jab molassie rhythm. Orville had another uncle named Nelson who for Carnival played bat. And one they called Crappo who was a stickfighter and drummer. And these people could also sing and dance and play cricket and football. Everything resided in these people; so, when, as one of the elect, Claude won the scholarship that would take him to St. Mary's College in Port of Spain, he decked himself out with the heroes of that world; while St. Mary's fellars were mimicking the Irish priests and getting the images of themselves from them, he was walking with stickfighters' drums beating in his belly, he was hearing Shango rhythms in his head.

And that must have done something to his mind, because although in elementary school in Cascadu he couldn't beat Orville or Sammy running, at St. Mary's, forced into the athletic program, Claude discovered that he could run faster than nearly everyone in his class. It became at first almost an embarrassment to him. He did not expect to run so fast; that was for Orville from Cascadu to do, that was for Sammy. He would run against fellars in scratch races, feeling himself a representative of that world; but he refused to run for the school. Let them represent themselves. They believed the world was their own. The real people were outside this world. Let them run for themselves. He was not going to consolidate their idea that here was the world. He knew there was another world.

And he was waiting for that world. His attitude aggravated fellars. He got under their skin. They wanted to fight him; but there was about him something dangerous, some secret strength that they saw in him that made them hesitate to tackle him.

So in school he became a kind of a rebel, seen as someone who didn't play the game, and he grew up largely untested, never knowing how good a runner he was, not

236

caring to prove himself to them. He was waiting on that world. He became somewhat of a loner, a kind of odd man out, having friends, but when he tried to show them his world, they were on another beat, and he had to hold on to himself, because everybody, the whole tide was moving on and away and he was left in his elsewhere world. So, with the feeling that everybody was gunning for him, to bring him down, to civilize him, the masters and the boys, he put his mind to his schoolwork, in secret more than in class, studying not just to beat them but to make himself worthy of the fellars in Cascadu, his ambition to be accepted into their world, to have the right to stand with them by the street corner, or feel possessed of the authority to enter the steelband, barebacked with his jersey tie across his forehead, in the line of men beating iron, yes, he wanted to hold on to them, to let them know that they had a champion.

But he had to deal with the expectations the very people had of him. On weekends when he returned to Cascadu, the people of the town wanted to see what St. Mary's had done for him, for them, and he didn't have the heart to disappoint them; so he invoked St. Mary's in his walk, in his speech. When he was in Cascadu he represented St. Mary's and at St. Mary's he was the people of Cascadu. He would know how closely the people of Cascadu were watching him when one day, as he was going along the street, Marvel, a fella who had never spoken to him before, watching him walk by, said, "Like you putting on some size. You lifting weights or what?" making him feel buoyed up, recognized. When he got home, looking at himself in the mirror, at his chest and arms, *he was putting on some size.* After that he went past the corner a little slower, with greater certainty, with a greater sense of belonging to this place and these people.

Claude went through UWI with the confidence of his own opinions, able to outtalk anyone, with a tone of voice that insisted on being listened to and a fastness of mind to keep on the track of whatever point he was making, arguing incessantly with his friend Merrit who in order to keep up their debates, to make another point, to clarify another idea, allowed him to tag along with him and his girl until Merrit girlfriend Joy, so that she could get some time with Merrit for herself, set Claude up with a girl who was teaching in the same school as she, "someone who likes to talk like you." She was an elementary school teacher, a girl from the country, from Grande, teaching in Tunupuna. She smelled of Oil of Olay, young, clean, and when they embraced she encircled his neck with both hands like lovers in the movies, a gesture that did not seem natural to her, that she was making just for him. However, she didn't talk; she listened.

Sometimes for hours they would sit, he talking and she listening, her questions opening up new vistas for him. Next day they would take up again where they left off. Not wanting the conversation to end, when he got the job to go to Rio Claro as a Senior Agricultural Assistant, he decided that he couldn't leave without her. That was when he knew that in her he had found the girl with whom he wanted to face the world.

He went to her school in Tunupuna to give her the news and to ask her to marry him.

"You crazy?"

"Will you?"

"Will I what?"

238

"Marry me?"

She hesitated. What would her family say?

He had not thought of family. He had been talking about the future, about the world. He had not been talking of family, neither his nor hers.

"Yes," he asked. "What would your family say?"

Yes, what would your family say, not even saying what was in his mind: *You have not asked what would my family say, but you are asking what would your family say.* "What would your family say?"

"What you getting vex for? Is they, not me."

"Then why have you, my love, asked me such a question?"

She encircled his neck with that movie-star hug.

"Well, maybe we should ask them."

"Ask them? Ask them?"

"Yes. If we want to know what they have to say maybe we should ask them."

"Claude, you know what I mean."

"No," he said, "I don't know what you mean. Tell me what you mean."

"I don't think is a good idea to ask them anything."

And then it came out in little driblets, Hindu, Presbyterian, caste and family. Old-fashioned.

"But don't worry with them."

"How not to worry?"

"It doesn't matter to me. To me it doesn't matter."

He felt he had pushed too far. He held her. She settled in his arms.

"We are the new world," he said.

And that was the beginning. They never spoke to her father. They dodged it. He never raised it.

They married, his family alone. Her family absent. Her sisters absent. None of her brothers. And it became clear to him that here was another reason why he had to have a new world. She wasn't going to blame her father. "He is who he is, what he is, his experience, and I must be true to what I am, my experience," she said. "We have the future."

So he got married. They got married.

So he had a partner now, a pardner with whom to face the new world.

They would go together to Rio Claro, where in the first week of his posting he would witness the silent march of armies of hunting ants, his interest in them turning to alarm, to horror, as he saw lines and lines of them climb up into the apiaries and return with bees held in their jaws. Instead of being diverted from their business, the bees kept on flying into the hives to deposit their nectar and flying out again to gather it, while the ants, with the same implacable efficiency, kept marching in and seizing them and making off with them.

He had looked on with interest, expecting the bees to struggle, that they would somehow mass and call upon their own soldiers to repel the attack of the ants, but instead of being diverted from their business, the bees kept on flying into the hives to deposit their nectar and flying out again to gather it, while the marabuntas with the same relentless efficiency kept marching in and seizing them and making off with them. And he soon realized that if something wasn't done, the waves of ants would overwhelm and destroy the hives of bees. It was his first posting as Agricultural Officer. He did not know enough about bees, and nothing had prepared him for this sight.

"Is there nothing we can do?" he asked the Beekeeper.

The Beekeeper seemed almost pleased to answer: "Nothing, Chief."

"Nothing. No spray, nothing? Aldrex, Sevin, nothing? There must be something."

"If you say so, Chief." Already in the worker the sense of indifference, a surrender, a fear of even thinking of using initiative.

"How you mean if I say so?"

"If you spray the ants you will kill the bees." He was enjoying this. Yes, I was the fool, I was the arse, I would get in trouble; already in his voice, his smile, *Trouble*, saying it in his mind, *this chief heading for trouble.*

"But you see they are dying, Carlton. They will all die." Claude had read of the marabuntas, he had seen the movie where these ants cleaned everything in their path, big animals ran from them, snakes had to get out of their way, cockroaches, grasshoppers, sometimes even butterflies perished in the sweep of these armies.

"They going to clean out the hives, Carlton. Is there nothing you can do?"

"I don't know, Chief."

No, you don't know. What you know is to eat and shit and come to work here and scheme as much as you can to get off as much work as you can, though when I think of it ... when I think of it, that is what they teach you, that is the way they control you.

"Maybe a little insecticide spray will kill them. A little spray below where the ants are climbing. Give the ants a threshold of insecticide that they can't cross. Go for the insecticide."

"You think that will work, Chief?"

As if I don't know that I stepping out of my crease, as if I don't know that this was where the whole fucking conversation was going to lead ... You going to get in trouble and I have to be sure I am safe I not in that. I not offering no advice you do what you want to do that is what they paying you for me am just a charge hand just a worker just here to see about the pigs and the cows and the goats and these bees you are the one who went to university I am just a laborer here, so I just helping you out anyway.

"Well, you're the beekeeper, tell me what to do."
"Anything you say, Chief."

Yes, so we arrive where you want us to: anything I say. Anything you say, Chief.

"Anything I say? What do I know? Anything I say?"

So this was how it was going to be. I surprise you. Anything I say.

"You sure, Chief?"
"Just a little."
"A little, Chief?"

Well, of course you don't know what a little is. Of course, of course, you don't want to have no part in it, that is your wisdom, so when they come to ask anything you would be able to say "was not me, I was just following orders."

"Give me the can, *yes, give me the fucking can.* Give me the can of Aldrex." So that was to be how it was going to be, he was the one who had the call and he made it too. "Give me the can," and he sprayed the area.

But it pained him. He felt let down. He felt let down by the people he so admired. My God. Afterward he began to blame them. How could they? How dare you

242

do this to yourself? How dare you? I know you. He knew them. He knew they were better than that.

"Here, let me do it."

Next morning not an ant, not a bee. They had all disappeared. It was an omen of his own helplessness, he would realize later, as he watched agriculture go to pieces, the coconuts in his area dying of red ring disease, the bananas falling to moko disease, the pawpaw to dieback. There was no longer any market for pigeon peas. And he found himself supervising nothing.

The Land Settlement Division to which he was posted had its activities frozen. The land, the land. People were building houses on the land. The drops of sweet peppers and anthurium lilies that had been expected never materialized. The great things they were attempting were all fizzling out to nothing: the pineapple project, the sorrel project, the anthurium lilies project, the tomato project. The demonstration stations were closing down because they were too expensive to run and farmers were left without example, to depend on themselves since the demonstration stations had long ceased to demonstrate any practice worthy of emulation.

"It's a plot," his wife Arlene said. "They want to frustrate you."

He read the reports. He heard the stories. In the Nariva swamp thousands of acres were squatted, the rivers were drained of fish, the conch in the rivers harvested almost to extinction, gravel mined and the land abandoned, its deep wounds eventually turning to pools of mud.

He went from division to division, transferred each time with promotion. He wrote papers, he spoke at meetings of the Agricultural Society. He went hiking. He took photographs. He talked about agriculture in the twenty-first century. And he realized that he was in a limbo place. To keep up the appearance of well-being, he took Arlene to Grenada, he took her to the St. Vincent Carnival, he took her to the baths in Tortola, to Virgin Gorda, among the rocks, its beauty something he could feel only not even speak. He brought her necklaces, rings. They played mas with Minshall one year. Another year they played fancy sailor with Jason Griffith. He went to the cricket Test matches in the Oval. But he soon realized that all this was just a way of seeking to hide the profound disappointment with himself, his job, his life.

He had to face it. He was trapped in the death throes of a system he had been trained to contribute toward, but that was no longer viable. Now he thought of his childhood, of the people there, of Orville and the Baachacs. All that life, that energy, that color, that creativity, what had they done with it. St. Mary's had won. He changed his car regularly. He bought a hat that he never put on his head, but that gave a certain style where he placed it on the rest above the backseat so that it could be seen from outside. In Cascadu, he witnessed the aging of his parents and the confusion of his sister. He looked for Orville. But he hardly saw him now Orville had a small business as a builder. He made regular trips to the United States, where his workmanship was valued, where he could find every tool he needed for his work. And make some money.

Claude felt overwhelmed, the future behind him. The world had not turned out as he had expected it to. The people had not come into their own. Power was being taken away from them, centralized into the hands of the wise. Yes, St. Mary's had won.

The Hard Wuck Party had interested him. It promised a new world. Arlene had joined with him. They found people who were interested in ideas, who wanted to save the people. They had been educated to believe that they were naturally suited to rule and so had expected that the people would come flocking to them. It did not happen. They had already affixed their hopes to an earlier version of the Hard Wuckers who were already in power. They were already in power. What the people wanted was not better rulers; what they wanted was not to be rescued from themselves, what they wanted to be given was themselves. And where was their future to be found? Where it always was in what they had been doing, in the struggle they had been making, in the struggle to retain themselves. But what worried him was not only the Hard Wuck Party's confident assumption of its destiny, it was the people's willingness to be saved. So he had withdrawn from them, along with two couples who were to become his close friends, Orlando and Shirley, Hamid and Carla, the six of them ending up by being liming pardners, going together to fêtes and shows and playing mas together.

It was Carnival that would save him.

One Jouvay they were playing in Three Canal Jouvay band when they stopped at the roadside to get some beers and something to eat. When they finish eat, they start looking for the band. They can't find the band. Everybody they ask giving them different directions. They start to walk. It was seven of them. They meet up with three fellars and a woman, one fella beating a du-dup, the next fella beating a brake-drum iron and the woman blowing a whistle. The fella on the du-dup know Orlando, so he pulled Orlando into that band. Orlando pulled them in. Out of nowhere a fella appear beating a piece of iron and join them. So now they have a band. They swing down St. Vincent Street. People sitting on the pavement, some resting, some sleeping, some waiting for their band. Among them is a short stump of a woman, her curvaceous body painted yellow and white, a bucket of yellow mud at her feet, who as Claude was about to go past her, responding to what he thought was the desire to join them in her eyes, stretched out an inviting hand. She grasped it with both of her own and pulled herself up to a standing position. With both hands, the woman first dust off her backside, then pat her bosom, heaved the mass of her breasts into a more seemly alignment, dipped into the bucket of mud and began to anoint him, then Arlene and Orlando, other members of the band dipped into the bucket of mud and anointed themselves and each other and with the iron beating and the du-dup sounding, the little woman assumed a half-stooping calisthenics position, cocked the promontory of her bottom in the direction in which the band was heading, turned her head sideways as if to look back at her bottom, put her hands up like somebody ask her to surrender and start to wine and, still wining, she slipped herself between Claude and Arlene, hold them round their waist, and take them with her to the front of the band. Claude take off his shirt and tie it round his head, and is so, moving to the waves of the rhythm from the du-dup and iron, Arlene, Claude and the rest of them moved through Port of Spain, sharing rum, dancing, singly and sometimes one with the other or in an embrace, the line of them, hands round the shoulder and hands round the waist. And for Claude that was his best Carnival.

He drink rum. He dance, he jump up. He wine, he beat iron, he hug-up woman, woman hug him. It was the greatest time. And when the sun come up he see in the eyes of the people on the roadside looking on at him the magnificence of this ordinary raggedy bunch daubed with mud, knitted by this love and community and peace, the feeling inside him so holy it raised in him again the sense of people, their beauty. By the time the morning was over, Claude felt touched by everybody in the band. He was ready to go again.

And he saw that this was what would save him, this little Carnival Jouvay band. All the grandiose dreams he had about the future were collapsed into this little band. Later when they got to Adam Smith Square, and about to split up, all of them confessed it was the best Jouvay they had. And Claude said yes and Hamid say yes, man. Yes. And the little half-pint woman wining on Orlando say yes, and the fella on the iron and the man on the du-dup and everybody had such a great time, they decided to meet again the next year.

Yes, Adam Smith Square at four o'clock on Jouvay morning of the following year. "This time, I will bring the mud," Claude said, and they took their leave of each other with hugs and pats, Claude and Orlando and Hamid and their party walking back to their place in Woodbrook with such a feeling of fullness, walking on the whole town, sailing on the air, Claude hugging up Arlene and she with her two hands around him.

Claude had a cart made that he could push or pull, and he placed buckets with mud on it. When he and Arlene and his little group reach Adam Smith Square next Jouvay, some of the people were there. But the majority hadn't turned up, though they had the man beating iron and they had the du-dup man and they had the cart with mud and people came off the streets and joined them; but they didn't have the inspiration of the little half-pint of a woman.

Next year Claude gone back again, he and Orlando and Shirley, Arlene didn't get up on time. Hamid decide to go back and play with Three Canal. But now Claude have this pushcart with buckets of mud, so he gone with this little cart with the mud. This time when they meet Adam Smith Square is only the man with the iron. The du-dup man gone. But people join in and they daub themselves with mud and they had a band.

In the next few years, is only he and Arlene alone from the lime. By this time, Claude, anticipating the possible absence of the iron or du-dup, placed pieces of iron and a du-dup on the pushcart with the mud so whoever was around would be able to beat iron and du-dup and make music for the Jouvay band. Fewer people again. The cart was a hindrance. Arlene rebelled. She was prepared to go to Jouvay with him. It was all right, the two of them going out and finding a band, but what was he doing, carrying a cartload of mud when the people not going to be there. But Claude had made a commitment and he would keep it. After that year, he set out for spite with the cart with the buckets of mud.

"For what?" Arlene had asked. "To show what?

"If you know they not going to be there, what you carrying mud for?"

"Just in case they come," he lied. Because by that time Claude was carrying the mud, expecting the people not to be there, carrying it as an act of reproach, as a testament to his faith, as an accusation, almost as something to martyr himself and hold it against them. As evidence of his faith and their failure. *To show how they will disappoint me again.* And that year and the years after that he had walked martyred all over the city, pushing a cart in which he placed buckets of mud and on which he had as well iron and du-dup, so that he had all that was needed for the band, except a set of people he was sure of. And although he tried not to do it or he did it less and less, he spent his time looking around for the people from the original band, waiting for the people, on the lookout for them. And although every Carnival a band coalesced around him, he still kept looking for the original members he had found years before. Each year one or two or three of them would turn up, but never enough to challenge his theory that the people had no responsibility, no commitment, nothing to dent the shield of his heroic martyrdom. I listened to Claude. I suppose it was a confession of sorts, that he had good reason for losing faith in the people. But I didn't have the impression that he had given up. I felt, though, that he was trying to convey the idea that he wanted to believe in the people. I felt that he was looking to me, looking to us for some direction that would help him.

The Martyrdom of Dorlene

From that day Claude became friends with Sonnyboy and me. I think it was his attempt at establishing roots that he had never been able to properly develop in the town. I suspect also that he had a feeling of guilt at abandoning the people and he wanted to prove to himself that he had not surrendered his interest in them. He wanted us as witnesses. When he came to Cascadu to visit his then ailing mother he dropped by and we went over to Sonnyboy's place to eat or at Mendoza's to have a drink. He invited me to play with his Jouvay band and I accepted. That brought us even closer.

He was concerned about Dorlene. After that day on the hill, she had returned to Cascadu and had thrown herself into the business of the steelband, arranging tunes, organizing trips, visits, exchanges with other bands – all of it done with a new compensatory zeal that drained her resources and left her exhausted, since increasingly the band depended on her for everything.

But it was a mission that consumed her. She had missed so much, she said to me. She had been so blind. She had wasted so much time. Now she wanted the music to speak not only to the people, she wanted it to speak for them. And she managed it. The music started to make a way into the hearts of Cascadu, so that when my aunt Magenta hear the band playing, she say, "Wait, this is me," because in the music she could hear the Shouters' hymns and she could hear the call of she spirit, and hear her own voice preaching and feel a calm sense of belonging to a big big world. And for a time she pack her basket, put on a straw hat and get into the bus with the people and she and Clephus went down to the savannah to push the pans across the stage.

Feeling herself on the right track, Dorlene left her job at the library. She had this idea about wanting Cascadu to be an example where panmen and women and people from their communities could employ themselves in the Carnival and pan industry, making the instruments, but also producing the beads, feathers, sequins and other accoutrements of Carnival. Claude didn't like it. You can't do this by yourself, he tell her. "Dorlene, these people will kill you, they will suck you dry. They have to take responsibility."

She took no warning. Her mother nagged her about her health, she wasn't eating properly, she wasn't really taking proper physical exercise. She had no man. She had fainted once or twice after musical sessions. She had fainted at Panorama, but she hushed it up, got to her feet and went again. She was getting thinner and thinner, her eyes puffy, tired. She was having problems organizing the business. She was running out of money. She was asking Claude to help her to convince her mother that they should mortgage the house.

Claude tried to bail her out, but as he said to me, "I don't want to encourage irresponsibility. I have my own problems."

Arlene's Zipper

Early in that Carnival season, Claude was about to leave with Arlene for the fête Orlando was having for friends of theirs who had returned to Trinidad for Carnival from the various continents of their exile, when in attempting to zip her up he ruined the zipper on the back of the dress she had put on to wear to the party.

To Claude, it was a catastrophe so perfect in its untimeliness, so subversive of the gesture of tenderness and regard he intended that he didn't put it down to accident, as it appeared to be, but recognized it as the familiar rebuke visited upon him every time he tried to extend himself beyond the confines of a habitual restraint that established his competence without challenging his imagination, or risking error.

Years ago, in the few football games that he played for the Agriculture Department, whenever he played a restrained game, it was OK. But he wanted to make the plays only a skilled player could bring off with consistency. Nine out of ten times he failed, often comically, so that whenever he got the ball, a buzz went through the crowd in anticipation of the disaster to follow. Sometimes even when his efforts made perfect sense, once they failed to produce the result he intended, hoped for, he was the one given the blame. He was not really discouraged. He put it down to a culture that had every respect for gift, and pity, if not contempt, for effort that did not yield excellence. And on the occasions that he played, while he never mastered the skills, he never tired of trying to make those extravagant plays that he could visualize but that could only be achieved by a superior player.

Claude had taken this attitude of adventure along with his ineptitude into his relationship with Arlene. To her, in the beginning, his awkwardness seemed charming, and his attempts at extravagance – in dancing, in cooking, in romance – brought into her life the unexpected, even the alarming. But after many disasters, she began to watch him and to feel she must guard herself once he involved her in his adventures, for she discovered that the things he was trying were not only new to her, they were new to him. After she had twisted herself into so many contortions to accommodate his search for another superior position in lovemaking, or sought to overcome her reluctance for display so as to keep up with his extravagance on the dance floor, whenever she realized he was attempting anything out of the ordinary, she would caution, "Wait, Claude. Wait." Claude would feel stumped, his good intentions would appear to be mocking him and he would shrink and turn away, wounded that he was rebuffed, and sad that he couldn't involve her in his adventure.

And the reason she was not alerted as he got at her zipper was that she had, just that moment, looked away from the mirror and did not see him come up behind her.

Claude was ready. He was wearing a new Carnival shirt, a blue silk affair with huge red roses on the front and back, the fashion that year, white pants, white shoes, a white sailor hat with a fringe of blue swan's-down and the golden insignia of captain, shaved, his little goatee, scented, ready. He had marched into the bedroom with the great sense of hurry she accused him of employing whenever

253

you have anywhere to go that you want me to believe is so important that you have everybody around you on edge, and had met her sitting on the stool in front the dressing-table combing out her hair with a sense of leisure as if she did not know they were due at the party maybe an hour ago and (he had not told her this) that they were to pick up his cousin Sybil and her husband on the way. *Why you only now telling me that?* said her posture; and as if his presence did not move her, she went on combing her hair with the same deliberate and fluent ceremony, glancing up now and then to look at him reflected in the mirror, not taking him on, as a kind of taunting, almost as if I wasn't there, as if she was deliberately establishing that she was her own person and the time she was using was her own. Ordinarily Claude's impatience would have served to convince her that the great world teetering on the edge of a cliff would fall and disappear if they did not hurry, but this time he felt alerted to something in her that he hadn't quite sensed before, a self-possession, a resolve, a determination that conveyed to him that she did not care even if he got angry, this awareness making him pause, sensing danger, not worrying now that they would be late, concerned now with her. And he stood behind her, scenting her perfume, watching the skin of her back where the dress was open, the zip still undone. And it occurred to him all at once that they had been drifting apart, that he had allowed his concerns with his sister, with his job, the people, the country, to make him lessen the attention he should pay to her, and it came to him that he might be losing her, just an inkling, a thought, something triggered by the quality of calm with which she readied herself. They had left so many questions unresolved, so many issues they had not discussed, hard things. Now, instead of looking to her with exasperation, as the one to be blamed for their being late, instead of that, he felt a fear. He looked at her and he saw a person on her own, disconnected from him; and he looked again, looking for the woman he knew, and it came to him as a surprising truth that she was leaving him. And now that she was leaving him, as he now thought, believed, knew, something occurred to him that he had paid lip service to but now understood for the first time: that she was with him all the time.

She was with me all the time. All the time. And he had not listened to her. He did not know her. Did not know what she had to offer beyond what she gave. All this time this woman had loved him. She had left her family and friends for him, her world to love him. And what had he done with that love? What had he asked of her? Not anything, not enough. Not enough.

Their eyes met in the mirror, hers injured and resolved, almost as if she was looking to see if he had comprehended the change in her, and he knew that his analysis was correct, in that moment wondering who might the other man be, then realizing quickly, no, that was too easy a way out, if it was not a man then it was her thinking. What was this thinking that had entered her head? He saw what it was; and for the first time he had to admit to himself that he had given up the world they were to build together. What had he given her to follow?

Where was the new world now? Instead of feeling angry, he felt a sweep of compassion for her, for him, for them both, thoughts of the party receding. He watched her finish her hair, her makeup, select and put on her jewelry; and the only remaining thing he saw that she had to do was to fasten the zip at the back of her dress. He watched as she put both hands behind her back to zip herself up, he saw the ripple of muscles under her skin and felt in his own heart a melting at his remembrance of her body that took him back to the memory of their first embrace when her arms went over his shoulders and around his neck like you see in the movies, not as something natural to her but as something she had practiced, feeling flattered that she had sought to master this gesture for him, feeling it as a performance, but thinking of it as the potential of what she wanted to give to him, of her will, her surrender. He believed that she thought her self-assertion would challenge him, but he was calm.

He saw the back of her dress open and he moved with a studied tenderness, not wanting to give the insinuation that he was doing this because of time, time was not on his mind then, not even caressing her back as he wanted to, sensing that that wouldn't do, that it would be a kind of trespass that was inappropriate at that time.

"You ready?" he asked softly, not really to hurry her but for want of something else to say, feeling himself on the edge of a knife, on the edge of a cliff, on the edge of a loss.

She watched him in the mirror. She didn't give an answer. That slowed him down; it challenged him to respond in a hurt way, as to a rebuff; but instead he rose to the occasion and softly, softly, and he felt it, this affection for her, this idea of affection, this idea of his contrition, he went behind her back and softly put one hand on a shoulder, she allowing him patiently, *Let me see what you go do now* must have been the thought in her mind, and with the other he grasped the zip with the intention of doing it up, casually, all of it, affectionately even, forgotten all his urgency.

The zip slipped out of the groove. He did not move. He remained behind her looking at the zip, his hands, her back, the dress, then trying without success to get the zip back on track.

"You spoil the zip, Claude."

He heard it not as a question but as an explosion, a statement of fact, exhausted, gentle and damning, as her body sagged with a sigh.

"You spoil it," as a statement waiting to be affirmed. As if it was something she could have forecast, not because she could have blamed it on his carelessness or hurry, but because it was something he had no control over, something that had to happen, that happened to express, quite apart from his intentions of the moment, his true relationship to her, as a sign, an event in its own right, for them to witness together the blight that had ensnared their relationship.

"You spoil it?"

Not even considering that the fault might have been in the zip, not even blaming him, saying, "The zip was good all the time. It was good all the time," as she breathed out the breath, dismissing him, leaving him in his world that she had escaped from, as if she was not simply uninterested in his world but had, on her own and unknown to him, found another world, her own world in which he not only did not figure but into which she had no wish to invite him. But he was not going there, not now.

He had said to her, "Do you have another dress you could wear?"

She looked at him, knowing he was expressing the exaggerated sense of guilt he was wont to display by accepting blame for being in the wrong even when he was uncertain that the error really was his. He was sorry, he said. He didn't know how this thing had come to happen. Did she have another dress that she could wear?

"Do you have another dress that you could wear?"

She looked at him.

She looked at me.

And he watched her first remove her necklace, carefully, take the clips out of her hair, then victoriously peel the dress off her body. Not a word. Then he himself went to the wardrobe and selected a dress that he liked.

He asked, "What about this one?"

Seeing what he thought was her disapproval, he selected another:

"Or this?"

Then he found one he thought that she liked:

"This one. What about this one? You always liked this one."

She looked at him.

I looked at him.

She looked at me.

"No." (She had bought a dress for the occasion and it had been ruined. And yes, she wasn't going anywhere.) "You could go."

"You don't like this?" He heard himself like a child.

Now she let out her hair.

"You go."

And before he could gain the kind of control that he had utilized just a while before, he found himself on his way out the door too late, because he did not mean to go without her. He did not mean it. *I did not mean to leave without her. I did not mean it.* But he was gone. Sybil and her husband were waiting on him.

And, later, at the party, without her of course, for he had left her sitting before her mirror at the dressing table, after the dancing and the drinking, thinking how he really missed her and then thinking that maybe he had been too hasty to leave so abruptly, he began to consider returning to get her. The distance came to his mind, her preparedness, her state of mind, would she be ready, and would she still want to come? He argued with himself, and then he got into one conversation, then another and all at once he found himself listening to his friends from long ago, relatives who had not seen him for years, people reminding him of the same things again, of the strides he had made in his career, the make of his car, the importance of his new job, bad-talking the government, remembering again how odd he was as a child, how lonely and stubborn, remembering him in St. Mary's with the king sailor walk and the muff in his hair and the badjohn attitude that made fellars want to fight him. Everyone had his own recollection, some of it true, that is to say, that he could recollect as really happening, others, stories, just things they made up, all of it said in jest, to give them a sense of superiority as the way of dealing with him. He overheard himself talking to them of the coconuts dying of red ring disease, of the witches' broom in the cocoa and the die-back of the pawpaws, of the problems, the stupidity, the loss, and he triumphant through it all as if he were a spectator, as if he wasn't there, and all of them as if they were not hearing what he was saying, complimenting him on how well the country was developing, with a sense of regret for being elsewhere, as if they had miscalculated, that there had really been a place for them here in the island that they had left for Canada, Britain, the USA, consoling him with the observation that at least he was still here, so he didn't have the heart to tell them about the depth of his disappointment with the people, with his Jouvay band. He didn't want to blunt his triumph entirely, so he find a way to tell them as if is a joke in which he remained triumphant, of himself, the man carrying the mud and waiting for the original members of the band. And it came off, the joke, everybody laughing, their teeth showing, their stomachs pulled in, as if they knew their faces would be in the papers next day.

When Claude returned from the Carnival fête he found Arlene curled up on the sofa watching television. He tried to make conversation with her, talking lamely, as if it was a lie he was telling, of who was there, of how she was missed, of who had asked for her. Merrit was there. Merrit. He had met her with Merrit. And she listened with a judgmental and disinterested silence, as if to express interest was to provide him with a relief that she was not prepared to grant.

That night when they went to bed, she took her side and drew her body away out of his reach so that she wouldn't have to touch him, and if he wanted to touch her he would have to make a deliberate move. He lay in bed debating with himself whether to lean over and touch her, or bring his body close to hers, but he remained on his own side and drew further away from her, lying on almost the very edge of the bed, hoping that by establishing such an absurd distance she would see the gulf between them. She did not move. He knew she wasn't sleeping. She did not exaggerate the distance, she did not draw closer, she slept with a sense of innocence as though she had completed the most absolutely satisfying day. He knew she was waiting for him to move closer to her. But he had established too great a distance between them. And he noticed, with some alarm, that the distance could not now be crossed casually. How to cross that distance now? He had crossed that distance many times before, out of understanding, out of love, out of appreciating that she had come with him, alone, abandoned by her family for marrying him. But it did not mean that because she had stood up to them in respect of her choice of him everything would be perfect. It did not follow that they, he and she, would not have their own challenges. He did not want to believe that she used this being alone, this being abandoned by her family as a lever to manipulate him. And although it was not something he was responsible for, he felt that he had to take responsibility. She did not have the option of other brides to threaten him with, *I going back home, I going home by my family.* Her family offered her no home. If she had to seek a haven it would be on her own. That was the horrible choice they gave to her. And for that she resented him at the same time she needed him. Because they had abandoned her, all she had was he and that was why she expected him to be perfect. It was too much. He had no room. That was his jail, the jail of perfection and it was because of this that, in order to be himself, that he strayed from that perfection. And what of the world? What of the new world of which they had dreamed? He began to see that to arrive at it they had to struggle with each other.

He thought to yield, as he had done at times before, to cross the distance and hug her and say "I'm sorry about the dress" and confess to his hurt over her remark. But he felt that her response had punished him enough already. Claude in his mind became the heroic and committed victim who had a right to his hurt. Suddenly, in that mode, outraged, he said, *Fuck that! Sorry for what?* He said it aloud in his mind. But he acted as if he had said it aloud in reality. In the same flow of vexation, as if he believed he had spoken, he got out of bed, went outside into the living room and turned the TV on.

He lay on the couch in front the TV.

What had they done with the love, with the dreams with which they begun? What had they learned from each other? What had they shared? He had exposed her to his family but her family was shut away from him, the sharing they had expected to take place, why did it not happen? He drifted off to sleep with these questions on his mind.

Sometime later he awoke, realizing that he had dozed off, and he returned to bed. She had not moved a millimeter. He lay for a while on his side of the bed, then he rolled close to her and put an arm around her, hoping that it was not too late to begin to deal with this woman, this love.

He was still awake when the telephone rang with the news that his sister was in hospital. She had collapsed after playing with her steelband at Panorama. As he dressed to go to see her, it occurred to him that once again something had come up to save him (save?) from having to engage things between him and Arlene.

His sister's collapse did not so much surprise him as it angered him. Dorlene had driven herself to the point of a breakdown. And the people? They had allowed her to run her blood to water to take up a burden that was really theirs, her house and money used to provide for the Brothers and Sisters who had no one and nowhere. They had allowed her to take on a burden greater than she could bear.

262

Claude couldn't indulge his anger; a more pressing concern had arisen. When he reached the hospital, it was to be told that Dorlene was dead.

The steelband people gathered around him, anxious, frantic. He did not bother with them. He had reached his end. Finally he knew what he would do. Dorlene would be honored with the grandest funeral ever seen in Cascadu; and he would surrender. He would beg his wife to go away with him for them to start. Again.

Funeral

It was a splendid funeral, with schoolchildren lining the streets, the church overflowing with people. Claude's family had come in from every part of the globe: Abigail from England, Ebenezer from Liberia, Leon had come from his liquor store in Brooklyn, the twins Dido and Aneas from Washington, DC, his brother-in-law Alpheus Brown, the welterweight boxer, from Miami, Ann Marie from Tacoma, Washington. The clergy was represented by bishops of every denomination, the Shouters church with its three archbishops, the Orisha faith with three Babalawos, the Hindu swami. From politics, the leader of the Opposition and his three deputy leaders, and three of the five deputy leaders of the National Party, each one same height, same puffed-out chest, so that despite their difference in racial stock they looked like triplets.

The only person of real consequence absent was the Prime Minister, who was locked in his residence writing the letter of resignation he had begun in 1970, after that period of dreams and vitality, when revolution appeared possible and he had worked it all out in his mind, how the people would take over and there would be full and unqualified democracy and a West Indian nation from Cuba to Guyana with a West Indian university, and he would be the one to blend together the different strands of what was his nation, those who had resisted the colonial structure by confronting it, those who had tried to equip themselves for life (not without their own challenges) by following the path it had set out for them, those who had been beneficiaries of its structure of privilege. He worked on his speeches through the Carnival (while the population was fêting), preparing for the debates in the Public Library, the all-night discussions, arguing with activists and politicos from the Left and the Right, confronting Regionalists and African and Indian nationalists, Chinese ideologues and the French Creoles, as he came to grips with the constituencies of people that he needed to understand – as he faced the challenge of blending the discipline derived from the order imposed by the plantation, the creativity that came out of resistance and the anarchy of individual rebellion, and at the end still come up with one nation.

He had written it to lay blame that had been heaped on him at the door of colonial history, its injustice, prejudice and waste that left Blackpeople so impatient for an equal place, that less than six years after he take power (power?) he would find the army in mutiny, the youth, unemployed and trade unions demonstrating on the streets, productivity down, business people packing up to leave, and a set of Black Power drums vibrating in his head. His prophetess had not yet entered his life. Papa Neeza, the great obeah-man whose advice had guided his decisions, was sick in bed. But he couldn't do it. He couldn't allow the country to start its Independence with the military in charge and rabble rousers at the helm. No, sir. No way, Jose. He call a state of emergency. He get the police and the loyal part of the army to do their duty. He put the dissidents in detention on Nelson Island. He make sure they get a fair trial. And he wasn't going to be no frightened dictator either. To show his self-confidence and because he understood the matter,

265

he released them into the society, and so as not to lose the radical presence, if not the thinking, he attempted to bring into the fold of the Nationalist Party some of the more sober-minded of them, but they too had replaced thought with ambition, were now giddy with the sound of their slogans. They had grown accustomed to being the headlines. So they would remain parading their martyrdom, soaking up the applause as to who was the brightest, the most revolutionary, as if they didn't know whose backyard they were in, until the massacre of the government of Grenada torpedoed the ambitions of the more left-leaning of them, and left those who described themselves as cultural activists trying to convince Blackpeople that their salvation lay in making the journey back to who they were before the Middle Passage.

And if, as he wrote in the aborted letter of resignation: '... if I had not transformed the country to everybody's satisfaction it was because I resisted ruling with an iron hand, but allowed my people enough space, enough liberty so that from their own error they would come to understand that they needed to establish boundaries for themselves, that they could not be corralled by law alone ...." Before the people could learn these lessons from themselves, the world had taken another turn, and he wake up to find the country bamboozled into accepting what they called multiculturalism, that divided up the country into ethnicities and classes, with all the suspicions about each other planted in colonialism in full bloom, everyone with their own culture, their own music, their own worship, with less and less to share, nobody responsible to nobody else. All the work he had done to produce a narrative that included everybody as equal victims of a system unraveled. Instead of excess being used to correct itself, excess established as a way of life, on the roads, in business, in the very government: the laws applied to the meekest and the poorest. Everybody waiting for him to disappear, for his party to mash up like everything else Blackpeople put their hands on, all reduced to frivolity, corruption, emptied of their resolve and spirit. And in his ears, the voices of the cynics: *is Independence you want, take independence. See if you could manage these people with charisma, with talk, let's see you, as you say, put full and unqualified democracy to work*, and all he was left with were the people who had made their personal investment in him, the little people, folk from the underclass, the jamettes, the Shouters, the Shango; people from the steelbands, calypsonians, ole mas Carnival characters, Best Village people, who, sad to say, were the least politically conscious. He had to give them political education. He had to take charge of things, put everything in his own hands safe from corruption, select the senators, decide on the parliamentarians, choose the aldermen, the delegates to the party's convention, run the general council, head the committees, identify who should be given national awards, who should be given scholarships, sift through the contractors. But was he alone. When he open his eyes, it was to find the nationalist movement tottering under accusations of corruption, its supporters still waiting for salvation, colonialism christened with a new name: Globalization. In that election, he get lick-up bad bad, his party reduced to three seats in a Parliament of thirty-six.

After twenty years he find himself alone. The militants, the ideologues, the intellectuals and the trade unionists had silenced themselves.

And he sit down to write a letter of resignation, this time to the party, according to the convention in the British

Parliament. And he start it, yes, he begin it, in his own hand, *To my faithful party members, it is with great sadness that I speak to you tonight. After reviewing the problems that beset the nation I think it incumbent on me to return to private life and take no further part in political activity. I go knowing I leave the party in the capable hands of … of … of … of who? Who?*

The pen freeze in his hand. The pen didn't want to write. Then he burst out a big laugh. What madness was this? Who he going to leave it to? How many years it take Britain to come up with their holy conventions? How many kings get killed, how many priests murdered? In America how many Native Indians get slaughtered as cowboys win the West, how many Blackpeople get lynched before they settle down – and not even to convention, to law? Well, he needed time too. And he tear up the blasted letter and he turn his attention to winning the next election.

He set about making alliances with people who had been on the sideline of politics. Those who was out of power he bring them back in, those who was in, he throw them out, those with new money he let them know it would be worth their while to give him their support. He appeal to those who was fed up with their role as perpetual opposition. He leave academics out. Too much damn trouble. He bring in secretaries from the civil service, managers from the world of free enterprise. But these alliances didn't come without a price. Yes, if wealth had to trickle down, it had to stand on some foundation, his new advisers tell him. So, in for a penny, in for a pound, he couldn't go in two directions at the same time. He had to start to forget the past. He had to stop what they called his anticolonial rhetoric that made important people uneasy. He had to cull from his vocabulary divisive words like *oppression* and *resistance* and *injustice* and *reparation* and *poverty.* He had to accept the fiction that every ethnic and religious group in the country had started off with equal opportunity. He had to agree that privilege was earned and poverty deserved, that people had chosen the state in which they found themselves ... how you make your bed, et cetera, et cetera ... Yes, all that he had to do to come up with his victorious new all-inclusive nationalism.

But things didn't turn out how they were supposed to. After four and a half years the miracle of prosperity glimpsed on the horizon by his spiritual adviser had not turned up. He had to play for time, slow down the game, put out white papers on local government, set up commissions on race relations, send ministers on economic missions to Norway and Singapore, invite the Prime Ministers of the region to talks on Regional Integration.

But time run out on him, and he wake up one morning to find trade unions ready to strike, the IMF in his backside, the Chamber of Commerce pressing him to privatize industries his government had acquired during the first escalation of oil prices (when money ran through the belly of the country like a dose of Epsom salts), the Opposition party complaining of discrimination, alienation, marginalization, his constituents in the East-West corridor questioning his commitment to their welfare, the sister island Tobago threatening secession from its union with Trinidad, his eyesight getting dim, one doctor telling him about the rise of his blood sugar, his dentist asking: *So what we going to do with this front tooth that's shaking?* His spies whispering in his ears that the party was angling to throw him out as leader, his adviser on policy reminding him that elections were constitutionally due in

269

six months; and the final straw, the dagger to his heart, the words of the handwritten letter left on his pillow that morning by Marlene Spicer, his mistress of ten years, *Let us end this thing. It was never enough for me. I don't want what you are offering, I deserve better*, that after he read it make him want to resign in truth.

Yes. He went into his study, poured himself a drink of brandy (to hell with his blood pressure), called his secretary and instructed her to advise his cabinet ministers that not one of them was to contact him by telephone or in writing unless the miracle of prosperity that his spiritual adviser last sighted on the horizon had entered the Port of Spain harbor – or those idiots in Tobago hoisted their own flag.

For days he sit down before the paper, searching for words for this resignation, but the words wouldn't come. He move to his living room, he try the veranda, he lie down on his bed. Everywhere he sit was uncomfortable. He put a desk on the balcony and sat there at his computer but instead of writing he found himself looking out at the sea, this time with a pair of binoculars, trying to locate the miracle of prosperity that his spiritual adviser had assured him was on its way to land. And is there the news of the miracle would find him. But, that is for later.

Sweetie-Mary at the
Funeral Service

At the funeral, Sweetie-Mary left a multitude of mourners outside the church where the Picoplat Steel Orchestra was playing hymns in bolero tempo on the walkway beside the flower garden, and carrying the muted steeldrum rhythm in her body, she entered the hot crowded church and made her way up the center aisle to the front row where her nieces and sisters had already taken places beside the family of the deceased, not out of any forwardness, but in their own right as dignitaries, since over the last seven years three of her nieces had represented the district as Carnival queens and had been accorded the status nearly that of cabinet ministers, granted the privilege to sit in the front row at any public function, to be entertained in the VIP lounge and to be photographed by the press.

For what was to ensue, providentially, that front-row seat placed Sweetie-Mary in direct line with the coffin, and she could see a bit of Dorlene's upper body and all of her face.

Mr. Godwin Constantine, proprietor of Cascadu's recreation club and Chairman of the Village Council, dyed hair, lisped speech, fatigued face, was reaching the end of a eulogy in which he traced Dorlene's life from the shelter of a stable home where she mastered the piano, played the steelpan, conduct the church choir and give support to the Cascadu steelband that moved it from a pan-round-the-neck band with fifteen players to a conventional steel orchestra with seventy-five players. Sweetie-Mary listened with sadness as he talked about Dorlene's earnestness, her disappointment in love, her struggles with the band, the abuse of her goodwill, the more she give the more they want from her, when out of nowhere, startlingly, a single tenor pan began to play, the notes drawing to themselves the strings of a new thrilling silence that made the church heave out a breath and elbow for itself a grander space. In that space and silence the choir began to sing and Sister Cynthia Salandy, a nun now, began to weep, deep heartfelt sorrowful tears for the Dorlene she knew when together as young women they entertained the sick in hospitals and the children in orphanages. Sweetie-Mary listened to her weep for that Dorlene. Just so Miss Ella's high-ringing voice cry out in song:

Zion, Zion, mi lord
Zion Hill is a shining glory

And down, out of the belly of the congregation came Brother Ken's answering plaintive wail:

Zion, Zion, mi Lord
When the power come down from glory
Zion Hill is a shining glory

This was for the Dorlene Sweetie-Mary had come to know, the Dorlene who after she came back from visiting Clayton went into the panyard to play music that when Sweetie-Mary hear it, she say, *This music is me*; because in it she could see the Shango dances, the hefty women's rhythmic bumping. She could feel the heat of the fire crackling in the coalpot, the oil frying the red fish, the tawa roasting the roti, the raindrops and the chickens with their fluffed feathers sheltering the rain, she could hear the love call of

Sonnyboy's whistling, she could see Franklyn batting, she could hear the roadside preacher ringing the bell outside the market and the young girls ambling down the road with short dresses showing their lean thighs. And she join the people who take the bus and go down to the savannah to push the pans across the stage there until things change and it became a hassle for them to go with the band on the stage. Because now they had police to keep supporters of the band off the stage, and as much as she love the music, she say, You see me I too precious for this business. And for Carnival now she stay home and look at it on TV, but it wasn't the same thing. Poor Dorlene. Without the people there the music begin to change, to lose its spirit, the dancing going out of it. Dorlene begin to grieve. You could hear it in the music, the lament, the confusion. Dorlene keep getting thinner and thinner and paler and paler as she try to bring back the spirit to the music.

Zion, Zion, mi lord
Zion Hill is a shining glory

Sweetie-Mary felt tears fill her throat, her body breaking and her head set on fire; and feeling that she was about to go into the spirit, she squeezed her eyes shut, tried to control her breathing and commanded her mind to focus on something happy. She found herself thinking of herself and Sonnyboy, before he created the distance between himself and those things that used to make him and her alive and happy, the early years before he distanced himself from Carnival and tried to find his more perfect world in Africa, imposing on her a lifestyle that make her sisters ask her if she join the nunnery. Yes, she was thinking of that time before this time, when he took her with him into that world of the island: the Carnival that had so much confusion and beauty, with the old mas and the pretty mas; the Camboulay and Mardi Gras; a stage for the haves and the haves not, for the Blackpeople and the Whitepeople, for the rich and the poor, for the imitative and the creative, for the Glories of Greece and Sailors Ashore, for the Jab Molassie and the Ice Follies. For brass bands and steelband, and she see this was the place, this was the place, this bacchanal space where it had everything that he fight against and was fighting for. This world and vision that she couldn't let him surrender; because it was against the background of this world that they really see each other, when his eyes on her was a hymn of praise and the anointing of a blessing, and his fingers softly grasped her hair and they surrendered themselves to long patient kisses that make time disappear and their love was a continent to explore and they loved everything about each other, their skin, their scent, the very feel of their blackness. And they went out together to a fête or to a show dressed in the same colors, black and black or beige and beige, and after the fête they lie down together and he caressed her with his scandalous hands that healed her wounds and sent her crazy. And right there in thinking, she feel those hands on her body and the scrape of the hairs on his chin under her neck, going down her breasts, meandering over her body, and she realize *Oh, God, I in a church!*

Frightened by the sin of her thoughts and desperate to fix her mind on something less disturbing, she was about to turn her attention to the coffin when she feel a tug on her hand from her sister Mercury who tell her that her son had just said that he had seen Dorlene's eyelid flutter. She was about to dismiss it when in looking at the coffin she sighted the cloud on the glass pane over the face in the coffin and quickly realized that the cloud could only indicate that there was hot air that would only have gathered there if someone was breathing in the coffin.

Excited by the possibility that Miss Dorlene might be alive, she and her sisters looked around the church frantically for someone in authority to tell. The person they decided to reach was Claude, Dorlene's brother, who was sitting on the other side of the church. Not wanting to cause a commotion she whispered her observation to the person next to her who whispered to the person next to her until by such relay the message reached across the pews to the ear of Claude Cruickshank, "Look at the cloud on the glass of the coffin. Miss Dorlene breathing. I think she is alive." His response was to shake his head and open his eyes like he think she and her sisters crazy. Until she take it upon herself to squeeze past people and go herself to him in the pew where he was sitting to whisper to him what they had seen, for him to express his disbelief: "Look, darling, I hear you. I hear what you say, but Doctor Bissessar has pronounced her dead. The District Medical Officer has signed the death certificate. There is nothing I can do."

She couldn't believe it. Right there she start to bawl. Her sisters joined in and they became so loud and appeared so afflicted with grief that they had to be led outside the church, where they let it be known that Dorlene was in her coffin breathing.

In a little while the news swept like a fire through Cascadu, reaching people on the roadside waiting for the funeral to pass, so that one man, Dalton Bobb, Big Dee, who had lived a quiet and apologetic life attending church and working a piece of land with great diligence, hardly

275

saying a word to his wife, repenting for the time fourteen years before when he gambled away the money he got from selling twenty-seven bags of corn one day, and to pay off this debt had undertaken to cook and wash and attend church with her and be at her beck and call, as his relatives would complain, like a little puppydog: this man, seeing the occasion to be a hero and so break out of his humble prison, hearing the news that Dorlene was alive in her coffin, went into his house and come back out with an axe on his shoulder and a cutlass strapped to his waist and set off for the church with the intention of freeing Dorlene from her imprisoning coffin.

Seeing which, people, who a moment before had seemed unable to make up their mind what to do, grabbed up sticks and stones and set out behind him, their march picking up people on the way; so that by the time they reached the recreation ground they had grown into such a noisy and purposeful procession that spectators, watching the football match in which the local team Penetrators was surprisingly ahead of Cross Winds 2–1 for the first time in three years of contests, believing that some disaster had hit the town, ran out from the pavilion into the street. Aji, the Penetrators goalkeeper, seeing people leaving the pavilion, looked up the hill to see what was going on and in his moment of inattention, Hing Wang put in one for Cross Winds just as Manding, the referee, blow the whistle to call off the match. All the players run up the hill, to the street and join the band which was on its way to the church. By the time the band reached the police station, it had maybe sixty people in it.

Constable Stephen Aguillera and Ramona

In the police station on top the hill overlooking Main Street, Constable Stephen Aguillera, buttoning up the last few buttons of his tunic in preparation to taking up duty at the funeral, heard the hubbub in the street below. He went to the door of the station, looked past the palmiste trees and see this multitude led by a man with a cutlass in one hand and an ax on his shoulder.

For twenty-five of his twenty-seven years in the police force, Constable Aguillera had pursued his resolve not to make an arrest.

In the beginning he just turned his back on the misdemeanors that people committed, but afterward, he began to think of people, why did they break the law, how did they get to be who they were, what examples of fair play and justice did the higher-ups set? What choices did they think they had? He saw past the little schemes they tried to get over one on the other, the small transgressions that ended in grief, the stupidity, the jackassness, the pride, the shame, and he found himself feeling toward them as much compassion as outrage. The exercise of what the villagers saw as his leniency made him the favorite police officer in the district, *a sweetbread,* according to my aunt Magenta, and in their parties, the people of the town always had a place for him. He was asked to speak to errant children, to stand as godfather to numerous children of women and men he had spared from arrest. A number of women had their eyes on him, and although he was more than willing to engage in the occasional encounter, he held himself back and didn't encourage them beyond a certain point because he felt settled as a bachelor, the only person with a chance to make him change his mind Ramona Fortune who he expected one day to turn up. So much so that he had developed the habit whenever he went to cricket in the Queen's Park Oval or at any event where there were plenty people of always looking around, thinking that by some chance he would see her. He aged, not getting gray, getting bald, taking fewer drinks, speaking his mind in a more philosophical and humorous way, saddened by the losses of the West Indies cricket team but always hopeful, on the lookout for a new captain, a fresh talent, better management; and even when his hopes were not fulfilled he would feel the sting of disappointment that made him glad it had something in his life that could make him feel.

One day, in the effort to settle a dispute between two of the villagers, he went to the community center where preparations were taking place for a Best Village show. Asked his opinion, he immediately began to critique the show. Impressed by his insights, the villagers asked him to join them. That year he helped them to reorganize themselves and to put aside old village grievances. The following year he wrote and directed a skit, entitled *Today For You, Tomorrow For Me,* for which he himself composed the songs. The success of this skit motivated him to turn his hand to writing calypsos, which he sang at the annual police calypso competition, using the soubriquet Lord Constable.

He was never in winner's row but he made people laugh.

Then, last year, at the annual Police Carnival Calypso competition, he placed a very close second with

Pain pain pain
I want to feel you again.
You gone gone gone
Let the memory of this love remain.

And "Don't Take My Coverlet":

I pay down on some furnitures
I want my place look nice
I had the intention to bring in a lady
To make me a wife
But I had some problems and run in arrears
The people come to repossess items I paying on for years
You could take my bed
But don't take my coverlet
Repossess the stove, the furniture, the fridge
The pillow where I rest my head
But please leave my coverlet.

His performance so impressed Assistant Police Commissioner Dowden, who was present and who had joined the police service at the same time he did, that he was prepared to intercede on his behalf to get him promotion that would enable him to retire with some measure of dignity and with the benefits accruing to at least a corporal. But ASPC Dowden felt he couldn't do that for a policeman who had not made an arrest in *how many years?* *Twenty-seven years.*

Despite the clear temptation to go out a corporal, Stephen Aguillera had his principles and it didn't feel right to him, out of convenience, to arrest a man (or a woman)

279

for an offense he had earlier overlooked in another; also, he felt that to start arresting people now would be too obviously self-serving and make him look like someone who had been simply a slacker. But this afternoon, as he buttoned himself up into neatness and strapped on his gun-belt in preparation for leaving the station, it occurred to him as he saw the noisy procession down the hill that a man with a cutlass in one hand and an ax on his shoulder, leading a mob of sixty people through the main street of the town, was a genuine candidate for arrest. Constable Aguillera put on his cap and without hurry, started down the steps. He followed the crowd and caught up with it in front the Catholic church, and was moving toward the armed man to question him. When he got to him, he saw it was Big Dee.

"What is this?" he asked. "Eh? Just so you going to start a riot, eh?"

It was then that he got the explanation for Big Dee's action from the crowd: Dorlene was alive and her brother wouldn't open her coffin.

"So you take the law into your own hands? You is the police here, or me?" he asked them. "Well, all-you better disperse before you force me to arrest somebody. And, Big Dee, you better give me that ax, and keep that cutlass in its case and go to the police station and wait there for me."

Constable Aguillera turned away to face the formidable sight of Sweetie-Mary and her sisters sweeping toward him. He stood where he was. He saw them speaking but he didn't hear anything because – and he couldn't have imagined it more perfectly – there, in her dress of mourning, looking up at him was this woman with the gentlest smile that came out of her throat, the full lips across her face, the huge eyes with their hint of sadness and pity, as if she was fighting hard not to cry.

"Ramona? Ramona Fortune?"

And yes, there before him was the Ramona Fortune of nearly twenty-seven years ago. Following on his happiness to see her, he felt an overwhelmingly tender desire to weep. Because it all came back, the days of coming out on the gallery of the police station to watch her walk to the taxi stand to get a taxi to go to school, and to be there when she returned, no words between them except those spoken by their eyes, until he take it upon himself to write her a letter expressing his feelings and give it to a girlfriend of hers to give to her and waited for her reply, only to discover that the friend (her name was Imelda) had out of mischief or naiveté handed the letter to her in plain view of her mother. She had showed her mother the letter and at the mother's request read it aloud before the family, who were listening and laughing. She herself laughing and crying (*what else could I do?*) but secretly triumphant that his words had such feeling and intelligence. It must have been that feeling and intelligence that indicated to the mother a potential for danger. They sent her to stay at a relative outside the district. He did not see her and heard nothing about her until Imelda the Traitor come and tell him that Ramona pass the examination and as reward her parents had agreed to let her play mas in a Carnival band and she would be leaving on Ash Wednesday for England to study. It was the only opportunity he would have to be with her before she left. And that was how he had come to lock up the station and go to look for her in the band. He had found the band and then had found her surrounded in the band by a phalanx of relatives who would never

281

leave her side. He followed her for most of the day without being able even to put his hand around her waist. Band members offered him drink, he bought drink, he drank, but he couldn't touch her. And he awoke to find himself sitting on the pavement in the middle of the afternoon with the band nowhere in sight. The rest of the day he spent looking all through Port of Spain. They had disappeared. He never did see her. As if that was not penalty enough, he was found guilty of dereliction of duty and as punishment, had been stationed in this remote district of Cascadu.

Now she was here. Constable Aguillera was so off-balanced that he did not ask anything. Almost as an act of defense, he reached into his pocket for his notebook, because by then it had penetrated that they were complaining that Dorlene was alive in her coffin.

"Tell me," he said to Sweetie-Mary, who appeared to be the spokeswoman, "how you get this information?"

He checked his pencil to see if the point was writing.

"Yes. You can begin."

She tell him how she had gone to the church, the observation by her nephew, the insistence of her sisters, their discovery of the cloud on the glass of the coffin, their concern, their appeals to Claude, his dismissal of them.

"And you think," Constable Aguillera asked her, "you think it was deliberate, that he deliberately chose not to examine the coffin to see if his sister was alive?"

"I don't know. Look him there. You could ask him that yourself."

She pointed to Claude, who was one of the pallbearers who had brought the coffin out of the church and had rested it down for a moment, before they took it up and carried it through the town, to the cemetery.

"He?"

"Yes, he self."

"But that is the brother of the deceased. What could his motive be?"

"You will have to ask him. Is Cain that kill Abel."

I walked over to him: "Claude Cruickshank?"

"Yes."

"You are responsible for this funeral?"

"Well, yes."

"Can I see the death certificate?"

"Yes." But even as he is putting his hand in his pocket to get it, I realize there is a problem. "I don't seem to have it," he tell me. "I was sure there was one signed by the District Medical Officer and issued to me."

"So how can we be certain that she is dead?"

"You have to take my word for it."

"With respect, you are not a medical doctor. If you don't have a death certificate to prove her death officially, you can't proceed with this burial."

"Look, Sir, Doctor Bissessar has pronounced her dead. The District Medical Officer has issued a death certificate ..."

"But you don't have it."

"No. I don't have it on me."

"Well, what are we to do? I can't allow you to proceed without a death certificate."

"Sir, people have come here from all corners of the island. We have the Minister of Festivals, Members of Parliament, people from the clergy, the arts. You don't believe these people know my sister is dead?"

"And what about the law? We have people here claiming she is alive."

"Sir, the District Medical Officer has issued a death certificate."

"What you want to do? Open the coffin here to see if she is alive? I am not a doctor."

"Nor am I."

And that is when the idea of arresting him and stopping the funeral occurred to me. I was about to resign. I needed to arrest someone. Who better than a big shot? And what better charge than one nobody had ever been arrested on? Burying someone without a death certificate.

"The woman is my sister, as you well know."

Cain killed Mabel, I thought. However, this was no time to joke. My mind was a blur. Ramona Fortune was there beside me. I was thinking of her ... *I glad you come back ...* of all the times I had placed myself on the front gallery of the police station to watch her go to school and to watch her return, remembering the time I had danced with her at the harvest in the school, not caring really about dancing, just so glad to hold her hands, touch her waist, the both of us not so much dancing as happy to be so close, holding each other.

Remembering her hands trembling and a tremor in her body as he held her, remembering the polkadot dress she was wearing and her hair pulled back and divided in two with two plaits at the back of her head and her eyes hardly daring to look into his because her mother and father were watching; remembering too the time by the river when she was there with her sisters and although the water was muddy he dived in, just to have something to do, and grazed his chest on a stone and came out like if it was nothing and showed it to her and she touched his chest with her fingers and he was healed.

The things we would have done together (he was thinking as if he was speaking to her) . . .

The things . . . He could hear her thinking, dreaming, her thoughts the same as his: *The Fisherman fête in Grand Rivere, the Calypso show in Skinner Park in Sando, the Jouvay mornings in Port of Spain, holding you in Desperadoes steelband going down Frederick Street . . . The things I wanted to show you . . . The beautiful funny things, the things to see through your eyes to share with you, to laugh with you.*

"But you didn't fight for me," she said.

"You went away."

"You let me go."

"If I did only know."

"I was still in the world."

"I didn't hear from you. I had to believe that you didn't want to see me, that that was how you wanted it, that somehow that would be better."

"That was how I had to want it. I didn't see you. I didn't hear from you. You didn't fight."

"My life would have been quite different."

"And mine as well."

"One slip and your life change forever."

"You have children?"

"Five. Three girls and two boys."

"You was busy."

"But we should be grateful. We should be glad. In life this thing doesn't really happen, you know. People don't get a chance to start again, to go back again to find the one they love again. When things go they gone – forever."

"And isn't that so now?"

"All those things I missed showing you. All those things I didn't see because you wasn't there to see them with."

285

"You didn't ask me if I married."

"I don't want to know."

"I didn't expect to find you here."

He saw that she had seen from the absence of stripes on his sleeves that he was still at the same rank she had left him. "You know, since I in Cascadu I have never made an arrest. I never arrest anybody."

"I'm sure you're a good policeman."

And then he knew that he wouldn't do it. He couldn't make up in one day what it had taken a lifetime to accomplish. He couldn't arrest this man. Let the promotion go. He could face himself as a man of principle, of values, of resolve. It was then he finally made up his mind. Yes. He would go out as a constable. As a big man. Maybe that would be some kind of record.

With a new calm, he heard himself talking: "So what we going to do?"

"You is the boss," Claude said.

Constable Aguillera let that pass.

By the time he reached the cemetery he was so moved by her presence, so deep into remembering and imagining, so filled with the sadness and beauty of life that he felt his own sadness over loss, over death and felt that he had been too hard on Claude, requesting the death certificate. And Dorlene would have been buried as a matter of course but for the bawling of Brian Algood, Sweetie-Mary's second sister's youngest son, a child of seven who maintained that he had seen her eyelids flutter, so that when it came time for the gravediggers to ease the coffin into the grave the little boy put on such a bawling that his father who was assisting the gravedigger threatened the boy with a flogging if he did not shut up. The boy bawled even more and it was only when the man who everyone called Dollar, because all his conversations included talk of money, began to take off his belt to menace the boy with the promised flogging that Constable Aguillera was given the opportunity to get into the story in a way that satisfied everybody.

"OK." For by then all eyes were on this boy and many voices were saying, "Well, at least you could look in the coffin just to show him, just to assure him."

Constable Aguillera was patient, almost casual:

"Dollar, why you don't just go and open the coffin and make sure the woman alive, eh? Why you don't do it?"

Dollar had turned not to Constable Aguillera but to the boy, who was still bawling. "OK," he said. "OK. I going to go myself down inside the grave and open the coffin and you better pray to God she is alive. Because if she is not alive, today your backside is mine."

With men at the graveside holding the rope, Dollar let himself down onto the coffin. After a while, he signaled for them to pull up the rope. When he came up he directed them to continue pulling because he had attached the rope to the handles of the coffin, and he joined those pulling, until they heaved the coffin out of the grave.

And yes, it was true, there sitting up in the open boat of the coffin was Dorlene Cruickshank, white as a sheet and alive.

Resurrection

If you see confusion. People fainting left and right, people running away from the cemetery, some falling to their knees to pray, others, doubting that Dorlene was really flesh and blood, pushing forward to pinch her to see if she was real, others, wanting to hug her, until Evrol Chance, the only one of the government ministers who had neither fainted nor run off at sight of the living Dorlene, pushed his way to her side, Constable Aguillera clearing the way for him, saying in the voice of authority, "Let the boss pass. Let the Minister through."

As if he had been preparing for this occasion all along, Evrol take off his jacket and put it around her. He signaled for the crowd around her to open up and give her fresh air and with one knee on the ground he calmly took her hands into his own and began rubbing them to increase the circulation of the blood until a tap on the shoulder made him turn and see from the stethoscope around her neck that it was the medical doctor, Melvina Thompson. The doctor signaled for help and some men came forward. Evrol was going to assist but the men waved him away and lifted Dorlene and carried her out of the cemetery to the car that would take her to the hospital. The crowd had not moved. Evrol knew he had to speak.

And he spoke, in the up-tempo declamatory style of the Black Power days, bringing back to me the noises of those days, the sparkle of words dancing in the sunshine, the drumming lifting us up, both of us walking in front the single car, the Volkswagen with the flags on it and the loudspeaker. The sun hot, the day bright. Crop time, with the pouis yellow and the flamboyant red and our voices over the loudspeaker talking, telling the people, *This is a march for you, this is a march for peace and justice.* And people looking at us as if we gone mad, others with astonishment that we so brave that we had the courage to march for the human rights that Blackpeople had forgotten we had a right to, for the dignity that we had refused to forfeit with Independence. We came upon a Blackwoman who had rice paddy drying in the sun, who when she see us coming hurried and gathered up her rice, and was about to run.

"No, Mother," Evrol tell her. Because she was not quick enough to escape us entirely, "We are not here to harm you but to liberate you."

Liberate you ... Liberate you, the words echoing in the vault of those years. And now at the funeral, he was speaking all these years after: "It is your love and your faith that have brought Dorlene back to the land of the living. Because even when she was in the coffin you refused to let her lie there until you had satisfied yourself that she was not alive."

When he was finished talking, he went to my aunt Magenta and stood before her, almost hesitant, wanting to greet her, to hug her perhaps. But, unsure of his welcome, he stretched out a hand for her to shake.

His hand was before her. He could see her grief. He could see her looking at him, her eyes asking with sadness if this was what it had come to. Words? Speech? After his friendship with Franklyn from a childhood in which they had grown up together, in and out her house the two of them, like brothers? What did he have to say to her, after the government of which he was a member had chased Franklyn through the bush and bring him out with his head shoot off? This was it? Was this it?

When after the Black Power rebellion was put down and Evrol was plucked, as the newspaper's report stated, from the ashes of the revolt and made a government senator, my aunt Magenta wanted to understand how Evrol could remain silent on the killing of Franklyn.

I wondered how she could ask that question of Evrol and not ask it of herself. Or was she in asking it of him trying to get an answer for herself. In the twenty-one years in the National Party as Evrol moved from backbencher to cabinet minister, I did not hear him once address the subject. He kept away from Cascadu unless on official business and then he left as quickly as he came. He went to live in Port of Spain. We didn't see him and didn't look for him either. We saw him on the newspapers in those years as he went from dashikis and long loose hair to braided hair, to dreadlocks, his tone of righteousness, his outrage modulated, the ring of sincerity losing itself in confusion of statistics, his passion castrated by calm.

My aunt Magenta looked at his outstretched hand, and, sorry for him, for herself, for all of us, she took the hand and drew him to her bosom and held him in an embrace, like she was holding the son she had lost and the son she was losing.

Above the poetry of that moment, the bell start to ring, *balang balang,* and Brother Ken raised a hymn and Aunt Magenta begin to pray. And even as the singing and the praying going on, the drums start up in the background, then out of nowhere Blue Boy, the calypsonian, cut in with his own song/chant that was to sweep the island, *"Get something and wave,"* and Miss Ella, who had sung the wonderful solo backed by the choir at the church, as if touched by a new spirit, joined in, her voice further lifting up the song, *Get something and wave,* like a resurrection morning call, getting people up from their knees, opening their eyes, women taking off their headties and their veils, men taking off their jacket and loosening their ties, the song rising still, with the bell ringing again *balang balang baling.* The Orisha drumming cutting and keeping time, and I don't know where they get the iron from, but somebody start beating iron and then the steelband fellars take up the tune, first the du-dup and then the bass section, until the tenors start to ring and the whole thing come together. And that is how people start out the cemetery, everybody, Shouter and Shango, Presbyterian, Muslim, Hindu, Catholic, Anglican, all, everybody *Get something and wave.*

It was a most beautiful sight. People who had been out of Trinidad for years and forget what it was like to be in Carnival were out in front waving wreaths and shawls. Peter Minshall the famous mas man, who had come up from Port of Spain for the funeral, and was standing beside me, watching spellbound this mass of humanity, individual and diverse celebrating this triumph, said, "My God, Calypsonian, this is the mas. This is the mas. Boss, this is it, The River, mas in black and white. Let them tell me that we can't rejoice in black and white. Look at the beauty, look at the majesty! Look!" And he raised up the tail of his shirt with both hands as if he want to take it off and go barebacked into the band, all the time singing, *Get something and wave!*

"Come," he said, holding me by the hand, wanting me to join him, "let's go."

And as I hesitated, "What happen, you can't sing?"

But when I open my mouth, is like the weight of all the years just fall on me and strike me dumb. No sound came out and I was back in Grenada and all I could hear was the roar of planes, grenades exploding and gun mouths flashing murder. What I was hearing was the noise of death as we sat in a circle with bowed heads hearing the radio playing over and over again the Becket calypso that was big in that season, *Vincy mas: whole night we fêting, whole night we jamming* ... while the bullets sang through the hibiscus hedge and the women huddled in fear crept through the doorway of our shelter to go outdoors to relieve themselves in that pitiless afternoon of our shame. Where was everyone running? Where was everyone going with those books of psalms, where was everyone going with buckets of water, where was the fire in this evening of disaster? And I was seeing me everywhere. That is me, there and over there and over there ... I am the military commander with the pips on my shoulder and the gun in my hand. I am the dedicated comrade, the revolutionary worker standing under the avocado tree with a smile from his teeth one moment before a gunshot ripped through his thigh and before he could shout another slammed through his windpipe. I am the man in the field of bananas, unraveling the sheets of cellophane with which to wrap the green bananas so the sun wouldn't scorch them, handling them gently so they wouldn't bruise, so we would get the best prices in the markets of Europe. I am the woman in the market dressed in the khaki of the militia holding on to the revolution that is gasping for breath as the shots rattle and boom in the afternoon of grief. And all the time I trying to sing *Get something and wave* so I could join the rejoicing.

292

But my voice is not my own. Everything is mixed up together in my mind. I could feel words of speeches reverberating in the tomb of my head; but no song. And I am trying to whisper with my mind to hold on to myself:

My name is Kangkala, maker of confusion, recorder of gossip, revealer of secrets, in the same skin I am victim and victor...

And I am seeing Franklyn dragged down from the hills dead, the long-haired girl beside him, my aunt Magenta chanting, *I will not let you go until you bless me,* I am hearing the song to herald the leader of the Grenada revolution, "Forward March, Forward March." Where was forward now? I am seeing Clayton Blondell's grandfather toting up the little track to the place that they would name Beverly Hills, the sheets of galvanize for the roof and the concrete blocks and the cement and sand, bucket by bucket, one by one, men diving for black coral in the blue-green waters in front the hotel at Gran Anse with the huge rooms and the circular bed with its bedposts plated with gold where the women of the Prime Minister flopped in surrender. I am hearing the voice of the Comrade Leader coming over the radio in that promising dawn, saying, *This is the revolution, resistance is futile.* Who could have forecast the dirge of machine guns wailing in the hills above the harbor, or imagined the people they call *the masses* holding their belly in grief, singing *God bless America, thank you, my Savior President Mister Reagan, for taking away this curtain of fear, thank you for helping us take back our minds from the confusion of so many rulers of the Central Committee and the party bureaucracy, the secretaries and chairmen of everything. Thank you for making it possible for us to get a rest from the political education that give us a headache and the fine print of the Communist Manifesto that water we eyes.* I could feel words in my head, but my voice had no sound.

I found myself alone, walking. I meet Aunt Magenta and Clephus going home from the festivities that the funeral had turned into. "Donny, what happen? What happen?" And from the alarm in her voice, I know how she frightened. "Look at you!"

I look at myself. I was shaking. My skin was hot with fever. I had a cross on a chain round my neck. I had beads round my neck and a bracelet on my wrist. My shirt was buttoned with a safety pin.

"Come, we have to see about you."

My lips felt dry and my mouth tied up like the time in Washington, DC, when I was trying to whistle outdoors in winter. I must have mumbled something that sounded like Grenada.

"Grenada?" Aunt Magenta said. "That disaster happen so long ago. Well, anyhow, they say these things does affect you later. I tired tell you, you must settle down, get someone to care for you instead of having these women flitting in and out your life. You not getting younger, you know."

In the distance I could hear the church bells tolling, the steelband and the people in the street celebrating Dorlene's return from the dead. It was like a new spirit had found its way into the island, the feeling of miracle.

Clephus, she called. Come and help Donny here.

But I waved him away. I could still walk.

We reached the house. I sat down and she brought me a drink that I thought was medicinal. It was rum. Drink it, she said. And wanting to be of further service, she added,

294

let me turn on the TV. Something big like this bound to be on the news.

When she turn on the TV, it was to find the dimple-cheeked television newscaster, Lauren Beausoleil, in a black jacket, white blouse and with red hibiscus flowers in her hair reporting on the resurrection of Dorlene. She had been taken to the Mount Hope Medical Complex for treatment for dehydration and exhaustion and for observation. While there, they discovered that three patients who had come into contact with her – Iris Mendez, a midwife from Valencia, Molly Logan, a waitress from Maloney and George Khan, a Pentecostal minister from Mausica – found themselves healed of their illnesses. The whole hospital was in an uproar because instead of waiting on the doctors and nurses to treat them, all the patients who could walk were making straight for the ward in which Dorlene was. The police had to be called out to keep order and experts invited to assess the claims of healing. Dr. Alan Tim Pow sought to dismiss the whole thing as a hoax that indicated the deeply held wish by the population for miracles. But Professor Hamid Mohammed from the University of the West Indies, Dr. Neil Cureton, psychiatrist at the St. Ann's Mental Hospital, and Albert Faraah, president of the Society for Transcendental Meditation, the three experts contacted to discuss the resurrection of Dorlene, had no reason to doubt the claims made by the three persons. They affirmed that there was scientific evidence to show that people who had a near-death experience generally received powers to heal for periods from as short as twenty-four hours to as long as five years, though taken on the average this ability persisted for a period of between nine months to a year, after which it could become erratic, wane or suddenly disappear. It was their opinion that this was a situation requiring government intervention because once the news gets out, Dorlene Cruickshank would be in demand throughout the world. And the three experts agreed that unless this country moved quickly the country would lose Dorlene to the USA where she would earn millions of dollars as a healer.

But, even so, callers to the program were skeptical and urged Dorlene to take up the offers made to her and go.

"Go, girl, and make your millions," encouraged Aunt Magenta. "Not just for the money, for the respect. They don't respect you once you stay here."

"A prophet does not have any honor in your own country …" began Clephus. Before he could conclude his statement Aunt Magenta jumped up again:

"Oh, Jesus! Look!"

And when we looked it was to see …

Yes, the Prime Minister, his face drawn, his lips dry, his face the washed-out house color of a man whose skin had not received the benefits of sunshine for months, moistening his lips with licks of his tongue, in his eyes the sparkle of excitement, around his mouth a slight tremor that made us know he had some great pronouncement to make, in his eyes the hurt that made my aunt Magenta say, "Yes. Is like she leave him in truth." The *she* referred to was Marlene Spicer who, rumor had it, three months ago had ended her ten-year relationship with the PM. And that it was for that reason he had withdrawn to his residence and had instructed his cabinet ministers that not one of them was to in any way contact him unless Tobago – which at that time was threatening secession – hoisted its own flag.

When they got his instructions, senior cabinet members who had known him for years and had watched him develop an attitude of careful calculation that with all its perambulation served an inflexibility of will knew not to argue with him. They took him at his word, as he expected them to. And although the rising from the dead of Dorlene was an event that had the country abuzz, none of the cabinet ministers wanted to be the one to break his injunction, especially as the majority of those who had been present at Dorlene's funeral had either fainted or run at sight of the risen Dorlene and had no desire to emphasize an event that would show them in such unflattering light.

Evrol

Evrol Chance, however, had returned from the funeral of Dorlene Cruickshank with the chant *Get something and wave* going on in his head and the satisfaction that he had left the cemetery in Cascadu with a sense of being if not a celebrated son, certainly a forgiven one. That event, he felt, was something the PM needed to know about, not only for the part he Evrol had played, but because it occurred to him that what he now called The Rising of Dorlene was the miracle if handled well would help the PM untangle himself from his difficulties, get back into the good graces of the people and rekindle in the consciousness of the nation the sense of miracle that marked his earliest years in politics. When he raised these points with one of the ministers who was said to be close to the PM (after he had revived after fainting at the sight of the risen Dorlene), he was told, "Boy, if I was you I wouldn't say anything to the boss." Another simply muttered, "Hmm," and went on dusting dirt from the knees of his trousers that had attached itself there when at the sight of the risen Dorlene he had fallen to his knees to pray. Later, on his way home to St. Joseph, Evrol found himself stuck in a traffic jam created by hundreds of vehicles on their way to the Mount Hope Medical Complex to get to Dorlene before her healing powers started to wane. He reasoned that the matter was already in the public domain, and, order or no order, he decided to risk letting the PM know of the fortunate events that had taken place.

The PM

"No no no," said the PM with the upbeat energy and rhythm of a calypsonian:

"We say no to the countries with their big money tempting her to go. This is our miracle."

Dorlene was to be declared a national treasure and he was inviting those who wanted to benefit from her healing powers to make the trip to this island.

"And, my friends," he declaimed, because by this time he had nothing more to fear, the miracle had made land, money was no longer the problem, his faith had been rewarded, "my friends," his voice cracking with hurt and pride of self-congratulation, his lips twisted with the determined willfulness of a child who believes that not being given his due has freed him to pursue a course of his own choosing: "I had to do it alone. Where are all the movements for change that sprang up around '70? Where are the Black Power people? Where is Moko and Tapia and National Joint Action Committee and URO and Young Power and New Beginning? Where is the United Labor Force? Where them? Where they gone? What has become of them? Into their harbors of tribalism: Movement for People of Indian Origin? Society for the Welfare of Africans? Chinese want a public holiday too. The whole country descended into an ethnic limbo? That is what we come to? I alone am left with thee. I alone carry the national promise. So what can they tell me? Eh?"

And if they wanted to look for their future in the past,

he would seek his future up ahead. Now was the time to leave behind all the confusion and resentment brought on by history and press on with development. He wasn't going to pamper the ethnic nationalists and he wasn't going to tolerate those who wanted to reduce everything to bacchanal. No. He was going to set them on the road to the development of a modern civilization, a road that has no ethnic association.

And that was why he was using this opportunity to urge the nation and particularly the striking workers in oil and sugar and others who were threatening disruptive industrial action to open their eyes and see that the miracle of Dorlene was a signal sent to deliver the island from the clutches of individualism and unreason, to halt tribalism and to bring us all together in a new and beneficial relationship, labor and capital, government and people, rich and poor, black and brown, yellow and white, Trinidad and Tobago. Let this be a healing moment in our history.

He had spoken to the Archbishop of Port of Spain, yes, who had greeted with enthusiasm his request that Dorlene's name be put forward to the Pope, to have her declared the first saint from the English-speaking Caribbean. Yes.

Already, he said, the news of the resurrection of Dorlene had spread far and wide across the globe. That meant that, henceforth, our small island would be under the microscope of the world's scrutiny and be host to the world's peoples. As I speak, he said, news media people from all over the world are heading for this island, pilgrims have diverted their trips from the holy sites in India, the Himalayas, Israel, Cancun, Palestine, Las Vegas, St. Lucia, St. Vincent, Barbados and Grenada, others have

300

already booked to come for Carnival. The eyes of the world will be upon us, he warned. The news media of the world will be at our doorsteps. Scientists, sightseers and trouble-makers are going to come into our midst, tricksters, students and people afflicted with illnesses will land at our front door. Financiers are ready to lend us money, investors are coming to invest in the development of the country. All this means there will be opportunities never imagined before, not only for business but to show our culture to the world. And since the only occasion on which we celebrate together as a nation is Carnival, Cabinet has decided to make this a special Carnival at which we celebrate ourselves and Dorlene Cruickshank. In this cause, he had ordered moko jumbies, dragons, jab molassie bands, chutney dancers and tassa drummers, steelbands, stick-fighters and jab-jabs in unprecedented numbers. For this reason he was extending a special invitation to every community, religious, ethnic, social, to join together and make this Carnival one grand truly national celebration in which every community will involve itself as we celebrate Dorlene Cruickshank's good fortune and ours.

"And we have agreed that we cannot pass up this opportunity to invite people from the world to come and see the progress we have made as a society. And so that we may kill two birds with one stone, we shall take the opportunity to hold the constitutionally required general elections on the Monday after Ash Wednesday ... to show the world the strength and transparency of our democracy."

My Aunt Magenta

At the home of my aunt Magenta that night, the telephone did not allow any of us in the house to sleep. Relatives were ringing us up from other parts of the island and the world, people calling to say they had seen the story of the miracle on the BBC and on CNN. People had heard it on the Voice of America. My aunt called from Caracas, Venezuela; my cousin Pete in Canada; my cousin Louis in the United Kingdom; Lystra from Australia, Eileen from Amsterdam and Gordon from Nigeria. And we realized that the PM was correct and the story of the miracle of Dorlene had reached the outer sections of the world. These calls confirmed the expectation of a flood of visitors and Aunt Magenta cleared the dining table and she and Clephus sit down with a copybook to note how much oil, flour, baking powder and shark they would need to make bake-and-shark to sell to the tourists who would be visiting. The prospect of profit so fired the imagination of Clephus that he set to working out how much money they would save if they rented a boat and he went out with his nephew who was a fisherman and catch the shark himself. He was only brought back to reality by my aunt Magenta, with a wink of her eye, and a chuckle in her voice saying, "Clephus, don't worry to fish; let us just *buy the shark*."

I fall asleep in front the television while my aunt and Clephus continued their mathematics. I jumped awake at her voice shouting:

"I know it. I know he had to spoil it. Look at the TV. Look! Everybody else happy to come together, but he decide to object."

And there on TV was Mr. Bissoon, leader of the Opposition, with a red shirt and his head bound with a red kerchief like a Fyzabad stickfighter.

Mr. Bissoon:

Here is a Prime Minister who is prepared to make capital of the rescue of a poor sick woman who due to the incompetence of their health system would have been buried alive but for the alertness of people in the congregation and the diligence of the police constable who in his more than twenty years in Cascadu – Are you hearing me? twenty years – has not made a single arrest (you see how the police service works). Having nearly murdered the woman through official negligence, the Prime Minister is ready . . . ready to use her to further his political ends. Suddenly, the woman is a saint. Suddenly she is a healer. And to lend credence to this fiction he has employed well-known supporters of his party to declare themselves healed. They are well known to us: Molly George, a defeated County Council candidate, George Khan, ex-preacher and party activist from Mayaro, Iris Mendez, boss of a road mending project and party boss in Sangre Grande. And the university backs him up and the press falls for it. And all this is happening when the statues of Hindu gods are drinking milk and oozing blood in the villages of Lengua, Caripichima and the towns of Rio Claro and Chaguanas! Why they don't go to Debe where people lined up by the hundreds, lame sick people are being healed by the blessings of the goddess Lakshmi?

My aunt watching in disbelief, shouting: "Clephus, you know about any statues drinking milk?"

And Clephus, equally attentive and bewildered, shaking his head, no. She was about to turn to interrogate me

303

when she must have remembered that I couldn't speak, so she shouted at the man on the TV, "When did your statues start drinking milk?"

But Mr. Bissoon was continuing:

And this thing about Carnival: are we going to be excluded from the national celebration because we don't have moko-jumbie and douens and jab molassie and jab-jabs? Because we don't have babydolls and jamette women and king sailors and dragons? Is the community I represent to be penalized because we have not succumbed to the bacchanal culture but have retained our rich cultural heritage? And isn't it laughable the arrogance from a nation not yet fifty years to a people with the Mahabharata and the Ramayana and 5,000 years of civilization?

My aunt Magenta turned to me as she made her way to the TV to, I suppose, turn it off: "You want to see this program?"

I didn't dare nod my head.

But before she could touch the knob, Joshua Little, a member of the African Empowerment League, appeared on the TV saying:

Once again, yet once again you have ignored the African's claim to proper representation. Every other group in these islands has been granted a space of respect; we alone have been denied one. You have broken everything we brought, spit on everything we tried to construct. We have been forced to twist our gods into shapes to fit into the spaces we have been allowed to enter only because they represent your festivals, whether Christmas, Carnival or Easter; and now we want to untangle them from the history of degradation, you want to tie us down to moko jumbies and jab molassies, you want us to accept as our inheritance the bacchanal.

"You too?" Aunt Magenta asked the television screen. "You-all doing your best to get the PM vex. They doing their very best. You invite him to come in and that's a problem; you don't invite him that is even more problem. Well, let's see what he will do now."

She had finished calculating her requirements for the bake-and-shark and was planning now to clear out what used to be Franklyn's room and furnishing it so she could let it out to one of the visitors.

And as I looked at her, "You not listening to what he saying?"

Before I could make a motion, a clap of thunder rumbled across the sky. The lights went out, and we heard the sound of the wind like a thousand galloping horses running ahead of the rain.

"Oh, Lord," Aunt Magenta cried, "let us get candles, make sure the gas lamp have gas in them, that the matches can light. Tie up the animals; pen the dogs and we better board up the windows. We should really cut down that rubber tree. We have to look out for the house."

For that whole day it rained. The river flooded over; you couldn't pass, cars had to stop as water swallowed the road, and the whole place was a mess and we heard the clatter and clanking of galvanized-iron roofs as they struggled to resist being blown off buildings. A deeper darkness covered the land and lightning pitched across the sky. And all over Cascadu was the rattling castanet of teeth as people trembled at the thought of the disaster that would follow the vexation of the Prime Minister.

"You see what they cause?" my aunt Magenta said.

"This look like earthquake weather," Clephus said. "You think it will happen now."

"What?" Because Aunt Magenta couldn't hear well in the storm.

"The earthquake that they predict will split the island in two."

The PM appeared next day on TV; in the calm, the rain cleared.

"Do not feel you have to manufacture a miracle in order to be included. The miracle of Dorlene is a Trinidad and Tobago miracle. It is a miracle for all of us. All will have access to her, all will benefit from her healing powers whether or not your statues drink honey or milk.

"There is not an iota of discrimination intended. What are being highlighted are cultural forms that were developed here in the island and shared by people of all ethnic persuasions. If any community would identify any of their cultural creations that we have ignored we would be happy to include them in the program.

"Let me repeat: in order that nobody feels left out or overlooked or offended, we want to encourage people to wear their native dress and present their native culture. Wear your own clothes, eat your own foods, display your own culture. Do, as you say in your local parlance, do your own thing. And, yes. We will pay. We will stand the cost of your costumes."

"You mean they will be paying for everybody to play mas?" asked my aunt. "That will cost a lot."

"Money is not the problem," said Clephus. "Now we will see who we are."

"So what mas you playing?" Aunt Magenta asked.

I pretended not to hear her.

In the first few days following the PM's speech, libraries were bombarded with requests for books on Africa and

India, so people could determine which part their fore-parents had come from, so they would know what costume to wear. Overnight, fabric merchants descended on the town selling scarves and cow whisks and headties, ohrinis and sandals, displaying styles from Ghana and Nigeria and India and China. And soon, all over the land, there would be the whistling of sewing machines stitching fabric, the rustle of hands sticking sequins and feathers onto papier-mâché constructions.

Many of the mixed population went about in a daze wondering which side of their ancestry to relate to but others were signing up for the Fancy Sailor band that was to be brought out by the Cascadu steelband. Some were playing jab-jab with the gambler Japan and others had signed up with big bands in Port of Spain, where the covering of a costume made everybody the same human.

In Cascadu the Ministry of Culture set about constructing a tourist village that would be a permanent attraction for even people living in the island. In it was a calypso tent, a stickfight gayelle and a steelband yard where they had pan tuners demonstrating the process by which oil drums were turned into musical instruments. They mapped out a route along which steelbands would parade at certain hours and play tunes of their choosing but would as well engage in the steelband clashes as obtained in the early days of steelband history. In what they were now calling interactive culture, visitors would be allowed (for a fee) to join a band (Desperadoes, Invaders, All Stars, San Juan) and play the instruments. Those not wanting to play the pans would be invited to take part in the reenactment of steelband clashes in which visitors armed with bottles and stones would be given the opportunity (for a fee) to pelt bottles and stones at their opposing brethren or have stones or bottles pelted at them. In the stickfighting arena tourists would be able to sit and watch the duels but would also be offered the opportunity to learn the art of stickfighting from the Joe Pringay School of Stickfighting, where those so minded could taste the delicious experience of busting a man head or having the thrill of getting their own head busted.

Limbo dancing taught by the Julia Edwards School of Dance, King Sailor by Jeff Henry, iron beating, Midnight Robber, bat and moko jumbie performances as well as blue devils from Paramin and Fancy Sailors from Jason Griffith, tassa drumming and chutney singing with sessions on how to wine were all on offer. The calypso tent had appearing Valentino, Superior, Mudada, Stalin, Brigo and I, King Kala, was invited to sing.

While all this going on, the political parties were screening candidates, organizing motorcades, holding meetings, decrying corruption, promising a new world. Everywhere I turned the New National Party was booming its slogan, *The Time of Miracle is Now*. This was the time for me to sing. But at this momentous time in the history of Cascadu, I was dumb.

Dumb

I suppose there were those who were glad that I couldn't sing; but I like to think that everybody was sorry for me. People from my neighborhood brought me cures, honey and lime, chandelier bush tea, soft candle and nutmeg, aloes and egg. None of it had any effect on my head or my voice. My aunt Magenta got an Indian man to come and gharay me. He placed a burning candle on my chest to draw out the bad spirit. He twist my hands behind my back, turn my head wrong side, but still the pounding in my head continued and the emptiness of my voice prevailed. And I went back to sitting in front the television, watching people going into the rest house where Dorlene had been installed. It was unbelievable. People who had gone in bent over in pain come out skipping, throwing away crutches, and bandages. Eventually, my aunt said, I better carry you to see Dorlene.

At first, I was reluctant to go, believing that I did not have the faith required for this kind of healing, but when fever start to burn up my body and ague start to rattle my teeth, I agreed. As soon as we stepped out the door and walked a few yards we could see the traffic, backed up for what looked like miles. We walked through the town, which was being decorated with national flags and buntings. Along the road, on foot or riding bicycles were members of the Hard Wuck Party, giving out pamphlets announcing power to the Hard Wuck, picking up crutches and other items thrown away by the people who had been healed and shouting: *The miracle will not happen without the hard work. We will not achieve anything by miracles. We have to take the hard road forward.*

"You see why I can't vote for these people," my aunt said, looking at me as if I was guilty of the crime she was accusing them of. "The miracle is here. What they talking about? It is here. We can't send it back. The question before us is not how to avoid miracles, but how to deal with the miracle."

"All these people can't be ill," Clephus said when we drew closer to the rest house and saw the size of the crowd.

"Ill?" Aunt Magenta said. "These people not ill. They have other things they want to see her for."

Politicians wanted to know their future. Trade-union leaders had come to find out when was a propitious time to strike, aspiring politicians in dark shades and hats with the brim turned down wanted to know to which political party they should apply to put them up for election. Parents had come to get their children to pass examinations, calypsonians wanted to know what song to sing to win the crown. Reginald Reddy, a local scientist, had produced a pill from the bark of the bois bande tree that was three times as potent as Viagra. He wanted to know how he could get his work known to the Nobel Prize committee so he could be in the running for the prize in chemistry. Filmmakers with scripts, painters with great works, John de John with two cloth bags full of manuscripts of his twenty-four unpublished novels, all of them just for a blessing, just for her to put her hands on them. It looked impossible for me to get to see her that day. On top of that my head was bursting. I wanted to go back home. I couldn't make it that day.

Clephus saw my distress, but Aunt Magenta had a different focus.

"Try. Remember," she warned. "This miracle could run out any time."

But I really couldn't wait.

My aunt dispatched Clephus to walk along the line to see if he knew somebody who would let me slip into the line, but it was clearly something he felt uncomfortable doing and I myself wasn't too keen on it. People had been waiting there since before dawn.

Soon it was dark. I looked at my watch. It was five in the afternoon. I looked up at the sky, but I couldn't see it. There was a haze almost like fog or dust in the air above.

"It is a storm coming," Aunt Magenta said. "Don't tell me they get the PM vexed again."

"Not a storm, dust. Look how it sticking on my skin," said Clephus.

That was the first time I noticed the cloud over Cascadu.

I didn't get to see Dorlene that day. On that evening's news we saw the PM announcing the discovery of new gas and oil finds that would give us the means to take our place at the center of the world ... *and give us here everything they have there. That is why I am going to keep it all in my hand, Corporation Sole. The sole and only hands, because I know if you get your hands on this* ... He was addressing the Opposition benches.

"Live forever then," said the Leader of the Opposition who was good for himself too. "Live forever."

"Well, my friend," said the PM with a smirk of delight, as he spread open his hands expansively as if to show the evidence of this ability, "what do you think I am doing?"

Next day the buildings the PM had ordered from a catalog displayed on the internet began to arrive, with the plans for their construction, and the workers to assemble them, apartment buildings and office buildings in different colors and in different sizes, city or rural, upscale or downscale. He brought in technicians from the global marketplace to reinstall the railway system that he had closed down thirty years before, experts to establish a new health service that had been allowed to fall into disrepair, advisers from Cuba to reconstruct a new agricultural industry that had been abandoned, a school building program to have places for all the children, a new police service equipped with the latest equipments and retired Scotland Yard officers to show how to use them, cell phones, bullet-proof vests, helmets, burly woollen sweaters marked POLICE, guns. In the area of culture, he created a symphony orchestra from the steelbands and set about building an opera house, a monstrous structure to dwarf the savannah to produce the operas he had been writing in his spare time, to host the National Ballroom Dancing Competition and the contest for singers of sentimental songs, which as a young man he had participated in, winning with "Unforgettable," a song by Nat King Cole. He completed the horse-racing complex that earlier he had to abandon because corruption exhausted the funds. He constructed a Disneyland with Mickey Mouse and Donald Duck. The country was humming. Yes, builders from China, planners from Canada, policemen from the UK, Trinidad and Tobago nationals working abroad who he invited to return to apply to development the techniques they had learned from the world.

In the days to come, the experts continued to work

feverishly in preparation for the influx of tourists. They tilted the savannah to face the sea. They take what used to be Shannon cricket ground, where Learie Constantine, C. L. R. James and Pascal used to play, and make a car park. They build a curtain of buildings to drape the waterfront so that the working population would not be distracted from their labors by sight of the sea. They hang buildings over the street to block out the sun so that we would have the gloom of the city of London. They had wanted fog, but they discovered that due to a clerical error it had not been budgeted for. But that would be a problem easy to correct, the contractors said, since once the paperwork was done and the money allocated, it would be a simple matter to pipe in the vapors of sadness from the reservoir hanging over the slum settlement we knew as The Beetham.

I sat there in that front room before the TV, sometimes with Aunt Magenta and Clephus and sometimes with Claude.

"I suppose this is what you call moving on," Claude said. "However, we still have Carnival. We still have the big steelband show, where every band from whatever part of the island would assemble to proclaim and celebrate and exalt the creativity and ingenuity of the human. We still have a festival that anybody could enter in whatever costume they decide on. I still have my Jouvay band where I could go dressed in rags, covered in mud, beating pan and old iron. Let them build their buildings."

But even as we sat there, the announcement came that in order to put on an efficient show for the visitors, the number of bands in Panorama was to be reduced from fifty to twenty-five so that the program would be completed no later than midnight when the luxury buses would arrive to take visitors back to their hotels. For the same reason the Dimache Gras show that had featured ten calypsonians each singing two songs was to be changed to twelve calypsonians singing one song. Events traditionally held in the North would be put in the South. Those held downtown were now to be staged in the West. The whole place was turned upside down.

The wind and all start to blow in different directions.

One evening I am walking home from Sonnyboy's when I feel a chill in the breeze. I start to shiver. I didn't know then that it was the wind of sadness whose origin John de John had traced from the madhouse in St. Ann's. From St. Ann's, it had come over the Lady Young Road, passed over Laventille, through Morvant and down Caledonia. At the Eastern Main Road, one part of the wind turned left and swing up the Priority Bus Route, the other part turned right and headed for downtown Port of Spain, via The Beetham. At Laventille it met eighteen-year-old Akeil Blackman coming out of a snackette with a beer in his hand, a good-looking smooth-faced youth with his hair cut down to his skull, his sideburns tapered to a point just in line with his ears. He was wearing three-quarter-length pants without a belt, the waist falling down and resting on his buttocks so you could see the waistband of his jockey shorts. A set of tattoos covered his arms, the motif something between a serpent and dragon; but instead of looking fierce the dragon looked more like a worm breathing fire; and that was the observation made by Marvin Baird, a youth maybe a year older than Akeil, not as neat, nor as decorated, standing among three friends: "Hey, Sadist, what that worm doing on your hand? I never see a worm breathing fire."

Everybody laughed, but Akeil was not amused. He had put on the tattoos, selected his trousers and shorts and cut his hair in the style not really to establish difference, to emphasize sameness, to help mask his loneliness and confusion and poverty, but as the wind begin to blow, he felt exposed. He could barely read, he yearned to be valued, he had doubts of his sexuality, his manness, the quality of his courage. He tried to laugh it away, but the wind held him and twisted his mind and he was trying to hold on to himself, to be calm, to join in the laughing, but he didn't know how to laugh and he didn't have the quickness of mind to make the incisive repartee the situation required. He saw Marvin laughing. Akeil felt himself shrinking. He felt disrespected. Marvin was still laughing. Akeil could see his gums. The other fellars were laughing too. Akeil wanted to talk but his mouth was dry of words. He began to walk away but the laughing walked with him. He walked faster, the laughing kept up with him. He started to run. He had a pardner with a gun. He went to where it was in the hollow of a brick behind the water tank. He put down the beer and he take up the gun and turned back in the direction of the snackette. The group of fellars were still where he left them. They saw him coming toward them, his two hands at his sides, his body leaned to one side like a dancer about to glide, one of them said. Like an angel, said the other eyewitness. Like a ghost. Nobody didn't see the gun. In any event, their laughing was over, they were now talking football. Marvin had a smile on his face, not a smile of ridicule, a smile to placate. Marvin now wanted to cool it down. He saw that Akeil had tears on his face. He said, by way of apology, "Dude, don't worry with me, the worm is a dragon. Is just a joke I was making." Is a joke, Marvin said again. Marvin bent down to pick up a piece of paper that the wind had blown to his feet, as he righted himself, a cloud passed under the sun, Akeil lifted his right hand with the gun and aimed it at Marvin. Even then he might not have fired, but not to shoot was to confirm himself as a joker. He placed his finger over the trigger. There was nothing else to do but to pull it. That was the first one.

Mervyn Delice had come out of the house at the corner of Erica Street and Old St. Joseph Road. He was wearing his new sneakers and a gold chain round his neck and a wristband of gold. He had just come back from checking out his girl when a voice ordered him to give over his gold chain. Mervyn Delice hesitated. The shot made him sit down. When he was found he was sitting on the side of the road. He had no shoes on and his gold was gone. In the week it take for the wind of sadness to reach Cascadu, twelve young men lay dead, shot by other young men.

There were kidnappings, rapes, violent acts that I don't even want to bring myself to mention, crimes that Pastor Prue and other pastors said were the work of the devil, who had entered the hearts of idle and unambitious youth and given them guns and starring roles in gangster movies in which police arrived in speeding cars with flashing lights and sirens, and helicopters appeared hammering the sky above the buildings, in a confusion in which ambulances screamed and reporters shoved microphones in the faces of grieving mothers and sisters and girlfriends who were about to discover that their menfolk were dying real deaths in a movie that was unreal.

The Selling of Dreams

That week, Aunt Magenta and a few of her followers, as part of the national effort to clean up the embarrassment of crime, set out on a pilgrimage of prayer that would take them around the island. For their part, the government purchased a blimp that floated above the city and could see everything that was happening on the ground. They also brought in Scotland Yard.

They acquired the services of Professor Matthew Wrinkler of Nova Scotia, Canada, a criminologist of exemplary credentials who had done research in Haiti, New York and Johannesburg that demonstrated that it was not poverty or television violence or poor education or desperate communities that bore the responsibility for crime. His research had shown that 93 percent of those committing crime were people who wanted the impossible. They had allowed old, unreal dreams to clog up their head. His recommendation was simple. The state and private enterprise needed to join together to rid the people of unrealistic and stifling dreams.

"That is what I have been saying," said the Minister of National Security: "We need as a society to follow the example of the successful citizens, who, even though they endured servitude no less severe than that of some others, managed to get rid of their encumbering dreams."

"Yes. Yes. Yes." The politicians, the clergy, the business community, the police all agreed.

"Yes," said the PM at an election rally. "The world is

not going to change. At least not in a hurry. This is the age of technology. The leading nations have everything down to a science and there is no longer any need for their people to dream. Everything has already been thought through."

"Yes," said the experts from the university. "We don't need to think again. There is no point in reinventing the wheel. The technology is available and we have the money to purchase. We just have to follow."

Yes. And they explained the frustration, stagnation and resentment that engrossed people with dreams and the freedom associated with people who had surrendered their dreams.

It was for these very compelling reasons that a few days later the Ministry of National Security and Mental Health, at a ceremony in the County Council building, launched the program to buy up useless dreams. It was a grand occasion with the Prime Minister the featured speaker, with wine and cheese and crumpets and accra and those little things you eat with a toothpick. I didn't go, but Aunt Magenta make Clephus put on his jacket and a tie and go with her. They come back and tell me about this new system where you could sell your dreams. Something about assigning to each dream a number and being paid for it. Clephus and Aunt Magenta tried to explain it to me but I remained confused. I watched the advertisements they had running on TV, in a video featuring the Carnival queen lying on a couch surrounded by luxurious furnishings and handsome young men singing the theme song, based on a popular melody by the Mighty Sparrow, that ended with:

Dreams gone, development take over now.

With Dream stations in supermarkets and drugstores, and

advertisements running on radio, in the papers and on TV, the game captured the imagination of the population who at every turn were encouraged to exchange for money what were said to be old useless dreams that had no chance of being realized. People started to sleep early so they could dream, women started complaining about husbands and husbands started complaining about wives who wouldn't let them sleep. Births went down and the smoking of marijuana and the sale of sleeping pills went up. Our novelist John de John was once again catapulted into the spotlight, the only protester, with a placard around his neck, on which was written the words of the poet Martin Carter,

I do not sleep to dream
I dream to change the world.

But that didn't stop the long lines of people waiting to sell their dreams.

Reparation for Africans held in enslavement, a full and unqualified democracy, the removal of poverty, good housing, water for everybody, boats up and down the Caribbean, Caribbean Federation, a literature prize, the return of the pushing of steelbands on the streets at Carnival, all the steelbands in the world in the savannah for Panorama, a good bookstore, a bus to take poor people children out of the city to show them their country, a boat for them to sail to go down the islands, a victorious West Indies cricket team and various little dreams that people had kept in their family, for their children. But the selling of dreams did not stop the sacrificial slaughter of young men, nor the crimes of passion among the older folk. Everybody seemed to be on edge. It was as if in selling their dreams, people had been left empty. What had held them

319

together was gone and they were left unbalanced and on edge and they rode or walked around ready to explode.

My aunt Magenta returned from her tour of prayer to discover that the wind of sadness was circling our neighborhood in Cascadu. Mr. Maycock, the Creole fella who used to play all fours with Manick father was dead, Miss Dolly who was secretary to the village council was blind and one of Orville's son had been stabbed and was in the hospital fighting for his life. Down the street from us Manick father had fallen ill. His daughter and son-in-law Doon brought a Hindu pundit to attend to him, and from his house came the chanting of prayers, the smell of incense and the fine tinkle of a bell. A day afterward we saw Doon victoriously planting a cluster of slim bamboo rods in a corner at the entrance to the yard and we wondered if that meant that Manick father was about to die. Aunt Magenta get busy right away. She had already prepared herself by having Clephus rub her down with a mixture of Vicks, soft candle, rosemary and coconut oil so the wind would not be able to get through her pores, she put socks on her feet and wrapped her head with a headtie, lock up the doors and windows of her house and went past the flags to see Manick father to offer her prayers. His wife, Elsie, called her to come up the steps to the gallery where Manick father lay in a hammock from which he could see the cricket ground. My aunt Magenta said her prayers with Elsie standing next to her. And then she sat down and began to talk with Elsie and Manick father.

She came back shaking her head triumphantly. "He not going to dead," she said.

They had spent a long time talking. When she was leaving he had offered her cassava sticks, bodi beans and dasheen plants from his garden, and invited her to come over and help herself to whatever other plants she wanted. They had talked about cricket, about Franklyn and of the offer made by the Prime Minister to pay for the costumes of all who wanted to play in a band for that Carnival. She humored him by asking him if he was playing. He surprised her. He hadn't been waiting on the Prime Minister's offer. He had been preparing to join a band long years earlier.

"And what happen? You didn't have a costume? You didn't have a band?"

He lay back in the hammock as if contemplating how to answer. Then he said, "I was making my costume."

"I don't believe you," my aunt Magenta tell him. "I see you watching cricket. But I didn't know you wanted to have anything to do with Carnival."

"You don't believe me? Elsie," he called, "go and bring it for me."

Elsie hesitated, "But I thought you said you didn't want anybody to see it until it finish."

"Bring it. Let me see it."

What Elsie wheeled onto the gallery was an unfinished Carnival costume of bright red, yellow and black stripes, with mirrors on the chest and a sun on the back and a headpiece with three faces looking in three directions.

Aunt Magenta couldn't believe her eyes. "The man had a costume in truth," her astonishment palpable as she spoke to Clephus and me.

"So how come you never finish it?" she asked Manick father.

"Every year he would work on it," Elsie said. "But when Carnival come and he look at it he would find it not ready. And he would put it off 'till next year.'"

321

"Every year, hot and sweaty, and when Carnival come he find he don't like it."

"But it looking good," my aunt Magenta say.

"Good for you, but not good for him."

"It looking real good. With that costume you coulda join any band," Aunt Magenta tell him.

"Joining for him was not like jumping into a band, it was not joining a band, it was bringing something to the band," Elsie again. "He had to have something to give. That was the problem."

"You was shy?" my aunt Magenta ask him.

"Not shy. The costume was just not ready."

"He wanted it too perfect. 'You too perfect,' I tell him," Elsie said.

"Neighbor, you know how hard it is to come into a place where you meet so much things: Carnival, calypso, the steelpan. You see the great costumes them other fellars make and bring.

"I couldn't go with a half a piece of a thing. I had to bring something worthy – of me."

"That was something you keep to yourself. You never tell nobody. I living nearly next door to you and never suspect you was building a Carnival costume."

"And that is why it had to be something good, neighbor."

"Good or perfect?" asked Elsie.

"Time. I didn't have the time," Manick father said.

"And what time you had to make anything? Whole day you on the tractor and when you come home in the evening is your garden. Bring what you have, I tell him. People will appreciate it once you bring it."

"I didn't have the time."

"Now he have the time, he laid up in bed," Elsie say,

trying to laugh. "Now you have the time."

"So he find himself in a funny position. What he had to give is not perfect enough. So he put off joining a band until. Because if he join a band he would lose the chance to develop what he was developing. It would be our loss too. You understand?

"So he never joined. He never played," my aunt Magenta said, talking now to Clephus and me. "Because joining was not just jumping into another band, it was bringing something of his own to link with it."

As my aunt Magenta recounted to me and Clephus the details of her conversation with Manick father and Elsie, it occurred to me how little we knew of each other.

"I wasn't looking for him there," Clephus said. Then he added, "This Carnival going to surprise plenty people."

My thoughts turned to Manick.

Since going up for elections on a Hard Wuck Party ticket, Manick had gained increasing acceptance among Settlement people, the majority of whom were supporters of the National Party, not because he had done anything special but because of what they construed as his neutrality. So in any matter requiring community representation he was one of the first chosen because he had no special allegiance to either the National Party or the Democratic Party. It was this neutrality that evoked an unease from his brother-in-law Doon who insisted on reminding him of 1970 when we supposedly "spit him [Manick] out like a plum seed." But others of us were mistrustful of a man who didn't belong anywhere.

Manick continued to straddle the two worlds. He was a member of the Eastern Cricket League, and represented Chutney Bands on the New Cultural Council, as manager of Cascadu Chutney Band which was captained by his

323

nephew, Baldeo. Of late, I had seen him more and more at Sonnyboy's place, talking mostly about cricket and the disaster that the West Indies team was becoming.

I hadn't tried to talk to him before and I couldn't do it now. The distance created between us since '70 and the red flag he wanted to carry still remained.

If Manick really wanted something new and wanted to bring something of his own, why couldn't he say so? He was different from his father. He had grown up here. He had played cricket with us. He had limed on the corner with us. He was at one time ready to march with us.

Why had he not spoken? Why had he not corrected Doon, who was giving the impression that *We spit Manick out like a plum seed*, when he knew that the problem was not only with us, it was with him as well? Why didn't he speak? And I began to wonder if what kept us from moving out of our different harbors was that we were perfecting our offering to the world we had to enter.

But I had begun to stop trying to second-guess people. What Manick would do, I had no idea. He had not made his speech in '70 and he had not made it as a candidate of the Hard Wuck Party. I really didn't know where he stood. Well, soon he would have another opportunity to make his position clear. I found myself looking forward to the Carnival.

The Visitors

And then they came, the visitors, in planes at Piarco airport; and in Port of Spain three cruise ships, each one the length of the island, anchored out in the ocean, ferrying visitors ashore by dinghy. From every part of the globe, photographers and journalists, from Rome, from Paris, from London, from various parts of the United States of America, with cameras, camcorders and cell phones, in short pants and bush jackets with big pockets, businessmen, academics, sightseers, financiers, entrepreneurs, evangelists and is only when the camera (for I seeing this on TV) focused on the tags swinging from their necks I see the names of some of the people that had been invited: Christopher Columbus; Sir Francis Drake; General Sir John Hawkins; William Wilberforce, liberator of the enslaved; Friar Bartholomew de las Casas, protector of the Amerindians; Roume de St. Laurent, organizer of the settlement of French planters in Trinidad; John Steadman, painter of portraits; Sir Ralph Woodford, governor and developer of Port of Spain, after whom streets and our biggest public square were named; Gertrude Carmichael, who wrote one of our first histories; Governor Hill, who read out the Emancipation Proclamation. Architects from the World Bank, city planners to take us into the Developed World.

In those first days, they visited Dorlene. They had lunch with the Chamber of Commerce, made courtesy calls on the President and on the Prime Minister. They were taken to see the bird sanctuary at Caroni swamp, the Point Lisas industrial estate, the oil refinery. In Cascadu we welcomed them at our official welcoming post, the County Hall, where the Minister of Festivals and our Carnival queen, wearing her crown and the Miss Cascadu sash across her chest, embraced them and a line of girls all with the same slimness, the same hairstyle and complexion, contestants in the Miss Cascadu beauty pageant, gave them miniature steelpans as tokens of our appreciation of their coming. I saw them on the news responding to welcoming speeches:

> *We are indeed pleased to see how well your country has developed ... Happy to know the success that your society so wonderfully demonstrates is an achievement whose foundation is your stable labor force and your educated elite ... laid by us in an earlier time ... Glad to see that you appreciate our wisdom ... Thrilled to hear that unlike many developing countries you have not allowed the recalcitrant and the delinquents to compromise your development ... Delighted that the cultural forms, which had been used by delinquents and rebels to challenge and disturb the peace and welfare of the law-abiding citizens, have now been fashioned to provide us with such marvelous entertainment ...*

I listened to our Minister of Festivals letting them know that *it was a privilege and an honor to welcome you back, albeit in a slightly different capacity ... stlll a lot to learn from you ... immense appreciation of the help with our challenges ... pleased that you will get to see what we have done ... since you have laid the foundations of the society we now enjoy.*

I couldn't talk, I couldn't say anything. But I was thinking: *Then what about the ordinary people who resisted the colonial pressure, whose resistance gave us a sense of self, whose artistry speaks for our humanity and whose struggle turned plantations into the battlefields for humanness? The stickfighters and the masquerade players, the dragon and jab molassie, the Midnight Robbers, King Sailors and moko jumbie, all those maskers who come out of nowhere to speak for who we are, the caisonian and the creators of the steelpan, the dancers of Orisha and the Shouters?*

If we accept the contribution of Columbus, Drake and the colonizers' systems and governors with laying down the foundation of the society, how can we ignore the input of people who have made the society much more than the plantation they had in mind? It is to them we must answer. What have we done with what they have done? What have we made of their sacrifice, their inventions, their fight for freedom? What have we done with family, with the generosity, what have we done with steelband and calypso and the mas, what have we done with their love?

I heard a calypso coming:

Big big party, rum, food and music hototo
They invite people from Biche, Arima, Grande, Rampanalgas
and Oh-hi-oh-ho
But is only when they looking to make the toast
The party realize that it forget to invite the host.

The Season of Dreams

Before the Carnival could get under way in Cascadu, a dark heavy cloud appeared over the rest house where Dorlene was curing people, and spread over Cascadu. Some said it was dust from the Sahara, some said it was the spirits of Amerindians who jumped off the cliff in Arena, some talked about the Hosay riots in which a number of Indians indentured on the estates were killed, some pointed back to 1970 when Basil Davis and Franklyn and two revolutionists, Guy Harewood and Beverly Jones, were killed, some believed it to be the spirits released into the town from the people cured by Dorlene. Claude was certain it was the spirits of the old masquerade characters that had appeared to see what was being done with Carnival. Whatever it was, we only had to look to my aunt Magenta to be clear that something was not right in the world. Such things affected her keenly. If she was all right, then the world was all right; but once she began to sneeze, look out.

I knew something was seriously wrong when I hear my aunt Magenta quarreling with Clephus. Where he put the soap, if he bathe the dogs, little unimportant things. I watched Clephus respond with his patient smile, his extraordinary expression of love, doing everything he could to set her at ease, to get her out of that mood. He sapped her head with Limacol, massaged her shoulders and rubbed her swollen legs with soft candle and coconut oil but somehow she still managed to strike a discordant note, *it is my left shoulder, not the right ... you don't have to be so hurry. If you don't want to do it, don't do it.* He prepared her meals. She liked her rice strained and not sappy the way it is when you leave the water in it, the chicken had too much salt. Poor Clephus, as if he knew something was not right with her, saying little but forced to answer lest his silence be the cause of another onslaught. Now she resumed talking to Franklyn, not asking him for an explanation for his actions, but talking with a surrendering patience, wishing he was all right where he was, telling him of the seasons, that the calabash tree he had helped her plant was bearing at last, of the pain she had in her shoulder, of swelling in her legs, of all the things she wanted to do, bewailing the small scores the West Indies cricket team was making. *As if they forget who they is. You should be there batting. Oh, I hope you playing cricket in Lord's over there.* She sang loudly consoling hymns and Clephus joined in,

I must have my Savior with me
Cause I cannot walk alone,

singing and sapping her head or anointing her feet, all of it a sweet sad melancholy that I wished I could render in calypso.

She carried on dialogues with the PM, questioning him and commenting on whatever was the current business. If anyone opened their mouth to criticize any action of his, she would enumerate all the things he was doing: the schools he was building, the free secondary education he was giving, free tertiary education he was spending money on, money to help people start business, entertainment center, look at how much money he giving calypsonians, the place of importance given to the Shouters Baptist faith. I recognized that the one she wanted to convince was herself.

She had her radio tuned on to the talk shows and she carried on a debate with whoever was talking.

Mr. Bissoon had become her favorite target because he blamed the PM for everything. He was highly critical of the idea that people should sell their dreams. "This is the madness that you produce when you encourage people to sell all their dreams. At least we should retain some."

"Dreams? *You* talking about dreams," she said, addressing Mr. Bissoon's voice coming over the radio. "If to be PM of this country is your dream, you better sell that dream."

Clephus was worried about her too. He came to me to ask my advice on a matter he had been thinking about for the longest while. He wanted to ask her to get married and wanted to know if I would have any objection.

What did I think?

I indicated to him by way of signs that I still could not speak. And he left me without comment. I didn't know what he had decided until the morning my aunt Magenta woke up deeply sad, and called us all to tell us her dream.

In her dream, it was Carnival. She had a bonnet on with the peak turned down so you couldn't see her face; she had a short short skirt on, her legs all showing. And she had a baby in her arms, and she was pointing at a man who looked like Music, accusing him of not minding the child.

But the man was ignoring her.

"You," she shouted, and then when the man turned in her direction, the face she saw wasn't that of Music, it was the PM's. And closing around menacingly to protect him were the police.

Aunt Magenta was sure that dream foretold her death.

"I sure they come to bury me," she said.

She set about to instruct us what to do when she died, what preparations to make for the wake. She wanted bongo dancing and children playing games, and plenty rum and coffee. She told us who she wanted to preach the sermon, who was to ring the bell. Clephus and I were to share the house. I was to get a lawyer and see that it was done legal; she did not want any family coming and making any claim on her property when she was gone. She did not want anybody coming to put Clephus out of the house.

While she was talking, Clephus was trying to get a word in. But she did not give way, and it was only when she was done talking and let him speak that he proposed to her that they get married.

"Well," she said, "this is a good time, now when you know I going to dead."

"You not going to dead," he said. "Whatever coming for you coming for me." And he begin to tell her the dream he had dreamed.

In his dream, Clephus saw his uncle Abyssinia coming down the hill in Castara, his whole body daubed with black grease, a trident in hand and long pointed fingernails made of tin, and he had a tail and his uncle was dancing and wining like a jab molassie and he, Clephus, was behind him barebacked in a short pants daubed with the same black grease, and on a strap around his neck was a biscuit pan that he was beating with two sticks to provide the rhythm for his uncle's dance.

Then I remembered what I too had dreamed.

In my dream, I was seeing my grandfather Freddie, and he was dressed in a dragon costume. Fire was coming out his mouth and I was one of the men dressed as an imp

331

holding the chain, while he tried to break away. But, of course, I couldn't speak.

The rest of the day I puzzled over the dreams. That afternoon, I went over to Sonnyboy's place. I found his shop packed with people telling each other their dreams. Nobody could give a satisfactory interpretation of what this meant. Next day, the figures of our dreams appeared to the children in Cascadu Primary School. Seven children from Standard Three of the school had to be taken to hospital. One boy had collapsed three times after he had seen a short green man. "He had a sword and a pistol and a dagger and a cape. He was laughing, and I started to pee my pants," the boy said.

One of the girls, Avinisha Pariag, said, "I saw a green man with hooves like a goat and big red eyes. And it had a black sword." Another girl, Marlene Superville, had seen a man with wings folded like a black bat. Six other students, Charlene, Angela, Debbie, Kerry, Leanne and Kamla, are reported to have fainted over the last week. The school principal, Mrs. Sharlene Jagroop, reported the incident to the authorities, who ordered that the school be closed until the Ministry of Education could provide the children with a safe environment. In the meantime they began investigating the cause of these spirits.

Acting on the assumption that the spirits removed by Dorlene from the sick had taken up residence in the town, some in our dreams and others in the heads of the children, the Ministry of Health ordered that small children and pregnant mothers be moved to other districts so that when the spirits were released they would not find the souls of the innocent to enter.

With this news made public, it set off concerns in

districts throughout Trinidad. The Tobago House of Assembly was concerned that the spirits would find their way over the sea and settle in the island. Also expressing worry, especially for their tourist industry, were the governments of the nearby islands Barbados and Grenada. Venezuela just seven miles away sent its health officials over to find out what was going on. In the meantime on their own initiative, people were consulting obeah-men and obeah-women and religious people who knew how to handle spirits, and in many homes we began to get the smell of incense burning, and on the trees blue bottles and red tied to the branches of trees to repel the spirits.

The Ministry of Health sent out men with spray-cans on their backs, which they used to spray for dengue fever and they sprayed a thin white mist into the air, which killed mosquitoes, had the place smelling stink, but left the cloud intact and the land dark.

Business persons threatened to move their businesses because of concern that bandits would be emboldened to use the increased hours of darkness to murder, kidnap and smuggle. The cricket Test Match, which was being played in Trinidad between England and the West Indies, had to be halted at four in the afternoon because of bad light, the English commentators starting to giggle and ask what kind of tropical weather is this, is better we had stayed in jolly old England. Pastor Prue on his own initiative brought in from the USA the Reverend Benny Henny, the famous evangelist. Benny Henny held one prayer meeting in the savannah in Port of Spain. But he stopped what was intended to be a crusade and rushed back to the United States since he found the spirits he encountered were too numerous and strong to be tackled with the resources he had at hand; he promised to return with the reinforcements to take them on.

The cloud was spreading over the island. The Concerned Citizens lobbied for Carnival to be postponed until the cloud was removed. Some wanted the elections put off as well. In order to put the population at ease and to ensure that neither the date for Carnival nor the elections was changed, the Office of the Prime Minister advertised worldwide for an obeah-man, occultist, spiritualist or holy person to get rid of the cloud before Carnival. This search committee shortlisted three persons – all foreigners – who were to be brought to Cascadu for interview, prompting Claude to take another swipe at the government, saying: "You see how they insulting and ignoring us. You mean to say you can't even get a competent obeah-man from Tobago or Trinidad?"

The spiritualist finally chosen was the Canadian who turned out to be a Trinidadian. Because of the shortage of hotel accommodation in Cascadu, he was brought to occupy the spare room that my aunt Magenta had for rent. The man was Victor S. Rooplal. He had put on weight around his middle and his hair had thinned considerably, but Aunt Magenta recognized him right away by his deep engaging eyes. She remembered the danger he posed to women who gazed into them.

"No. I don't think you could stay here," she told him. "Your eyes. I know who you are."

"Lady," he said to her, "it is very flattering, your concern, but I done with that years ago. I am not the man I used to be."

"OK. I not doubting you. But, just in case your powers come back, you better put back on those dark shades."

334

That same evening I took Rooplal over to Sonnyboy's place.

"Wait," he said as Sonnyboy was about to greet him, "first things first." He pushed his hand in a pocket and brought out the twenty-one dollars he had kept for Sonnyboy for twenty years.

After that he told his story, beginning with that night when he escaped from Khalid's place with Khalid's daughter, of going with the truck and getting off at the Central Market, of getting into a card game and winning (the girl was lucky for him) and then going with the girl by relatives of his, moving all over the island to avoid the men Khalid had sent to kill him, until with money from his winnings, from family and the girl pawning her jewelry, he and she got on a plane to Canada, where they were granted entry as political refugees fleeing the discrimination of an African government that had done nothing to protect him and his family from rape, robbery, kidnapping and death.

"You tell them that?" an astonished Sonnyboy asked.

"Was the best I could do. I didn't have a better story."

In that land of opportunity, V. S. Rooplal worked as a janitor, a calypsonian and pan beater and a Midnight Robber speech-maker, graduating to become a toaster and later a motivational speaker dealing with young people who had fallen foul of the law. He had married (to the same girl), opened a roti shop and joined the Pentecostal church. His wife had gone to university and had graduated as a business administrator and he had taken courses in magic and anthropology. Later he had moved to Calgary where he ended up being a calypsonian, motivational speaker and toaster using, as poet, the idiom of Midnight

Robber speeches; and as occultist, giving people baths and charms to ward off evil spirits.

Trinidad was always in the back of his mind. Life had been good to him. He had done well and wanted to give something back. He had thought of returning and joining a political party and going up for election, winning his seat and serving the people. And he had actually begun to make inquiries of which political party would offer him a safe seat when Sookraj, who still kept in touch with him from Calgary where he was then living, call him up and as a joke said, "You don't hear what happening in your town of Cascadu? A woman come back from the dead and they have a whole lot of spirits roaming about the place and nobody to get rid of them, ha ha ha."

Next day Rooplal using his new Canadian accent called up the Consulate of Trinidad and Tobago to find out if the services of an occultist would be needed. In Trinidad they would have laughed at him, but here the officer herself, the Deputy Consul-General, hearing his Canadian/Indian accent was interested and told him they were in search of just such a person and if he would send in his curriculum vitae they would contact him. The Consul-General wanted to speed up the process by having him come in, but, knowing that a personal visit wouldn't do him any good, because once they found out he was a Trinidadian, his chances of getting the job would be quite remote, Rooplal pleaded his busy schedule but kept up their correspondence, and the Deputy Consul-General only saw him when, as an act of courtesy, he came to Toronto airport to see him off. V. S. Rooplal was dressed in a unique outfit – a black cape, a wooden sword, a dagger at his side, a hat out of the French Revolution, blue tights, gloves and pointed shoes

336

– and many people came up to him to ask him what country he was from; however, the Deputy Consul-General, being a Trinidadian, recognized it as a Midnight Robber costume. The man nearly fainted. But it was too late for him to change anything.

It became clear to Rooplal, after he had spoken to the schoolchildren and listened to what Sonnyboy and the rest of people had to say, that whatever its origin, the way to move the cloud from over the town was by dancing.

"Dancing?" Sonnyboy asked him.

"Yes."

He wanted all the people in the island to join together and dance. The heat of their exertions would rise, push the clouds higher up, leading to condensation and rain.

"This," said Mr. Bissoon, when he heard the proposal, "is just another effort by the government to drag my people into the bacchanal called Carnival that we have resisted for all these years. This dancing might save the town. My question is, will it destroy the moral fabric of my people?"

In the lecture he was invited to give at the University of Trinidad and Tobago in its Distinguished Lecture Series, Rooplal talked of his work in Canada as a Midnight Robber and a performance poet. He had returned because he had so much to offer to both art and politics in the country. He had no ax to grind for any particular ethnic community since he was six of one and half a dozen of the other. What was required was for the people to put aside ethnic loyalties and come together for Carnival and dance.

Next day his speech and a photograph of him appeared in two of the daily newspapers. He was hailed in their editorials as a patriot who had left his busy schedule in Canada to return to his beloved country to give us the benefit of his expertise in the resolution of this serious matter. And they suggested that we should not let a man of such important credentials and insight be lost to us. Next day the telephone in Aunt Magenta's house rang incessantly as one political party after the other sought to court Rooplal.

But later that week the whole thing turned around. It was discovered in delving into his background that when he left Trinidad years ago he had entered Canada as a refugee seeking to escape what he had described as "the terror of a Black regime and its supporters who had an agenda to rob, rape, kidnap and murder Indians." When he was further investigated, it was found that his PhD was fake and that he was Victor Sonny Rooplal, a petty magician and gambler who had spent his early years in Cushe and Cascadu.

After the story broke, V. S. Rooplal indignantly declared that he was returning to Canada to have his name cleared. He packed up his things, said goodbye to us and Sonnyboy and slipped quietly out of Trinidad, his only regret that after all these years he didn't even get to see Carnival.

Carnival

Jouvay morning Claude jumped awake in a cold sweat. He had been shot by Orville's son and was preparing to die. He was surprised not to be feeling any pain where the bullet had struck him and he found himself waiting with a kind of puzzlement for something else to happen before he died, and it was only when he hear the alarm ringing that he realized that the reason his mind was so clear was because he really was not going to die. He had been dreaming the same dream for the last seven nights.

In his dream, he had gone with Dorlene to the family house she had left to take up residence in the rest house, and found it filled with people they did not know and who did not know them, but as they were about to leave they saw the piano in the living room and knew for sure that they were in the correct house. And he began to wonder how had these people come into possession of the house. Then he remembered that he must have sold the house when he thought that Dorlene had died. He must have sold it, because when he went outside, there at the side of the house, heaped there to be thrown away, were the newspapers their mother had piled up for forty-five years to read when she had time. When he rummaged through them he found papers on Self-Government, on Independence, pamphlets by J. D. Elder, newspaper photographs of the Carnival portrayals of *Beauty in Perpetuity*, the fancy

339

sailor mas of Fruits and Flowers by Cito Velasquez, prints of Alf Cadallo's paintings that his mother had planned to frame and put up on the walls, pictures of Paramin blue devils, a photograph of Errol Jones as Makak and Stanley Marshall as Moustique in the Derek Walcott play *Dream on Monkey Mountain*, newspaper reports on the mutiny trial of Lieutenants LaSalle and Shah, a big Minshall poster of Man Crab from his Carnival presentation *The River*, a CD of Phase Two Steel Orchestra, featuring Boogsie Sharpe, a C. L. R. James pamphlet on *Party Politics*, Keith Smith *Express* articles, Merle Hodge interview on Grenada after the murders, André Tanker's music, old cassette tapes of the calypsos of Indian Prince and Drupatee and Popo and Fluke, cassettes of Neville Jules with Trinidad All Stars and ones with Rudolph Charles, the general from Desperadoes, and Clive Bradley the arranger of the same band, music cassettes from the extempore singer Big B and the calypsonians Lord Blakey and the Mighty Duke, the newspapers she had kept from 1947 with the story of the Boysie Singh trial, the Mano Benjamin trial, the Black Power papers from 1970, the papers on the trial of the Muslims who sought to overthrow the government in 1990, the *Evening News* articles of the poet Eric Roach. The picture of a black Jesus that she had bought from a Rastafarian peddler whose looks she liked. As they stood up there watching, one of the women who no doubt was trying to be helpful came up and asked if they wanted any of the things.

"You can take anything before the garbage collector comes."

"Claude," Dorlene asked. "Whose house is this?"

Before he could speak, he heard the sound of a steelpan; when he looked in its direction, he saw Orville as a small boy, barebacked, standing near the pile of things. He had a steelpan on straps around his neck. He was holding the pan sticks but he wasn't playing anything. It looked as if he too was left to be taken away.

Then he heard a gunshot. Orville held his neck and began to fall, and Claude raced toward him, at the same time looking to see where the shot had come from. Another shot rang out, Claude found himself holding his chest, watching the blood spread and waiting to die.

Awake now, Claude lay in the quiet of his bedroom and heard Arlene changing; then he remembered it was Jouvay morning, the first day of the Carnival. He put on his Jouvay clothes, old pants, old T-shirt, his sneakers still caked with mud from last Carnival, put a rag in his pocket to wipe his glasses, and he was ready. He had prepared everything since the night before, had placed the buckets of mud on the pushcart as well as the du-dup and the two pieces of iron as instruments for any casual musician to play for the band. The mud had settled to the bottom of the buckets, with the water on top. All he had to do was stir the mud to the required consistency so it would be easy to be daubed on. He headed out with Arlene to Adam Smith Square where the band assembled each year, in his heart the same awkward feeling of anxiety, wondering who of the people would be there. There were not many of us when he arrived. He plastered the band members with mud, but we didn't set out right away. We milled around. Then we set out, the few of us that were there, not really dancing to the music of the du-dup and the iron, but ambling with a heroic resolve, Claude, still looking around for the people he expected, making little forays of enthusiasm that he expected to pass for dancing.

We had been going for about half an hour when I hear a scream and there is this blur of a woman jumping into Claude's arms. I recognized her as the little half-pint of a woman with the curvaceous body and her short little shorts. Beside her are two women equally curvaceous, dressed in pretty much the same way.

She had been away. Out in the country, had a baby . . . She was so sorry she couldn't come before, but every Carnival she thought about the band.

"How is the band? Where the people?"

"The people," Claude said, upping the tempo of his voice and sweeping a hand to include the few of us around him, "we are the people."

He said it with an ironic pride that didn't seem to register on her.

"Well, what you waiting on? Mud us up."

He dipped into a bucket of mud and he plastered her body and he anointed her face and hands and he did the same to the two women who had come with her. At the end of the ceremony, the fellars on the du-dup start up again with a new energetic beat as when a new stickfighter enters the ring, whistles start to blow and the iron start to ring, with a fresh joyful, exalting rhythm. One woman, calm as a priestess, straightened her legs, pushed out her bottom, bend forward, her hands down, like she going to touch her ankles and she lift up from that position, looking back behind her delighting in the contour of the bottom attached to her body, and with that admiring look, as if to celebrate its presence, she stepped off into the Jouvay morning dance, the sight so appealing that women and men invite themselves

342

into the band. Seeing Claude as custodian of the mud, they asked his permission, and this time he wasn't reluctant, he was so accepting that he himself began to mud them up; and I figured it must have been at that moment that it hit him, the sense that we were the people we were waiting on.

It was an awesome feeling and frightening and grand and so simple. I suppose Claude noticed it, because he was embracing the people who had invited themselves into the band, mudding them up, as if he now knew who he was and where he was going and what he had to do.

When the mud was done, he held on to Arlene and she held him in consolation, her head on his chest, both hands around his waist. Orlando opened a bottle of rum and passed it around. I take a shot. Then I feel a hand round my waist and holding me is this woman who had come with the half-pint into the band. I hold on to this woman, lifted and sobered by the welcoming and saluting touch of her hand so that I put my arm around her and embraced her with a deserved and cherishing love, and we went down the street, slow, joyful, me and she and all of us, sailing on the town.

After Jouvay, we drive down to Macqueripe Bay and wash off the mud in the sea. At one of the roadside eating-places we had bake-and-shark. After that the lime mash up. Claude and Arlene went back to their place; the half-pint of a woman and her friends were going to play mas in Port of Spain later in the day so they couldn't accept our invitation to come to Cascadu.

When I get back to Cascadu it was late. Night was beginning to fall and people were going home. I didn't mind it, though; I had a good time and a tomorrow to look forward to.

Carnival Tuesday

Tuesday was the day of pretty mas, on the streets, all the big costumes of the imagination, all the grand themes of life, the splendid limbs of youth, the celebration of spring, the affirmation of life, women and men in the finery of feathers, beads and skin, bands celebrating the events that had impressed our history: pirates, knights of the Crusades, nobles of the Elizabethan court, New Guinea totems, pilgrims, conquistadors. My aunt Magenta and Clephus were at the front of their Africa Band, with their pharaohs, their princesses with locksed hair, the pyramid they had ostensibly labored on, their masks, sacred birds, their musicians; Gypsies, Red Indians and Black Indians with their tepees embroidered with their history, China's dynasties.

In the midst of all this pretty mas, I hear the pitch-oil tins beating the frenzied jab molassie beat and when I look I see coming through the crowd the fierce jab molassie band blackened with black grease, people getting out of their way, and behind them, another not discordant sound, the tassa drumming and the chutney music and the red flag in the air above the heads until at last they come into view for me to see Manick with his red flag waving, surrounding him, a band of barebacked men and gaudily dressed women dancing with delight and spirit, and Manick in the costume that I recognized as the one described by my aunt Magenta as the one made by his father, with mirrors and glitter and swan's down, Manick himself dancing not so much with abandon, with care, with an exultant sobriety, turning this way and that so that we could see all sides of the offering of his costume. I stood and watched them pass, the flag bobbing like the mast of a ship that had lifted anchor and was making its way on the rhythm of the waves, out the harbor.

Up to that time I can't talk, I can't say nothing, I just drinking in everything that was happening, and then they call me on the stage. And in my mind I am repeating my mantra, trying to summon my voice from the darkness of silence:

I am King Kala, maker of confusion, recorder of gossip, destroyer of reputations, revealer of secrets. In the same skin, I am villain and hero, victim and victor.

I reduce the powerful by ridicule. I show them their absurdities by parody. I make their meanings meaningless and give meaning to meaning.

I am the protector of the people's vexation, embalmer of their rage, Singer of their praises, Restorer of their Faith, I am a stickfighter come out to dead, I am a warrior come to bust people head. I assassinate the mighty with melody and arm the people with laughter.

And I see them all there, the big band of contraries and togetherness in this temple of soul, and I begin to feel my voice back in my throat. I could talk.

And what will I tell them? What will I sing? Because before me is the audience in the VIP stands, the politicians and business people, the lords of the land. And for a moment, the temptation is there: now is my chance to wine on them, now is my chance to crow. Now is my opportunity to let them know that I had seen the foolishness of their pride, the performance that is their importance. But I was better than that. I had traveled far to get here. With the melancholy of discovery, I am seeing past the costume of their skin and status to the people inside them, the people inside their heart, playing roles according to their script, everybody rehearsing for a play they playing in their heart but don't yet have the heart to play. I look out on the monument of people:

"People," I cry out ... "People, are you ready to dance? Are you ready to get on bad? Are you ready to mash up the place?"

And I sing now about harbors we had found and harbors we must leave. Of the optimism we need not fear. Of the care we must take not to blight our adventure with cynicism, or devalue our experience with blindness. I sing for the band of hefty big-bottomed women holding on to the railing and wining, for the little jab molassie masqueraders beating tin pans and threatening for money, for the gathering that come into this grand cathedral of song and spirit to celebrate that self of themselves that they get a glimpse of on this occasion each year.

Ash Wednesday

Next day was Ash Wednesday. The campaign for the elections had the town busy, with people now in the costumes of their parties waving their flags and their emblems, trumpeting their logic and their passion for their version of the Promised Land. These programs went on, with calypso singers and chutney singers, with moko jumbies and Midnight Robbers and then they came to an end.

Victory at the Polls

Then, the elections. After the votes were counted, the New National Party had triumphed and the PM was PM once again. Up and down the islands car horns were tooting and supporters celebrating the victory. We watched it on TV. The next day was the swearing-in ceremony. That was what my aunt Magenta and Clephus wanted to see. I went with them to Port of Spain, to Woodford Square where the swearing-in ceremony was to take place. We were there from early morning, because Aunt Magenta insisted that she wanted to sit in a spot where the PM would see her, so he could, if he wanted to, tell her something about Franklyn. We got her the spot. But, although she was right there when he waved at the crowd, I don't think he saw her.

It was a good display with a stage for his swearing-in, and the bleachers used to seat the guests. It looked fine, the stage covered with a red carpet and cushions on the chairs for the dignitaries, the judges, the religious leaders, the champions of business and the political representatives of the people.

The Carnival characters were pressed into service. The moko jumbies, towering above everybody, seeing far ahead and seeing far behind, led the way, preceding the PM's entrance into the park, and ahead of them the Paramin blue devils in a ritual clearing of the space, scaring evil spirits away, these spirits portrayed by the bat and the dragon and the jab-jabs and the imps. And then he came, escorted to the podium by king sailors with huge headpieces, the fancy Indians, burroquites and the monumental creation that looked like what Peter Minshall called Tan Tan and Saga Boy. This time, however, Saga Boy had a razor in his pocket and a knife in his shoe and Tan Tan wasn't a tantie, she was a jamette with a long wig of yellow straightened hair and a voluptuous body. Music for the ceremony was provided by the National Steel Symphony Orchestra, its members in bow ties and dark suits, and the National Tassa band. The National Chutney Singers sang, the bele dancers danced and the President spoke. They didn't have a calypsonian.

After the program was over and the PM sworn in, I saw the Carnival characters hanging around, the jab molassie and the devils and the dragon and the king sailors, walking aimlessly as if expecting that more would be made of them, like actors unhappy with their performance, sitting around remorsefully, wishing that they could be called back to act their roles again, so this time they would do them better. This time they would show them. This time they would mash up the place.

Lunch had been prepared for them, and they were given lunch boxes and they sat on the bleachers in the park and had the meal.

The Cruise Ships Leave

Two days later, the cruise ships began to leave the harbor and we all went down to the wharf to see the visitors off. It had a lot of speech-making and sad goodbyes. But we needn't worry, the PM said. Be of good cheer. They had left behind plans that should we follow them would enable us to construct for ourselves a world as wonderful as the one they had built for themselves.

Later that month, I went with Claude to help Dorlene move from the rest house back to her home. Her powers had begun to wane, and although they weren't exactly putting her out – if she wanted she could stay – she felt she might as well make a clean break of it and go back to her home, like Makak in *Dream on Monkey Mountain*.

Wedding

At home, my aunt Magenta had accepted Clephus wedding proposal and had already been measured for her bridal dress. For the wedding, church people came in to scrub out the house with lime and red lavender and whitehead broom, and to smoke it out with incense. And all around there was softness, the days cool, the sun bright. The couple didn't want anything too fussy and too big and they wanted to do it and get it over with quickly. Even so, all our neighbors were there and although he wasn't too sprightly, Manick father and Elsie. Clephus family had come in from Tobago with a wedding cake in the shape of a horseshoe, three good-sized lobsters and seven bottles of the aphrodisiac, pacro water. Aunt Magenta had Shouters people from churches all over the island, with drums and tambourines and bells. For the wedding, my aunt Magenta had chosen for her dress something African, with an elaborate head tie and yards of colorful cloth that would be drawn around her body so that you could see the richness of her skin and the heft of woman. Clephus hair was getting thin and the entire top of his head was getting bald. He shaved his head so that the whole was shiny and smooth but he left his sideburns which he had shaped out with a razor to resemble that of the Blackfella who had starred in the movie *King Solomon's Mines*. He had an African outfit as well. I rented two tents from Manick and we set them up in the yard. All around there was a Sunday calm and softness.

At the wedding ceremony, the Shouter Baptist leader officiating called us all together and talked about love and enduring. Then it was time for speeches. Clephus spoke about what my aunt Magenta meant to him and my aunt Magenta talked about how much of a companion and support he had been to her since that Easter he passed and helped her catch the chicken. I wished them well, and everybody in Clephus family from Tobago wished them well, and I talked a little bit about the example the two of them had given of people cherishing each other, that I must say brought tears to both their eyes. We had lunch, curried goat, chicken, lobster from Tobago and pigeon peas and paratha and chataigne and bodi and corraili that Manick's wife sister make, then a program at which Constable Aguillera sang in a slow, sentimental tempo "Lady" for them to stick the cake. Then, when the dancing started, he sang, by public request, what had become a hit song for that Carnival, his calypso "Don't Take My Coverlet."

And we drew closer to each other like family. Claude and his wife, Arlene, were there, deep in conversation, as two people who had just met and were getting to know each other. Claude didn't talk to me about going away, and I didn't ask him any question. Constable Stephen Aguillera and Ramona Fortune were talking earnestly to each other. During the course of the afternoon, he had been very attentive to her, getting her drink, bringing her cake; but now he sat beside her with a transcendent satisfaction, not trying to convince her to stay or anything, just exuding delight at their being together, she holding his hands in her own and stroking his fingers one by one with the gentleness of someone who wished it were otherwise, but now had to say goodbye.

I was thinking of Sweetie-Mary and Sonnyboy. Just after that Carnival, Sweetie-Mary had packed her things to leave Sonnyboy. I saw her at the grocery when I was buying drinks for the wedding.

"I can't live the life he want to give me," she told me. "You know what it is. He think he spiting the people for not recognizing him. But how could you be spiting people by letting them force you into becoming somebody who is not you?"

When next I went to their business place, she had not left yet, but there was a coldness between them, and her leaving was imminent. Sonnyboy was very hurt. He hardly wanted to talk.

He couldn't understand why she would want to leave him at this time when the business was better and they were so much more comfortable. He spoke to me about their life, the things they had been through together, the future they could have. Somehow the conversation turned to the time when he volunteered to be arrested as a freedom fighter, and I reminded him of the movie in which his magnificient dying did not find favor with the director.

"Yes," he said, tiredly, as if a new insight on life had been revealed to him, "King, it is just a movie."

"Yes," I said.

He had a rag in his hand and was wiping the counter. He looked up sharply, with a bit of surprise.

"But with you as the star."

He looked at me, looked away, then looked at me again; but he didn't say anything.

I was still looking out for them.

Afterward we stayed together in the yard, the old fellars in a tent with enough food and liquor to keep us happy.

Inside, the young people were dancing. Outside it had grown darker and still, with overhanging clouds giving off a heat that had you feeling the need for hurry, all of us talking, everybody telling their story of these last years, of who did what, of how things made them feel.

In the middle of the remembering, we hear a roaring.

"Rain," I said. "The weather change." And everybody looked to the sky.

"Look," Claude said. "Look! They going," pointing at the clouds. "They going."

"What?"

"You blind? Look them there: the jab molassie, bat, robber, jab-jab, babydoll, pan man, dragon, moko jumbie."

All I saw were drifting clouds.

"Yes," I said, pretending to see what he was pointing at.

I could feel the wind blowing. Then the rain that had drizzled a bit on Carnival Tuesday started falling in earnest. Most of the company went inside the main house where people were dancing; Manick wife wanted to dance and he and she followed them but I sit down in the tent, hitting the grog and going over in my mind the stories that each one of us had to tell, thinking how I might put them into calypso.

After a while the place begin to grow lighter and the music from the house and the chatter from the dancing people to sound louder and more inviting. With a few drinks under my belt, I was charged up now, ready for dancing. I stood up to go inside to join them. When I look outside was to see Sweetie-Mary holding Sonnyboy by the hand, coming in from the rain that was easing up now, with a new music that when it stopped would leave a clearer sky.

Acknowledgments

In salute of steelbandsmen Neville Jules, Boogsie Sharpe, and my friend Nestor Sullivan; calypsonians Slinger Francisco (The Mighty Sparrow), Leroy Calliste (Black Stalin), Winston Bailey (Shadow), Emrold Phillip (Valentino) and David Rudder; writers Keith Smith and Jennifer Rahim; masman Peter Minshall; my artist friends Jim Armstrong and Eddie Hernandez; George Baboolal from the Valencia days; Hollis Pierre and the Matura villagers; Baas, Aji and the Rio Claro crew; and all who provided inspiration and support for this book.

Special thanks to Norvan Fullerton for allowing me use of his robber speech, Barbara Temple-Thurston and Pacific Lutheran University, Kelly Hewson and Bill Schwarz for support; Laurie and Tessa Watkins for their unforgettable hospitality; Margaret Busby, Funso Aiyejina and Alake Pilgrim for reading and responding to the manuscript; and Derek Walcott for the generosity of his presence and work.

About Haymarket Books

Haymarket Books is a nonprofit, progressive book distributor and publisher, a project of the Center for Economic Research and Social Change. We believe that activists need to take ideas, history, and politics into the many struggles for social justice today. Learning the lessons of past victories, as well as defeats, can arm a new generation of fighters for a better world. As Karl Marx said, "The philosophers have merely interpreted the world; the point however is to change it."

We take inspiration and courage from our namesakes, the Haymarket Martyrs, who gave their lives fighting for a better world. Their 1886 struggle for the eight-hour day reminds workers around the world that ordinary people can organize and struggle for their own liberation.

For more information and to shop our complete catalog of titles, visit us online at www.haymarketbooks.org.

Also from Haymarket Books

Field Notes on Democracy • Arundhati Roy

Notes from the Middle World • Breyten Breytenbach

Essays • Wallace Shawn

Black Power Mixtape • Edited by Göran Hugo Olsson

Palante • Young Lords Party, photographs by Michael Abramson, introduction by Iris Morales

About the Author

Robyn Cross

Earl Lovelace was born in Toco, Trinidad, and has spent most of his life on the islands of Trinidad and Tobago. He has been a journalist, has been Writer-in-Residence at the University of the West Indies and at universities in the United States and Britain, and has given lectures and readings and participated in conferences internationally. His books have been translated into German, Dutch, French, Italian, Japanese, and Hungarian, and his short stories have been widely anthologized. His books include *The Wine of Astonishment, While Gods Are Falling,* winner of the BP Independence Award, the Caribbean classic *The Dragon Can't Dance,* and *Salt,* which won the 1997 Commonwealth Writers Prize.